THE MISFIT MAGE
AND
HIS DEVILISH
DESIRES

MN Bennet

THE MISFIT MAGE AND HIS DEVILISH DESIRES

DIABOLIC ROMANCE BOOK THREE

MN BENNET

Paperback ISBN: 979-8-9901493-7-3

Ebook ISBN: 979-8-9901493-2-8

Edited by Charlie Knight (CKnightWrites.com)

Cover art by Miblart (miblart.com)

www.mnbennet.com/

DEDICATION

To everyone who has followed Wally and Bez, you really are absolutely wonderful!

AUTHOR'S NOTE

Thank you so much for returning for the final installment of the Diabolic Romance series. I'm delighted to share more of Wally and Bez's journey in this wonderful world of magic. There's so much to enjoy about this Diabolic Romance, but I do want to offer a note on the content included in book three. If you've read book one and two, many of the warnings are similar. Lots of bad humor to love and steam to warm you up. That said, there are some elements I always prefer making readers aware of before diving into a book. For those interested, I've included a list of content warnings at the bottom of the page.

This book contains the following elements:

Foul language
Graphic violence and gore [descriptive]
Torture both mental and physical
Blood
Murder [some brutal]
There are several open door, descriptive sex scenes between adults
So Much Spice!
Depression and anxiety
Self-mutilation [magic based]
Cannibalism [magic based]

1

Wally

Bez bucked against my hips, resistant and clearly a bit uncomfortable beneath me. I didn't mean to be so rough. This wasn't exactly a position I was used to. With my legs wrapped over his thighs and my arms tucked under his, I held Bez in place. This was the first time I'd been on top. As he fidgeted, I steadied my hold over him. Pulling my arms up while I kept them wrapped under his and pressed to the back of his head. It forced his back into a deeper arch.

I wanted to run my fingers through his shaggy black hair, play with it, tease him a bit by grabbing a fistful all the way to his neon orange roots. But Bez was already squirming, and something told me he wouldn't react well to me yanking his head back like he did to me a thousand times over. No, that was something I enjoyed—even when I didn't.

I pushed all my weight down and pinned him to the soft floormat. Bez bucked again, but it did nothing with my thighs squeezed over his. His muscles tensed, yet the warm skin of his back remained soft when pressed against my chest. When he flexed his arms, though, the muscles constricted against mine, and then he stretched them as far out as he could; his fingers gripped the matting of the floor and ripped through it once his essence transformed his human fingers into their more demonic claws. It didn't help steady his position beneath me, merely a defiant need to resist. Bez grunted, biting back a feral groan.

Was I hurting him? I didn't want to hurt Bez, but this felt too good. I couldn't relent, not when I was this close to… I sucked my teeth, taking in a deep breath of all the Mythic residue in the atmosphere. It strengthened my body, fueling the mana my mortal coil contained, and sparked the devil essence that'd become entwined to my very being on a cellular level. The more magic I fed into the Diabolic power, the more it surged through my veins, strengthening me.

"Walter." Bez ground his teeth so hard the crunch snapped in the air. "You probably think you're hot stuff right now, don't you?"

"Don't ruin this for me, Bez." I sighed. "You're gonna ruin this for me, aren't you?"

And just like that, one of Bez's tails coiled around my throat and whipped me back, pulling me off Bez and knocking me to the ground. In a flash, Bez darted on top of me and pinned me to the floormat.

Fuck. Between his arms, his legs, and his three tails, I couldn't wriggle loose for the life of me. Bez loved it. His heart pounded against my chest, faster with each second that passed, which made mine speed up, desiring to match his rhythmic pace. It was one of the few things I'd mastered purely on instinct, hence why we trained like this so I could navigate all my powers and learn to hone them at will.

I didn't understand how wrestling was going to help me improve my Diabolic abilities, but I really enjoyed the homoerotic positions we found ourselves in each time. Plus, it was one of the few times Bez dressed down—no damn suit and tie. Only a pair of gray joggers that barely reached past his knees, and since he wore them baggy, they often left the deep V cut at hip bones exposed and the crack of his ass too. Not to mention, he always went with gray because he liked the way it framed his monster cock, though I believed some of that interest had to do with social media influence. He easily had a dozen gray sweatpants dick memes saved on his phone.

"Yield?" Bez grinned, cocky and carefree. But I could see him panting, using the Mythic residue around us to compensate for his state of exhaustion.

If I could summon my tail, I'd be able to break his hold around my throat. His tail coiled tighter, constricting my breathing—breathing I didn't need but still had such a forced habit of taking. Or maybe I did need the oxygen. It was difficult to discern how much a mortal body fueled entirely by base insentient devil essence worked. How much of it was rudimentary based on my instinct and history, and how much was an actual requirement since the essence merged with me?

Bez thunked my head with the tip of his second tail while his third remained wrapped around my legs. "Gonna yield?"

My face burned from frustration and failure. "Yes."

"Good boy." Bez released me and leapt to his feet in a swift motion. He relished our sparring matches. And even though he darted throughout the training room at blurred speed, reassembling everything we'd knocked over, in a matter of seconds, I tracked his movements, each step like a collection of flickering still photos. Like a Claymation movie.

How come my senses worked automatically, observing the most minute details, but I couldn't simply trigger other abilities?

"If it hadn't been for your tails, I would've had you."

Bez rolled his eyes. "Unlikely. Though, I admire the effort."

"I was closer this time." Not really. I barely felt the essence stirring inside me. It was there. It'd been there for over a year now, circulating throughout my body and doing its own damn thing. That said, what I did control had managed to nearly overpower Bez. Sort of.

"Do you wanna know where you messed up this time?"

"Got confident?"

"No—well, yes, because obviously, you'll never best me." Bez flashed a grin and strutted back toward me now that he'd returned everything to its proper place. "You're still internalizing your Diabolic abilities."

Since Bez cut the devil essence from his being and poured it into me, he'd made it his mission to teach me how to cultivate and control its every whim and make the power bend to my will alone. That hadn't gone great, no matter how much we trained or I studied—not that there was a Diabolic devil-taming manual lying around.

As Bez lectured about ways one feels their essence, I let my eyes drift around the training room. He wasn't the best teacher, or I wasn't the best student. Okay, that was a lie. I was an amazing student. Top marks in nearly all my classes from kindergarten all the way through college and my magic academy.

Seriously, I'm a rockstar student.

Well, except for implementing theory into practice. Gaining the devil essence and my inability to master it bogged me down most days like a constant reminder of the years spent trying to wield my mage magics.

"When we're training, you need to let loose, stop thinking, stop holding back, and just focus on eviscerating your opponent."

"And what happens when I do eviscerate you?"

"Cute."

"Fine. What if I destroy your special training room?"

Bez scoffed, completely offended I'd make the accusation. This was his special room, too. He didn't lift a finger to clean at home but made sure to take care of everything here, from combat tools, portraits, and furniture all the way to stocking the fridge daily. Even the intricate sigils that he'd taken the time to set up himself—a big shocker since he was so lax about magical maintenance—worked to contain our strikes in this area so they didn't spill out into the store.

He probably would've built this at home, like a personal gym, but Bez knew me too well and figured most of my days would be spent at the Well of Wonders, where I studied and fixed rare artifacts all day, every day. He wasn't wrong. *Still wish he didn't drag out his post-training lectures to eat into my entire break.*

"Are you even listening to me, Walter?" Bez had his hands on his waist, and I found my eyes drifting along the muscles of his abdomen to the exposed happy trail leading to his crotch.

"Yes." I stood up. "I just need to—"

"You need to learn how to manifest your Diabolic extensions at will. Wings. Tail. Claws." Bez waved a dismissive hand at my desire to return to work and put an end to his post-training lecture. "Any of those could've and would've surely helped in maintaining your position."

"Oh? You think my little cherub-sized wings would've kept you pinned?" I definitely added a heavy lilt of sarcasm to my question, but he'd mocked my tiny wings every time they'd randomly sprung out.

"Certainly. With a precise flap of those wings, mixed with the Pentacles of Power surging through your body—I mean, Walter, you could've summoned elements to strengthen your attack. You could've spread your saturation around the terrain, claiming this area as yours."

I huffed. "Fine. The wings would've been useful."

"Or your tail." Bez used one of his own tails to tickle my chin while using a second to weave an incantation in the air. "They're perfect for sneaky, delicate work such as drawing a swift spell to assist in whatever you need."

The incantation glowed and suddenly knocked me off my feet. I grunted as I hit the floormat.

"Ow."

"With mastery over the Pentacles of Power and access to Diabolic essence, you need to learn how to use them in tandem."

"Yeah, yeah." I dug my hands into the floormat, wishing I could shift my fingers into claws and slash the thin padding to ribbons. I mean, technically, I could. I knew a dozen incantations that'd offer me elongated claws for such a purpose. My mage magics worked just fine. "But after damn near eighteen months, I haven't made an ounce of progress on my Diabolic abilities."

I didn't need to mutter the rest of my thoughts; Bez knew them.

"You'll get there once we get you outta your own head." Bez looked down at me, not with judgment—not like he was actually looking down on me, but more of a carnal gaze, a primal stare. Suddenly, he was slinking toward me with less of a lecture on his lips and more of a smirk. "But let's be honest, your mind wasn't on training today."

"Well, there's just so many orders I need to go through at the shop, and there's a shipment of artifacts I need to catalog, plus I've still got to inventory—"

"I don't mean work." Bez knelt, crawling toward me on his hands and knees. "Your mind wasn't there either. No, no, no. I could feel exactly which head you were thinking with while we trained."

"Huh?" My face burned.

Bez swiftly circled me, his eyes locked onto mine one second, and then his smirk appeared in my peripheral the next. "Dirty little mage only had one thing on his mind."

"I'm not sure what you mean." I shivered when Bez's tail caressed my neck, and then another wrapped around my inner thigh.

"I could feel your boner pressed against my ass." Bez whipped around, straddling my waist and shoving me onto my back. "Sort of like this, well you were on top…momentarily."

I didn't usually get aroused by the idea of fucking Bez. I mean, *I do*, but not with me doing the fucking. The most thrust-happy I usually got involved his face or throat on occasion, and even then, I often preferred being the one in a satisfying position meant to satiate his needs. That brought me pleasure.

Yet here I was, getting hard as Bez rubbed against my crouch. I wrapped my hands around his waist, desiring to control the pace of his thrusts. He looked at me with this smoldering expression. The red of his irises expanded, pupils shrinking, and black veins highlighting the pinks of his sclera. Gods, when the pinks of his eyes got glossy ever so, I found myself even more enamored.

"Do you wanna fuck me, Walter?"

"W-w-what?" I bit my lower lip because I'd never fucked anyone. I mean, yes, I'd had a lot of sex with several different individuals in my lifetime, but I'd always known which position I preferred, and that hadn't changed over the years.

"I can feel the urge." Bez kissed me, his lips pressed so rough against mine, it distracted from my need to mumble, my need to fill the silence with words, because he'd filled the quiet with passion. "The desire in your hold."

I strengthened my grip around Bez's waist, one hand sliding down his joggers and getting a firm grip on his ass. Gods, what an ass it was too.

"The thrust as you fought to pin me," Bez whispered, and when I went to speak, he nibbled on my lower lip, silencing me. "But if you wanna be in charge, you're gonna have to be a bit more assertive."

Bez slid off my waist in a blur and flipped me onto my stomach. Running his hands down my spine, the sensation of his claws tearing at the fabric of my shirt incited the deep arch of my back.

"I think you like me being in charge too much to show off that dominant nature in combat." Bez pressed against me, slowly wrapping himself around me. His thighs squeezed against mine. His arms wrapped under mine. His face was buried in my neck, sharp jawline rubbing against mine before he bit my shoulder, then kissed it, then bit and licked and tore into my flesh just enough to provoke the essence to knock his teeth from my skin.

"Dominant?" I shook my head. "Sex and combat are completely different."

"That so?" Bez ripped off my jeans and smacked my bare ass so hard my tail sprouted out and coiled around his arm.

The muscles of the Diabolic extension were unlike any other in my body. It was as if the tail had senses of its very own, from sight to sound to sensation. This piece of myself squeezed tighter against the flex of Bez's bicep, like a serpent unyielding against a potential threat.

"Seems you still require a physical touch to enact your essence."

Bez knew exactly how hard to hit me, more force than a playful slap, but not so hard he'd actually hurt me. Suppose there was probably a way to quantify that. Though I doubt I'd wanna extrapolate data on how to harness my abilities based on sexual kinks. However, I would like to test pain receptors to summoning power, but Bez often held back and still managed to always knock me on my ass. Or, in this case, leave me face down on the floor with my ass in the air.

"Someone's lost in his head, thinking. Always thinking." Bez kissed the nape of my neck gently.

"I can't tell if you're teasing me or taunting me or teaching me."

"Why not all of the above?" Bez stopped resisting the grip of my tail, and eventually, I released my hold on him, but it continued twitching, smacking against the floormat, and asserting the Diabolic power within me.

"I take it we're done training?"

"You're gonna take something all right." Bez chuckled, sliding down my body until his face rested at my ass. With his clawed hands, he spread my cheeks and spit on my hole.

I moaned when his tongue reached inside me, lathering me, soothing me, sending a warm, radiating charge through my entire body. A jolt of energy mixed with a surge of desire, yet I lay on the floor, completely stripped of clothing like putty in Bez's hands, all for him to play with, to taste, to have his way.

Bez trailed his way back up with light kisses serving as his footsteps along my skin, then rested his cock against my ass as he lubed me up. I shivered at the cool liquid covering my hole and dripping down me. When had he grabbed it? He must've telekinetically—

"Fuck," I moaned when he stuck his fingers inside me. It didn't matter when he retrieved the lube, only that his touch felt so fucking good.

"Looks like my Worthless Walter has lost all his assertive energy."

I growled, partially from irritation and partially because that fire hadn't been entirely quelled. In a blur of fury and fighting, Bez and I rolled along the mat until he ended up on his back, and I straddled his hips.

"Remember, you're only in charge because I like it that way." I eased myself onto his cock, wincing as he entered me.

Bez locked his eyes with mine, the expression was subtle, but I could always tell when my own eyes had gone completely black. There was a curiosity in his gaze, along with caution and concern. Bez never wanted to lose me to the devil essence, which was why he spent so much time forcing me to master a power even he didn't fully grasp after hundreds of years of containing it.

I pressed my hands against Bez's pecs, fingers twisting into gnarled claws from the sudden thrust of Bez's cock entering me. Each nail dug into Bez's flesh, cutting through his demon essence. Blood dripped from his chest, yet he didn't resist or fight or heal. Bez remained in the moment, lightly continuing his thrusts and motioning me to move my hips and sway to his pace. Taking a deep breath, I reminded myself, reminded every cell of my body that might've forgotten, that there was a pain that came with the pleasure of sex. This was not an attack; this was not a threat; this was exciting, enticing, exhilarating.

It took a moment, but my essence eased as my body adjusted to the length of Bez's shaft, pumping in and out at a steady pace. The sensation made me shiver, desiring the throbbing pleasure that came with Bez's fuck.

"Harder," I gasped, finally retracting the bulk of my Diabolic claws, leaving only sharpened black nails and charcoal-dusted fingers.

Bez sat up, slapping his arms around my back and pressing our chests together as he pounded into me. His wings sprang loose, wrapping us in a cocoon of sex as we tumbled on our sides. Bez fucked me faster and harder. I panted, lost in the taste of sex in the air, the sensation of power radiating all around us.

"Let me hear you beg, Wally." Bez nibbled my ear, teasing and tugging. "Tell me what you want."

"Bez." I bit my lower lip, fighting back the desire to answer because I didn't want the pleasure to end.

Two of Bez's tails wrapped around my thighs, forcing my legs wider. Bez kept one hand firmly pressed against my back, squeezing me closer, while his third tail reached around my neck and tilted my head. He wanted my eyes locked onto him with every single thrust.

My cock throbbed as he gripped it with his free hand, jerking in motion with each pound.

I panted, holding onto the ecstasy that came with finishing. And as such, Bez continued edging me closer and closer to a climax before drawing back momentarily. This went on for what felt like forever. In reality, it was about ten minutes based on the wall clock that revealed I'd gone past my allotted break time.

"Bez," I whined as he shoved the entirety of his shaft inside me before stroking my cock to completion.

I came hard, so hard my entire body convulsed while wrapped up by Bez's arms and tails and wings. Incapable of containing myself, I wheezed as Bez stroked my dick, milking the cum out onto my stomach. The satisfaction in his gaze as he watched each pearl thread pool together and the head of my dick soften entirely in his fist.

Bez smirked. "Now that my little mage has been satiated, I think it's time the demon gets his dues."

2

Bez

Once Wally had climaxed, I retracted my wings and pulled out of him, cock throbbing and ready to return to his beautiful hole. He lay on the mat, covered in his own sweat and cum, leaving me utterly ravenous. I flipped him onto his stomach, relishing the whimper from his lips and the splat of his sticky stomach hitting the mat.

"Oh, Bez." Wally panted heavy exhales into the mat that only further enticed me.

"Now that you've had your release, it's time you offer me mine." I positioned him on all fours, adjusting the alignment of his hips and ass and arch of his back, so I could slide inside him with ease.

Using my clawed fingers, I spread his cheeks wide, staring at his hole as I buried my cock into it. Gods, I loved the sight of watching my dick vanish inside him all the way to the base where our skin touched, and the most subtle spark of electricity surged between us. Not Diabolic, not even magic. Merely chemical, chemistry, something euphoric in the air every time our bodies did this little dance.

Wally moaned, his back rising momentarily until my sharpened nails encouraged an obedient arch.

It didn't take long to find a steady, pleasurable rhythm in pounding out Wally, but I found myself eager for more, wanting to relish in his whimper, make him bend to my will, and work a bit harder to satisfy my needs.

I yanked him by his blond curls, jerking his head back. "I'm gonna rail you until you buckle."

Wally nodded his head, which remained in my grasp. His pleading hazel eyes held this desire to offer approval, to satisfy my every craving. Good. Admittedly, I missed the glasses he no longer required, the pair he ultimately set aside since the essence coursing throughout him enhanced his senses, sharpening them intuitively.

I shoved his face into the mat, and then I gripped him by his hips. Pulling out with only the head of my dick inside him, satisfied by the warm tight embrace, I allowed the nerves of our bodies to tingle from the sensation for a moment before I slammed the entirety of my cock back inside him. My teeth chattered in sync with Wally's quivering body. I repeated this several times, from tip to base, feeling invigorated each time I thrust deep into Wally's guts and hearing his moan, his whine, and watching his body bend to better accommodate me.

Oh, how he worked so hard to please me. Still, as I continued pounding away, pouring all my energy into railing Wally into the floor, I found myself returning to the spark of our training. There was a moment, the briefest of seconds, when I found myself eager for him to overtake me the same way I currently held him down. The exertion of his muscles, his magics, and his masculinity all conjured this beautifully intoxicating aroma that left me eager to delight in his needs. Yet here I was, fucking him to meet my own delights.

He was no longer the timid twink incapable of anything except wordy nonsense.

"Bez," he gasped, enthralled by the thrust of my hips yet still desiring to speak, to explain, to tell some factual anecdote. Utter nonsense, his chaotic craving for conversation.

I leaned closer, tilting his head and holding his strong jaw in my hand. Gods, his hazel eyes had this beautifully delirious look to them as I fucked him, and his lips called out for mine, desperate for the silence I offered.

I kissed Wally, tasting the sweetness of his lips and relishing the pained pleasure he murmured into my mouth.

Surely, I jested about his obscene need to talk, always talk, talk, talk. In truth, I craved his words almost as much as he desired to speak them. His voice offered me solace from the world in every way, an escape from everything else, and one continuous constant from a companion unlike anyone else.

I ran my hands along his torso, continuing to kiss him. Wally had grown quite handsome. His physique had become more muscular, yet still posing his natural slender form. His shoulders were broader, easier to grip and hold while ramming my cock faster and harder into him. The rhythmic panting made his abs tighten, flexing and revealing his perfect physical state. I took swift breaths alongside Wally, syncing our bodies. It meant so much to him to feel unity, like when the essence shared between us stirred sensations from the Diabolic bond.

With Wally holding the devil essence all on his own, we could never perform the bond again with my essence, but I'd never felt more united to him and his will. Every stroke brought me closer to him, every pump of my hips elicited a familiar reaction, every gentle touch across his tender flesh sent a quiver through my spine as I gauged his response. For the last eighteen months, I studied Wally in the same ways I had when perched atop a mantle and bound inside a Diabolic orb, realizing I didn't require a link to know what brought him joy, didn't need a bond to understand his sensations, and didn't lack in the pleasure of feeling his satisfaction with my every action.

I indulged in every delight that crossed my mind, exploring Wally's body, mind, and heart to the deepest facets, ensuring we would remain forever close. The Diabolic bond meant nothing to me. I didn't require it to feel like one with Wally. I only needed him nearby, and that completed me.

His desires had grown and subtly shifted over the months, the more we trained and the stronger he became. No. He'd always been strong, powerful even when underestimating himself, but something had blossomed in his heart, in his cock, and I found myself eager to explore the new roles our future might offer.

As my mind wandered to the potential reversal, my chest heated, my breathing hitched, and I pressed my hands down between Wally's shoulder blades, holding him in place. My muscles spasmed, tightening like a wet cloth being wrung out, and then all the tension in my body fizzled away as I came inside Wally. I took twitchy thrusts, cumming and indulging in the satisfying pleasure of my stiff cock softening inside Wally.

When I pulled out, I smirked at the white droplets that dribbled down Wally's crack to his sack.

"That was quite fun." I slapped Wally's ass—not hard enough to provoke his tail but enough to rouse a response from him.

"Uh-huh," he said with a wispy breath.

"I think I fucked you unconscious."

"No," he panted. "Just gathering my bearings."

I zipped across the room and retrieved my black suit and tie. Wally continued lying on the floor while I dressed, all his energy spent. A part of me desired to roll around with him for a second round, really unload on him, but I'd never hear the end of it if I fucked him through his shift and he fell behind on whatever random artifacts he had on the agenda for today.

Once I'd buttoned my shirt, I strutted toward Wally and knelt beside him. Since he kept his face pressed to the mat while taking deep breaths, I kissed his cheek. A wet and sloppy peck meant to convey love and lust and maybe a laugh. He remained too exhausted to chuckle, so I took my leave.

I left Wally flat on his stomach, ass up and snoozing with his legs spread and arms outstretched as he gathered his bearings.

"See you at home, my love." I adjusted my tie and exited the sparring room.

I'd simply wait until he came home to cum again and again, with a second and a third and possibly a fourth round. The idea alone was invigorating, and I intended to indulge to the fullest.

Following the gloomy lighting of the stock room's hallway, I made my way through the various stacks of knickknack oddities Wally would spend countless hours fawning over.

If he spent half as much time focusing on the devil essence circulating throughout him as he did fixating on these so-called artifacts, then he'd practically be a masterful devil. Well, devil adjacent.

Whatever. I'd already done my job. Deliveries were all dropped off, and my boyfriend was piledrived—and trained in casting—so that meant the rest of the evening was mine.

I lounged in the breakroom, rifling through the fridge to put together a little snack. While I didn't have everything I wanted, there was enough to make a half-decent sandwich.

Wally's mysterious little shop generally had a decent amount of foot traffic, which was why I stayed in the back. I didn't have the patience for customers. I didn't have the patience for these artifacts and antiquities either. Nope. The only puzzle I enjoyed deciphering was the array of flavors I created in my salted ribeye fried tomato peanut butter sandwich. It had everything. And thanks to the panini press, I could smother all of it together into a warm, crispy bite.

Luminescent green light reflected off Antoninus' black shell as the tiny scorpion scuttled into the room. He hissed, carrying a dozen different boxes.

"You're in a mood." I took a bite of my sandwich.

The boxes shook, potent Diabolic essence gripping their delicate edges and crushing the finely wrapped packages until the creepy crawly bug eased the flow of his telekinesis. Such a bizarre sight. Not the scorpion. He wasn't bizarre, merely fucking irritating.

No, the strangeness came from their familiar bond. Sure, mage magics allowed them to draw upon the Pentacles of Power and establish links to animals by sharing their mana with the little beasts, but I'd never met a Diabolic who could do such things. The essence demons unleashed often overwhelmed the mortal animals, poisoning them, rotting them from the inside out, yet Wally's connection remained unfazed. In fact, it seemed stronger. Antoninus didn't have Diabolic essence coursing through his body, but this somewhat phantom form of Diabolic abilities, like a ghostly connection to Wally.

If I were to be a Walter about the situation, I'd hypothesize that since he'd established the familiar bond before absorbing the devil essence, it allowed him to continue his familiar link. Since I wasn't Walter, my actual theory was that they were both fucking weird.

"This is why Wally can't control his essence." I snatched away the packages Antoninus carried here. "You're teaching him your sloppy technique, you annoying insect."

With a click of his claws, he summoned a black gust and knocked my sandwich out of my hand before scurrying out of the room.

"Fucking coward!" I shouted.

I crouched low to retrieve my splattered snack, but that damn bug had ruined it. I sighed with defeat, then looked at the boxes he'd left. I had some deliveries to attend to.

"Which would be easier if some people—*bugs*—didn't just scribble the addresses all illegibly!" I gathered the boxes and made my way out of the stockroom. "Guess I'll just starve now."

And yes, I didn't require nutrients, but I wanted them. Needed them to be happy. Antoninus had taken away my happiness.

As I stepped outside, I winced at the harsh burn of the setting sun's light. Such a shift from fake light indoors to over-emphasized daylight trickling through the dimensional walls of this city. I preferred this pocket realm when Mora first created it with her witchy wife. The blueprints were wonderful, and Wally analyzed the Fae magics, tinkering with the mechanics to streamline things. The realm was truly euphoric. It was eternal nightfall, glimmering rainbow stars and colorful comets and glittery rainfall.

But no, the whiny citizens Mora continued to invite to live here craved sunlight for normalcy or routine or cheer. I hated it, especially this slow-setting sun.

"Just fucking go to bed already, daytime!"

I spread my wings, using the gray feathers to block the fading light until the night finally took hold and the moon's gentle illumination filled the city below. There was a calm, perfect silence for the flicker of three seconds before the nightlife ignited.

Neon lights to rowdy businesses switched on, cars weaved between each other as their brights flashed, and vast buildings stacked atop each other lit up in the strangest patterns depending on who sat at home.

And just like that, the Diabolic Oasis had come to life, sparkling under the moon's beautiful light.

Mora's city didn't look anything like an oasis. Well, if the snow surrounding the veiled city served as a sandy substitute, I supposed the resemblance wouldn't be too far off if it weren't for all the tech and plant life.

I stretched my wings wide, enjoying the cool evening breeze against my dark gray feathers. Even if artificially created. This dimension, while and isolated temporal fold, worked exactly like the mortal realm thanks to the spell craft put in place to make it tick-tock on the same scheduled clock as the mortal world along with the technology meant to keep everything synced with the rest of society.

A society the Diabolic Oasis had intentionally removed itself from. And I certainly didn't understand Mora's obsession with time. It was dumb and boring and constraining. Schedules were ugly things that often got in the way of joy. I hated time. The idea of dealing with it forever. I shuddered.

Perhaps I could convince Wally to find a pocket portal dimension where we could simply be, no structure, no linear lines of day through night back to day, no million and one Xs to cross off a calendar of to-dos.

It was something I'd push for in a century or two once Wally had grown bored with his menial tasks as a shopkeeper of exotic antiquities. Speaking of menial tasks, I took a deep breath and unleashed a wave of telekinesis to wrap the packages in my grasp, and then I soared high into the sky and flew through the city.

I weaved between buildings wrapped in giant vines, plants sprouting flowers in every color, and roots that burrowed into concrete to claim a foundation. Despite the stranglehold the wildlife here had, it never slaughtered the city as it should to assert dominance.

Instead, it seemed nature and technology intermingled in this weird form of symbiosis, as Wally called it.

His curious voice buzzed in my mind as I approached my first destination, dropped the package on a porch, punched the door buzzer, and bolted ahead to my next stop.

"You see, the Fae place integration incantations—or their magical equivalent—into the spell work used for pocket dimension creation," he had rambled. Quite often, in fact, composing a new theory or test every day. "The process behind how they cultivate miniature worlds is the most fascinating form of preservation. The Fae altered malleable life so it wouldn't encroach but also wouldn't simply accept being wiped out—say from Mora's constant construction. There were augmentations placed in every plant and animal to enhance their survival instincts by adapting them to… Well, for lack of better words, become more adaptable. It's what keeps the things in this pocket world from going extinct. Again."

Personally, I didn't think of the plants and animals as symbiotic with the city so much as a plague. A virus of overwhelming strength that'd learned how to become innocuous. Sure, the plants and the birds and bees and the other damned fluffy-tailed beasts seemed harmless now, working around the streets and the lights and tech, but one day I believed they'd devour Mora's carefully crafted city.

I shuddered with delight. Maybe I was wrong, but I hoped not. With no real challenges or conflicts or combats, my days had turned into paranoid hypotheticals to maintain some semblance of entertainment. How I hoped the bunnies revolted, sitting atop armored flowers and carrying blades made from the bones of their enemies.

I sighed, tossing another package onto a porch, and resigned to accept this daydream as nothing more than a fantasy. Despite the joy the thought brought, it seemed unlikely I'd be so fortunate.

Everyone seemed to coexist so well here. It was exhausting. Not that the Diabolic Oasis didn't have problems. Mortals and Mythics were inherently awful beings, selfish and simple, but the looming threat of the mage Collective didn't turn every day into a paranoid battle of glancing over my shoulder.

In fact, most seemed to fall in line with Mora's authority, her reign, especially since it didn't interfere with their vices, and no one targeted Wally or me. No one who knew my name, my history, challenged the phony devil who no longer wielded Beelzebub's stolen essence. No one sought to attack Wally, the only known mortal to possess devil essence. A few Diabolics had challenged me when the Oasis first opened to residents, but now… Now, everyone seemed annoyingly content with leaving us be.

Most waged wars with each other on whether nature, magic, or tech would rule with supremacy in this tiny pocket world, yet even that had an obnoxious balance as innovators sought to ensure the three elements melded into interwoven nonsense. The Mythics loved breathing in the magic that seeped throughout the atmosphere, and the mortals indulged in every technological privilege meant to level the playing field. Seriously, if a spell could accomplish something, then suddenly, someone on Mora's tech team created a Googly app to do the same thing.

And the witches, who remained the highest in the population here, craved nature above all. Sure, they liked their finery and their modern living, but if they sought to fully harness the Four Corners, then every witch required Nature's Blessing. Nature wouldn't offer her blessing, her casting, her touch of primal magic, without a bountiful stage to exude her presence. Hence, why so many goddamn plants had become overgrown vegetables that wrapped around every building of the Diabolic Oasis.

My phone buzzed, catching me off guard as I threw another package. It curved a bit too far, so I took a deep breath and unleashed a subtle current of black wind to knock the package back onto the path I'd intended.

It slammed against the door knocker and landed on their welcome mat with a heavy thud. Delivered. Easy peasy.

I swiped the green camera icon, and Mora's eyes fluttered and filled the screen of my phone as she adjusted the lens to fully frame her face. She raked her long pink fingernails through her blonde locks and treated this video call like more time in front of her mirror, fawning over her own lustful desire for the mortal flesh she possessed.

"A pleasure as always, Bezzy." Mora pursed her lips, checking her makeup more than attempting to appear flirty. Her gaze hadn't even met mine yet as she only had eyes for herself at the moment, examining every feature of her newest host body.

She kept a collection of mortals to possess larger than my wardrobe of suits. I had one for every occasion, much like Mora had a body for every day of the year. Hell, every day of the century, based on the vast collection she kept in storage. This week, she wore a petite blonde with vibrant green eyes, not to be confused with Mora's actual Diabolic green eyes that matched her demon aura just as my aura radiated red. Despite growing more comfortable living her demon truth here in a city of her making, Mora still didn't indulge in displaying her Diabolic features, though, keeping her essence coiled beneath her delicate mortal flesh.

All the same, her royal arrogance had flourished when returned to a throne. A throne of her own making in a kingdom smaller than most cities, but thanks to her carefully calculated cunning, she'd already cemented this Diabolic Oasis as a vital silent partner to many outside the dimension.

I tossed the final package into a mailbox. Perhaps a bit too rough as it dented the metal frame. Whatever, their cheap homes didn't concern me, so long as Wally's protective wards held up the artifact in the parcels would remain unscathed. "What do you want?"

"Having an issue with our security lines, and I thought who better to handle it than…"

I rolled my eyes. Issues. Meaning she'd undoubtedly invited someone with a ploy into the realm again. Mora indulged too many foes, offering them opportunities I would never. In fact, it was the one benefit of her scheming.

"With the witches already circling, I don't have time for this drama," Mora continued.

"Wait." I smirked. "Have the witches finally risen up against you?"

While, more often than not, the residents of the Diabolic Oasis coexisted well enough, there were times when people acted out and needed to be put in their place. Their place being a grave that I got to put them in. Sanctioned murder wasn't the same as impulsively ripping out someone's heart for touching my man, but it quenched the bloodlust.

"The witches are fine." Mora waved a dismissive hand. "Plotting their coup while I placate them with concessions until I decide what the most lucrative solution will be."

"Your solution should be bloody."

"Perhaps." Mora pouted her lips, posing for her camera as if my presence on the telephone didn't exist. "They're under the delusion that since the city lacks Collective authority, there's a vacuum in power. I believe with a few polite meetings, I can quell this hubris without the need to slaughter them all. However, I'm always prepared for a bit of carnal carnage should the discussions not go accordingly."

"Well, call me when bloodshed is on the table, not diplomacy or whatever."

"I'm not calling about witch drama. Though, that is becoming irritatingly high on my list," Mora said with an edge in her voice. "My concern is for the unknown intruder waltzing into *my* city."

While serving as a delivery service for Walter's silly shop was my main occupation, I also freelanced for Mora, handling issues or threats when they arose. Technically speaking, Mora could handle them herself, but apparently, it was unbecoming for a king to soil her hands with unruly peasants, so she'd declared me an official lord or knight or thug—some absurd title I didn't ever use or announce when eviscerating enemies.

Plus, I struggled to pay attention when Mora went on about the semantics of monarchs and the roles of her society. At least Walter was cute to look at when he rambled. Mora had this unpleasant scowl as her expression shifted into a sour face whenever I didn't listen to her. Sort of like right now.

"Bezzy, did you hear a word I said?"

"Yes, all of them, in fact." I huffed. "Someone's doing something to cross you. Blah, blah, blah biddy, blah. Kill 'em for your king. Wait, don't kill 'em. Hang on, maybe blah blegh blob."

"You never listen."

"Maybe you never shut the fuck up." I squinted at her telephone face. "Ever think of that?"

"There's a demon that's torn through the dimensional barrier."

"I thought that was impossible."

The whole point of this tiny pocket dimension was to create a completely self-sufficient world that allowed its residents to weave in and out of the mortal realm as they pleased while creating a precise locking mechanism to thwart intrusion.

"So you want me to kill this demon?"

"I want you to locate them first." Mora frowned. "I have questions. And concerns. No demon should possess the strength necessary to tear through my dimensional walls."

"They're not really your walls," I said. "It's not your essence permeating at the edges of the realm. Hell—pun intended—it's not even held together by Diabolic power anymore. Just a bunch of Fae and witchy magics."

"Semantics, Bezzy. It's my realm, and I'd like to know who dared attempt to infiltrate."

"It's not really an attempt if they're already roaming the streets."

Mora bared her teeth, her pearly smile fizzling away to a frustrated grimace only I could cause. I batted my lashes in response.

"Talk less, kill more."

I smirked. "Finally, you're saying something I can agree with."

3

I scrambled to toss my clothes on, rifling through a drawer of spare shirts since Bez had shredded mine. At least he had the decency to strip off my jeans this time. Once I finished, I rushed out of the sparring room and toward the front of the store, where Tony sat perched atop the incantation I'd crafted. He alerted the patron to what they owed and whisked the cash they offered into the register.

The sigils allowed about a thousand different talking points for Tony to express through the simple activation of the various sigils weaved into the incantation. It was mostly for me. Not so we could communicate, but so I wouldn't have to spend all day working in the front of the store.

"Sorry," I said, a bit haggard. "Got busy back there."

The click in Tony's claws carried a very judgmental "uh-huh," or perhaps that carried through the psychic link I shared with my familiar. He didn't exactly have tangible thoughts, but I felt the words, the feelings knocking at the edge of my brain.

Tony finished up with the last customer, using the incantation to bag their golem hammer artifact, and then sent them on their way.

Even though we didn't get many customers—the place currently emptied out now that the most recent patron had left—working the front of the store was my least favorite thing. Thankfully, Tony didn't mind dealing with customers. What he did mind was the extended sparring sessions I had with Bez several days a week that often put me behind track on inventory requisitions. And honestly, I didn't care for the inventory components of our store. I just wanted shiny things to research, analyze, decipher, but the more we dealt with clients, the more opportunities we had when it came to expanding our own inventory.

The bell at the front door jingled, and an elven woman walked inside, bulldozing directly to the checkout desk without so much as perusing the stocked items. She approached and tossed a pouch of jewels onto the counter. Definitely jewels based on the lumps in the small coin purse and the fact elves switched over to dragonic currency after forging a mutually beneficial alliance a millennium ago. Something about dragons possessing no desire to attend Mythic Council meetings and elves requiring the aid of sheer indomitable force to safeguard humanity didn't truly obliterate the wonders of the world.

"Welcome to the Well of Wonders. How can I assist you?" I asked, to which Tony scoffed. Actually, he let out a little chirpy hiss of judgment as if I couldn't handle one customer.

And sure, I often avoided the front of the store because it reminded me of my time working in the repository with demanding superiors. Plus, Tony had a knack for customer service. He always picked the most polite 'fuck you' phrases from his glyph selections that still ensured he didn't tell a customer off. Part of why Bez wasn't allowed to work out front anymore. That and the last time Bez interacted with a patron, the ogre ended up losing his tongue.

"I gave him a choice, Walter," Bez's snarky voice rang in my head as fresh as it had that day, where he stood over a gasping ogre who rolled in his bloody muck, clutching his mouth. "He waltzed in here demanding a manager—as if I'd ever be managed—and then had the audacity to berate me."

I recoiled at the memory of him holding the flailing tongue, an organ that resisted Bez's grip as an ogre's limbs and pieces never lost motor function unless the brain and heart were smashed.

In retrospect, Bez was pretty considerate…for him. He'd offered the ogre the option to walk away with or without his tongue. It was how the Mythic responded afterward that led to Bez's impulsivity. Hence, why he handled deliveries now.

The elven woman snapped her fingers. The jewelry bedazzling her hand shimmered close to my face, where she held it to draw my attention.

Did she just treat me like a dog? I shook it off and smiled. "Sorry. How can I help you?"

"As I was saying, I'd like to see the Fae relics you have in stock. Something exquisite and exotic. A conversation starter." Her eyes drifted to the pouch of jewels she set on the counter, indicating her intention to spend big.

I supposed she hadn't read our barter policy. Dragonic jewels were fascinating but worth about as much as human gems. There was nothing to be gained for me and my research by her gaudy currency.

"I've already arranged something with the owner." She waved a hand, dismissing me from my post. "So go retrieve the shopkeeper."

I quirked a brow. I'd never met this woman in my life. "I'm actually an owner."

"And I'm here about employing the services of your nymphs."

"We don't have any employees."

Tony clacked his claws.

"We don't have any Mythic employees," I corrected myself. "Tony's basically the manager here. And I, well, sort of run—"

"Again, put me in contact with the person in charge."

"Again." I raised my shoulders, trying not to turtle my neck. "I'm an owner. The owner. Well, one. Um…"

"I need to speak with someone in charge about the nymphs." The elven woman waved a hand as if to shoo me from her presence and send me off to fulfill her request. Well, her order. More like her rude command. "I'm hosting a gala and could use their services on my gardens."

A bell chimed, indicating someone new had stepped inside, but I didn't catch sight of them when they turned down the nearest aisle up front while I stood locked in combat…conversation with this elf.

"Um, well, I'm in charge. Mostly. Sort of. I handle a lot of in-charge things. Books and inventory mostly. Valued exchanges. Paperwork. Legal documents. Artifacts. Employment records—which there are no nymphs in."

"I've seen your nymphs tending to that hideous tree outside." The elven woman lifted her head high, holding her nose up with a commanding flair and a disgusted expression, as if everything in the front of our store not only lacked in wonder but created an eyesore she forced herself to endure. "I don't understand why you built this store inside a tree and named it after a well. It's confusing. Unless that tree ate the well like the signs suggest."

"Funny you should say that." I chuckled, running a hand through the back of my head to ease my nerves by brushing my fingers through my blond curls. "There is an actual well in the back—mostly unused except for the occasional explosive experiment on relics by Kell. Hence the name of the store. Well of Wonders. Which is a fusion of the owners, myself—Walter and Kell."

Kell suggested we'd get a lot of pushback on the name, but I figured it'd make for an interesting anecdote, a bit of a puzzle for our guests to solve, something unique to spark curiosity. Personally, I loved our mysterious little shop set up inside a strangler fig. Even if I had to put up new signs every week to warn folks about the dangers of the tree.

Normally, they didn't cause harm, aside from the tree it grew around and literally strangled the life out of to become a gnarled beauty and proof of the many wonders of nature. But this particular tree attracted a lot of woodland nymphs that imbued it with the strength to strangle anyone who wandered too far off the path leading to our front door.

"Oh, those nymphs." I nodded. "Yeah, so we don't employ them. In fact, Kell and I have actively discouraged them casting…" Well, I'd asked since I worried Kell would either create something destructive to scare the nymphs away or tell Mora, who had an even deadlier impulsive attitude than Bez. She merely sat on a throne while slaughtering those that annoyed her.

"I must've spoken with this Kell fella then, as he ensured me I could procure the services of the nymphs for my party."

I frowned. "I don't think you spoke to *her*."

"I'm absolutely certain I spoke to her." The elf cleared her throat, staggering for time as she piled on more bullshit to her request. A request I couldn't even assist with since I didn't have the contact information for the nymphs.

"But I do know when woodland nymphs patrol plant life, spreading seeds, pollinating, augmenting, altering wildlife." Seriously, they were like the organic version of Fae as they always kept the shifts they conjured with magic within the realm of possibility for the plant or animal in question.

"You clearly do not understand who I am or the power my opinion wields in the Diabolic Oasis." The elven woman glared, shooting dagger eyes down at me. "I personally know the king of this city."

"So do I."

"You know of her." The elf scoffed. "Everyone does. But she'll be attending my event along with so many others. Unless you wish for me to run this business into the ground, I suggest you get me the contact information for those woodland nymphs."

"We don't actually require clients to keep this shop afloat." I grimaced. "I mean, it's a wonderful perk, but the business is more about cataloging our own inventory and inviting others into a library-like bartering exchange."

"You listen here, you little bastard." She pointed her finger, jabbing the air and stirring the store with the radiance of her elven magic.

I took a deep breath, quelling the immediate impulse my Diabolic essence had to surge outward. It buzzed beneath my skin, itchy and synced to the anger I buried. Controlling my devilish powers at will wasn't the easiest, but finding how they linked to my emotions served a vital lesson—even if it meant having to temper my own feelings to keep from slaughtering someone just because they were annoying.

"As a matter of—"

A hand swiped so swiftly past the elven woman; her aggravated expression didn't even have a chance to lessen once the Diabolic strike beheaded her.

I gasped, taking in the sight of her lopped-off head whirl with this annoyed face before finally bouncing on the ground with several heavy thuds.

"Fuuuuuuuuuck." I dragged out the word, blinking away the shock as I stared at the hand coated in Diabolic essence and a trickle of blood.

Speaking of blood, the elven woman's exposed neck sputtered blood upward like a little fountain. I backstepped, ready to hurl at the intoxicating smell that sprayed through the store, painting the floor with sweet, sticky red blood. Yuck. Blood was not a yum factor. This was my devil essence coursing through my veins, demanding something gross while tampering with my senses to alter my tastes—quite literally.

If this weren't such a dire situation, I'd consider performing a study on my tastebuds in various situations to see what stimulated the essence to circumvent control while rewriting my natural programming. No hijacking, though. Once I swallowed the lump in my throat, the desire to lick the floorboards clean faded, which meant the sensory tampering from my essence was short-lived. A working hypothesis. But right now, I had bigger issues to contend with, unfortunately.

"Bez," I snapped. "You can't just kill customers. I don't know how many times we have to discuss…"

I paused my tangent—one I'd given Bez multiple times when he threatened to eviscerate a customer. There was something off about his nails. Black essence coated his bloody hand down to the wrist, but his nails were painted. Bez didn't paint his nails. They were sharper, longer, and more curled than Bez's, too.

I looked past the headless elf corpse still standing and spurting blood out and found a shirtless, powder blue-skinned man standing behind the body. A body that finally tumbled forward.

"Um…" I widened my eyes. "You're not Bez."

"Apologies. I simply found her behavior atrocious," the powder blue-skinned guy said with a raspy voice and a wicked smirk. His teeth were sharklike and added to the smile that quickly filled his face. "I'm Prince Corson, here to greet the devil of the Diabolic Oasis."

"Huh? Greet with a beheading? You can't just…" I fumbled with words as I took in this Diabolic's features. And he was a Diabolic, too.

The hands coated in essence was an obvious indicator, so his very human aesthetic was probably a partial possession, hence the skin color, or he had a humany demon body similar to Bez. Like Bez, he also had a very muscular build.

He wore a thin leather strap across his chest on an angle that connected to an armor plating on his right shoulder. His left shoulder remained exposed, perhaps to reveal the many tattoos that covered his entire arm, along with his very large bicep, easily bigger in circumference than my entire head. Between his muscular physique, his bloody hand, and his menacing smile, I took a tense breath from all the intimidation his mere presence radiated.

The guy looked like he'd stepped out of a Roman warrior catalog, wearing only a black leather skirt, easily a modern version of the pteruges the soldiers wore to battle, and a pair of caligae which was sort of a mix between a sandal and boot, at least the black pair he wore.

He ran his bloody fingertips—well, clawed tips—through his ruffled shoulder-length hair, a dark blue with white and gold streaks. His nails matched the streaks in his hair, with every other nail being either white or gold.

"I find it quite surprising that you endured the elf's dreadfully dull demeanor for as long as you did." Corson waved his hand, casting telekinesis with his demon powers to toss the elf's corpse into a corner of the store. "Bizarre even that you didn't simply obliterate her upon the first offense she dared to utter at you."

"Offense?" I found the tremble in my legs and attempted to appear as nonchalant about Corson's arrival as his wicked demeanor did. "Wouldn't have many customers if I killed them every time they annoyed me."

"Yes, but the ones who did continue their customer services would be more respectful of their betters." Corson shrugged, his expression aloof yet definitely curious by the way his eyes studied every subtle shift in my body. "Whatever. A docile devil should make what comes next easier."

"Easier?" I swallowed hard. "What do you want? Who are you, exactly?"

"I'm here for you, Walter Alden, devil of human mage origin," Corson said before he pressed a hand to his chest, feigning insult. But despite how his mouth twisted into this offended expression, his eyes still had a smile. "Do you not remember me?"

His bright sapphire blue irises shimmered with the whites of his eyes a sky-blue barely a few shades different from his complexion. It made his dark blue lashes pop and the vibrance of his irises all the more intense.

"I haven't forgotten you since our last encounter where I tried to murder you." He chuckled. "I sort of braced myself for your wrath, anticipating vengeful ire from you at mere presence, yet you have this lovely, fidgety, frightened expression—sort of reminiscent of the first time we met."

"Met?" I thought back to every Diabolic I'd encountered, which mostly consisted of Bez and Mora here in the Diabolic Oasis. Even with other demons in the city, they avoided me, whether because I had devil essence or I had Bez or both.

The only time I'd really encountered other Diabolics was when I was trapped in Baron Novus' villa, where the demon knight Eligos released demons to help him slaughter Bez, me, Mora, and Kell. There was the demon possessing the pink-skinned Fae, but she had red eyes like Bez. There was the creepy sunshine-yellow demon that blew himself up, but I'd never forget his creepy, hungry voice.

"You were the one possessing the birdlike Fae," I answered, finally recalling this demon who attempted to kill me in the maze tunnels before Bez ripped out his heart and then devoured him with Mora. "You're dead!"

"I was." He tsked. "I fucking hate Oblivion."

The empty void where all dead Diabolics went, eternally resting.

"How'd you get out?"

"My mommy brought me back," he said with this mocking, pitchy voice.

"Your mother?" I trembled. Only one thing could pull a demon from the depths of Oblivion. "She's a devil?"

"Sort of a big shot devil, too. Lilith, the mother of macabre and mayhem. Maybe you've heard of her." His minxy expression shifted into a menacing smirk. "She's certainly heard of you, Walter Alden. And she wants you."

"Me?" My voice cracked.

Corson held up his hands, summoning black flames between his palms.

Without an ounce of hesitation, I traced a protective sigil in the air with my fingertips. I poured mana into a written incantation, preparing to summon a barrier that'd absorb even the strongest Diabolic elements unleashed. Usually, their essence rained down with such tremendous superiority against magics, nature, and technology there was no way to compete. And while I didn't have much control over the essence bound to my being, all the experience I had with Bez, plus my love for experiments, allowed me to find innovative new spellcasting combinations to redirect, deflect, or counter Diabolic abilities.

"What's your damn problem?" Corson roared, loud and visceral, as he ground his teeth.

Between his fury and the flames he conjured falling to the floor, I panicked and stepped back. That was when I realized it didn't matter how quickly my brain had reacted, how swiftly I'd channeled mana or written the incantation because my Diabolic essence had reacted faster. Pure instinct took over—which Bez would undoubtedly rub in my face—and my tail had sprung out, piercing through Corson's wrists and nullifying the threat of his attack.

I gulped.

Not the entire threat. My anxiety surged as the black flames flickered and fluttered to the floor. They were Diabolic made, which potentially meant only a few embers were required to set the entire store ablaze.

"Not happening," I muttered.

I didn't even need to formulate a plan because the sharp tingle beneath my shoulder blades indicated the instinctual summoning of my black cherub-sized wings. Another Diabolic feature that moved of its own accord for my needs. Each flap carried a dark gust of smothering wind that devoured the oxygen and magic the flames Corson had manifested.

"This would be more helpful if it wasn't so unintentional." I huffed as my devil essence performed feats and techniques I couldn't muster despite my best efforts.

"Are you seriously trying to fight me?"

"Are you seriously trying to challenge a devil?" I swallowed my trepidation, shifting my stance in the process and attempting to look badass.

But I scrunched my face, worrying the creak in my voice when I spoke hadn't sold the confidence bit. I mean, he knew I wasn't an actual devil, so what was stopping him from calling me out for the incompetent little mage who cried Diabolic.

"Fuck it, you wanna go, let's go." Corson gestured, arms wide, flames exploding from his palms. "Even if you get lucky and kill me again, at least I can tell Lilith what a fucking fool she was for—"

My tail zipped ahead and sliced off Corson's left hand. As it fell to the floor, my essence devoured the fire and continued lunging toward the demon who'd dared to face a mage coursing with the power of a devil in his veins.

"I'm so sick of you." Corson roared, unveiling six powder blue scaled wings. Each flap carried a subtle black gust. Hot, dry wind whirled until flickers of embers mixed and sparked and set the entire store on fire.

"Motherfucker!"

"As if I'd ever bed my shrew of a mother."

Ignoring his nonsense, I focused on flames and traced a dozen different incantations meant to shield artifacts and suppress Diabolic elements. Instead, black lightning zapped and snapped from my fingertips. It zipped throughout the store like a thousand hungry serpents. Each bolt tackled fire, surged and coiled around the flames, and then consumed the demon's magic in a way only a devil truly could.

"You made a seriously grave error attacking me." I studied my essence circle and devoured Corson's continued futile casting. I only wish I were more involved in my own defense. I muttered techniques my body adapted to instantly without my input and made a mental note to actively learn how to do that.

Corson ignored my mutterings and continued destroying my store in an attempt to strike me. This wasn't gonna work. I couldn't allow him to trash the Well of Wonders. And as the thought swirled in my mind, the devil essence lunged ahead, knocking the demon through the door and leading us into a battle outside.

Too bad none of it was my doing, my knowledge. Nope.

Seriously, even with the power belonging to me, I'd still somehow become a damsel forced to rely on my devilish abilities. They acted on instinct—instinct that merely required me to stare in awe. I didn't have to participate a bit in my own survival.

I still had so much to learn, which, at the very least, I could study during this fight. If one could call it that.

4

Bez

I lunged from the Diabolic threads laced throughout the Oasis. When a demon or devil covered an area in their essence, it allowed them to control the territory in a subtle manner, establishing a foothold for their dominion. These invisible webs of essence weren't mine, so much as Mora's, but I darted inside them for the fast travel it offered, instantaneously returning to the Well of Wonders where Wally clashed outside with some blue-skinned demon whose heart I ripped out of his chest immediately upon my arrival.

"Son of a bitch," the foul demon shouted. "Again? Is that your fucking go-to move? Taking hearts?"

"I am quite charming." I grinned, then took a bite out of the still-beating organ.

It sparked a memory. I recognized this essence from when I first encountered the demon, devouring him alongside Mora. Back when that fool Eligos sought to slay me and use the trace amounts of

Beelzebub's essence entwined with mine to challenge the devils in their own Hell domains.

"Fun." I tightened my gaze, locking eyes with this audacious prick. "Guess I won't have to share my snack this time."

"I'm a tasty treat for sure, but I'm not here for conflict or conquest." His fanged teeth twisted into a sick smirk. "The name's Corson, and I'm merely here to—"

"Shut up!" I crushed his heart in my hand.

Corson bit the air, playfully panting. "Bossy."

"You attacked Walter. There's only one recourse."

"How'd you know I was in trouble?" Wally asked.

"Now is not the time for your inquisitive prodding."

"Hmmm." Corson wiggled his eyebrows. "I'm always up for a bit of prodding."

I snarled.

Corson huffed. "The tension here is so not my vibe."

As much as I'd like to say my investigative skills had improved, how I'd solved Mora's mission about the intrusive demon that'd broken into her Diabolic Oasis, my arrival was purely happenstance. Whenever Wally activated his devil essence, my body shuddered ever so subtly, recalling every day spent with the devil's might coursing through my being, reliving every eon spent at Beelzebub's feet, serving the god-king who reigned with a callous cruelty unlike any I'd encountered since my lifetimes in his Hell.

Despite the fact essence remained veiled and hidden from detection, my instincts were synced onto every movement of the devil essence radiating within Wally. And since he'd acquired it, he never accessed the power so heavily, potent and destructive in the air. It served as the only proof I required that he was in danger.

"To be clear, he attacked me." Corson pointed a gold-painted clawed finger at Wally as if he'd ever provoke a fight. "I came in peace, merely attempting to deliver a message."

"Liar." I lunged forward, slashing my claws at his throat.

"Bezzy, no!" Mora leapt from the finely hidden threads of her essence, positioning herself between Corson and me.

Of course, she proclaimed herself the only demon allowed to weave her essence in such a manner, but she allowed anyone of a Diabolic nature the privilege of accessing her threads. She said it was a sign of her graciousness. I said it was further proof she loved having as many people inside her as possible.

"What is your problem?" I growled. "You're the one who told me to kill this guy."

"Of course this is a case for Mora." Wally pouted. "So much for chivalry."

"Are you whining?" I glared. "You're the one always telling me not to kill folks."

"That's before he attacked me and tried destroying my shop."

"I did no such thing," Corson commented.

"Bezzy, focus. Perhaps on his official banner of passage." Mora kept her telekinesis trained on me, an effort to deter me should I attempt to strike this foul demon.

I scoffed. As if she could.

"I didn't realize Lilith was sending an ambassador." Mora curtsied.

"Why would you?" Corson shrugged. "You don't even have an embassy in this shitty dimension. How is one meant to be greeted upon their arrival?"

"Well, usually they arrive at one of the official gates," Wally interjected, a moody expression on his face and a tangent ready to explain the sophisticated complexities of how the Diabolic Oasis had several points of entry for incoming and outgoing traffic.

"A truly disgraceful display on my part." Mora smiled, adding this cutesy inflection meant to come across as delicate, which only made her sound pitiful.

Anything involving devils resulted in Mora's immediate submission. Not that I could blame her. If one deemed her world a threat, they'd shred the walls and burn the magic holding this place together until only cinders remained. But I figured the Diabolic Oasis wouldn't catch any devil's interest, a meager pocket portal at first glance and barely anything more than a tiny realm veiled inside another world. Our dimension wasn't even linked to the infinite web of dimensions creating the ever-expanding universe.

Mora's city was more like a downloadable content to the mortal world. I shivered at the idea of the game of life that was being a boring, basic mortal. Yuck. But unlike DLC, Mora's world would never become anything more than an added extension. Downloadable Loser Content because only losers paid extra for game add-ons when they were just gonna buy the special edition that included all the add-ons later anyway. I stared at Walter, the truest victim of DLC syndrome. Unlike him, I had the patience for slow-moving mortal time and always waited until I could make Wally procure the deluxe special versions of the games I indulged in.

"What's this about an official banner?" Wally asked, squinting his eyes as if that'd somehow assist. It wouldn't. Even I didn't notice the display right away since I no longer lived in Hell or entertained demon delegates sent on Diabolic business.

"When a devil wishes to speak to another, they often use a proxy since so few deign to step foot outside the glory of their own dimension," I explained, biting back my sarcasm as best I could.

"And Lilith is constantly jerking herself off over the *glory* of her Hell realm," Corson added with a snicker.

I glared. The audacity to speak about his devil in such a manner. Even if she were a vile shrew—I'd had the misfortune of Lilith's visits to Beelzebub's Hell on the rare occasions when she deigned another world worth her ventures. I'd bet if she heard this Corson's cocky comment, she'd toss his ass back into Oblivion.

"Okay, but where is this banner?" Wally gestured everywhere, searching for the hidden cue on Diabolic etiquette when it came to a situation such as this.

"Oh, sweetie." Mora crinkled her face and spoke with a pitchy lilt. "Still can't channel your Diabolic senses? His banner's practically on your lap."

"Hence why I figured you were berating me." Corson grinned. "Maybe you didn't like my display, didn't like me slapping your face with my big, thick Diabolic energy."

"I'm about to slap you, demon." I snarled.

"Apologies." Corson raised his arms in feigned surrender. "I'm terrible at diplomatic policy, yet Mother continues to drag me into this stuff. I'm merely attempting to be friendly."

"Don't want your friendship."

"Boo." The arrogant blue demon pouted. "Here I was hoping we'd stay up late, braiding each other's hair and sharing secrets while eating the ice of cream."

Wally continued searching for the banner, stepping right through the translucent fabrics. Since Wally hadn't come close to mastering control over his Diabolic abilities, he couldn't enhance his vision to see between the dimensional layers of reality where the banner of diplomacy floated. Each strand of fabric moved like a floral flag, some pedals coiled inward while others stretched out far, revealing emblems unique to Lilith's Hell. Beacons of her devil's signature. These intangible pieces of energy conjured by a devil weren't exactly the essence of Lilith's being, but they carried her scent, radiated her aura, commanded her authority.

"What exactly brings you here?" Mora asked, cautious but too curious not to investigate.

"An invitation, of course." He reached into the satchel hanging at the side of his leather skirt, meant to evoke some warrior garb from a long-forgotten culture. Retrieving a piece of parchment, he opened it with essence and unveiled the flaming orb that served as a key to Lilith's dimension.

Beelzebub would make similar ones for his demons venturing outside the realm. It was linked directly to the full power of a devil. Even as such a tiny item, Lilith's being oozed through each flick of the fire, casting an immense palpable presence.

I clamped my jaw, teeth ready to crack under the pressure.

"Lilith has decided to hold a banquet in honor of Walter Alden's ascension as a devil, per se, and would like to extend him an invitation to her Hell." Corson bowed, raising his arms and offering Wally the fiery orb.

"Oh, fuck me," I groaned.

Corson cocked his head. "Maybe if you ask nicely, phony devil."

"Stop talking to me, or the next thing I rip out of you will be your tongue."

"He's jesting." Mora laughed, then elbowed me not-so-subtly and shot me a glare that absolutely meant I needed to shut the fuck up, but I had no energy or desire to placate this prick at our feet.

Correction, at Wally's feet. Wally, who stared at the flames in awe, curious and cautious and calculating every observation that'd likely turned all the gears in his overly active mind.

"She's having a banquet for me?" The flickering fire danced in Wally's eyes, illuminating the hazel irises until the black void of essence completely overtook his sight. The black orbs studied the fiery invitation. "Why? How?"

"As the newest devil, Lilith wishes for an audience with you," Corson explained as if Wally should grasp such things.

"She knows I'm not a devil devil, right?" Wally raised an eyebrow and bit his lower lip as he did his very best not to elaborate on the unique complexities of his situation. His forehead crinkled in the cutest way as he held back the extra notes he wanted to add to the conversation.

Honestly, devils so rarely birthed themselves into existence, it made some modicum of sense Lilith would crave to have one of her carnal festivities with a knock-off devil. True devils were consciousness constructed in the dead, empty spaces of the universe. They filled the void of nothingness with tangibility, conjuring a Hell realm for their being, for their world, for their eternity. But the last devil rising I'd heard of was more than a thousand years ago. With so many infinitely growing dimensions, there were few empty spaces to carve out Hells in this universe.

"She knows all," Corson answered Wally's question. "Lilith can never be deceived."

That wasn't a response so much as a warning, a threat, a promise she'd learn the full extent of Wally's being. I could think of no other reason for her to offer him a key to her Hell, a party in his honor.

"Here is all the information on the Devil's Banquet." Corson handed over the flaming orb, which Wally carefully cradled between his hands. "During the event, you'll be expected to present yourself to Lilith's Court and declare war, alliance, or neutrality with her realm."

"W-w-what?"

"It's all very standard," Mora said with a smile. "Most devils choose neutrality with each other, alliances becoming demanding."

"And most devils are too cowardly to attend a Devil's Banquet and declare war," Corson added.

There was one devil in existence who attended Lilith's ceremony and declared war in the midst of a party—Beelzebub himself. It was before my time, but the recounting of the tales passed for eons from the mouths of the demons who attended the banquet with Beelzebub as he tore his way through Lilith's Hell to challenge her. A sign of his boldness but also a sign of her strength. Beelzebub only believed in war, conquering, and death. Yet, he left Lilith's realm at a stalemate where the two clashed for millennia in between other wars.

"I look forward to your attendance, Walter Alden." Corson took a bow, waved a hand in some frilly bid to add levity to his formal behavior, and then used a tail to rip through the dimensional barrier of the city.

Lilith's added strength to her diplomat allowed him to slice through the intricately woven layers of this hidden world with ease. Corson backstepped and vanished as the tear in the dimension sowed itself shut as swiftly as it'd fallen apart.

"Is this real life?" Wally blinked several times at the fire in his hands, wondering about a million things based on the frazzled expression. "Did I just get invited to Hell?"

"You did," I answered, resisting the tremble in my voice.

"I mean, that's cool and all, but I'm not ready for Hell." Wally grinned. "I'm totally gonna study this key, though. I bet I can figure out the frequencies Lilith harnessed to hack into our dimension. Maybe even find a way to prevent it in the future. Actually, I bet—"

"You can't," I interjected. "You can't say no to a devil's invitation."

"What?"

This Devil's Banquet sent an icy chill of horror through my being. Hell was unlike any experience. Lilith's domain might not be as horrid as Beelzebub's, but none were gentle on the mortal coil. A single step into Hell would shatter a human's sanity beyond repair. Would the devil essence coursing inside Wally be enough to protect him from such horrors?

5

Wally

Each flicker of the fireball in my hands cast a shadow of intrigue, of mystery, of utter fucking confusion. That demon—Corson—had snuck into our city to invite me to his Hell. Correction, his devil's Hell. Lilith. A devil knew me…Walter Alden…and she wanted to throw a banquet for me. One I couldn't very well reject.

"Wait." I tilted my head, still studying the movement of the fire, which danced more like the gentle ebb and flow of waves on a beach than of actual flames. "What do you mean I can't say no to the invitation?"

"Lilith is temperamental like most devils," Mora said. "She would deem it a slight, and such offense can only be met with measurable retaliation."

"She'd likely eradicate this entire dimension," Bez said nonchalantly, though his gaze was lost on the flaming invitation I held. There was a sadness in his crimson eyes, his expression devoid of charm and hiding concern.

"Wait." The reality of their comments sank in. "What part of destroying an entire world is a measurable response to me rejecting a party invite?"

"It's not a party. It's an opportunity to assess you, dear." Mora sauntered toward me, fixated on the same flames that captured all our attention. The key to Lilith's Hell. "This is Lilith's way of reminding everyone of her authority in the universe while she evaluates your place in said universe."

"You make it sound like I'm…" I bit my lower lip, unsure what it made me sound like because nothing whirling in my mind even came comparatively close to the level of power Lilith suspected me of possessing. My place in the universe? My attendance was the difference between an entire world living or dying? "What the fuck."

"Basically," Mora continued, ignoring my muttered outburst. "Rejecting her is like saying she holds no interest to you, and as such, her natural response would be to express how little interest your world is to her."

"How is that a natural response? Destroying an entire world! That is the opposite of no interest. It's very spiteful. Spite requires interest." I studied the key that would access Lilith's world, the key that would take me to the Devil's Banquet she had planned. "How do I use this?"

"Easy to activate with any essence," Bez said softly. Too softly for him. He moved closer and traced a clawed hand along a zigzag pattern of flames burning against a fiery core. "See here. It's locked right now. I suspect the banquet has not begun yet."

"Knowing Lilith, this is a last-minute invitation," Mora said. "She did the same thing to Bael. It was awful. He scrambled to prepare himself before dragging me with him."

"You've been to her Hell?"

"I've been to nearly every Hell, darling."

"Well, that's good." I exhaled, releasing a bit of my trepidation. "Having your insight there will be good."

"Oh, I'm not going to Hell," Mora said with a laugh. "Only a fool would willingly attend one of Lilith's banquets."

"So you don't think I should go?"

"No," Bez said.

"I didn't say that," Mora clarified. "A willing fool walks to their death. You're not a willing participant."

"And we don't have to be complacent," Bez said, stepping in front of Mora. "If your instinct is to not attend, then we won't."

"We can really do that? What about what you said?"

"We'll keep a lower profile, make it harder for anyone to find us, learn of us. Vanish entirely." Bez's eyes were wide and wild. "Living somewhere called the Diabolic Oasis is like having a beacon on us to begin with. We can do better."

"There's not really anywhere to hide if Lilith would destroy our whole world."

"This world," Bez clarified. "We can find a new one. I can cut through a hundred different dimensions at once and let you have your pick of new, wonderous treasures to explore."

"What happens here if I just leave?" I asked. "Would Lilith pursue us? Would she retaliate on this dimension? Would she…I don't even know. No, I can't abandon an entire world."

"What's the world ever done for you, really?"

"Bez, I can't just let the entire world burn in my place."

"I could." Bez turned away and extended his wings, hiding his face behind the large gray feathers. "Even if Lilith doesn't kill you for one singular misstep in her realm, you're still a mortal Walter."

"One who's apparently quite devilish." I reached out, delicately running my fingertips along the contour feathers; they were darker and bigger than most others. "I just have to make sure I don't misstep in Lilith's Hell. I can behave. I can be proper. I'm an Alden. Formal ceremony is part of the lineage."

"You don't understand." Bez paused, his voice cracking. "Stepping into Hell is irreversible. It could shatter you the second you arrive."

I quaked, less from the strength of Bez's words and more from the tremble as he said them.

"Take some time to consider your options, Wally." Bez flapped his wings, hovering in place. "It's okay to let the world fall."

"No, it's—"

And just like that, Bez soared off into the night sky.

"I wish he would've stuck around to talk about this."

"Oh, Bezzy's fine." Mora waved a dismissive hand in the direction Bez flew. "Worried about the world is all."

"He only seemed worried about me."

"That's what I said." Mora gave me a matter-of-fact look.

I was Bez's world, and he was mine. But letting the entire dimension be destroyed because of the possibility a devil might kill me… That was a tough choice.

"Do you think stepping into Hell would actually hurt me?"

"Definitely." Mora grinned. "But I also think it's impossible for a mortal to live with devil essence. I think it's pure fiction that Bezzy would be in love. There are a lot of absolutes I would've declared before encountering you, Wally."

"So, you think the essence will protect me?"

"From the effects of Hell itself, perhaps." Mora rocked her head side-to-side. "From Lilith's ire when you inevitably wrong her through mere mortal behavior, unlikely. But maybe you'll get lucky."

"On both counts."

"Fleeing isn't an option, however." Mora squared my shoulders, tilted my chin, and adjusted my head until our eyes were locked onto each other. "I've known demons who've fled from devils after crossing them. They don't escape. They don't hide. They merely leave a trail of ruined worlds in their wake as a devil drags out their death."

"But Bez said—"

"Bez is pulling from his own experience with Beelzebub, the devil he escaped." Mora's eyes flickered emerald green for the briefest of seconds before returning to the softer green of her host body. "A very different circumstance."

Of course. Bez hadn't been to Hell, to any Hell, since escaping his own ruled over by the cruelest of all devils. He didn't only flee, though. He took a piece of Beelzebub, the essence now circulating through me, and thus forever locked Beelzebub away in his own dimension. After all, only complete devils can open the doorways to and from Hell realms.

"This is a lot to consider."

"Take your time. It's just your life, the world, and a few trillion souls at stake." Mora sauntered away, lightly laughing. "I'll let Kell know you ruined her shop. Maybe she can stop by and help clean the place up."

"Our shop." I huffed, turning back to the broken glass and small flames eating away at the entrance of the Well of Wonders. "Suppose I can fix this up while I ponder."

No amount of cleaning cleared my head. I'd never had such an insurmountable decision before. Hell might possibly be the death of me. Entering the dimension itself or simply annoying the devil hosting the banquet in my honor. Which wasn't really to honor me but to study me.

Tony crawled over the back of my hand, his steps cautious yet familiar. They evoked a memory, our first encounter, our first time working together with a familiar bond. A bond that had grown tremendously since then, allowing me to share a phantom form of my essence with the scorpion and allowing him to share his thoughts with me. Even if they weren't words, the sensation struck a chord that reverberated through my entire being.

I had faced choices like this before. When I first worked with Tony, I used a spell to merge his shell into a makeshift patch meant to mend my broken arm. An arm broken by Bez, Bez who was under the thrall of Ian, Ian who sought to slaughter The Collective, The Collective who believed me to be a traitor.

"What do you think I should do?" I lifted my hand, staring into his tiny collection of eyes.

He drew upon my mana and activated his sigils to spell out his scarlet words. A vibrant choice meant to convey his feelings on this decision. "Be cautious and remember the world has done nothing for you."

"Ouch." I pouted. "Never thought I'd see the day where you agreed with Bez."

Tony hissed.

"I'm not sure I could actually say 'screw the world' and run," I said, to which Tony hopped off my arm and floated to the floor with a light breeze before scurrying away. "And I guess that's the end of the conversation."

"Oh my goddess, I can't believe you were attacked!" Kell burst into the store—quite literally as she summoned a gust of wind through Nature's Blessing and flew inside, causing nearly as much damage as I'd just repaired.

Thankfully, chaotic Kell had sorcery sigils at the ready. Their bright glow illuminated Kell's brown skin and made the fabric of her puffy blouse a bit transparent. Not that the top wasn't already quite revealing as it cut off at the shoulders and exposed her stomach.

Bristles of her broomstick flung free, controlled by sorcery, catching and restocking anything knocked off a shelf by the mini tornado whirling inside. In fact, the second she landed beside me, her broom fluttered off like an animated cartoon character and went to work tending to the parts of the store I hadn't cleaned yet. I needed to learn that spell. All my cleaning incantations usually created a bigger mess.

"Wally, how could you!" Kell rushed toward me.

"How could I get attacked?" I raised a brow. "I didn't really have much say in the matter."

"What're you talking about?" She shoved me aside and reached for a box sitting behind the front counter. "How could you nearly let this place burn down with my babies inside?"

"Seriously?" My face fell flat. "You're worried about stuff? What's even in here?"

Neatly tucked in the box sat three of Kell's witch's hats. They were similar in shape to the one on top of her head now, but each had its own color and differing lengths of curl in the stem of the hat.

"Really?" I eyed Kell up and down, scrutinizing her with my judgiest squint.

The hat she currently wore had green stitching that matched the shade of emerald looped in with her braided black hair.

"You're more concerned about an item than me?"

"Says the guy who literally let a goblin attack me last month while he prioritized saving some old trinket."

"First of all, you provoked the goblin," I replied, biting back every fact on how docile goblins were, which meant Kell really went the extra mile to piss one off. "Secondly, I was saving a one-of-a-kind ancient—"

"Blah, blah, blah." Kell stuck her tongue out. "There's countless one-of-a-kind thingies in here."

Kell squeezed a hat, and it chirped. Another one meowed in response.

"Do you have animals in there?"

"Worry about yourself, Walter." She chucked the hats back into their box and returned the box under the counter.

I should worry about myself. About everything that'd unfolded today. Gods, one minute, it was just a normal day, and in a blink, this momentous decision had been thrown at me. The worst part, I couldn't quite discern if it was an obstacle or an opportunity. It seemed more like foreboding death, but there was so much to consider.

"You're worried." Kell's shoulder bumped me, casual yet caring.

"Yeah," I dragged out the word. "It's a big decision. Not exactly the choice I thought I'd be making today. Here, I figured topping Bez or not was by big debate for the month, week, something. Year? Ever? All time?"

"Wait, what?"

"It's nothing. I mean, it's something. Big. Not outrageously big."

"I didn't ask for your measurements, Wally."

My face turned hot, and I let out a flustered tsk. "Not what I mean. I just mean it was a big choice."

"Oh, I know." Kell smirked. "From what Mora's said, she spent the better part of two centuries trying to coax Bez into bending over. Guessing you're gonna have your work cut out for you if you're trying to switch things up."

"What? No." Suddenly, the room was sweltering. Usually, when the conversation of sex came up, it involved Kell sharing her many exploits with Mora and occasional adventures with a third partner, or fourth, or fifth, or that time she talked about the Mythic orgy she hosted that somehow resulted in The Collective setting their apartment on fire. Or maybe that was the ifrit rolling in her bed. More often than not, I tuned Kell out when she talked about sex since her conquests ended up quite descriptive.

"Lemme get this right… You were trying to convince Bez to bottom when the demon attacked."

"Not exactly." I shuffled a few trinkets displayed on the front counter around, not really liking the placement of anything since picking everything up. "We'd already…yeah. The attack came after."

"Ooooooh, so you've worked up this whole 'pining for top' thing in your head?"

"No, it was a mutual thing. Like a moment."

"Uh-huh." Kell eyed me, judgment in her gaze. "That boy is a toxic top."

"Well, he seemed amiable."

"Ugh. Does Bez like this clinical dirty talk?" Kell shook her head. "It does nothing for me."

I huffed. "I'm not trying to fuck you."

"Fair. And honestly, total respect for the conquest." Kell winked. "Thick tops like Bez need to be bottomed out and railed. Why else would the universe gift those boys with such glorious butts?"

I chuckled. "I think that's mostly his host bodies."

"That he chooses. Plus, I've seen him undressed, and lemme tell you—those human guys he slips into don't do that devilish demon half as much justice."

Kell had a point. Bez picked his host bodies. Plus, they shifted based on the composite, taking on his features as best a human body could, dependent on the demon inside.

"You've seen Bez in his demon form?" I asked, having only seen snippets of his true form in memories he'd shared with me.

"Briefly," Kell clarified. "Usually jumping from one body to another. You know demons don't like going undressed."

Their essence reacted differently to our world; they couldn't feel anything without possession. In their true form, they moved like ghosts, able to interact but numb to every experience.

"As much fun as distracting small talk on the ass to be or not to be banged"—Kell conjured the illusion of a skull in her hand through sorcery—"there's still a serious question looming in the air."

"How much lube to use?" I jested, feeding off Kell's playful banter because she was the most casually comical person I knew in the world. Well, besides Bez. But Kell wasn't nearly as murderous.

"Funny." Kell tossed the illusion behind her head, and the skull banged against the wall and hit the floor with a heavy crunch of a thud.

"Wait, was that a real skull?" So much for an illusion. She must've used some type of transmutation or teleportation or something wicked. "Whose skull was that?"

"Doesn't matter, it's theater." She shrugged. "What matters is what you plan on doing. Are you attending a Devil's Banquet in your honor, or are we watching this world go up in flames before dodging an offended devil?"

"We?"

"Mora filled me in, and I'm definitely not hanging around for global eradication." Kell playfully clapped her hands. "I'll stick around long enough to watch the prettiest explosions, make a few smores, and then I'm outta here."

"Well, you don't have to worry about the world," I said. "I mean, technically, you should be. There's tons of catastrophic things constantly ticking by on a natural or human-made clock, but as far as vengeful devils, that was never an option."

"Not even for a second?" Kell cocked her head knowingly.

Sure, for a second. A minute. For a few lingering moments, I considered whether I wanted to roll the dice on my chances of stepping into Hell versus abandoning the world.

"But ultimately, how far would I get?"

"With a wicked witch like me and the baddie boyfriend you plan on bending over?" Kell asked, dimples deepening from the smile that filled her face. "I think we'd make quite a showing outrunning some petty devil."

"I'll let Lilith know how little you think of her when I go to her banquet."

Kell shoved me. "Your banquet, little devil."

I smirked, letting the weight of this decision roll off my shoulders. "Thank you for the distraction."

"Thank you for not destroying my things."

"Well, if you showed up to work regularly like you're supposed to, then—"

"I hate to interrupt." Bez knocked as he sheepishly stepped inside. So the opposite of him. He'd even tucked away all his Diabolic features, from the horns on his head to the wings on his back to his three tails, his clawed hands, even his crimson eyes held less luster.

"You're fine." I half-smiled, hoping to encourage one of his playful grins, his minxy smirks, or his beaming, full-faced, wicked expressions.

The stoic look he had didn't shift, but his eyes softened some when he saw my smile.

"You boys talk." Kell strutted past me. "I'm just gonna sneak a peek at that fiery key Wally received before I head on home."

"What?" I asked. "No. No tinkering with a devil's invitation."

"Not tinkering." Kell averted her gaze and hid her smile. "I just wanna make a copy of the frequency layers."

I blinked at her, conveying my most befuddled expression. "You'd like to tamper with a flame created by a literal devil meant to only be used to and from her Hell at her bequest?"

"Yeah. Imagine the breakthroughs in interdimensional traveling I could make."

"Or you could set yourself on fire a fourth time."

Kell hopped onto the front counter, kicking her legs up as she crossed them and sat with flair. "Life's too short to worry about trivial things like burning alive."

"Says the immortal witch."

"I'm just throwing it out there." Kell gestured with her hands, reaching out for the intangible idea that'd likely only flitted across her mind a second or two—after all, the more impromptu the concept, the more enthusiastic it made her. "As a baby devil mortal mixture walking into Hell, it might be wise to have an extra key if you needed to slip out early."

"You're gonna get yourself killed." I flitted my gaze to Bez, who silently watched. "Or us. You'll get us all killed."

Admittedly, I itched with curiosity, too. But Bez was already so worried about this Devil's Banquet, about me choosing to walk through Hell, about how Lilith might very well slaughter me the second I stepped into her world. I didn't want to add to his concerns. However, devils had an innate way of carving through any world with ease, yet their Hell realms required tremendous strength to open.

The whole reason Beelzebub couldn't chase Bez was that a fraction of his devil essence had been stolen. That tiny missing piece locked his Hell behind a door that could only be opened by a fully formed devil.

But the Diabolic Oasis? Mora's hidden kingdom proved no challenge for a devil to slip inside. Well, her proxy diplomat by extension.

"Admit it." Kell kicked my knee with the tip of her heel. "You wanna know how they got past our system."

She knew me as well as I knew her.

And it didn't make any sense. We had countless layers of security. The spell required to make the dimensional walls came from ancient artifacts and darker magics only Kell could harness. It pulled together Diabolic essence, witchcraft, and Fae magics to make something completely unique. Archaic and new simultaneously.

And to top it all off, we added security measures. Spent months upon arriving cataloging every possible way to slip in or out unnoticed and created the most advanced technological checkpoints that tied together the best magical detections to analyze every variable.

"No," I said firmly. "No messing with stuff."

"Do you think you could successfully make a copy of the frequency used by the invitation?" Bez asked, leaving me shocked in silence. I'd expected him to play it safe, cautious, careful, calculating.

"Hehehe, yes!" Kell clapped her hands, then took off her hat to rummage through.

She dug her arm in all the way to her shoulder, reaching far through the pocket portal of storage, and tossed a few business cards onto the counter. Not cards. Customized parchment sigils. Sort of the personalized magical house key we'd created for residents of the Diabolic Oasis.

This place wasn't a prison, Mora wanted people to come and go as they saw fit, but we had to ensure no one unannounced stepped through the barrier. These allowed us to track any movement in or out of the city.

It also kept people from leaving or entering with undocumented items. No need for relics to be removed and returned to Collective hands.

"Make your copy," Bez said as he approached the front desk to join us. "I will have a request once you achieve that."

"If," I interjected. "If Kell achieves making a copy of the devil's invitation and it doesn't like self-destruct or something."

"You assume a devil would feel the need to safeguard their work."

"Exactly." Kell shot me a smug smirk. "Nothing better than stumbling onto the so-called invulnerable. They're always the easiest to exploit."

"It's actually how Kell first met me." Bez shrugged.

"What do you mean?" Kell winked. "I always stab boys before I kiss them."

"Ha," Bez snorted. "Didn't you screw Wally's brother?"

"Once or twice or five times." Kell laughed.

"Wait, what?" I widened my eyes.

"But we never kissed." Kell playfully poked Bez's chest. "No need for stabby stabs."

Bez roared with laughter while Kell cackled, and I couldn't piece together how much of this conversation was nonsense banter between friends and how much of it was the truth because they both had sordid dealings romantically and otherwise.

"You two are impossible." I glowered. Not at their history of fucking. Their past was their past. But this desire to playfully tamper with primeval powers.

That didn't sit well with me. Somehow, our roles had returned right back to where they started. I was the overly cautious one, and Bez was once again willing to risk it all on some impulsive idea.

"What is your idea?" I asked him as Kell walked to the back of the store to retrieve the fireball key meant to open a door to the Devil's Banquet being thrown in my honor.

"It's a discussion to have later," Bez said. "Right now, I'd like to apologize for not initially supporting your decision."

"You're fine," I said. "I mean, I hadn't even really made a decision."

"You did," he said. "You made it the moment you found out others would be at risk if you hesitated. Your compassion is your biggest flaw."

"Thanks?" I raised an eyebrow. "I wouldn't call it a flaw."

"I was hasty when suggesting we run," Bez said. "There is no running. And as much as it frightens me, the idea of what could happen to you stepping into Hell—the voyage itself, the intricate layers of the dimension, and the inhabitants themselves—I know we don't have an alternative."

"We've been forced into challenging situations before."

"This will be unlike anything you've faced. It's imperative you treat this seriously."

"I'm not you, Bez." I grabbed his shoulders and squeezed. "I treat everything seriously. Too seriously, sometimes."

"Know that I will serve as your right hand, your commander, your personal vanguard of protection." He delicately traced his hand along my face, gently rubbing my cheek. "I will ensure your safety against any and all foes in Hell."

"And I'll follow your lead completely." I tilted my head, leaning into his hand, the soft touch, the longing. "While we walk through Hell itself, you'll be in charge."

"How's that different from any other day?" Bez chuckled.

"Excuse me?"

"Come on, Wally." He shrugged with this obnoxious expression of arrogance and cockiness. "We both know I run this relationship."

"Is that so?" I pursed my lips in this questioning disdain.

"It is, and while my natural dominance in the relationship is obvious, we'll have to downplay it while in Hell." Bez adjusted his tie. "It must appear that you run things between us."

"You're such an ass."

"I am what I love." Bez slapped my butt with his hands and squeezed tightly until I yelped.

"Hey!"

"Is for unicorns." He playfully batted my cheeks. "And we're fresh outta of those."

"I'm glad your mood has lightened."

"I can drag my feet as we face Hell, or I can walk hand-in-hand with you, smile on my face, and something provocative swimming in my thoughts."

I smiled, giddy and annoyed. Annoyed that his immature charm always soothed me. While I had no idea what to expect in Hell, at this Devil's Banquet, or from Lilith herself, I would step into danger with ease, knowing I had Bez at my side.

6

Bez

Since Kell needed more time with the flame to make a copy of Lilith's signature, I dragged Wally home. A short reprieve as we'd need to grab the essentials before heading to Mora's and then to Hell itself.

"Weather!" Wally called out as the iron-spelled gates opened. They reached nearly two stories in height and proved the only way in and out of our manor since Wally had created a towering stone fence to keep our Cerberus locked inside while we went to work. Apparently, the hound had the behavior of a Husky, which was a Mythic beast I'd never heard of until Wally mentioned it. But they dug holes and jumped fences and whined about everything and pretty much did all the other annoying things that Weather enjoyed.

"Weather," he yelled again, adding a smooching sound with his lips. The name held affection and absurdity as Wally sought to give the Cerberus purpose behind the personas of his identity.

Three heads that make up one being. Just as the weather changed throughout the day, Weather's personas differed from hyper, hostile, and calm.

The giant lumbering hound with short, coarse black fur darted toward us once he heard Wally's call. He towered over us and was nearly half as tall as the front gates, with shoulders easily twenty feet wide and almost too wide for the only entrance in or out. With the flames that reached an additional five to ten along each of their thick necks, Weather was definitely too big. But he'd often jump or burrow his way out of the yard until Wally started adding invisible incantation barriers to put an end to that behavior.

Sunny, the center head, immediately went to lick Wally.

"Stop." I pointed a finger, halting the beast in his steps.

Antsy steps with claws bigger than my fucking torso bounced back and forth for affection. Purple flames burned brightly around the ankles and matched the same purple fire that framed Sunny's head and filled his eyes. The fire at the Cerberus' feet turned blue, indicating Stormy had taken full control.

The aggressive left head always demonstrated the most self-control. A difficult task when he had a flighty other self that demanded kisses and playtime every second of every day. He nipped Sunny's ear until the hound settled, and the blue flames burned brightest along his body.

Fiery collars, each a different color to represent where Weather's three persona drew upon their power. Sunny's flames had the most magical energy, whereas Stormy's flames contained the most heat and ferocity. And while Cloudy kept his head low and sniffed Wally's extended hand with soft eyes that held the gentle heat of orange flames, there was a pureness to his fire, unlike the other two personas.

Wally pet Cloudy's nose, getting the wet slobber of the beast all over his hand. I shivered and let out a visceral, gagging protest.

"You need to stop babying him," I said.

"Someone has to." Wally stretched his arms wide so he could wrap them over Cloudy's snout and hug the beast. "You're such a bully to him."

"It's called obedience training." I snapped my fingers. "Heel."

Cloudy yelped when he accidentally shoved Wally off, but his body obeyed my command, and Weather sat at attention with his shoulders squared and his three heads looking straight ahead. Blue fire covered his ankles and chest and trailed down his back, but as the three formed a proper consensus, purple and orange flames joined the extensions of the body.

"Good boy." I nodded. "Go fetch your favorite toys and bring them for our trip."

Weather bolted through the yard with Sunny panting excitedly as he led the way to the best toys they'd buried for later while we made our way to the house.

"So…" Wally lingered at the front door, eyeing me with a suspicious amount of questions hanging on his tongue. "I don't need to pack or dress for the party, but we need to find Weather a babysitter?"

"Do you wish for Antoninus to watch him the entire time we're gone?" I gestured to the scorpion hanging onto Wally's shoulder.

"Tony can totally watch Weather for a few hours. He could watch him for a few days." He turned to his familiar. "Isn't that right?"

The bug clacked his annoying little claws.

"Okay." I shrugged. "Is he fine watching the mongrel for the next six months or six years?"

"What?" Wally's eyes widened.

"It's a Devil's Banquet," I said. "It's gonna be a long trip."

"But it's a banquet. It's a party." Wally blinked with this dumbfounded confusion. "I've been to like a thousand. It's…"

Watching him go speechless as his brain processed the information was priceless and a rarity.

"You have been to zero devil parties," I replied. "I've been to plenty, and most last at least a year. The decent events go for a decade or more. Beelzebub refused to attend a gala that didn't come with blood sports and the guarantee of a timely commitment."

"That's absurd," Wally said, muttering a dozen other half-thoughts. "How is this a thing?"

"We can still run," I said with a sly smile. "Pack up the pets, light the house on fire, and kiss this world goodbye."

"No," Wally said glumly, defeated, persistent, yet confused.

"Don't worry." I patted his free shoulder. "Lilith will definitely keep the event short since you're a no-name devil unworthy of her time. This is all a formality."

I hoped. I desperately hoped.

Wally insisted on riding atop Weather's back across the city, claiming the pup needed to get some of his energy out. Weather wasn't a pup. He certainly was a baby, but that had more to do with Walter's need to cave to all the demands the tyrant of a beast made. More food. More playtime. More walks. More affection. More fire. More. More. More.

"Good luck with that at Mora's," I whispered into Stormy's pointed ear, which was met with a snarl.

The muscles of the beast flexed, and he bolted faster through the emptied back streets like he could actually outrun me.

Fine. I'd play the game. I flew alongside the Cerberus until I outpaced him by several leagues and awaited the sluggish arrival at the front entrance of Mora's mansion. By far the grandest built and biggest residual space in the city, but despite my vocal protesting on the matter, size truly meant nothing to me. Location, location, location reigned superior. There were particular star alignments Wally enjoyed, so I ensured we had the best corner of the sky where he could revel in late-night research while pondering the infinite universe our tiny dimension gleamed when he stepped out onto the balcony.

Sunny panted; Cloudy yipped; Stormy growled. My feral overachiever was held back by the weakness of his personas. Part of me wanted to pet him, commemorate his achievements, but he'd find it insulting. As he should, something the clingy Sunny didn't grasp as he brought his nose close to nudge me for affection.

"Indoor size." I snapped my fingers and watched the gigantic Cerberus shrink down to a modest size like a black bear.

Wally nearly crashed until a black gust cushioned his fall, which was a comfort. The devil essence inside him continued to defend for the most minor threats. I could only hope it'd protect him in Hell. I could only hope we'd survive this voyage.

"Come on, Weather." Wally hugged the hound as they walked through Mora's guarded front gates together, Sunny licking, Cloudy nuzzling, and Stormy growling.

One look at us and the elite Mythics and mages on patrol quivered. It was nice knowing some people still feared my presence and the mischievous threats of my misfit mage of a boyfriend. Even if most of the rumors surrounding Wally were outlandish lies. I savored the anxiety his presence provided.

The front door swung open, and Mora immediately greeted us, a martini glass in one hand while she waved us inside with her other. "Come along now. You two can get settled in the study while waiting for Kell."

"Where's she at?" Wally asked, rifling through his satchel. "I'd like to show her Weather's schedule while getting him settled for the night. He acclimatizes well to new environments, but it's imperative that he sticks with his routines, especially since Bez and I will be…"

I nodded as Wally rambled. I tried to listen. Really. Truly. I even recalled a few things he'd said previously while we packed up Weather's belongings. But Wally was stress chatting, and that meant there was no end to the nonsense.

He held up a laminated folder of papers and beamed pridefully over the schedule he'd tossed together this evening.

"It's eight pages," I said with wide eyes. "And color-coded."

"Truthfully, it's only fifty-two bullet points with a few subsections explaining the importance of said marker because while some of these seem trivial, it's all important for Weather's routine." Wally finally paused for a breath. "It's really not that long."

"That's what she said." Mora chuckled.

Wally rolled his eyes. "Anyway, where's Kell?"

"In her workshop." Mora pointed. "Tinkering with projects."

Wally went to find his bestie with Weather at his heels and Tony perched on his shoulder.

"Aren't you going to join your man?" Mora pushed between me and the door, quickly closing it behind us and ushering me away. "You'll have to get used to sticking close with him in Hell. Wouldn't want him to wander."

"Why are you rushing me?"

"I'm not. Merely assumed you wouldn't want to miss any of Kell's work on copying that damned invitation Wally received." Mora folded her arms, keeping her expression even, but the subtle shift of a scowl formed at her brow. "The unnecessary risk you always bring into my life, Bezzy."

"You love it." I grinned. And exploited it. Mora had turned nearly every major event in my life since arriving at the mortal realm into a serendipitous fortune of favors for herself. "I'd think you'd enjoy your witch finding a way to circumvent devil abilities."

"I don't like anything that lands their attention." She sighed. "I assumed my little pocket world had a few centuries before even my devil deigned to acknowledge its existence. Now, thanks to your misfit mage baby devil adjacent boyfriend, I'll be contending with ambassadors from Lilith's realm likely forever."

"It could always be worse," I said. "You could be dragged to this Devil's Banquet, too."

One of the guards under Mora's employment stepped into the foyer and whispered to her.

"Bring them to my office." She waved the guard away, then turned to me. "I might welcome Hell again if I get dragged into another meeting with these damned witches."

"Perish the thought." I smirked. "If you like, I could handle your problem before my departure. It'd be nice to get my hands a bit bloody before the party. Practice and all that."

"Tempting." Mora traced a finger along my sharp jawline. "But until the witches do more than bully their way into overtaking other Mythic territories, I think it's best to be civil."

"What's the real reason?"

"These witches might also be studying Diabolics." She fluffed her hair, fighting the growing frown on her face in the process. "It's not unheard of or unwarranted. I actually met a witch a few centuries back who streamlined possession thanks to her research. Obviously, I had to kill her for other reasons, but I'll always be grateful for the wealth of knowledge she provided."

"What are they studying?"

"No clue. Nothing of Novus' caliber, not that I've observed, but when people try to analyze essence, decipher demons, I pay attention."

"You should do yourself a favor and slaughter them. They can't research if they're dead."

"It doesn't benefit me to end them until they achieve the fruits of their labor, at least enough to pique my curiosities."

"You're placating their actions, and in turn, these witches are overstepping, intentionally testing how far they can push boundaries. This whole compassionate thing you're trying out is gonna get you ousted."

"Not placating," Mora said. "I merely wish to ensure that when I do move, everyone knows I did everything within my power—my vastly incredible power—to avoid bloodshed. Thanks to your ruthless presence, some have considered me a hostile ruler. In truth, your brief absence will do my image wonders."

"Bah." I stomped by her. "They think I'm ruthless when it's your orders for carnage."

Between Mora and Wally, though, I supposed my hands had been tied these days. Murder was always an alternative option, never the first, second, or even third option with them.

I left Mora to contend with this witch drama and prepare for my own. How I'd much rather spend my night ripping out hearts to help Mora maintain her kingly crown bullshit than navigate the etiquette of Hell.

"You okay?" Wally asked, joining me in the study now that he'd settled Tony and Weather somewhere for the evening. "Today has been long."

"I'm fine."

"Cue my go-to line for every exhausting family dinner I attended after feeling utterly devastated and defeated by literally anything in my life." Wally chuckled.

Even without saying all the things that used to get him down at every turn, I recalled them. I'd listened to much of his sadness vented aloud and alone inside the repository where he worked, and I lay imprisoned inside an orb. So much had broken him to pieces over the years until he was this tragically meek man with no will or wonder in his life.

As annoying as it was, I enjoyed seeing him happy, content, absurdly brave in the face of even more absurd threats.

"There's just so much happening." I sighed. "Not what I had on the agenda."

"Planning a trip to Hell certainly wasn't the direction I saw this evening going," Wally said. "I mean, considering the afternoon delight we had, I sort of expected an evening delight to follow up."

Me, too. I intended on lots of fucking.

"Oh, you wanted to spar again?" I teased. But how I genuinely wished we'd taken his training seriously. If I'd known he would land on the radar of a devil, then I wouldn't have been so lax with his understanding of the essence coursing inside him.

In all my years of existence, no devil had deigned to acknowledge me when I walked the mortal realm with a piece of Beelzebub's essence. The rumors of other demons holding pieces of their devils inside them, similar to how I held onto a piece of mine, were never met with a banquet hosted by Lilith herself. It never occurred to me Wally would be scrutinized in such a manner. I believed…no, I'd hoped, he would be nothing but a blip on the radar of devils reigning supreme across the vast, nearly infinite universe.

"You're worried." Wally shoulder-bumped me. "I recognize the internalized hyperactive scenarios likely flooding your imagination."

"They're not scenarios. They're inevitabilities given the dangers we face."

"Well, this crinkle right here." Wally pointed to my forehead, playfully brushing his fingers over the crease in my brow. "I've made that expression a lot over the years. If I recall, it's generally either because I'm worried about something or I'm worried about how someone isn't listening to me and my warnings. But I am listening to you, Bez. I understand your concerns, your reasons."

"I'm not worried about you listening; I'm worried about you keeping your mouth shut." I stared at his pouty lips, the slight quiver in his lower lip. Already, his body anticipated the chatty little mage's need to bite his bottom lip to hold back some rambling intel. "Even now, you're ready to mutter a slew of protests."

"Ut-uh." Wally shook his head, pouting his lips further out until they appeared ridiculously puckered and delightfully delectable.

"I do admire your efforts." I stepped in close. "But in Hell, one wordy misstep could be our end."

"I know." Wally pressed his forehead against mine, and the scrunched frustration I held washed away in the warmth of his touch. Essence fueled him, buzzed with this euphoric splendor, and he sent a spark of his excitement through me. "It's obviously serious. Stressful. But I've faced the worst with you more than once. I've resisted the Collective. I've defended myself against you while enthralled under another's control—and also when you just casually tried to murder me."

"It wasn't casual." I shrugged. "It was intimate."

Wally scoffed, then smirked, then gave me a quick peck on the lips before grimacing. "I've fought other Diabolics with and without you. I've died in your arms. I've walked through Oblivion itself."

"And none of that compares to the threats that lie in Hell."

"My point is, I wouldn't feel capable or comfortable walking through Hell itself with anyone else." Wally wrapped his arms around my waist, bucking our hips together. "With you, though, I know I can handle anything. You make me stronger every single day."

I kissed Wally, slipping my tongue in his mouth. "You will have to follow my lead."

"Done," he said between kisses. "You're in charge."

"Yes, but you must present yourself as the lead." I ran my fingers through his curly blond locks and yanked his head back. With his neck exposed, I gently kissed his Adam's apple and worked my way along his collarbone. "You are the devil; you must evoke authority. Do you understand that?"

"Done." Wally locked his eyes with mine and planted his hands on my shoulders like he planned to push me beneath his authority.

"You'll have to be more convincing than that."

"I can be take-charge," Wally snickered, then muttered a hundred whispered side thoughts he had about this instance. His mind was already lost on recollections, theories, concerns, curiosities, and so many other obnoxious things.

I glared. "And the rambling seriously has to be reined in."

"Maybe you can help with that." He grinned, hand reaching for my belt. "Sometimes, when I'm extra talkative, I simply need a distraction."

"Walter."

"Are demons opposed to such things?"

"No." I huffed. "But you can't exactly suck my cock every time you need to stop yourself from a blundering babble fest."

"Why not?" He unfastened my belt, whipping it off my slacks in a quick motion. It clacked with a snap against the hot air in the room. Heat conjured from our essence that stirred, intertwining in this small space, craving the feel of each other. "I'm a devil, right?"

"Yes, technically, but also—"

Wally pressed a hand to my mouth, silencing me.

"As a devil, I get what I want, right?" he asked, yanking my pants halfway past my thighs, exposing my semi-hard cock and ass.

"Yes."

"Now, what I want is for you to teach me a little lesson on what happens to good boys who talk too much."

I smirked. "Insatiable."

"Or I could give you a detailed account of my research on—"

I gripped Wally's shoulders and shoved him to his knees. Before he could lean forward and playfully take in my cock, I slammed my growing erection into his mouth and savored the sound of his startled choking. In a few moments, his gagging lessened as I continued pushing his head and inching my cock further down his throat.

Each time he gurgled and slurped, it sent a shudder of ecstasy coursing through my being. I thrust my hips, relishing his struggle to take the entirety of my shaft. Brushing the watery tears building in his eyes, I craned his neck. It helped ease my dick further down his throat, and it forced his gaze to meet mine.

The whimpering and yearning and desire to serve made me crave more. I hungered for satisfaction almost as much as he hungered for my cock. A feast I granted him with each pump of my hips as I face fucked him.

Wally gagged and drooled on my dick, gasping in instinctual breaths from a habit of oxygen he couldn't seem to quit, even if the only thing he wanted to breathe in was my scent. A musk of primal desire that demanded more from him.

"Nope." I gripped my dick, stroking my erection and keeping it away from Wally's lips. "Earn it."

Wally crawled closer, mouth reaching for my sack and kissing my balls. He held them in his mouth one at a time, sucking until he fit the entire sack in his mouth. Panting, he released them and lightly ran his tongue over my balls.

"Good." I kept a hand on top of his head, tilting his direction and aiming his mouth back to my cock, which he greedily went to work on again.

He ran his tongue up and down my shaft. When he reached the tip of my dick a third time, he finally played with the head, rotating his tongue around and teasing me with his puckered lips.

"This is what you want, isn't it?" I pulled my cock away from him and slapped it across his face, smearing precum and spit on him.

Wally moaned, begging, pleading for more. "Bez—"

"Uh-uh." I shoved my dick back in his mouth, groaning with satisfaction at the gulp of surprise he released when choking. "We're here to make sure you learn how to shut the fuck up, Walter."

Gods, the quiver of his body when I scolded him sent one of equal delight coursing through me. I grabbed the back of his head and shoved him forward, ramming my cock all the way down his throat. I held his head there, watching him struggle to breathe through his nose that was pressed against my groin.

"Take it all. Take every fucking inch." I kept my grip steady as his body wriggled instinctually, yet Wally grabbed my thighs and steadied himself. Gods, how I loved when he struggled on it. "You love this, don't you?"

When his tail sprang out, I used two of mine to coil around it. If he wanted, his essence could resist, fight back, overpower me, but he submitted. I pinned his tail with mine, mounting it, so to speak, while I continued face fucking Walter with my dick buried all the way down his throat. I couldn't pull out, not when he felt this wonderful.

I ran my free hand along his throat, massaging his neck with each pump. His throat muscles constricted, making me moan when he gagged again.

"You want it all, don't you?"

Wally gurgled something incomprehensible, and I moved my hands to the sides of his head, subsequently holding him by the ears as I jerked Wally back to the tip of my dick. It edged me right to the precipice of release, and then I slammed every inch back in, repeating the motion as each gasping stroke brought me closer and closer until I finally burst.

My entire body tensed, warmth spread, and I came down Wally's throat with two shots before pulling back and unloading with a third splat in his mouth. When I pulled my dick out, a string of cum hung from the head and connected to Wally's lips.

He didn't wait for me to comment, immediately and hungrily licking my cock clean. He held the head in his mouth, just the tip, as he suckled my softening erection. Part of me wanted to jerk myself hard again, shove it back in his mouth, but I waited. I allowed him to savor the taste of my flaccid cum covered cock as he played with it.

Once he'd had his fill, I pulled my pants back up and tucked my dress shirt in.

"Strip," I commanded.

He blushed. "Bez, we really don't have—"

"Thought you said I was in charge here."

"And I thought you said devils make the rules."

I leaned forward and growled into his ear, relishing the heat turning it red. "Strip."

More than anything, I had an insatiable desire to please him, fuck him, control him, hold him, love him, and a thousand other things I could and would only ever explore with Wally.

"I know this was where the night was originally going, but shouldn't we be preparing for Hell?" Wally asked as he lifted his shirt, obediently undressing.

Whether the longing in my gaze or the subtle gesture with my hand, Wally caught my desire for him to slowly strip. I wanted a show. I wanted to savor this. I wanted to hold onto this fleeting bliss because who knew what awaited us.

"There's no preparation we can make in the time we have," I said. "And with Mora tending to witchy bullshit business and Kell's timely tinkering, we could be waiting for the rest of the night."

Or the next several days if I were fortunate. In which case, I'd spend the entirety of them railing sweet Wally.

He unfastened his jeans, slowly working them down his hips and letting them linger at his knees before dropping them to his ankles.

"Knock, knock, knockity, knock!" Kell's voice rang loudly to the beat of her door knock.

"Aaaah!" Wally shouted as he fumbled with his discarded shirt and his jeans.

He tumbled forward with his head poking through one of the arm holes of his shirt, and his pants poorly slipped up to his thighs. Kell flung the door open wide, a smile on her face and a flame in her hand, while Wally wriggled on the floor into his clothes.

"Walter." I sighed and shook my head.

"Oh." Kell looked down at Wally. "Am I interrupting?"

"What?" He finally found the right hole—the number of jokes I could make—and slipped into the tee shirt as he wiggled his butt against the floor to squeeze his ass into his tight jeans.

"Shame." Kell pouted. "There's nothing hotter than watching cute boys smash together their cute parts. Speaking of hot."

She blew on the fiery key meant to lead us to Hell and sent it fluttering across the room on a gentle breeze. I caught the wisp of fire with a telekinetic grip.

"As promised, it's completely intact, and I've successfully made a copy of the magical signatures used."

"How'd you pull that off?" Wally asked. "There's not many spells in existence that can mimic energy without breaking it or stealing it or…yeah. Are you sure you didn't mess up the key?"

"I'm a professional, Walter," Kell answered. "And I used a Doppelganger Reflective Replica spell."

"Whoa." The embarrassment on Wally's face became replaced by intrigue, curiosity, and likely a hundred thousand questions based on the size his eyes had expanded to. "That's just a theory. No one's ever successfully done that spell."

"Well, I'm fabulous as fuck, so naturally I pulled it off." Kell ran a hand through her hair and flipped it over her shoulder before turning to leave. "Try not to die in Hell. Take lots of pics. I want to hear all about it!"

And with that, we were alone again in the study with a key to Hell and no reason to linger. The Devil's Banquet awaited our arrival.

"So, how do we do this?" Wally asked, staring closely at the flickering flame. "Like, is there a password?"

"Did that buffoon who delivered it give you a password?"

"No, but like, maybe there's some unknown Diabolic code I'm just expected to understand."

"It should instinctively react to your essence when you're ready to leave."

"Oh, but what if it's like subconscious preparation?" Wally frowned. "Because I'll never be ready. I mean, I'd need to complete a checklist of at least my top hundred priorities before I even considered being ready."

"More like top thousand." I folded my arms.

"Seriously." Wally brought his hand close, testing the heat of the fire. "Is it subconscious? Maybe I need to touch the fire."

"You don't need to touch the flame."

"Thank goodness because I don't like fire," Wally said. "I suppose there's always a chance that maybe she changed her mind. Or perhaps—"

The fireball erupted, carrying waves of Diabolic energy throughout the room until everything faded from the world, and we were dragged out of the mortal realm and into Hell itself.

7

Wally

The flame exploded in an instant, a fraction of a second, and engulfed the entirety of my being. And I do mean the entirety. Every fiber from physical matter, my magical extension, and the essence coiled deep into the roots of my cells. Everything burned with a blistering sear. I lacked the words to express the hot-white agony that I struck because as quickly as it'd stabbed me from all directions, it ceased. The only comfort came from a slow, steady drumbeat. It echoed and indicated an arrival, a delivery, an ending. Or so I hoped as I endured agony and followed the sound.

Suddenly, the flames bathed me with cool relief, shifting to a campfire warmth, then a day at the beach—usually not a feeling I enjoyed baking under a bright sun, but currently, I embraced it, hugged the sensation. Then, a blink later, the inferno returned, devouring everything down to my intangible thought process.

Pain didn't begin to describe the horrors. It peeled away my flesh instantaneously, yet when I glimpsed my hand between the infinite layers of light, I saw every cell. Each microscopic cell. Fully intact but divided, held together by thread.

Not thread. Essence. My essence. My devil essence that kept me wrapped up and safe as I crumbled apart and burned the entire trip. The voyage. The long-lasting eternal journey up the never-ending hill.

I screamed. I cried. I begged.

But my voice released nothing. I was motionless and moving. Flashes forever long passed in the tick of a second.

This wasn't what traveling between dimensions was. I'd read every account of dimensional travel I could get my hands on because, truly, I wanted to escape my life as an Alden. But this trip to Hell. This single step into a world unlike any other felt eternal, never-ending.

Perhaps I'd already died.

Perhaps I'd never lived.

Perhaps I'd only ever experienced this unyielding agony.

And as quickly as the pain had burrowed its way through every fiber of my being, it dissolved away and fell to dust at my feet.

The fire sizzled, and the intense blaze disappeared. It shrank and split apart into tiny blobs of liquid before evaporating into nothingness.

Here I stood in a sandy field. It stretched far from every direction, leading to large walls so far away, they appeared fuzzy. I squinted, which did little to alter the blurry splotches.

"Wow," I said, taking in the sound of my own voice, a voice that sounded so much crisper after what seemed like a lifetime of silent agony. "That was…"

"One Hell of a trip?" Bez snickered.

I glowered, which only made the smirk across his face grow that much bigger.

"Oh, come now, you're the one who insisted we make this voyage." Bez squared my shoulders and looked me over. "And don't start with the betterment of the world blah, blah, blah biddy, blah."

I wanted to argue the point, firmly express this wasn't some frivolous decision, but the phantom ache of a hundred thousand injuries inflicted over lifetimes or fractions of a second still clung fresh in my mind. "Is my skin on fire? Melted?"

Bez continued checking me over, his expression calm for the most part, but he maintained composure a lot better than I did. "No cracks or dents or obvious injuries I can see."

"It feels like there are needles poking every pore on my body and that there's spikes under my skin and that there's—I don't know—pain lurking." I trembled as Bez continued his examination. "You might've been right; this trip might be too much for my mortal body."

"No, that all sounds like standard passage." Bez grabbed my face, turning my gaze to meet his, then used his clawed nails to stretch the skin so he could thoroughly inspect my eyes. "Everything seems in order. Your mind isn't oozing out anywhere, so I think you're okay."

"Wait." My jaw went slack. "My brain might start oozing?"

"I said your mind."

"Which is—"

"Not the same thing," Bez clarified. "Mortals always attach everything to their organs like they're so special. I don't even have organs. Well, currently, I have some." Bez wiggled a bit, poking his torso from either side. "But they don't do anything. Except for the tummy. I like to use that one."

"Fine."

"The point is, if the voyage between dimensions was too much, your memories would've started pouring out, forming sentience. Like little ghost films floating around until all that was left of you was an empty husk of drool and living death."

"You certainly could've elaborated on the risks."

"I said you could die."

"Yeah, I was thinking quick and heroic, not like an agonizingly slow death that felt like a bajillion years only for my mind to fall out of my head and leave me what? A decaying mess of mortal mush in Hell?"

"Pretty much." Bez grinned. "Letting the world burn doesn't seem like such a bad deal now, does it?"

I scoffed. "Whatever. My essence and mortal coil are fine here, mostly, so what's next?"

"We wait for our host." Bez scrunched his face. "And by host, I mean some grimy demon lackey sent to escort us."

"Why's everything so fuzzy here?" I asked, and then the realization of a paranoid possibility dawned on me. "Wait. Did the trip use up all my essence? Is that why I can't see anything clearly?"

"No, don't you think I would've mentioned that while looking you over?"

"Right. Then what's up with the blurs?"

"You still suck at focusing your essence for the proper sensory experience." Bez waved a hand, creating a spark of black and crimson lightning, which conjured a pair of glasses. "These will help."

"Fascinating." I grabbed the glasses. It'd been so long since I'd worn a pair, I almost forgotten the feeling. After the essence adjusted my vision, enhancing all my senses, I sort of fell out of the habit. That and the prescription strength on the lenses gave my eyes a headache. "This is not the Hell I was expecting. We literally arrived through fire, but now it's all…"

The field of sand stretched far in a perfectly symmetrical circle with gated doors evenly lined in opposing directions. Pillars were sculpted into intricate designs, etched against the stone walls surrounding the sandy arena. The walls stretched so high, it'd require flight to reach the stands, which went even further up. They angled back and towered so high it blocked out almost all light above. This place reminded me of an ancient colosseum.

"Lilith has a filter on her realm, so even I can't see the full extent of her Hell," Bez explained nonchalantly as if warping the way a world was perceived wasn't a godly ability. "She's muting her dimension for us."

"Huh?"

"Basically, she carved off a piece of her dimension and lessened it—removing the truly exquisite aspects, then turned it into this place where we're attending the banquet."

"Because we can't see things fully?"

"No, we can. I'm Diabolic, and you have devil essence. You'd be more than capable of comprehending the full ratio of five-dimensional reality." Bez grumbled, stringing together a few quiet profanities. "This is meant to shame us. A note that we're from a poor, weak dimension, and she's extended this veil as a sign of pity."

"I mean, it's kind of nice." I shrugged. "Just stepping through was like a sensory overload, so if every second in Hell was like that…yeah, I'll take the filter."

"And the pity as she parades our weakness on display for all her children."

"Speaking of…" I bit my lower lip, looking around the empty area. "Where's our host?"

I was sort of expecting a party when we got here. Or at least the waiting room of said party. Looking around, there was nothing nearby.

"It's disrespectful to encroach upon a devil's territory," Bez explained. "This is yours. A modest gift for your arrival."

"Modest?" This arena would easily fit three or four football fields into it. "I mean, were they expecting more people?"

"Generally, a devil would bring a horde or legion at the very least." Bez rocked his head side-to-side. "Beelzebub dragged me to these events on occasion. Not Lilith's Hell, but generally, there's more on display when a devil arrives in another's realm."

"Like what?"

"Well, we got a continent to the last Hell I visited, a couple sacrifices, and I believe there was a feast of Fae magic before we traveled to the festival."

"Wow."

"But it wasn't much of a festival. Beelzebub used the invitation as a way to invade and obliterate another Hell to expand upon the nothingness and allow his Hell domain to grow."

"A monopoly on Hell." I shook my head. Bez's devil truly was the worst devil. Suppose he was my devil, too, since I held the essence of Beelzebub inside me.

Eight giant tentacles waved from behind the walls of the arena. Each one stretched high, wriggling at least twenty to thirty feet in length. It was hard to tell from the center of this arena. They gripped the edges with spiked suckers and dragged a bulbous head into view before the enormous body slithered down the stage seating. The sandy brown held a stark contrast from the white stage, but once the giant octopus-like demon plopped onto the ground, its tentacles and core blended, accentuating the sparkling gems in a variety of colors adorned across its entire body.

"Welcome, welcome, welcome!" The voice bellowed from the giant eyeball itself. The squishy sclera held a lime green hue, while the iris was a deep emerald.

"Blegh." Bez stuck out his tongue and made a yuck face. An expression he usually reserved for when I cooked something so bland it could kill. "He could've at least come dressed."

I cocked my head, studying the sheen-white fabric stretched across the tiny bulge that must've been the center—the core—of this demon's body because no octopus had such a part. I mean, they had a mantle, which connected their heads and arms, but the anatomy was different. I supposed, ultimately, I was drawing octopus conclusions for Diabolic anatomy, which was equivalent to comparing Bez's humanish shape to human anatomy. Not related.

"But he is dressed." I pointed, once I'd processed my observations, to the tunic pulled tight across the demon's core with frilly ruffles for the eight giant tentacle limbs. At least I hoped those were limbs. "When you say he's not dressed, do you mean he's exposing a certain appendage—appendages—of himself?"

"What?" Bez scrunched his face. "No, you pervert! I thought he might possess a host. Something out of respect for you."

"How would possessing someone show me respect?"

Bez rolled his eyes and went back to studying this grand arena we'd arrived in. While he might've played it casual, I could see all the mental notes he took, the calculations he made, the concerns he held back because Bez always preferred to shield me from worries.

"It is an honor to meet the esteemed Walter Alden, Devil and Mage of Misfit Hybridization."

My chest warmed. That was quite the title. It made me sound special.

The emerald iris of his eye moved every time he spoke, similar to a heart monitor.

"I am your host, Orias." He extended all his tentacles and nodded his bulbous head almost in a bizarre curtsy.

Unsure how to respond, I went to bow back until Bez flicked me with his tail.

"Devils don't submit," he whispered. "If you wish to accept his greeting, then merely allowing him to live is all the consideration you need to offer."

That seemed cold.

"Can I ask what's with the set up?" I asked. "Lilith seems to have an interest in the Roman Empire."

"As your host, the design of the banquet fell to me, so I thought you'd enjoy a mortal theme."

"This is a mortal theme?"

"Oh, yes." His iris wriggled alongside the excitement of his voice. "We are on top of all the current trends in mortality, having a panel of esteemed experts who recently toured your realm."

"Time moves differently in Hell," Bez explained. "Chances are a handful of demons dropped in a few thousand years ago and recently reported their findings. Hell doesn't change the way mortal trends do."

"I did peek at the current realm of mortals," Orias added. "A brief visit, and it seems more or less the same."

"The world appears the same as when the Roman Empire reigned?" I asked, blinking at the perplexed expression I felt growing on my face.

"A few distinct differences, certainly, but nothing too extreme based on my research." Orias' iris expanded so big the pupil filled his entire lime green eyeball, then tightened into a thin, shaky strand. "Is it not to your liking?"

"Oh no." I waved my hands back and forth, gesturing for Orias to relax. "I think it looks—"

"Acceptable," Bez interjected. "Walter will tolerate this blatant albeit cheap imitation of our realm."

"It's very homey." I nodded assuredly. "I mean, I wasn't even sure if I'd left home or arrived in Hell. Practically identical."

"Oh, lovely, lovely, lovely." Orias' eye wriggled as he clapped his eight tentacles together. The spiked suckers clicked and clacked against each other, creating an almost rhythmic tap dance beat. "If there are any changes you require, I will see to it immediately!"

He waved a tentacle, casting a gust with a sparkling black and green hue. It shook the ground beside us, carving open the earth and summoning walls that formed into a large room. With a click of his spikes, Orias created marble portraits and pillars to support the structure, making a modest temple.

"In theme with the festivities leading up to the banquet, I've collected every piece of knowledge possible for a proper human spa day treatment in accordance with a young emperor, which I hope is a close mortal equivalent to your stature."

"You think being a devil is like being an emperor?" I asked, holding my expression in a tight smile because I could feel my whole face ready to fall into this bewildered, dumbfounded confusion. "You think I'm like an emperor?"

I might've squeaked a bit at the end of my question, but I remained mostly composed.

"Hardly," Bez hissed. "But I suppose you would see the grandeur, Walter."

"Walter?" And then it dawned on me he properly addressed me the same way Orias had. No Wally here. Only the great Walter Alden, devil hybrid guy of unquantifiable ability that needed to be measured at a party with an ancient Rome theme since Lilith hadn't allowed any of her demons proper pilgrimage to the mortal realm in several thousand years.

Geez. This was already too much for me to keep up with.

The door to the structure Orias just created opened wide. and several humans stepped through. Not humans. Each had vibrant-colored irises, with the whites faded a similar shade. Bez had explained how demons had their own auras of magic since they weren't pure Diabolic like devils who radiated black essence. Hence why my eyes sometimes turned pure black without a hint of crimson like Bez or emerald like Mora.

Each person wore the bare minimum in attire, completely topless, no matter the sex or gender of the human they possessed. They all had on skimpy underwear, which, since they'd gone with an ancient Rome theme, had an authentic subligaculum cut. Almost skirt-like. Hmmm. Now, I began to wonder if the stretched fabric of Orias' tunic was actually a pair of skimpy subligaculum undies.

"We'd like to treat you and your…army of allies, should you bring anymore forth, to leisure experience accustomed to those under your reign." Orias' tentacles flailed a bit as his iris zipped back and forth with awkward pauses. The discomfort in his tone made me tense.

"He's wondering where your army is," Bez whispered.

"I know that," I said, feeling the second-hand embarrassment Orias had for asking the question. It reminded me of every time I had to do a chancellor's job when I worked in the archives and fill out requisition forms for the Mythics who'd inquired about artifacts the Collective had stolen centuries back. Ugh. The flashbacks to my complacency were mortifying.

"He's being polite," Bez said in a louder hush. "But he wants to know where they are, should you choose to invade."

"What? No!" I gestured a definite no with my arms. "We don't need an army to invade. No army required at all! I am not bringing an army to invade."

Orias' iris bounced back and forth so quickly I couldn't follow the movement. The words bellowing from his giant eyeball changed, no longer carrying a sound I could comprehend. Faint elements of it felt familiar, but as the essence in my stomach tightened, I figured he'd shifted to some type of Diabolic language. Which made me wonder how Orias had learned English. Gods, I wanted to ask. But the fact that he scrambled and shouted and flailed his tentacles at the human-possessed demons told me I would regret further inquiries.

I leaned closer to Bez. "Why's he freaking out?"

"You just said you didn't need an army to invade." Bez chuckled. "He's *freaking* that he just started a war with you."

"What?" I stepped forward. "I need to fix this."

"You'll do no such thing." Bez snatched me by the arm. "Let the minions fret. It creates mystique. Lilith won't hear. No one would inform her since all know the messenger always pays the price, and none here seek Oblivion."

"I do hope we can provide you a truly divine experience." Orias' eyeball gurgled, and the iris moved with a steady beat. "Perhaps we can provide you with proper accommodations for the spa treatment."

Several of the topless attendants weaved their hands around, stringing together their essence in the air and materializing various garbs. The clothing fit with the ancient Roman theme, from tunics and togas to various levels of armored materials. They had replicas of basic infantry to what a general would don. It was clear they didn't understand what a mortal would wear to a spa treatment.

"You should embrace the full experience." Orias waved a tentacle to the outfits on display.

I ran my hands over the soft wools and lovely silks.

Orias wriggled. "Would you like to undress? Surely, you must feel quite limited in this design."

Bez snarled and adjusted his tie. Getting him out of a suit and tie was a challenge most days. Usually, the only way was when we trained or screwed, which, more often than not, had a tendency of overlapping.

"I can assist." Orias scooted close behind Bez. "Help you undress for the full experience?"

"Oh, absolutely." I laughed a little, eyeing the demons dressed as oiled-up Roman attendants meant to see to our every need, and a part of me really wanted to see Bez rocking the subligaculum undies. "He'd love to strip out of that suit and into something befitting the theme."

"Certainly, Great Lord Devil Walter Alden of the Misfit Mortal Mage Hybridization."

Fuck me, that was a mouthful. Oh, man. Now I had to make that joke to Bez. Make him call me by that mouthful of a name.

Bez, whose eyes had gone wide with shock. He stared, perplexed for a second, and then furrowed his brow. "Walter, take it back before—"

The spikes of the tentacled suckers stabbed Bez from every direction and dug in deep before ripping him apart.

I screamed.

What had I done? What had I allowed?

8

Bez

"Son of a motherfucking bitch!" I roared as the spiked tentacles pierced my flesh and hooked in deep.

Before I could utter in protest, one tentacle wriggled down my back, slicing through the skin all the way to the core of my being and using the suckers to pull me out of my own skin.

Wally covered his face; shock and anguish and disgust merged his expression into this scrunched look of sour regret, which only further irritated me. The wry smile he had a moment ago had shattered into a thousand pieces of confusion.

I stood naked and bloody, staring down at the husk of my host body. Correction: former host body since some asinine demon decided to strip me of human form so I could feel Hell. Just as I required a body to indulge in the sensations of the mortal realm, possessing one here in Hell muted most of my senses, making my interactions with the world a mostly numb experience. Something I was quite comfortable with until Wally got my body shattered with his poorly phrased order.

Wally's unique physiology as an altered devil made from this unique entwinement of human and Diabolic energies must've shielded him from the worst of Hell's reception. That, and Lilith's need to bind her realities perception in this space as she feared the hybrid devil's unquantifiable limits. Even her dimmed dimension vibrated with a potency through my entire being.

Without a host, the dull sensations sprang to life. The touch of Hell's air lapped at my skin. There was no emptiness in Hell. Devils were born of nothingness, so every piece of space held tangible sensation, meaning the molecules themselves crawled over my flesh with a constant prickling flutter. Now, the taste of essence from a billion demons rested on my tongue, reaching out for acknowledgment. The wails of Diabolics bound beneath the intricate layers of the dimension called out, echoing like a thrum of a pulse against my eardrums. Devils loved to shatter their creations, smear essence along the cracks of their dimension to keep the flow of energy cohesive for every other demon worthy. Equivocally, they were the working-class cogs driven to their deaths to fuel a beast of a machine they'd never reap the rewards of fueling.

"What did you do? What did you do? What did you do?" Wally muttered to himself; his hazel eyes drowned in the black void of his essence. Every cell in his body radiated rage. The emotion hacked into the air, palpable and menacing. Orias and the demon attendant knelt in awe, in obedience. They didn't react with confusion to Wally's mixed emotions, for a devil owed no explanation to their mood, merely an outlet to unleash it. Essence bubbled inside Wally, ready to burst, but I caught him soothing himself as he took in the sight of my completely uninjured demon form. "Are you—"

"I am fine." I took a knee alongside Orias so I wouldn't be revealed as the devil Walter's vulnerability. Gods only know how Lilith would exploit my little obsessive boyfriend's love for me. "Apologies for the outburst. I'd grown attached to that silly little host body."

"I didn't realize when I said—"

"Yes," I interjected, with a very 'shut the fuck up' glare because we'd already established his talking would be the end of us if he didn't obey my discretion. "I suppose this Orias could use some training when it comes to undressing guests from their host bodies."

"Of course, my lord." Orias' tentacles wriggled and went to work retrieving the entrails of my former body. "The layers upon layers upon squishy layers that make up these carbon dwellings are so difficult to interact with. I will do more research on ways to repair this host body."

He pushed the muck of mushy meat that my hollowed-out former body had transformed into around until it made a neat, goopy pile.

"Pass," I snarled. "I don't want that body."

"Perhaps I can interest you in another." Orias swung his tentacles and hooked two males by the throat, damaging the bodies he put on display for me. "These are similar to your former vessel."

"No." I waved a dismissive hand. Possession was such an intimate process, delicate and patient work. Plus, I doubted any of Lilith's demons knew how to appreciate a body from one of the lesser worlds they were exclusively told not to venture into. They were sheltered by their own Hell and devil's authority. It showed in their every action or lack thereof. "I just got that one all cozy. I'll wait until I return home."

"What if I repaired this one?" Orias began weaving his essence through the goop. "I'll stitch it back to perfection."

"No," I said with conviction because politeness didn't go far in Hell. "Provide me and Walter a mirror and the privacy befitting his station for this sacred event."

"Certainly." Orias' eye, embodying the bulk of his being, stopped shaking when he noted the change in pressure from Wally's essence.

He'd calmed down since my demeanor shifted. I'd have to be less impulsive to avoid the ire of not one but two devils. The wrong reaction on my part could offend Lilith or worry Walter. In either case, the results weren't something I wanted to see unfold.

"Befitting my station?" Wally asked, his voice light and chipper. "That's a total Roman empire nod. I see what you did there."

"What I did was get us some breathing room from these fucking cuck demon lords." I rolled my eyes. "This way, none will be foolish enough to eavesdrop as we spend a little time cleaning up and playing dress up."

I gestured to my bloody naked body.

"You look hot." Wally grimaced, fighting a smile, which only made him extremely kissable in this moment.

We stepped inside the constructed room where Orias had quickly scrambled to teleport the wardrobe he'd had on display onto a neat rack that didn't seem to fit this ancient Roman theme, but I didn't know shit about Rome. Other than the fact I'd wasted a few seasons screwing and slaughtering mortals, mages, and Mythics alike while in their city. But that was nearly a century ago, and from Wally's long-winded explanations, ancient Rome was far older than that. A few thousand years based on his wet dream expression.

"This is the epitome of luxury during the rise of Rome." Wally gestured to the swimming pool and pointed to the separate tubs, each big enough to hold us and a small group. "Hygiene hadn't exactly become what it is today, but there was…"

Wally's worries washed away as random facts for every element of this magically constructed bathhouse replica spilled from his mouth. This continued with every single thing we walked past between the door and the mirror, where I finally examined myself.

I stood hunched since I'd grown used to squeezing into most of my host bodies, finding the more compact ones easiest for composites overall. Still, straightening my posture drew Wally's gaze. He looked up at me, taking in the difference in our height, awed by the nearly two-foot difference. Or perhaps it was my muscles that shocked him. I'd always maintained a muscular shape in his presence—even when decapitated and a meager pint-sized version of myself. But now, Wally tilted his head, like he was measuring with his eyes how his head compared to my large biceps. Then, his attention fell to my abdomen, studying the added definition created by splattered blood.

My light gray skin appeared even paler in the stark contrast of bloody remains dripping down my body. With a wave of my hand, I channeled telekinesis and pulled the droplets of blood off one by one, pooling them into a large blob. Wally watched with intrigue, studying my actions, noting the ombre effect on my hands extend and reach about halfway down my forearms. Controlling essence without a host body was more physically revealing, the notes of power. Black essence had even coated my feet and lower legs, creating a similar effect as with my arms. That helped keep me grounded in myself, reeling my senses inward toward my core so I could block out the bulk of Hell's overwhelming sensations.

PLOP.

I dropped the bloody mess into the center of the large pool that filled the bulk of this bathhouse spa, savoring the loud splash and lovely scarlet stretch throughout the clear water. It held the most beautiful allure as the blood painted beneath the tiny rippling current my disturbance had caused.

"Seriously?" Wally huffed. "So much for going for a swim."

"Please, makes me wanna take a dive even more now." I smiled, staring at my watery reflection before turning back to the mirror and taking in my fully nude, natural body. A body created in Hell and formed through the will of my essence and the tutelage of my devil. I ran a clawed hand along my sharp jaw, my throat, and rested it on the center of my chest.

The biggest drawback to walking through Lilith's Hell in my own skin was knowing how everyone would see every fault in my form. Every weakness I'd tried to improve over the centuries, every flaw I'd hidden beneath host bodies, every detail of my essence I despised. A complex created after eons of Beelzebub parading his shame, undercutting my successes, showing what his truly superior demons were capable of.

But while I hated my appearance, hated the inferiority my body possessed in comparison to some of the strongest Diabolics dwelling in Beelzebub's Hell, it didn't compare to Mora. She was stuck with a body that wasn't hers, never fit her right, never reflected the demon she was. Oh, what I wouldn't give to have Mora at my side during this Devil's Banquet. She was more than a king of Hell. She was a political genius, a savvy entrepreneur, and a cunning tactician.

Wally's curious, quiet gaze called to me. Even looking away from him, I could feel his need to speak, yet just as I sensed his antsy energy, he sensed my desire to take in my form. Or perhaps he simply felt guilty for the bad order. "You okay?"

"Yeah." I placed my hands on my hips and wiggled them to shake my dick and get a laugh out of Wally. "Just wondering what I'm gonna wear or if I should rock out with my cock out."

"May I make a suggestion on a personal favorite?" Wally held up a pair of skimpy clothed underwear that all the demon attendants awaiting us outside wore.

I didn't care for Wally's choice, but I could see his eagerness in me flaunting my body. He didn't see the blemishes across my gray skin, the need for improvement in my muscles, the faults in my features, or anything other than perfection. To Wally, I embodied beauty, confidence oozing from my pores, so I sauntered over to the rack of clothes, swaying my hips and relishing Wally's eyes locked onto my diabolically sexy bubble butt.

I wouldn't wear the togas or tunics. But I didn't care for the full-scaled armor either. Sifting through the selection, I found a piece I enjoyed here and there. I grabbed a smaller set of gauntlets for my wrists without detracting from the ombre effect of my essence coating my arms. I snapped a crown of leaves into pieces and adorned the golden shimmers between the feathers of my wings. Then to hold the outfit together, I slipped on a dark brown leather skirt divided into several slit straps.

"A gladiator's war skirt." Wally nodded approvingly, biting his lower lip and likely holding back some random factoid about the clothing. "It's very becoming."

"As in you'll be coming while I'm in it?" I winked.

He snickered. "Exactly."

"And what're you planning on wearing?" I batted my lashes. "And don't think you can escape the themed wardrobe because of your devilish station."

"Actually, I always wanted to do a Greek or Roman-inspired costume, so this is kind of like a dream." Wally rifled through a few of the clothes on display. "Aside from the fact that one misstep in said dream will turn the entirety of this into an absolute nightmare which would potentially lead to my death, your death, the death of everyone in the Diabolic Oasis, the death of everyone in the world, and yeah—sort of taints a bit of the daydream factor."

Wally grabbed a black tunic with a golden robe to tie around his waist, along with matching gold-laced sandals that tied to his knees and a crown of leaves to set atop his head.

"That said, I look pretty stylish." He popped his hip, looking cute as fuck. And I do mean fuckable in the cutest way.

Using my tails, I pulled Wally closer. His cheeks burned red as his lips nearly pressed against mine from the swift shuffle. Then, I tore the front of his tunic open, exposing his muscular chest, and ripped the sides of the tunic's skirt bottom to reveal his lovely thighs.

"Hey!" he whined.

"Now, you practically look perfect." I kissed him, shoving my tongue in his mouth and massaging his before he could protest a hundred complaints about how I'd ruined his choice outfit. "The only thing that'll make you look better is when I bend you over and hike your skirt up."

He huffed and went to retrieve a new tunic. His brow furrowed, likely hating the color choices.

"Might as well keep on what you have." I bumped my pelvis against his butt. "I'll just end up ripping apart whatever you choose next until you're all sexy for me again."

"Not if I order you to behave," Wally teased. "As the devil here, I am the one who makes the rules, right?"

"That so?" I spun him around, closing the distance between us so our crotches touched. Only the fabric of his short tunic and my frilly war skirt divided our skin. "What orders do you have, Lord Devil Walter Alden?"

"Um..." His face scrunched, flustered yet aroused.

"Should I get on my knees and worship at your altar?" I dropped down without awaiting his command.

I'd craved Wally's authority for some time, and when better than in Hell, where it might all come to an end? And if it was coming to an end, I wanted to cum with him one final time.

"Wait," he whispered. "What about the demons out there?"

"They're not listening." I ran my teeth along the golden belt tying his tunic and tugged at the knot. "They wouldn't dare."

Wally held his breath, watching me with excitement. Delicately, I traced my clawed nails up Wally's legs, rubbing the hairs, and rested my hands under the fabric of his outfit. He'd have to assert himself if he sought more. My thumbs rested close to the inside of his thighs, near his growing erection.

"How may I serve you, Walter?"

He released a swift and heavy breath, exhaling all his nervousness, and then lifted his tunic to reveal his rock-hard cock. Without a word, I went to work. I held the tip in my mouth, resting the head on my tongue, rotating to massage the nerves. Wally sucked his teeth, immediately entranced by the sensation, but I'd just begun. I swallowed further, taking in the whole shaft to the base of his crotch.

Wally moaned, stifling the noise as he slapped a hand on the back of my head, hoping to hold me here longer, keep the feeling from fading. I swirled my head, keeping Wally's cock in my throat. He wasn't small or large, but even if he were, my gag reflex didn't really exist. I could swallow a sword if I were craving it, so Wally's seven inches didn't exactly choke me.

Though when he started pumping his hips, I gulped and gurgled at the suddenness. It enticed him, and he slammed his dick faster and further in a frenzy. He grunted, which sent a shiver through my warming body. I quivered, drawn to his energy, surrendering my mouth to him to use how he pleased. He bucked and grunted louder the deeper he pushed his cock head into my tight throat muscles.

He slid his hand between my curled horns and played with my ruffled hair. Then with a tight grip of his hand wrapped between the locks, he yanked me back, pulling me off his cock. Not quite entirely, but back to the tip where I licked and teased the head until he ran his hand under my chin and pulled me forward with both hands. He slammed me back to the base of his dick and thrusted.

Each time he pumped his hips, the fervor inside him swelled. Usually, Wally was calmer when I sucked him off, merely enjoying the affection, the shift between my eager and aggressive nature in bed, yet now this primal beast grew from him. Each second that passed, Wally tested himself a little more, adding a touch more assertiveness as I continued pleasuring him.

He smacked the side of my face lightly and held his grip there. He massaged my hair before raking his fingers through and pulling my head back by the roots. He yanked my mouth away from his dick, teasing my lips with the head. With a playfulness, he rubbed the tip of his cock along my mouth and then stuffed it back in.

I choked, taking in the swift thrusts.

Oftentimes, I was the overzealous one, relishing in his whimpering satisfaction, but now he carried himself with this commanding need for dominance. Submission was never something I offered to a partner—satisfaction, yes—but I preferred to remain in charge. In control. Too much of my existence was met with service in Hell's battles and so much more, but with Wally, serving obediently offered a high unlike any other. It washed away the world outside this room.

All that called was Wally and his cock.

I tilted my head, adjusting ever so to make it easier for Wally to face fuck me. He pounded into my throat, pulling his cock almost all the way out, leaving just the head in my mouth before stuffing every inch of his shaft back in down to the base.

I gripped his hips, steadying the erratic, brutal thrusts to create an almost rhythmic pounding.

He panted, taking faster strokes and edging himself right to the point of release before slowing down and rubbing his hand along my jaw.

"Fuck," he muttered. "You feel so good."

I stretched my mouth wider, taking him in entirely. Wally continued, using my throat to meet his needs and finally cumming.

His teeth chattered, and he groaned. I let him slowly hump my face to shoot out a few more jets of cum, savoring the taste that filled my mouth.

He pulled out, wiping the last drops on my lips, rubbing cum and spit with the head of his dick over my face, then he shoved the tip in once more to suck until he'd fully finished. Until his body stopped craving satisfaction. Until he stopped vibrating from the orgasm. Until he'd felt the full extent of his release. I played with Wally's cock, taking it back into my mouth as it went soft. I continued sucking until he told me to stop. I would please him until he ordered something new.

9

After Bez and I finished—well, after I'd finished—Bez summoned Orias and the other demons to join us in the bathhouse. I sort of expected Bez to want or desire a little mutual satisfaction. But Bez beamed with delight, requiring nothing in this moment, satisfied entirely by my completion. Not that he was a selfish partner; it was just that our dynamic usually involved me serving Bez's needs. I craved it, craved him, always.

Yet now I found myself stirring with new desires, new ideas, passions and wants and primal needs. Needs that sought to control Bez, use him, bring him the same subservient satisfaction he'd offered me since the first time we'd been together.

"Get out of your head, Walter." Bez flunked my temples from either side with the points of his tails and reeled me from my thoughts.

I adjusted my tunic, covering myself as best I could since Bez had ripped the sides all the way to the top of my hips. My ears burned when the demon attendants gazed, only comforted by the eager delight in Bez's crimson eyes while he kept his attention locked onto me.

Orias squeezed past the entourage of demons and shrank in size so he could fit inside the bathhouse.

"I have a Cerberus who does that," I said, thoughts spinning into a hundred concerns for Weather.

While I definitely doted on him, chances were he already missed Bez. For whatever reason, the hostility Bez demonstrated appealed to all three personas of our Mythic beast.

"Fascinating. Size manipulation is a standard ability for Diabolics," Orias replied. "I didn't realize other creatures possessed the skill."

"You can change your size?" I quirked a brow at Bez, recalling the only time his stature had dramatically shifted came from a decapitation incident and a lack of essence to reform his full size.

"But of course." Bez looked down, towering above in his demon form—at least a solid foot in height difference. Possibly more because, despite my best efforts, spatial awareness wasn't a strong skillset I possessed. "Which part of me would you desire I change the size of, Lord Walter? I can enlarge anything to your specifications."

His teasing smirk made my ears burn even more. Yes, he maintained a completely composed demeanor with no hint of snark in his voice, but his sass cut through to the deepest core of my being.

"No." I grimaced. "You're sized just right. Not too big or too small or…um, yeah. Just right."

"The three bears will be glad to hear that." Bez winked, which only added to the flustered scrunch of my face.

"A Cerberus and three bears." Orias nodded. "You must crave a zoo of beasts for a collection. Perhaps we can acquire you some unique oddities of exotic beings."

"We don't have bears," I said. "I mean, we have them in our world, but I don't personally have any bears."

Orias' iris wiggled into an almost rounded shape, possibly a sign of his confusion, so I went to clarify until Bez interrupted.

"It's a mortal expression, you wouldn't understand."

"Ah." Orias nodded his bulbous head. "Mortals do say the strangest things. Perhaps the satisfaction of the three bears would make more sense in one of your many other languages."

"How do you know our language?" I asked.

"Research," Orias said.

"He probably devoured a few hundred humans to gain an understanding of our world," Bez whispered.

"That's awful."

"Surely, the thought occurred." Bez grinned. "You don't think these host bodies are volunteers, do you?"

I recoiled a bit, turtling my neck, then buried the thought. There was nothing to be done about it. Nothing by me. These demons might fear the wrath of Walter Alden, hybrid devil guy, but I didn't want to cross anyone while here in Hell. Lilith's Hell. The devil still yet to reveal herself since my arrival.

"Allow us to offer a bit of relaxation and wonder before escorting you to the first course of the Devil's Banquet."

I twisted my lips into this anxious, scrunched, puckered confusion because, in all my time with Bez, I'd never seen him enjoy a normal meal. Since it appeared nothing other than demons and devils survived within the walls of Hell, I could only imagine the most disturbing cannibalistic meals ever conceived.

Bile built in my throat at the thought, and I did my best not to hurl.

"It's rare for them to import food into Hell." Bez raised his brows. "It's such a lower being need to require sustenance and all that."

Well, that was slightly comforting, but then Bez's concoctions and ideas behind seasoning rang in my head, and I hoped his chefly ways were far from what other Diabolics considered appetizing.

"Let us begin with a few treatments on the physical extremities." Orias clapped his tentacles together, using the clack of the hooked spikes to usher the demon attendants, who used their telekinesis to shift the room's arrangement.

"Hmmm. A spa day in Hell." I chuckled. "This isn't the horrors I expected."

"Remain on your guard all the same," Bez whispered. "Everything is a test, an evaluation of how you hold yourself. I plan on being insufferably demanding."

"How's that different from any other day?"

Bez scoffed, then smirked, then let his gaze drift from me. His eyes gleamed with excitement at the supplies telekinetically carried into the bathhouse by the demon attendants. They all huddled around furniture where Orias encouraged us to rest. I sat in the cushioned seat, studying the equipment. I placed my hands on the nearby table positioned so I could lounge while they worked.

"Mani pedis?" He fluttered his fingers with dazzle, adding essence to the sheen black of his growing claws. "I'm here for the pampering, but it doesn't seem very on point with the theme."

"Actually, manicures date back to 3200 B.C., which ties into some of the earliest forms of hygiene, cosmetics, a desire for…" I bit my lower lip when Bez's eyes glazed over. "All right. Let's enjoy a little pampering."

I carefully lifted my feet and set them in an empty tub where someone went to work cleaning my feet. The entire experience was well beyond my comfort zone. Strangers touching me. Working on me. It was something I'd rather tend to independently, privately. But something told me devils weren't modest or concerned about burdening someone else with serving them. I let my mind spin to every fact I knew about manicures because my thoughts had immediately drifted back to how hot Bez was when he served me. Served my cock. My cock that was already getting stiff at the idea of once again—

"What color were you thinking?" I asked.

There were hundreds of nail polishes arranged on racks and presented in a similar fashion to opening a crayon box.

"Something bold and stylish." He hummed for a dramatic pause, but we both knew the color he'd choose. His favorite color. "I'm gonna go with neon orange."

He eyed the assortment on display, resting on the several shades of orange in selection.

"Or perhaps I'll settle." Bez feigned offense. "Walter, must we settle for subpar oranges?"

"Um…"

"Never." Orias' tentacles flailed, and his essence went to work, conjuring a new collection of nail polishes to fill in the gaps in colors he'd offered. Not sure how he managed to create so many other shades when he'd already practically included every color in the rainbow spectrum. Watching him work was like going to a paint store where they had fifty types of white to choose from that only differed on the most microscopic level.

"And what color would you like, Great Lord Devil Walter Alden of the Misfit Mortal Mage Hybridization?" Orias levitated half of the nail polish bottles, providing a circular catalog for me to sift through as they whirled slowly around.

"Hmmm." I tapped my chin. "Probably just the clear polish for a nice clean look."

"Wonderful choice!" Orias applauded me, which made me feel less like a devil and more like a toddler, but given the tantrums devils were expected to have over any tiny whim, I figured the toddler comparison was too generous.

Bez rolled his eyes and then flaunted his neon orange polish.

"On second thought, let's go with black." I nodded affirmingly.

I'd attempted a rocker style back as a teen for all of, like, five minutes. The wardrobe required a lot of laidback glam, which was a difficult look to accomplish when I had an obsessive need to be anything but casual. Plus, the first time I painted my nails, my mother had *opinions*. It wasn't the femineity or the queerness. No, she was always fine and accepting and open to any lifestyle her children chose. Except for failure, which I majored in. The real judgment came from the fact she considered me dull as dishwater. It was bad enough I was a failure from a lineage of the most elite mage pedigree, but to change my style to something edgy and alternative made me nothing more than a tragic try-hard in her eyes.

Critical, menacing eyes that still haunted my memories. With the brush of the black polish over my thumbnail, the expression of my mother's gaze blossomed in my mind. A hateful expression of pity that burrowed to the depths of my soul and made me squirm in place. Even with her long gone, locked away without her magic, I'd never truly escape her years of venomous disgust directed toward me.

"Looking cute, Lord Walter." Bez puckered his lips, stealing me from my own self-loathing and reminding me in an instant how much I'd grown, changed, and left behind that person who blundered everything he tried. I wasn't the apprentice who failed every time he applied himself. I was a devilish hybrid with the most darling demon at my side.

I crinkled my forehead. "Are devils allowed to be cute?"

"I don't see why not, Great Lord Devil Walter Alden of the Misfit Mortal Mage Hybridization," Orias interjected. "Lilith often strives to be seductive, professing herself the most unattainable harlot of lust and love."

"Yet she's most commonly known for ripping out still-beating hearts and strangling her lovers with their entrails." Bez chuckled.

"Precisely." Orias' iris wriggled and set almost into a sideways smile. "The complexity of devils is truly unique to all lesser beings."

I frowned. That didn't make devils sound complex at all. It sounded very human, which Bez obviously agreed with based on how he rolled his eyes and then mouthed "petty bitches" before returning to his mani-pedi.

The demons breezed through Bez's treatment, literally moving at a blurred speed and not spending nearly half the detail on him as they did for me. Not that he complained. His voice dropped deeper, and he bellowed weird noises that I couldn't comprehend, but it made my essence react. Each growl commanded faster work, a retouch on something already finished or something else Bez relished in ordering.

When Bez's nails had finally dried, he skipped the massage table they had set up at a nearby station, using a tail to flip it over, and then he strutted over to one of the smaller tubs surrounding the big pool he'd spilled bloody remains into.

"Hurry up, Lord Walter." Bez unfastened his armored skirt and dropped it to his ankles, standing completely nude with only the gauntlets on his wrists.

Without any hesitation, Bez jumped into the tub. He rifled through the assortment of bottled products lining the tub and squeezed a bunch all at once, releasing a medley of sweet fragrances that created bubbles in the boiling water.

It was quite inviting, and when Bez glanced back at me, grinning, I desperately wanted to get up and join him. Instead, I paused when another demon grabbed my hand and went to work filing my nails yet again.

"Actually, I'm pretty sure this is finished." I half-smiled. "Mostly. Looks good. Great. You don't have to do the whole thing again. Do you? I wouldn't want you to have to feel the need to work on redoing all of this again."

Gods, that was wordy when, in reality, I simply should've said "no" because I wanted this to end. To be over. To completely conclude. To wrap up, so I could hop in one of the hot baths with Bez and make obnoxiously loud groans of satisfaction in bubbly water.

"No worries," the demon said, filing faster. "Just a final touch-up to ensure everything is precisely perfect."

The file zipped back and forth against my nails, jumping from one to another and back again so quickly it required my essence to track the demon's movements. I knew it was essence, too. The sensation of reality stalling, slowing down as my eyes widened and locked onto the action at play. There was a recklessness to their haste until suddenly, the tip of the file jabbed the cuticle of my index finger when hopping around.

I winced, sucking in a sharp breath when a drop of blood pooled at the tip of my freshly painted nail. Hard to see the difference between scarlet blood and black polish, but again, my essence fueled my vision, adding layers of nuance I never realized was possible.

It took everything in my power to reel back the building essence. It surged through me, seeking retribution and ready to explode.

The pain reminded me of the horrors I'd endured when picking at a hangnail, only for it to bleed and tear and ache and threaten eternal agony until the end of time. Seriously—if walking through Lilith's doorway to Hell involved a hangnail, I might've actually considered letting the world roll the dice against a devil.

Okay, dramatic, but it hurt like fuck. I prepared to put my finger in my mouth and clamp down until the blood clotted and the pain subsided, but essence trickled out in a tiny weblike thread, stitching the little tear in my flesh while dragging the droplet of blood back into my body.

"Cool." I widened my eyes, entranced by the active essence working like a colony of cells determined to keep me, my body, and the kingdom optimally functional. Since I refused carnal destruction, resisting every impulsive urge to eviscerate, the essence changed strategies. Maybe I was getting the hang of this stuff. Little by little.

"Deepest apologies, Great Lord Devil Walter Alden of the Misfit Mortal Mage Hybridization." Orias thrashed, shoving aside every demon attendant in his path, whether they were performing entertainment, tending to Bez, or preparing for the next spa treatment. "This is a travesty of the highest proportions!"

I held up my hand, showing the healed finger. "It's all r—"

"Unacceptable." Bez leapt out of the tub, wings outstretched and tails snapping. Each one flicked against the floor with a crack and thwack from the water. They hit with such force, they sliced through the marble.

In a flash, Bez lunged forward. He moved so suddenly, even my vision struggled to keep up, recalibrating to slow down reality and study his movements. Did I actually slow time, or did my essence merely alter the perception of my brain receptors so I could comprehend super speed in a digestible manner? I'd wager on the latter. Either way, I'd confer with Bez in private so I could gain a better grasp on this continuous growth in my Diabolic abilities. But first, I needed him to calm down.

"Bez, I'm fine."

He stood completely naked, drenched in water and covered in soapy suds that didn't hide his most private areas. Not that it concerned Bez to swing his dick while also swinging that menacing attitude. Part of me wanted to giggle, reminded of the first time he'd kidnapped me and threatened to chase me buck naked if I attempted to flee while he showered. But his furious expression made me swallow that humorous thought and keep it to myself.

"You dare presume to attack Lord Walter?" Bez snarled, glaring down at the demon who'd accidentally struck me.

The demon shivered, dropping the file. It clinked almost as loudly as the demon's hands that slapped the marble floor when they knelt to apologize.

"I meant no harm."

"Bah." Bez waved a dismissive hand, his tails flicking in unison and smashing nearby furniture. "As if you could ever harm my great lord. It is your audacious nature, your impotence, that infuriates me."

"Bez." I grimaced and bit my lip because I'd agreed to follow his lead here in Hell. If that meant staying quiet while he verbally ripped this low-level demon to shreds, then so be it.

Whether for the show of authority or indulging in his own ego, Bez's antics reminded me of every time a practitioner emotionally eviscerated me when I worked in the archives. The number of times I'd been called an "incompetent fucking moron who can't do anything right" could fill a calendar. All three-hundred and sixty-five days, not the monthly spreads.

Bez slashed the demon across the face, watching the essence lash out defensively as the host body was hacked through. In one swift motion, Bez had torn open flesh, bone, muscle, and brain matter. All things the demon's essence could restore, but Bez didn't offer the chance.

As quickly as he'd leapt over and attacked, he summoned black flames between his hands and dropped an inferno of fire down onto the demon who'd struck me.

I bit my knuckles to stifle a shocked scream. Not that anyone would hear it over the horrified wails of agony unleashed by the demon Bez incinerated.

10

.

Bez

Wally nearly gave away his compassionate heart a dozen different times. But thankfully, he recalled my warnings and silenced his protests while I burned this daring demon to cinders. It wasn't that there weren't kind devils. There were. There were plenty, in fact. They'd been birthed into the universe to balance the scales, perhaps, but the universe underestimated the wickedness of the foulest creations.

Devils like mine, devils like Lilith, devils who reigned superior through the test of time, didn't tolerate compassion and deemed it an easy weakness to exploit. The devil Walter couldn't be considered weak. Not if we wanted to walk away from this unscathed. He'd want his life back, a life without Hell, without Lilith's authority, without the ominous threat of death for daring to exist, and as such, it fell to me to ensure I evoked a level of terror befitting a devil.

I served as commander and needed every demon in the vicinity—not simply those in attendance to serve, but also the tens of thousands watching from a safe distance, studying and composing theories for Lilith on whether they should strike or submit. It was a delicate process, one I'd contributed to many times for Beelzebub over the eons. Demons conspire, cautious and obedient and always willing to take the fall for failure.

"Bez, what the fuck!" Wally ground his teeth, nostrils flaring because he loathed the smell of charred flesh. Always so sensitive, but I loved it almost as much as I loved him. "It was an accident!"

"It was an overstep, my lord." I dropped to one knee, arms swiped to the side to bow in submission, and hoped for the love of everything simple that Wally caught the cue. "But this audacious behavior could not be tolerated."

"Absolutely!" Orias wriggled and went to bow himself. "Lilith does not tolerate such obstinate failure. These demons were hand-picked for their precision of flattery and understanding, and I am ashamed to have considered that fool to be even remotely…"

Orias' iris zipped erratically, and his voice slipped into the Diabolic language, the singular tones we shared across every Hell, proving that, despite immortality and massive power and dimensional travel, we lacked uniqueness like the obnoxious mortal Walter pitied.

"Enough," Wally snapped. "Out. Out. Everyone out."

I stood along with all the demon attendants, preparing to leave as I needed to appear as obedient as everyone else under the order of the devil's command.

"Stay." Wally seethed, pointing a finger to the broken floor I'd smashed, and honestly, there was something so hot about his rage in that singular second. *Stay*. I nearly dropped to my knees again.

Once everyone had exited, Wally's enraged expression fell flat into a frazzled panic of disarray, and suddenly, my desire to kneel fizzled away along with his confidence.

"What the actual fuck, Bez?"

"No actual fucking thanks to that panicked pancake face."

"What?"

"Nothing," I mumbled.

"You can't just kill someone over a mistake."

"It wasn't a mistake." I locked eyes with him so he'd truly listen. "Nothing here that happens will be unintentional. The theme picked carries a message. These demons picked to tend to our needs are the best of the best. They wouldn't make a mistake in a million years and probably lived that long at Lilith's side tending to her needs."

Wally swallowed, losing confidence in whatever retort he'd had bubbling in his thoughts. "So, you're saying the accident was on purpose so they could see how I'd react?"

"Did you not listen to a single warning I gave you?" I cocked my head. "This is Hell. Lilith's Hell. A Hell where everything you do is observed, studied, scrutinized, and evaluated."

Wally's face turned pensive.

"But don't get a woody over it," I continued. "These aren't musings like your artifact studies. Lilith's goal is to determine your power. Right now, she can't quantify your strength. The reaction for any demon to acquire a devil essence varies dramatically and is rare enough. But to find another being, a non-Diabolic, to possess a piece of the most powerful devil in the universe? That fear she holds is the only thing affording us privacy right now."

I didn't say it, didn't tell him how Lilith herself had watched since we arrived, but I could feel her looming above us, intangible and merely goosebumps in my paranoia. All the same, even without being able to detect her, I sensed her through the sheer horror-struck awe I held for devils.

"It's my goal to make sure Lilith realizes Walter Alden isn't a gnat on steroids," I said. "I want her to see you as the potential nuke that could eradicate anyone who poked too hard."

"You think I can pull that off?"

"Wally, I've seen you slaughter when pushed. Stop empathizing with demons. They'd gut you the first opportunity to lay at Lilith's feet in the muck of fallen foes."

"Yes, yes, yes, I know. Very dramatic." He nodded reluctantly. "One misstep could be our deaths. You're in charge."

"Thank you," I said. "But remember, as far as they're concerned, you're in charge. I'm just an eager pleaser jumping to defend my devil."

"Yes." Wally sighed.

"It's important that you remember, you can't tolerate any slight."

"So all devils strike down for the tiniest flaws?"

"Any devil who wishes to keep themselves and their demons out of Oblivion does."

"Well, I don't have demons." Wally pouted.

"You have me."

His pouty lips fell into a frown. "Sorry. I know I need to follow your lead. I know I need to just be a dick to everyone. This shouldn't be so hard."

I smirked. "There's a joke there."

"As an Alden, this whole entitlement thing should come easier to me."

"If you're having trouble coming, I can help." My grin widened, hoping to elevate the tension with terribly dirty puns, which worked when Wally finally broke into a smile. We might be risking our lives, our very existence, but I didn't want him to panic the entire time. We could die at Lilith's whim any second for something we did or didn't do or a billion other factors that suited her mood, so I needed to hold onto any brief moments of happiness here in Hell I had with Wally.

He stood tall, squaring his shoulders. "I'm going to make a solid effort to be imposing moving forward."

"Just don't be complacent or tolerant or kind or considerate or nice..." I rocked my head from side to side. "If you find yourself wanting to Walter the situation, do the opposite."

"Don't turn me into a verb."

"Why not?" I shrugged. "I turned you into a devil."

He huffed. The cutest, breathy little exaggeration. Now, if I could get him to add a scowl with that attitude, we might be able to trick a few demons into thinking Wally was a threat.

"Just ignore any instinct that seems rational," I said. "Impulse is honestly your friend."

"You would think being all-powerful beings would afford devils a bit of resistance in their moods."

"When has anyone with absolute power proven to be anything other than absolute trash?"

And with a glum tsk, Wally concurred, and we took our leave from the bathhouse. Orias left a trail of glitter meant to guide us to our first destination on this trek through Hell for the Devil's Banquet.

"Whoa." Wally adjusted the glasses meant to help alleviate the strain he had on taking in the sights of Hell. Thankfully, Diabolics didn't have much understanding of where mortal parts began and ended, so they likely assumed the lens was merely an extension to the eyeball. "It's so pretty."

We walked a trail leading out of the stadium. It led us into the heart of a lush field of plants, trees with bright and vibrant barks reflecting the false sunset projected nearby. Lilith's many filters cloaked the intricate layers of her deadly dimension, cloaking it with an aesthetic meant to lure guests. I couldn't see beyond the three-dimensional design she offered, but I trusted nothing. Wally, on the other hand, found himself entranced by the splendor and beauty put on display. This design emulated the parts of the Diabolic Oasis Wally loved most, having a fondness for the exotic plant life that grew alongside Mora's expanding city.

Clear evidence that Lilith had spies observing Wally's interests prior to the buffoon she sent to deliver our invitation.

"Hell's not all bad." Wally brushed his fingers along the pedals of several different flowers. "Fields of plants with several extinct species, guessing to highlight some of our natural beauty."

"You give Hell too much credit," I said. "It's all part of your mortal theme."

"It's nice. You think they imported some of these, same with the human hosts?" Wally chose to delude himself with grand hopes that those human host bodies would be treated with similar kindness as Mora exhibited to those she possessed. "Obviously, some of it's magic. I mean, unless they did like hybrid cloning for the extinct flora, but that'd require—"

"It's just essence that's been spruced up."

"Wait, what?"

"Diabolic essence." I gestured to the grand field of flowers. "My guess, by the size of it, a few hundred demons shredded and reshaped. Well, there's also the stadium."

"Wait." Wally's eyes bugged out. "The stadium was made of demons?"

"Oh, yeah. A few thousand at least." I shrugged playfully. "Probably why the stands were so empty."

"That's awful."

"It's a joke." I laughed. "Because the audience would've been slaughtered and shredded and seamlessly reshaped into all of this. If there was ever an audience. Probably just some lesser, forgettable Diabolics."

Wally's expression turned queasy, which was a good indication the reality of this horror show sank in fully. "Wow, that's disturbing."

"Well, it's not funny if you have to explain it." I ignored his internalized turmoil because he needed to reflect on this while seeing me maintain a light-heartedness to the dire situation we stepped through.

Wally's hand retreated from the flower like it'd somehow snap its pedals around his fingers and devour them.

It wouldn't. The Diabolics used to paint the walls of Hell rarely kept sentience. The few centuries I spent with my essence spilled out to create a diamond-floored entryway were a blur of nonsense. There was an occasional flicker or flash of footsteps from that time, but otherwise, simple silence. And pain. Constant agonizing pain with no understanding of the purpose. The duration. The existence of nothing else.

"They're fine," I said. "Life as a flower is a pretty easy existence."

"I guess." Wally sulked. "Just seems kind of sad."

"It's only sad if you dwell on it." I shrugged. "Like most things."

"Are there animals?" Wally searched the fields, his pupils dilating then tightening to view the many intricate layers of plant life stretched for miles upon miles.

"No. Plants are already too lively," I answered. "Personally, I think devils simply enjoy the stillness in their beauty."

"So, no animals?" Wally asked. "Not even insects?"

"Thinking of yours?"

"Tony's an arachnid, not an insect."

"In either case, an animal—a beast of any level—would require a level of sentience not afforded to the essence of any particular demon when divided and reshaped in such ways."

"Is everything here just Diabolics in one form or another?" He kicked the dirt at our feet. "Essence?"

"Yep." Hell itself was the soul of a devil, their greatest organ, and as such, it fueled their infinite power to layer their realm with the essence of their creations.

"The air we're breathing?"

"We're not breathing." I widened my eyes to clue him in on the obvious secret that he'd stopped breathing.

"Only I haven't stopped," he muttered aloud because he had to share his internal ramblings. "Breathing requires a constant flux of reflexes formed by instinct with the complex motor function and neuromotor control and so many other pieces of the body. But I'm not taking anything in, am I?"

Suddenly, the air around us felt so stale and hollow. Bursting his bubble on the reality of life here, if one could call living in Hell a life, somehow added to the emptiness of this realm.

"Would you like to know what the stars are?" I teased.

"Probably just more essence since everything is just essence." He sighed. "Even your magic is just twisting your essence into another form, right?"

I nodded, then gestured up to the twinkling stars shimmering around the setting sun. "Just as the stars are an after-effect of Fae births in your reality, they are merely infantile Diabolics too young for sentience. They watch from the heavens above, far from easy reach, so they can observe and study the world."

"That's kind of sweet, showing them all of Hell, but kind of sad they have to stay billions of miles away all by themselves. Of course, this assumes the distance is similar to the mortal world."

"It is. And the method is to protect them," I explained. "Babies are violent and stupid on top of being ugly and boring, so it makes for a deadly combination. If thrown together in a playpen, they'd devour each other."

"Geez." Wally squirmed. "Demon babies are ruthless."

"Like human babes are any better," I said. "But it also removes Diabolic infants from the weak, feeble demons who might be tempted to feast upon defenseless babes to enhance their own essence."

Wally's expression twisted into this desire to yack. Despite all the warnings I'd given him since the day we first met and the ruthlessness I'd demonstrated upon our first interaction, he still didn't quite grasp the full extent of Diabolic destruction. We were beasts of primeval power, pioneers of carnage and mayhem, warriors born and bred into eons of savagery. Even in Hells such as Lilith's that professed diplomacy over combat such as mine, no dimension of embodying virtues of compassion and consideration survived.

We approached a large building meant to host our first course. Wally mumbled audibly loud approval over the structure of this place. This temple, according to the string of words that escaped his lips held fine authentic craftsmanship that balanced mortal and Mythic influences.

"Now, remember." I squeezed Wally's bicep. "You must maintain a level of control, dominance. Show no hesitation if possible."

"I got this," he squeaked. "I'm totally okay."

"I'll serve as a buffer, but I can't appear the one calling the shots." It was hard enough to portray myself as an arrogant demon high on my devil's reign.

I'd met demons who deemed themselves equals to their devil because they were treated as lovers or brothers or both. Anything to delude themselves into thinking they were significant in their devils' eyes. They weren't. To a devil, anything beneath them was merely a whim of entertainment. Whether they were kind or cruel, the emotion was as fleeting as a mortal's existence.

"We got this." Wally led the way. "Just the first course of what'll be a long day or century or forever."

"Relax." I pressed my claws to the small of his back, guiding him until we reached an audience, where I changed my demeanor to something aggressively subservient. I reeled my essence outward, close to the ground at Wally's feet. I kept my head lowered with my eyes locked on everyone nearby. I even hunched my shoulders while keeping my wings upright and high to add to the flair of the devil's arrival. Even with a small entourage that embodied only myself, I needed to appear imposing. Not a hard act since I'd walked this line into a hundred Hells at Beelzebub's side.

When we arrived at Court, the demon lords in attendance had this aristocratic air about them. Yes, they dressed in garbs suited for the best Roman parties, but with all my time spent in Hell, the most notable mortal comparison came from the wealthy nobility. Those truly seeped in opulence to their very core, high on their title, on their station, on their divine purpose gifted by fate over effort. Few in Hell who toiled ever succeeded beyond what their devil deemed they deserved.

"Did you know the Romans had several distinguishable types of banquets and parties?" Wally said nervously as all his collective knowledge spilled out as we crossed the threshold of white stone pillars to the temple we entered. "They had public feasts which were referred to as an epulum and drinking parties known as comissatio and banquets of all kinds that were really more than simple dinner parties."

"Well, let us hope this isn't one of the orgy parties." I grinned. "Everyone would be clamoring for a piece of the new devil."

"Orgies actually weren't very common practice," Wally said with this matter-of-fact bravado on the plethora of knowledge he possessed. "Banquets were, though. In fact, when the Romans hosted a banquet, it was never meant to be a frivolous gathering. It was a spectacle, a display of authority and status and worth."

Wally paused as the realization of his words sank in, and suddenly, the choice in theme rang loudly. It was called a Devil's Banquet for a reason. One misstep in front of these demon lords, and they'd feast upon Wally. They'd rip us both to shreds and devour us down to the last speck of our being, dropping what remained of our consciousness into the void of Oblivion, where we'd lay dormant until the end of time. If such a thing ever occurred.

I stood confidently as we approached the crowd. The demon lords exuded authority; it seeped from the fibers of their being, danced on the edges of their essence, and radiated from their Diabolic cores. They were not merely the rulers over the vast territories in Lilith's domain but the best of the best meant to provoke a reaction.

Thankfully, Wally fixated more on their appearances than he did their power. "Is that demon just a collection of triangles?"

"It's symmetrical aesthetic." I shrugged. "Some prefer their essence appear sleek as a sign of control."

"It's like a geometric nightmare." His eyes locked onto the other demons who pointlessly wore togas over their assortment of clustered shapes. Then, he studied the beastly bodies similar to birds, reptiles, felines, and so forth. He mouthed the various species he recognized.

At the core stood Orias, iris curved in a demure sign of respect. Not for Wally, the devil in attendance, but the demon Orias passed the baton of hosting duties off to.

I ground my teeth at the sight of that blue demon, Corson, who'd delivered Lilith's invitation. He stood at the center of the banquet, surrounded by the best of the demon lords, posturing as if this event was in some way a celebration of his ego.

"Is it rare to look mortal?" he asked quietly, worried about eavesdropping, but based on how well the demon lords kept their essence coiled and away from our path, I suspected none dared listen in on Wally's musings.

A few—a very small margin, in fact—possessed a human shape and appearance. Only a handful here at the banquet and not many others throughout the many Hells I'd had the misfortune of visiting.

"Seems more like you lot aimed to look like us." I puffed my chest and strutted with some extra swagger so my tails and wings swung wide. "The best-looking bunch, at the very least."

The added span in my steps afforded us more space from those who'd already cleared a path for our entrance.

"Hmmm." Wally strummed his fingers against his thighs, thinking. "Right, because so many Diabolics predate human existence. Predate a lot of the animals you're guised as—not guised because skin isn't a disguise. Well, it is when possessing a body, but no one is doing that here. Well, not *here* here, anyway. The point is"—he released an exasperated breath not meant for the lack of air in his lungs but the crowded words in his brain—"this all begs the question of how much of the mortal realm's development is happenstance and how much was influenced by Diabolics?"

The room quieted, and Wally's question echoed loudly in the silence offered. He swallowed the lump in his throat and bit his lower lip to silence the need for clarification resting on the tip of his tongue.

This whole ordeal might have me in a stranglehold of anxiety, but I couldn't help but smile at Wally's quirky excitement and curiosity.

"It reminds me of a paper I read about the influence of Mythic magics on biological evolution and the symbiotic connection between the pair. After all, magical entities often replicate themselves to share some distinction with nature," Wally whispered, shrinking in on himself because he still struggled to accept everyone's eyes resting on him. This was the type of thing he did when he worked in the archives. I had witnessed him bury his thoughts because those who outranked him treated his every musing as prattling drivel. "Or um…oooooooh. Maybe Diabolic features evolve and change to replicate the realities of others. I mean, your bodies differ from every other species in existence, magical or not, basically being nothing more than goopy energy that willed itself into a preferred aesthetic."

"I'm so much more than goopy energy."

"A fascinating theory," Orias said, joining in our conversation as we approached the room's center stage. "It reminds me of findings by Alloces in Belphegor's Hell. Oh, you must be quite close with Belphegor's demons."

Wally raised a questioning brow.

"Not particularly," I said. "Walter does not often make time for demons on a quaint pilgrimage."

Much like Mora's devil, Bael, let his demons come and go as they pleased, Belphegor had a notorious reputation for sending his demons to travel and chronicle every lesser world. Truthfully, an invitation from Belphegor would've been fortuitous since he was the only devil equivalent to a nerdy explorer like Wally. Unfortunately, devils with kind or aloof or lazy natures were few and far apart. And devils like Bael and Belphegor didn't concern themselves with oddities like Wally.

"They researched the soul of your most popular planet and presented a hypothesis that she traveled various dimensions before settling on a realm with more malleable inhabitants."

"You mean Nature?" Wally's hazel eyes shimmered with excitement. "A demon talked with Nature herself? Kell's gonna be so jealous. Wait, did you say Nature traveled interdimensionally?"

"As all higher beings, certainly," Orias said. "It's Alloces' belief she presented her collection of perception to some of the earliest devils, and they offered the images to their demons."

"Though, who really remembers after all this time?" Corson side-stepped in front of Orias. "And who would be brazen enough to ask a devil?"

"Only a fool would speak to a devil so cavalierly," Bez said.

"And we are no fools, which is why my tongue only moves for you, Beelzebub." Corson winked. "Bez. Bezzy. Phezy? That stands for Phony Bez, if you were curious." Corson turned to speak to Orias and the other demons. "Composite names are quite popular in the mortal realm from what I've gleaned."

"Bez is sufficient." My nostrils flared, but I held back the need to snarl and shout and slap this fucker right across the face.

He wasn't actually that bad, but I simply found his arrogant aloofness so irritating.

"I see." Corson nodded playfully, letting his hair bounce dramatically. "It's just so hard to know the name you go by. So very hard."

Never mind. He was the fucking worst.

"Don't do that," Wally snapped, quick and sharp, so concise it carried a wave of silence.

Every demon took a pause, eyeing Wally, whose eyes had turned black. Hollow and haunting and fueled with Hellish power. It was unexpected and hot. So damn hot watching Wally exude his authority over the tiniest slight. Something I didn't believe he'd ever do being so kindhearted. I supposed he didn't like the false flattery thrown at me.

"Apologies." Corson knelt to one knee and lowered his head to Wally's feet. "I merely jested. Mother calls me her favorite jester. A foolish waste unworthy of your reprimand."

The title might be insulting, but he meant to reveal his mother's love for him, Lilith's awareness of his existence. Not something the trillions upon trillions of demons in this Hell could lay claim to. Her favorite jester implied acknowledgment and likely a desire to change Corson's ways so he'd be less of an embarrassment.

"I want space." Wally waved at Orias and the demons who crowded by him.

"But Great Lord Walter, we planned on a proper introduction before the first course."

"Space." Wally's voice deepened, and a spark of essence added an echoed layer to his demand.

Every demon backed away. Corson backed away on his hands and knees, seeking not to offend further. If I were a guessing demon, and I very much was, then I'd bet he'd been threatened with Oblivion for the slightest mishap. His trip to our world probably made him believe Wally a pushover—rightfully so, given his docile behavior—and he wanted to boast in front of his fellow lords with subtle jabs. Prove himself. And now, he crawled away, afraid of the ire he'd sparked.

Wally gripped my shoulder and pulled me close. His black eyes stared out at everyone, menacing and casting essence meant to sting anyone foolish enough to reach out with their own.

"I gotta say, I didn't expect the demonstration this early," I said without the whisper, knowing full well every demon kept a cautious distance from Wally, going as far as dampening their senses so as to not intrude or observe something above their station. "We can play this to our advantage, Corson being a cocky cunt and all, so it won't look like you're emotional over lil ole me. Merely a devil displeased with lowly demon antics."

Not a single demon here would dare eavesdrop on an angry devil.

"Bez, I can't turn it off." Wally's expression remained firm and hostile toward anyone who met his gaze, but there was an anxious crinkle in his forehead. One I'd seen a thousand times over without the show of toughness. This authority was him doing his part to appear devilish, but the fear—the fear was real. "My essence is boiling. Like it's trying to eat me from the inside."

11

Wally

Bez always worried the devil essence would eventually attempt to overtake my body. It lacked sentience, so we hoped the drive for control would remain dormant while I learned to control my powers. Control. Mastery. Skill. If I had the ability to direct my essence I could stop this agonizing feeling.

Sharp pains stabbed at my insides, at first like the worst stomachache, but soon, that gnawing feeling hit every muscle of my body one by one. It was as if the essence struck my insides and squeezed out all the mana I harnessed. Not only mana. I quaked as it shredded my insides, the horrifying sensation of my organs being gutted and devoured and then rebuilt by essence.

Pain met with relief, then pain again.

Every part of me wanted to lash out, to strike Bez, to strike every demon here simply for some type of soothing distraction.

When I thought I'd buckle, tumble forward, and collapse, the essence sprang out of me. Only it didn't. I stifled a gasp, expecting to feel the wriggle of living tarlike energy funneling out of my mouth, but there was nothing there. I feared looking down at my chest, prepared to see my exposed heart as surely my bones had exploded outward, and my ribcage turned into an open floor plan for the essence that sought an escape. That hadn't happened either. All the pain fizzled away, and the sensation of release hit like the gentlest hug after the hardest day, yet it was as if nothing had happened at all.

Was I imagining this pain?

"What's happening?" Bez asked, his voice the only thing grounding me as the world washed away.

"I'm not sure." I clamped my jaw, biting back a snarl that nearly slipped out of my mouth or the twist of pain that almost covered my face. "I think your concerns, the trip itself…"

Was my mortal body having a negative reaction to stepping into a Hell world?

The layers of this dimension vanished, but not before allowing me another bout with the agonizing infinity of passing through Lilith's dimension. Had I fled from Hell? I shook my head. No. I stood firmly in the temple, surrounded by demons who maintained a distance, but my mind had splintered and traveled beyond this world.

That was why my essence had this bizarre confusing feeling. It reeled my consciousness—an invisible and intangible form of energy—out of Hell and back to the mortal world. Not simply the mortal world, but through the gates of the Diabolic Oasis.

I floated through the city more a ghost than a devil, zipping past every single building in a blink and appearing within the walls of the Well of Wonders. My store. I couldn't explain it, couldn't comprehend it, but this didn't feel like I was breaking apart. The essence melded with my being on a cellular level, soothing the anxiety before it had a chance to stir inside my head. There were no answers from the base power coursing through my veins, but I knew everything was fine. This weird development was natural, or as natural as a mortal devil hybrid could be.

Once I entered the store and my being hovered over my familiar, Tony, the jarring confusion finally settled. The tiny scorpion skittered across the floorboards, utilizing telekinesis he'd borrowed from our bond to access Diabolic abilities. Was that what this was?

Nothing I'd ever studied about the Pentacles of Powers suggested a familiar bond would result in this dual-like vision, so it had to be a Diabolic development. Because honestly, while I might not hold mastery over my mage magics, I certainly knew every component, including the rare outliers, because I spent years wishing I was a late-blooming outlier.

"Not the point or the focus at the moment," I muttered, pulling my vision away from Tony and back to the temple of demons. It was weird because I could still see Tony like an overlapping faded image of what I physically stared at.

"Quite fascinating." Corson waltzed forward, no longer frightened by my command to back away. His voice was lighter but still layered with the same deepness he usually spoke with, too.

Every demon had offered space, turned their gazes, and stood in silence. And I meant complete silence. There was a stillness to them which made everyone in this temple appear statuesque, awaiting a reprieve from the command I'd yelled a moment ago.

Bez went to intercept, froze for a second, and then turned away from me and the blue-skinned demon without a word. He stood motionless with the demon lords in attendance. Even his essence stilled.

"Is this your first takeover?" Corson asked, the sapphire in his eyes washed away into complete blackness. They were as black as mine probably were right now, with so much essence surging throughout me. "I don't recall my first takeover. Time has withered that experience. Such confusion is permeating from your scent. It's curious and concerned yet confident, too. Such a sweet fragrance."

"What?" I threaded the dual vision of following Tony's clicking steps while observing Corson, who studied me with a deep fascination. His expression had changed entirely, almost making him appear like a different person. It wasn't only the change in his expression; his essence had a different radiance to it. Deeper and darker with no hues of blue like when I'd first encountered him. "Who are you?"

"Of course, introductions are to be made." Corson extended his arms, gesturing to himself. "I am Lilith, ruler of Hell and overseer to the remaining emptiness of the universe."

Lilith. The Lilith. She was here. Well, she was housed inside the body of one of her demons.

"How are you possessing him?"

"A devil's takeover allows us complete control over anything created with or containing our essence," he said—correction, she said. Lilith spoke through Corson's body. "Our takeover is most potent when in our dominion. We stand in my Hell, and as such, Corson is easy enough to access. A quick pluck of his strings and his being is mine until I choose to relinquish it. If I choose so."

"Could you keep his body forever?"

"I could." She examined Corson's muscular arms, channeling essence to coat her blue skin, creating deadly blades from the pooled tar. "But what good would such a weak form do me?"

She shook her arms, waving away the weapons she'd manifested with Corson's essence.

"How are you controlling him without sharing your essence?" I asked. "I mean, your essence is here, but it's not."

It was bizarre, like I could see her very being coiled around Corson's body, but not in a tangible sense. Still, it held a very tangible grip over the demon's will. She wouldn't share her essence because, according to Bez, no devil did such a thing. That was what made my existence such a rarity. Even demons with devil essence—such as Bez previously—were few and far apart.

"He is created by the grace of my willpower. I birthed his existence as I have with all the Diabolics of this dimension." Lilith circled me, black eyes studying every part of my being. It took all I had not to tremble, to ooze with weakness, to collapse from terror in her presence. "I'm more intrigued by how you control your beast."

Beast? She meant Tony. My familiar. "Do you mean because of the distance?"

"In part. But also, my connection is through creation. Everything I've created is mine by extension if and when I so choose to repurpose it to my desires." Lilith stared at the translucent thread of my essence stretched infinitely far to link my sight to Tony's. "You have not created this beast or given it your essence."

"Well, I am sharing it in a sense." I ran my fingers through the back of my hair, scratching my head nervously and trying to find the most simplified answer possible. Wordy rambles might bore or offend Lilith, and I didn't want to chance it. "We have a familiar bond. Or we did before I gained the essence. My current theory is that it allows Tony access to my Diabolic abilities."

"You share your power with this beast?" Corson's expression fell into confusion. Correction, Lilith's expression, since she currently possessed him. "Equally?"

"I don't share it exactly. I mean, I do. Um, it's still all my power, but I allow him access." I struggled to find the words to express how Tony had access without possessing essence. The familiar bond offered this almost phantom's touch on my abilities and gave Tony a link.

The only real example that popped in my head was how banks held money and Tony was the bank in this scenario but that didn't make sense because money would've represented essence which would still technically reside inside me not inside the bank and now my head hurt trying to make the terrible example fit.

Suddenly, the perfect example struck, one connected to Lilith herself. "It's like your key. It's your power, your way to and from Hell, but you let me and Bez borrow it. We only have access—"

"Because I allow it." Lilith nodded knowingly, then crinkled her brow with another questioning expression. "And even though my essence isn't in the flames, my power is."

"Exactly," I said.

"I'm more surprised you're capable of threading your sight beyond the dimensional walls."

"Because your Hell realm is locked?"

"No." Lilith waved away the question. "You still hold the key I've offered."

I did? I focused my essence inward, searching on a cellular level. Deep within me, deep within Bez, lay tiny flames meant to offer passage to and from Lilith's dimension.

"What's perplexing is the way you've reached out and found such easy unity with this creature of yours," Lilith said as if it were actually easy when I felt like my head was about to pop off. "I have reigned since the beginning of existence, and even I must make laborious efforts to gaze through the eyes of my children who step outside my realm."

"It's probably due to my familiar bond," I said, extrapolating the very limited data I had in an effort to teach the devil something neither of us had much insight into. "Since that's the only variable I can think of. I mean, there's a lot of variables. My essence belongs to a different devil—unless all devils are identical in power and ability. There's also the fact that I'm human. A mage, too. Magic is involved. Yeah, lots of variables, but really, I think it's the familiar bond because…"

I swallowed the next string of words bouncing in my head, worried I'd upset Lilith based on the glazed expression.

"Do continue." Intrigue filled Corson's face, and I shook away the self-doubt.

If I could offer knowledge to Lilith, perhaps she'd offer life and freedom and peace to me.

"You see, mages can share a magical connection with animals, offering them access to their magic. This sort of makes us joined—spiritually, emotionally—and that unity might extend beyond dimensions. It's only a working theory, but it'd make for an interesting case study."

"Are you suggesting your familiar bond is stronger than the connection I share with my children?" Lilith asked. The veins on Corson's body bulged and spread like a necrotic rot of Lilith's essence overtaking him entirely.

"I, um, well…" No. I needed to say no. Why was that suddenly the hardest word to utter? Any word. All words. I'd already blundered, offended Lilith. Offended a devil! She was going to kill me.

"Fascinating." Lilith cackled, her light voice bellowed alongside Corson's, and the two created a melody of chaotic entertainment with a dark undertone reverberating between the beats of their laughter. "Perhaps I, too, should get a pet for bonding. I keep Diabolic pets but have never once considered enslaving lower beings. Seems so wasteful. What could a creature so simplistic offer me?"

"Um, Tony's not my—"

"But I suppose even the lowest grain of dirt offers solid ground when gathered with the masses," Lilith said, no longer acknowledging my presence as she strutted in circles, adding a sway to Corson's hips. "I should like to learn this method of sharing essence without offering essence. Then, I will claim a million beasts from lesser realms and send them to scout worlds. Explore these pathetic realities without enduring the stink and filth of them. There must be something fascinating about those lowly realms. So many of my children crave the glitz and glimmer of these tragic dwellings."

I kept my opinions to myself. The fact she'd have to actually step foot into those lowly worlds to establish a familiar bond. The fact she was a devil and how the ability to link spiritually with an animal wasn't exactly a Diabolic skillset. The fact she'd need to possess a mage or witch or something beneath her stature to harness this power. Honestly, her whim seemed shortsighted and poorly planned. But then again, I overthought everything, so maybe Lilith had more ideas she simply didn't share when conceptualizing this plan.

"Come." Lilith extended a hand, gesturing for me to grab it. "Let us begin the first course while you explore Hell and your new takeover ability."

"Oh, so still having the banquet." I nodded nervously and fixated on the delicate blue hand instead of the tiny black scorpion scuttling about the room. Not this room. A room a whole dimension away.

"Surely, you can handle both tasks, correct?" The black gleam in Corson's eyes revealed how closely Lilith observed me, studying for any hint of a weakness in this new devil hybrid.

"Absolutely." I feigned a smile.

Bez sat on the floor beside me while I lay on a couch closer to the size of a stretched chair, doing my best to appear pleasantly at ease while navigating dual vision. Far away, I remained close to Tony, a ghost floating beside him while he worked. It was difficult to know if my connection waned at times or if the distance created a fluctuation in time, but Tony's position constantly changed in a blink. One second, he sat in the store; the next, he walked Weather; in the instant afterward, he basked under the hot sun, and then a single breath later, he stared at the starlit sky with longing.

Tony missed me as much as I missed him. More so, since it seemed days had passed for him, whereas only a few hours had gone by for me. Truthfully, I couldn't be certain if time had moved a sliver, as Hell didn't obey the laws of physics or really any laws unless Lilith deemed them appropriate to the current theme.

But I couldn't fixate too much on Tony and this second sight because I had to contend with where I currently found myself. I suffered silently in a dining hall surrounded by hundreds of demons who sat lined up at long wooden tables carved out of essence and made to appear properly themed for the Devil's Banquet and its Ancient Roman décor. The couch kept me positioned in the center of the room with a table between Lilith and myself.

A triclinium was a traditional Roman seating to indicate wealth and status, though they were never placed in the center of a feast. This was Lilith's way for the devils to exude power, attention, or whatever. Triclinium also had three small couches, which Bez knew not to fall for. We kept the third seat empty as only two devils attended this banquet.

"You must tell me how you acquired the essence," Lilith said, her head tilted ever so, turning the gaze of her haunting black eyes down at Bez. "I'd heard whispers of the coup for centuries but never expected Beelzebub would allow for such a rise."

"Beelzebub always liked a challenge."

"Still does." Lilith locked her eyes on Bez, veins fluctuating to heighten her senses. "If the rumors hold true."

She studied Bez's reaction down to a cellular level, but he gave her nothing.

His time in Hell still haunted Bez most days, even though he didn't mention it. Occasionally, our minds would meld when we slept, and I'd fall into one of his memories. This was a side effect of my saturation ability, a mage skill that hadn't been altered despite possessing essence of my own. It was how I'd first learned Bez paraded himself as a devil to the mortal world when he was actually a demon. It was how I'd learned a handful of the horrors he'd endured for eons.

Bez kept silent for a long pause, then grabbed a piece of wriggling meat with his tail from the table and chomped down. Delight filled his face when he chewed, and I shuddered immediately at the tiny, dying sound of whatever he shoved into his mouth. It was a whisper of a wail, one replicated from everything in the dining hall, from every bite of food the demon lords shoveled down their gullets. Or gullet equivalent in some cases.

I'd already hesitated about indulging in the meat, considering Hell didn't exactly have livestock, but I'd contemplated picking at the grapes in a bowl. However, seeing how clearly every piece of food, down to the fruit on display, was actually essence made to be festive, I lost my appetite entirely.

Either Bez and every demon in attendance were unphased by the dying gurgles of essence, or the noise was so soft, only a devil could hear the haunting howls.

"Interesting how a devil can lose a piece of themselves, and BAM!" Bez smacked the table before snatching another piece of meat. "The doors to the Hell are slammed shut forever."

"It is fascinating how such a tiny piece of power can be so potent." Lilith's gaze shifted to me. Was she doubting my strength? Did she suspect I didn't know how to use my abilities? Did she assume it didn't matter since I had such a meager amount of essence compared to hers? "Still, Beelzebub wouldn't be trapped if he knew how to make friends."

"Devils make friends?" I asked, ignoring Bez, who sucked his teeth. Did he want me to lean into the comment or to steer away from the bravado?

"We make the best of friends," Lilith hissed, soft and slow, so the sound of her voice alone slithered above Corson's and silenced his deep baritone. "That is why I've invited you, Walter. Being allies will strengthen our causes. It's imperative devils remain united and independent."

"Agreed." I extended my hand to shake. "It's a custom for unity, agreement, deals."

"I know what it is." Lilith chuckled; the haunting horror of her devilish tones rattled behind the girlish giggle she shared with the room. "May our friendship bring us closer together."

I grabbed her hand and squeezed it. "Even if we spend most of our time worlds apart."

"Even the briefest embrace can last an eternity." Lilith smiled, so genuine and gentle it would most certainly have deceived me in another lifetime. "I must take my leave for now, but I will find you for another course of the banquet. I plan to make the most of our time, Walter Alden."

And like that, the blackness of Corson's eyes vanished as his shimmering sapphire irises took sight of me. The sweet smile crumbled away, and confusion filled Corson's face.

"How I hate when she does that." The perplexed expression turned into a twisted smirk. "Then again, look at this fortune."

He took in the sight of the feast, the seating arrangement with us center stage for the demon lords and Bez on the floor.

"Well, well, well." He kissed the back of my hand. "Don't mind if I do."

Corson's tongue rolled out, and he licked my skin.

"And we're done." Bez's tail wrapped around Corson's throat, and he hurled the demon to the other side of the room. Others applauded the crash, and some mended the broken wall, with Corson still inside it, using a quick spell of channeled essence.

No love was lost for the demon or the action on Bez's part. It didn't seem anyone cared to note Lilith's absence or deign to acknowledge me as I sat alone. I grabbed Bez by the bicep and guided him to the empty seat.

"Wally."

"Sit," I demanded.

He didn't protest, and no one stared or shuffled to alert Lilith.

I needed to clear my mind, focus my split vision.

Flames from my phantom sight stole my concentration.

I blinked away the confusion of the dual sight I'd nearly buried while prioritizing Lilith's attention. But my connection to Tony persisted a whole dimension away, and I wanted to explore it. Every part of me wanted to panic, but I willed myself to be still, even steadying my breathing and hoping the patter of my heart didn't catch any Diabolic attention. Most of them likely didn't understand how or why organs functioned, so maybe they wouldn't notice the fear I quelled.

"Since my expectations here have lessened, for the time being, I'd like to study my new ability."

"Of course," Bez agreed. "I will keep anyone beneath your worry occupied if they approach for an audience."

"Thank you," I said as I let Tony's aggravation for the fire fill my sight.

Tony hissed loudly, clacking his claws at the flames which nearly engulfed him.

I tensed, stifling every desire to call out to Tony. He couldn't hear or sense me. But I had more than a visual connection. This devil's takeover allowed Lilith to embed her consciousness inside any Diabolic of her making. It allowed me to cross through the infinite layers of dimensional space and spiritually link to my familiar.

Carefully, he channeled mana and waved the flames away from himself. I tensed for the artifacts, but as swiftly as Tony had saved himself, he went to work redirecting the fire and sending it back toward the corridor it'd tunneled out of.

The click of heels intercepted him as Kell rushed out of her back-room lab and waved the smoke away with her hands, coughing.

Kell. Of course this was Kell. It'd taken her all of five seconds to find a way to destroy the Well of Wonders in my absence.

"Stop being dramatic," she said, adding a wave of icy mist with the flick of her wrist. Part of me thought she meant me, but then I saw her judgy stare fall to the floor and meet Tony, who clacked his claws.

The frost released in the room cooled everything, sucked up the air to remove the fuel for the fire, and ate away at the stray flames that Tony hadn't hurled to the back.

In the time it took me to scoff at Kell's nonchalant attitude, she'd disappeared, and Tony had reappeared at the countertop early in the morning, contending with a customer.

"Bez, when you said this banquet would potentially be six months to six years, did you mean because time dilation seems to be off entirely from one dimension to the next?" In the seconds it took to ask that question, Tony had upsold the customer and talked them out of several artifacts I doubted they wished to part with in exchange for a useless bauble. Honestly, he was less of a scorpion and more of a shark with the way he fleeced our clientele. That said, he acquired some really epic pixie products, and I couldn't wait to return home and study them.

Home, which seemed to change with every blink of my eyes.

"Time dilation?" Bez tilted his head. "Is time high or having a baby? What kind of dilation are we talking here?"

"What?" I asked with a squeak that I quickly buried by clearing my throat to appear gruff and confident and devillike despite the fact the demon lords continued offering privacy while they focused on their feast and conversation amongst themselves. "I mean, it's moving differently here and there. There—home—is moving faster. Is that why the banquet is expected to run so long?"

"Oh, fuck." Bez grimaced. "Yeah, I sort of forgot about time in the whole equation thingy. Devil's Banquets are painfully long. But yeah, guess that means we should expect a much more delayed passage of time when we return."

I sighed. A sigh that washed away the day Tony had and brought on an evening where he closed up the shop and tended to his usual checklist of tasks. This was a painful reminder my familiar was far too good for me and worked far harder than he should to keep this business afloat. A business Kell and I treated like an extracurricular while prioritizing our true passions for cataloging, analyzing, and whatever destructive tinkering Kell labeled as research.

The bell chimed despite the sign to the Well of Wonders clearly stating the store was closed—and not at all sorry about it.

"We're Closed. Come Back Later." Because Kell and Bez refused to apologize to people who showed up outside of working hours.

A group of cloaked people shuffled inside, levitating in fact, which meant mages or witches or possibly vampires if they'd fed on witches or mages prior to arriving. Not that it mattered. They barreled inside so quickly, they didn't even notice the tiny arachnid tucked away in the aisles as he dusted the artifacts.

Tony kept quiet and observed the situation.

They were witches, clearly based on how they circled around Kell's doorway and cast sorcery to check for traps. I furrowed my brow, offended they'd dare and perplexed they'd try. It was no secret Kell was married to the King of the Diabolic Oasis, and Mora did little to hide her bloodthirst. I mean, seriously, the number of odd jobs Bez had taken for her. It was like they thought I was too dense to piece together golems who threatened the status quo had suddenly vanished around the same time Mora would have a marble statue commissioned. Or the time mages mouthed off, and Bez came home with a new host body. There were dozens of examples. While life was mostly content for folks in the Diabolic Oasis, it was no secret Mora didn't tolerate rivals.

So why the fuck were these witches attempting to break into Kell's lab?

They managed to unlock her door—which I'd need to make a note to ask Tony if he jotted down whatever spell they used—and then they stepped inside. Not that I'd break and enter into Kell's private space, but she used top-tier traps to seal off and ward her belongings, which these witches managed to decipher almost instantly. I could use a spell like that when studying deadly artifacts.

One hooded witch approached a fireball sitting atop Kell's empty desk. The fire was kept in place through intricate sigils sort of locking it. This was the flame she'd copied from my invitation to Hell. Why was a coven of witches trying to steal Kell's copy of this key? And how did they know it existed?

My heart raced. Bez tilted his head, clearly listening in on the rapid flutter of my heartbeat that pounded against my chest with every word I held back. With every question I had about these witches.

"There are witches breaking into the shop," I said to Bez with a steady voice and deep breath.

"Mora is such a moron." He groaned. "This is what peace gets ya."

"So, she's aware of witches after Kell's fire?" I asked without explicitly stating Kell and Bez had the not-so-bright idea of trying to circumvent Lilith's abilities. "You know, the special fires Kell makes?"

A harrowing scream flooded my ears, and I leapt to my feet, spinning around the room. One demon lord locked his eyes with me, and I swore he could taste the fear pounding in my chest.

In an instant, Bez lunged and smashed the demon into muck, which he sprinkled onto plates of other dishes demons devoured. Everyone ignored the assault, didn't mind my outburst, and obviously never heard the scream since the sound came from my connection with Tony, and the scream came from a person he heard.

Thankfully, Bez didn't have to explain my bizarre actions because no one questioned them. Part of me was grateful for the horrifying fear the presence of a devil created, and another part found it disgusting.

"Well, this is fucking great," Kell said, pulling my attention to the second sight I glimpsed from Tony.

The scene had changed again—because, of course, it had—and Kell stood over three charred corpses, kicking one with the heel of her boot. The burned cloaks made it evident this was from the witches who'd broken in, and based on the fully intact fireball, I'd wager Kell kept even more intricate traps protecting her most recent experiment.

Kell glared at the bodies, held her flame in one hand, and turned her gaze to Tony. "Wanna help me find the rest of this shifty coven that has the audacity to try and steal from the baddest witch in town?"

12

Bez

Once this new devil ability faded, Wally recentered his attention on me and the dinner while filling me in on what'd happened to Kell. Nearly happened in this case. Wally still actively avoided the meal of essence they'd offered. Not that I blamed him. Their flavors were atrocious. The meat lacked in true savoriness. The meat had these phony grill marks while tasting like a steak Wally had murdered in a stove to the setting of overdone. Their fruits were so artificially sweet they may as well have tossed together a poorly crafted bowl of candy. If I weren't doing my part to blend with the honor of this feast, I'd have rejected this course much like Wally. Though, ultimately, he likely dodged nibbling because of morals or some shit, as if devouring essence meant anything.

"You murder cows every single day, Walter."

"What?" He raised a brow in confusion, and rightfully so. It appeared my Walter-isms were slipping in this stressful situation, and I ranted at him based on my own internalized aggravations.

"Nothing." I huffed. "So, what is your little bug up to?"

"Last I saw before the connection faded was Tony and Kell putting together a scrying board," Wally said, scrunching his face in a dramatic effort to reestablish this bizarre power.

No wonder I couldn't help Wally master his new devil abilities. He had access to skills only true devils were capable of. Yes, when the essence circulated throughout my Diabolic being, it elevated my access to essence and enhanced my demon abilities, but I never harnessed anything within the scope of a devil's actual power.

"The city is only so big," I said. "Surely, Kell and your beast bug will locate these treacherous witches."

"Yeah," he said, releasing the tension in his face. "And according to the detection system, no one has left."

"Not that the faulty system you lot created worked all that well." Corson strutted toward us, hands gesturing to his physique. "Check and mate."

"I think you mean case and point." Wally eyed the demon up and down. "But your snide arrogance is sort of deflated when you're covered in rubble."

"And spent part of the evening possessed by your mommy," I added. "Or quivering on your knees after running your mouth."

"What man wouldn't fall to his knees and quake when in the presence of the Great Lord Devil Walter Alden of the Misfit Mortal Mage Hybridization?"

I tsked at his condescending flattery. "Shame you clawed your way outta that hole so quickly; I quite enjoyed your absence."

"No worries." Corson winked at Wally. "I'm always looking for a new hole to bury myself in."

My tails went to snatch him by the throat and hurl him back through another wall when Wally's tail intercepted, wrapping two of my tails together and teasing the third. Though his was slimmer and shorter than my three, it moved with swift finesse. Something about Hell unlocked the block Wally had faced during our trainings. Perhaps the atmosphere of a Diabolic dimension or the fact my little mage always did his best when thrown into harrowing situations. The more dire, the less he overthought. Honestly, if I could keep him busy with a thousand tasks at once each day, Wally would become an unstoppable force.

Wally's tail went limp—shocker—and I redirected my tails to steady his stance so no demons would notice floundering. Alas, Wally's favorite skillset came from stressing over literally nothing.

Corson rejoined our table, continuing his suggestive innuendos as he picked over the best-presented food and ate.

"He reminds me of a certain demon," Wally whispered. "You know, with all the sexy murder jokes."

"Mora's not nearly this crass." I scoffed.

Wally's face fell into bewilderment. "Do you seriously not see it?"

I eyed this pampered prince of Hell, studying his blatant arrogance, recalling how much he despised his devil, yet publicly remained an obedient puppet.

"I guess they're both kind of prissy since they're royal Diabolics," I said, rocking my head from side to side.

"You," Wally blurted. "He reminds me of you."

"Walter." I furrowed my brow. "The audacity."

"The absurdity more like it," Corson interjected. "I'm nothing like this warrior of Beelzebub's. At least, I presume you're a warrior based on how you carry yourself."

"As if you know anything about the classes of Beelzebub's realm."

"Not much other than warriors and fodder, if memory serves." Corson bit into a piece of meat. "Though, given your hidden history and false name and whatever other lies you composed over the centuries, I'd wager a defective warrior."

"Don't say that," Wally said with a sharpness in his tone as his eyes went black.

"Apologies." Corson waved his arm round and round into a frilly, phony gesture of bowing as he sat at the table. "I merely meant to convey my understanding for the warriors of Beelzebub's world. In fact, breaking their bluster used to be a favorite pastime of mine before their Hell closed off entirely."

I barred my teeth.

The dining hall rumbled, and I turned to Wally, ready to calm him for whichever comment had finally set him off. Only it wasn't him. His essence circulated, protective, yet contained. This sudden overwhelming force came from Lilith's return as we wrapped up the first course.

Flames burst from the sealed doors, charring them and leaving nothing but a flutter of cinders that sparkled with the dying embers of the essence Lilith had eradicated for no other reason than it added a bit of flair to her entrance.

Lilith wore a sleeveless cream dress with an opening in the cleavage that reached her belly button. The cream held a cleaner white at the skirt portion of the dress that reached all the way to her ankles and exposed her bare feet. Feet coated in essence and gave her toes a clawed aesthetic.

"Nice dress." I crinkled my nose, fishing for a compliment.

"It's a stola," Wally said, already whispering a hundred random facts about whatever the ancient Romans called fashion. "A sign of wealth for sure, traditionally speaking, but usually they weren't worn independently like this. Too exposed."

I nodded to Wally's rambling asides and studied Lilith's appearance. She'd returned to the banquet in her own skin but not her own form. There was something strikingly familiar about her look. Skin the same light gray as mine. Longer hair, for sure, but a sheen black with neon orange roots. A pair of feathered wings sprouted from her back, the same dark gray as mine. Three tails, each playfully batting around the tables and causing mischief. Four curled horns atop her head, accentuating the jewels she adorned like a crown. Even her eyes had a crimson allure to them—an aura impossible for a devil to possess. They were pure darkness, utter black, devoid of any spark of any other color along the spectrum.

I leaned over to Wally to ask a question and confirm my suspicions. "Does she look human to you?"

"Yeah," he whispered. "Actually, kind of surprised she possessed a person, considering she seemed so against lower beings and whatnot."

"It's not possession," I said. "Merely an augmentation of her essence meant to reflect her appearance to resemble the person looking at her."

"Whoa. That's similar to how a siren song can alter sensory perception of smell or sight through sound. Also, the way succubi shapeshift for aesthetic pleasures." Wally adjusted his glasses, bewitched by the ability and likely curious if his devil essence could accomplish the same. "So, this is sort of a femme version of me?"

"Slightly more feminine, yes." I winked. "But I doubt she could rock that bossy bottom boy strut you've got no matter her altered presence."

Wally tsked, then grinned, then bit his lip to hold back a snicker. Once he'd settled, he eyed Lilith again as she approached our center-staged table. "The curls really get some nice buoyancy with more length. Though, not a fan of her glasses. The frames are kind of blocky. All in all, I make a pretty girl."

I studied my image from Lilith's perspective. In truth, I'd possessed a few female bodies over the years because Mora always made it look like such fun. But it never felt quite right, and the composites were never to my liking. "Personally, I think my femme fatale look is quite fuckable."

"I'd say your current form is quite fuckable, too." Corson smirked.

"Blegh." I mimicked a need to yack. "I forgot you were here."

As Lilith sauntered closer, her wings spread wide, cascading an air of caution to the demon lords. Perhaps they saw limbs or extremities matching their own Diabolic forms; then again, she might've shown her demon kin's actual essence flowing in a show of authority. Dominance. It worked.

Each and every one of the demon lords ceased their prattle, their feasting, their movements, and fixed all their collective attention onto Lilith. I paid respect to her presence and followed suit, keeping my body and essence stilled.

"Everyone, resume." Lilith gestured with a single raised hand like a conductor of an orchestra, and the melody of chattering demon lords who feasted upon the dishes comprised of essence continued. "We'll be moving into the second course shortly."

"Oh," Wally said, keeping his eyes on Lilith while his leg bounced. "I'm intrigued to see what could possibly top this already spectacularly outstandingly stupendously…"—he bit his lip and muttered—"that's a lot of adjectives." Then he quickly cleared his throat. "It's such a challenging menu to top. Because it's already so good."

"Well, I do enjoy topping things," Lilith said in quite the matter-of-fact way, so I couldn't determine if she was being playful with Wally or simply mimicking his word choice out of politeness. Neither seemed probable or positive. The Lilith of legend didn't do playful or polite.

"So, oh great and splendidus Walter, do tell," Corson commented, because of course he fucking did. "Which is your favorite dish from this course?"

Wally squinted and forced his lips into a tight smile to keep from scowling. All the while, I clenched my fists to keep from punching Corson through another wall.

"Such a difficult choice to make with what's been presented," Wally said through gritted teeth.

"It's not that difficult." Corson lapped up one of the more palatable pieces of meat provided and chewed with his mouth open. "Personally, I'm a fan of the steaks. I just love the feel of thick, juicy meat sliding down my throat. Don't you?"

Wally gulped.

"Shush, my sweet." Lilith brushed a hand over Corson's face and squeezed, breaking the skin and drawing essence out like blooddrops made of tar. "He is always voicing himself unnecessarily."

He growled and gurgled until complacently quieting.

"Do we need to hear your voice?" Lilith slowly shook Corson's head back and forth in a 'no' motion. "You're here to be a pretty and proper prince."

"Of course," Corson started before clearing his throat to silence himself.

"Much better." Lilith released him and licked the essence on her fingertips. "He's by far my prettiest child. Dainty and plain in most respects, but he glistens on a burning battlefield while dancing in dead dimensions."

An indication of Corson's station and where he served among his devil's army, and also a veiled reminder that Lilith regularly visited other realms with her demons to eviscerate everything in sight.

"Speaking of dances." Lilith's face lit up with excitement. Quite literally. Light from some meal of essence she'd feasted upon earlier illuminated her light gray skin or the projection of light gray skin meant to mimic my appearance in this augmentation illusion. "May the decadence of the devil's dance fill you with warmth and entertainment, Great Lord Devil Walter Alden of the Misfit Mortal Mage Hybridization."

"Wait," Wally squeaked, then squirmed in his seat. "I'm expected to dance?"

"Nonsense," Lilith said, strutting to join Wally on his chair, squeezing in close. "We won't share a dance until the ninth course."

He gulped, his eyes filling in the puzzle pieces with the fact that 'course' was an arbitrary term for anything deemed entertaining and appropriate for a Devil's Banquet based on the host, the guest of honor, and the theme. In Wally's case, it could literally be anything, as I'd never attended a feast in Hell with a mortal or mage or hybrid devil before.

"So, I *am* still expected to dance at some point?" he asked.

"You'll learn the steps during courses six and seven," Lilith replied. "Relax, darling."

Wally forced a thin smile. "Okay."

"For this dish, I've brought in another devil such as yourself," Lilith cooed, fawning over Wally like a lovestruck teen. "Well, more his former self."

Her gaze shifted, black eyes locked onto me, then the floor, then back to me and the seat I'd dared to move into with her absence.

"A demon with devil essence?" Wally asked, his tail instinctively wrapping around me and the seat where he wished for me to stay. "It's a fascinating topic that you consider them devils."

"Oh, I most certainly do not." Lilith chuckled, her attention for me and placement waning now that Wally had boldly and affectionately grabbed ahold of me. "They are…hmmm, mortal research. What would you say as mortal? Yes, they are gnats holding hammers. Entertaining but pathetic. You, however, are something different. Not me. Not him. Not our performer."

Her eyes flitted to me one final time when referencing my pathetic existence, how even when I robbed a piece of a devil and sealed him away for eternity, it meant nothing to her. All my achievements didn't even register as a threat. I was a joke. A stain.

A feeble attempt at power. As painful as that realization was, I took solace in the fact her gaze never turned sour like that when looking at Wally. There was admiration, fear, curiosity, but not disgust.

When her hand rested on Wally's thigh, I wanted to strike her, but if my essence even stirred with a threatening posture, she'd slaughter me. In truth, Lilith merely meant to treat Wally as furniture. I'd seen devils do this to one another time and time again. When I had the misfortune of being dragged to unified court assemblies by Beelzebub.

The events were filled with a multitude of devils speaking on the importance of their own Hells and the interference of lesser realms, while others argued the reprieve of tiny dimensions with nothing to offer but an escape. All the while, they tested their limits on each other, some subtly like ways Lilith toyed around, some directly like how Beelzebub would slaughter several devils to test the group's confidence.

"May I introduce Satan." Lilith extended a hand as the fire finally died down, and a bright red demon waltzed into the dining hall. "He's my favorite demon who survived the battle against Lucifer. Most have fizzled out, faded from memory, but not him."

"Ooooooh." Wally adjusted his glasses, studying Satan as he cocked his head ever so to show a sign of intrigue when listening to Lilith's story. "It's funny. In our world, Satan and Lucifer are actually considered the same person by most mortals. But they also assume he's the devil."

"Lucifer was *a* devil," Lilith said. "But Satan's merely a meager thing that looks good dressed in devil essence."

As she embellished the rebellion against Lucifer, much like the mortals did, I recalled what I actually knew about Satan. Millions of demons had banded together to overthrow and consume Lucifer. It was a tale of success, Satan being an incredibly popular pioneer among demons who bested a devil, despite the fact Satan worked with nearly all his demon companions to destroy Lucifer and consume his essence. It ultimately added to the battle cry Eligos and other foolish demons in my dimension shouted when rallying the masses against Beelzebub. Obviously, that tale didn't end with such celebrity.

Then again, seeing Satan's life had turned into a form of entertainment for Lilith, I wouldn't guess he'd been very successful either.

Physically, he towered over most demon lords here, standing with his shoulders hunched so his long, upward-curled horns wouldn't scratch the ceiling. A deceitful action by Lilith, who had modified the dining hall upon Satan's arrival. The vaulted ceilings had sunken inward with a droop like a wilted and withered flower.

Honestly, I was surprised Lilith didn't make Satan crawl on his belly, but she showed him some respect. None of her lords commented on his glittering attire not fit for the theme of the party. Wally would probably assume Satan was meant to be a star, but I suspected he was a trophy meant to be shamed publicly and loudly. It served as a reminder this fate could've been mine had I roamed in Hells after escaping Beelzebub instead of hiding away in some lowly mortal realm with only partial magic at its disposal. The only lower radar I could've gone was to a world with almost zero magic whatsoever, but even I couldn't live such a tragic life as that.

The lights flickered and flashed and focused on Satan's entrance. His scarlet-scaled skin shimmered. The bright red undertones of his complexion highlighted the sharp features of the oxen-dragon-like head. Coarse black fur covered his chest, growing wild and around his head like a mane with finely brushed hair over his forearms and lower legs.

Music played from older instruments Wally named off silently. His lips mouthed random factoids about the melodies created until he finally had to utter one or two or seven comments about the traditional verse popularized in Ancient Rome and the music they created.

Satan's steps were slow at first, elongated arms reaching the floor, so his claws dragged alongside his hooved feet until the swift slash created a spark of lightning. All the light vanished and suddenly only the electricity brimming from the essence of Satan himself provided anything other than pitch black nothingness.

Each clack of the hooves held a rhythmic step. The sway of claws cast trances on the audience, and perhaps at Lilith's bequest or merely for the sake of satiating his own appetite for carnage, Satan slaughtered a member here and there. No gasps followed. Not even by Wally, who'd quickly trained himself not to react to Diabolic carnage. A few cheers were met by the way Satan swirled the essence of his victims around the lightning.

Wally's eyes studied each move, enchanted and perplexed by Satan's graceful dance that blended death and fire and art into this elegant poetry where each step etched a letter in the lyrics of this performance.

I savored this calm entertainment where everyone's eyes had been drawn away from Wally, even Lilith herself as she watched her puppet perform.

Satan's movements reached their peak, and the dance slowed. When the final step was taken, the instrumental accompaniment died instantly with a sour thwack meant to silence everyone. Satan extended his arms high and wide, much like a warrior in an arena who'd bested a Diabolic foe, but now he only fought for Lilith's entertainment. His entire existence meant to serve a devil's whim.

Smoke captured Satan midbow, and he vanished in a swift act of teleportation, returning to whatever chamber Lilith deemed appropriate for her pet.

It was a sickening reminder of life in Hell, eternal agony or servitude or combat, and round and round it went.

The silence continued, only everyone's gaze had flitted from Satan's empty stage and landed on Wally, who did a masterful job of not squirming from so much attention.

"I'm floored by the level of research you all did," he said. "It's like you brought the era to life. With a Diabolic spin, but it's fascinating."

"But of course." Lilith smiled and with her features imitating mine, it made the phoniness of her sincerity all the more obvious. "Only the best for my guest of honor."

"You said I differed from Satan, from other Diabolics who possess essence." Wally turned his attention to Lilith. "How so?"

"We'll discuss it soon." Lilith brushed a hand over Wally's face, a delicate action but one met with a surge of Wally's essence as his eyes went black, meaning she must've circulated a pulse of her presence in the brief contact. "Or perhaps we should discuss it now. Privately. The third course isn't nearly as appealing as a conversation between devils."

With a snap of her fingers, Wally split into crumbling ashes, shattering to dust on the floor, which Lilith swept away with a flick of her wrist. Wally had vanished before my eyes. Before I could react, move, or question, Lilith blinked out of existence, disappearing as quickly as she'd stolen Wally away.

Up until now, I'd been terrified Lilith was looking for any misstep on Wally's part, a sign of weakness, a reason to shatter him to nothingness, but now, I feared it might be so much worse than that. Lilith had a curiosity for Wally's uniqueness. She saw him as a new trophy to claim…one she might desire to keep in Hell and put on display like her other Diabolic devil oddities.

13

Wally

My fragmented molecules corporealized, and each cell of my body tetrised together seamlessly, though thanks to my Diabolic senses, the experience was grueling and detailed. Each fraction of a second ticked by even slower. There was a low, slow whoosh of my body colliding from a billion puzzle pieces to one entity. And then, after the euphoric afterglow of vanishing from one location and reappearing elsewhere, I took in the new room.

"By the gods, is that what teleportation is always gonna feel like?" I asked aloud, partially because of this need to verbalize my thoughts and half hoping to hear Bez's snarky response sneak up on me. "But I hadn't seen him swept into the magic of Lilith's essence."

Because I had seen it. That was when my senses expanded, taking in full sight of the energy hurled by the wave of Lilith's hand.

I took in the new room where I'd arrived. It kept with the theme, cluttered with marble statues, decorative vases, and everything else that made this appear less like a room oozing opulence and more like a museum trying a little hard for authenticity. But this was a bedroom. The raised bed with a lavender canopy made of silk.

My vision flickered, and the essence that'd instinctually swirled into a defensive state had once again stretched infinitely long and pierced through the dimensional walls of Hell.

Flashes of my second sight, which linked me to Tony, to my world, showed a kaleidoscope of moments. Tony and Kell analyzing a map of the city. Sorcery searching for witches. Witches tracked in the dead of night. An array of bright sunlight and starry evenings. Weather's goofy smile. Weather's sad puppy eyes. Weather's grumpy growls. Moments twisted into snapshots, and the images seemed stretched infinitely long, like seconds spread out into a warped collage.

The passage of time in the city I'd left to attend this Devil's Banquet really became more apparent with each surge of connection that seized a hold over me. I couldn't make sense of what I saw, so I ignored it, waiting for the link to falter and fade, all while hoping my time in Hell would soon come to an end. I hoped even more that Bez and I could safely depart without incurring a devil's ire or an expectation of regular visits.

This one very brief trip had left my thirst for knowledge about Hell quenched. Well, not really. But I'd gladly bury my curiosities if it kept me and the whole world alive and unharmed.

"Walter, I do hope this room is to your liking." Lilith entered the room, a pep in her step, a bounce her long blonde curls, and a coy smile.

"Yes," I said with a strained smile. "The next course wouldn't happen to be scheduled nap time?"

She laughed, loud and bold and echoing throughout the entirety of this suddenly smaller room. Maybe it felt smaller because of her presence, or maybe she'd used some devil abilities to actually subtly shrink the size.

Something about Lilith's glamoured human form emulating my appearance reminded me of my sisters. Not that any of them really looked like feminine versions of me. Honestly, the only sibling who looked like my double was my brother, Alistair—minus being taller and buffer and the all-around jockier build.

Really, the only thing about Lilith that reminded me of my sisters was the carefree giggle that had this aloofness of my youngest sister. The innocent grin with a subtle mischief hidden behind it reminded me of my older sister. But the fierce, stern sharpness in Lilith's gaze was completely reminiscent of my oldest sister. But the confidence in her sultry swagger, the pop of her hips with each step, was definitely a move my brother would make. There was this air of bravado without effort in the movements. A carefree strut. Squared shoulders. Arched back. Cocky tilt in her neck.

A twinge of guilt hit me, dwelling on how little time I spent missing my family, how little time I thought about them, how much time had passed since I'd seen any of them, and how much more time would be lost while I attended a party in Hell and days passed every time I blinked.

What would they think of the mage I'd turned into? The fact that I wasn't very much a mage anymore at all. The irony of finally feeling comfortable with my proficiency over the Pentacles of Power only for a whole new set of Diabolic skills to consume my every waking thought. Devilish Diabolic abilities at that, ones that seemed to differ from known devils and pretty much meant I had no manual to rely on.

It was weird to think about my family while here in Hell. But this banquet, this party that required caution with every action, reaction, inaction, and instant contemplation for everything in between, brought all the Collective galas I'd been forced to attend as an Alden rushing back. A name that meant everything in my world, yet nothing at the same time. Aldens walked among titans in the world of magic, but to mere mortals, we were simple nobodies with too much old wealth.

The same could be said for my name in Hell. Alden would hold no authority to the Diabolics, to the devils, to even the weakest and most broken demons. But the name Alden tied to the title of a devil hybrid seemed to mean everything here. Here in Hell. Hell, belonging to Lilith. Lilith, who studied me. Me, the simple overthinking fool who'd landed a piece of devil essence he couldn't fully control and needed a few more centuries of studying to properly prepare for this Devil's Banquet in my honor.

"You spend a lot of time in your head." Lilith stood with barely a breath of distance between us.

Her essence burned so hot it hit with an icy sting, sending a shiver coursing over my body. My hairs rose. My legs quaked. My teeth chattered.

"Paradoxical cold is the sensation," I said, searching for any flimsy excuse that might've explained why I appeared so frightened and frail. Only, I probably should've led with an explanation to a question Lilith hadn't asked. "The reaction of my body is because your essence is cold."

"Is the temperature too much for you?" Lilith brushed her hand along my face, and I froze—almost literally from the cold but also in an effort not to react negatively. "Does contact bother you? You seemed quite content with contact earlier. Though, I understand some touching should remain civil lest your little demon find himself in a mood to slaughter."

"Oh, Bez is fine," I said, realizing Lilith referenced the demon he'd killed.

The demon he'd burned to a crisp. The demon who died when Lilith was supposedly nowhere nearby.

"Are you talking about the demon that pricked my nail? I'm sor…" I cleared my throat, swallowing the apology and my anxious need to fill the silence before redirecting my words. "I'm surprised you'd deign to acknowledge a demon in your service that'd failed so spectacularly."

The silence between us was haunting. Lilith's gaze was reminiscent of every judgmental look I'd ever received, threatening to rip me apart and reveal the awkward coward who desperately wanted to apologize for his sharp words. But this was Hell, this was my banquet, we were a pair of devils presumably on equal footing, and if I faltered, stumbled, then the most powerful force I'd ever encountered would devour me.

"No real loss," Lilith finally said. "A few centuries or eons in Oblivion does a demon good. How else will they learn to value eternity unless they're given a taste of nothingness?"

It seemed I'd done what Bez hoped, avoided a misstep. Now, I just needed to casually turn the conversation to a 'thanks for the invite, lovely party, but I should be moseying on home.' I tsked. Who was I kidding? There was absolutely no way I'd steer the conversation in that direction, so I might as well see how much curiosity I could lean on before this branch holding me up cracked.

Metaphoric branch, though, given how the entirety of my experience in Hell was filtered by this themed party, then technically speaking, I could be standing on literal branches without even knowing it.

"Speaking of glamours or filters which is just…" I bit my lip, realizing I'd muttered aloud. That had to stop. I didn't need one of my rambling tangents pissing off Lilith.

"Continue." Her black eyes locked onto my mouth. "Now."

"Um, yeah, sure. I was just thinking how, you know, I'm flattered by the human glamour, but you don't have to dress for the theme," I said because, quite frankly, even I'd grown tired of this tunic. It was already a couple of inches away from flashing my privates, and the slits Bez ripped into my clothes didn't help matters.

"I like the mortal getup." Lilith twirled a few times, letting her long blonde hair whirl and stretch further. By the time she stopped spinning, the curls had lost their bounce, and her hair reached past her knees. "I also wouldn't fit in this tiny dwelling."

"Oh." I quirked a brow. "Why not make a bigger building?"

"Orias insisted it was important for the theme," Lilith said. "Apparently, size is quite important to mortals despite them all being so tiny."

"I wouldn't say we're obsessed with size." I quizzically considered everything from homes, wealth, bodies, vehicles, reputation, partner count, partner parts, personal parts, measurements that needed to be smaller or bigger or… "Yeah, okay. Maybe a little bit."

"Though, part of me is curious if someone with the eyes of a devil can grasp the sheer magnitude of my glory." Lilith held a hand over her mousy smile, feigning this coy, girlish giggle. "Lower beings can't view the magnificence of my true form. The purity of my being overwhelms their senses and obliterates those beneath. Even my weaker children struggle to take in my full splendor."

"Wow." I gulped. "I'm not sure I wanna, um, test that theory."

"It won't kill you. Not one so strong, one who clawed his way out of Oblivion." Lilith strutted by me. "Not an easy feat for a devil. Retrieving our demon spawn, sure. But ourselves? Broken and no longer in existence. It's fascinating the Walter Alden devil managed such glory."

She heard about that? When I'd fought against Eligos, it took everything I had, including devouring Diabolic essence, which sort of overwhelmed my body, and since I'd ended up so entangled with demonic substance, I kind of unintentionally fell into the demon afterlife. Not that Oblivion was much of an afterlife, merely a dimension devoid of everything except the slumbering consciousness of every fallen Diabolic entity.

Still, it wasn't exactly something we advertised, but I supposed. in theory, anyone in Oblivion could've known about my brief time spent there. And, of course, Lilith's demon prince Corson was in Oblivion at the same time as me. Once she pulled Corson out of that nothingness afterlife, he could've told her everything. I mean, that was why he got assigned to deliver the invitation to begin with, since he *encountered* us at the villa.

"How about I unveil a layer at a time?" Lilith pursed her lips; the plump pink turned black as the soft peach skin of her face transformed into a deep purple. Flesh became scales. Essence coated her arms, and her fingers stretched far with seven nimble knifelike digits.

"Still humanoid, but I can see elements of something different." It was difficult to form into words, almost as if a phantom shape of Lilith's true body glimmered beyond the portrayal she slowly unraveled.

She peeled away her glamour delicately, but I carefully observed, ready to turn my gaze if I felt my insides ready to explode. I wasn't exactly sure what would happen, but it was safe to assume it'd be a painful reaction prior to being obliterated from glimpsing too closely.

"I knew someone of your caliber would be able to see a god queen in all her glory," Lilith hissed, the words slithering around me, coiling tightly and dancing against my skin. Each syllable sent a different sensation.

"Yeah, about that," I said, sidestepping from her intangible voice that seemed to follow me no matter where in the room I moved. "You still haven't clarified how I'm different from other devil hybrids."

"There are no other devil hybrids."

"That doesn't make sense. I've met some." Bez was a demon fused with devil essence. And now, I'd met or seen another Diabolic who'd consumed a piece of their fallen devil. "So, why am I classified as a hybrid whereas Satan would only be a demon in possession of devil essence?"

"Ah, yes. I heard you were an inquisitive devil. Few devils are curious of things outside their realm," Lilith said in this matter-of-fact tone. No condescension or contempt in her comment, which was something my curiosity often received over the years. "You differ from Satan and other Diabolics like him because they can never transcend with essence they take from a devil. Too much, and it'd overtake them, allowing the devil to be reborn in a meager body. Too little, and the power is futile, like what Satan possesses. Just a demon playing pretend."

Like how Bez pretended to be Beelzebub.

"The main difference is that while essence can remain intact inside a demon, it is merely a piece of power."

"That's not any different," I said. "I ingested a small portion, not too much to overpower my body, so it fused with my being."

"Not even remotely true, Walter." Lilith swished her clawed fingers back and forth in a 'no' motion. "The tiny piece of devil essence you merged with has swelled and grown. It's merely a fraction of a fraction right now, hardly noticeable or anything a lesser being would distinguish. But in a few centuries or a millennium, the evolution of your hybridized essence will spawn a new type of devil. A truly devastating force."

"W-what?" I trembled at the idea of a millennium of living. Of life.

I knew it was a thing. It was something always looming in my future with Bez, even when I shared his essence before acquiring this piece of a devil, but the idea of forever was a lot to comprehend. Who would I be in a thousand years? Who would I be if the devil essence inside me evolved and changed? How much would it change me?

"In all the eons of my existence, there has never been a new type of devil." Lilith circled me, always circling me as she evaluated me down to a cellular level. "Every single one of us was birthed into the universe identical in our structure and design, merely created with differing levels of capability. Even that was more by chance and training than anything else."

"That's fascinating." I meekly smiled. And bizarre, which I held back because explaining to a devil why their unchanging, unaltering, uniformed essence seemed unhealthy.

"Something about your lowly, feeble design as a mortal or a mage or both has culminated in something truly spectacular."

"Thanks?" I quirked a brow.

"It is a true honor. Something such as yourself would have never caught my attention, but now you've intrigued me, enthralled me, left me desiring my curiosity to be sated."

"Um…I don't know what to say."

"I suspect your lack of Diabolic origins plays a pivotal role in making the essence more malleable." Lilith placed a hand on my shoulder. "I wonder what type of demons you'll create."

"I doubt I could make any." I searched my insides, trying to quantify the amount of actual essence stitched throughout my cells, wondering how much was required to create a demon. "Plus, I don't really know how procreation works for devils. I'm assuming it's sort of like parthenogenesis—basically asexual reproduction—but instead of biology finding a way to keep a species moving forward, it's more of a magical quantifier established based on the vast array of Diabolic versatility in emulating and imitating other forms of existence while simultaneously maintaining its individuality in structured…"

I paused. I was talking a lot. Too much, probably. Possibly. Potentially.

"Sorry."

"Don't be," Lilith said. "I look forward to consummating our bond."

"W-w-what?" I choked on the question.

"Surely, the demon born of our union will be unlike any other I've breathed life into."

Lilith didn't invite me to a Devil's Banquet to determine if I was worthy of my newly appointed title as a devil but instead to figure out if I would make a suitable mate. A partner. A devil daddy.

"Fuck." I gulped.

"If you insist." Lilith sprawled onto the edge of the bed, poised in a seductive pose.

My eyes widened in absolute horror, having no idea how to politely reject the ruler of this entire Hell dimension that didn't result in me dying, Bez dying, and the world dying.

14

Bez

I excused myself from the feast and went to search for Wally. Common sense told me not to interfere, to overstep, to make a scene outside the expectations of my role, but Wally didn't know how to fully conduct himself—when to challenge, when to concede, when to call out for assistance. If I left him alone with Lilith, I feared she'd simply steamroll him into submission. Wally was far from timid, but he avoided conflict when at all possible, and I might've told him to put away his best weapon, which was his mouth. It was also his best asset. Aside from his actual ass.

I snorted at my own perverse humor, eager to ravish Wally once we'd paid our dues and escaped Hell. But first, I had to find him. Not an easy feat since I'd looped around the feast two times over despite taking deliberate turns down halls leading out of the temple.

"Why in such a rush to wander aimlessly?" Corson asked, continuing his patronizing attitude as he shuffled out of the dining hall to accompany me.

I sighed. "Is this feast going to be hexed until the very end of the banquet, or does this particular course require trapping the guests?"

"Mother does prefer her privacy."

I huffed in response.

"Even if you found your way out of this spatial loop—which isn't easy," Corson grumbled, feigning frustration, "what're you going to do if you find your devil? Sit on the floor like a lapdog again?"

"Lapdogs sit in laps." I took a sharp turn, almost gleaming a sliver of an opening in the corner of my eye before the illusion locked me in the infinitely looping pattern. "It's right there in the name, moron."

"You're welcome to sit on my lap if you so desire." Corson sped up, walking side by side with me.

"Pass."

"Shame. You look good in your own flesh." He arched his back and squared his shoulders so he could stand a bit taller, still a few inches shorter than me. And that was without the horns. "Quite fuckable."

"And you looked better dressed in that bloody feathered Fae," I said, reminding him of the last time we encountered each other, the briefness of our interaction, and how it led to his death.

"Those meatsuits you wore didn't do you near enough justice." Corson continued, ignoring my comment and nonchalantly peeking at my ass. "Though, the first time I saw one of your suits, it was already in shambles."

He was referring to my headless corpse that Eligos had propped up as a trophy or trap or both when attempting a ridiculous plan to assault and control all the Hells in existence.

"Gotta say that particular body was atrocious, but I did have fun sticking it to you." Corson nudged my ribs with his elbow. "Come on. Remember? I rammed you with a sphere or something."

"A lance."

"Whatever, it was long and hard." Corson snickered. "You took it well, as I recalled."

I joined in with the laughter, encouraging a bellowing reaction.

"Here I thought you were simply one of Lilith's many royal children." I slapped him on the back. "But you're so much more than that, aren't you?"

"Most certainly."

"You're her jester, too," I said, shoving him away and continuing my search for a chink in this hexed space.

All I needed was to find a sliver of an escape, and then I could scan for Wally outside the parameters of the illusion. I still didn't know what I'd say when I stumbled onto him and Lilith, what threatening tone Lilith might've used to sus out Wally's vulnerability as a devil, but as his commander, his champion, his right hand in Hell, it was my place to remain at his side. A fact Lilith wouldn't contest. Probably. Hopefully.

"How about we stop wandering in circles, and I bring you someplace where I can bend you over and appreciate that lovely Diabolic body?"

"Not on your life." I smirked. "Which I've already taken once."

"Oh, come now. An ass like that needs to be worshipped." Corson had the foulest grin. "We can take turns if you insist. I've bedded a few of Beelzebub's demons, and you lot tend to be the most ravenous."

"Flattery will only get you closer to Oblivion. Especially if you don't step out of my way."

"I simply thought we could enjoy each other's bodies while my mommy is busy bedding your boy."

"What?" I stopped walking, finally giving Corson the attention he craved.

"The things I'd love to try out on your luscious body." Corson chuckled; his grating voice reverberated loudly. "Think of the fun we'd have dancing and dueling and dying in each other's arms with each thrust."

I growled.

Corson slapped an arm over my shoulders, pulling me closer to him. "Bet I can make you purr so much better than that, darling."

My insides twisted in knots, essence uncertain of whether to lash out or curl inward at the realization of this news.

"Come now, you must've realized this wasn't a typical Devil's Banquet."

There was an air of overly considerate demons who didn't scheme or conspire nearly as much as anticipated. Though, I didn't attend many events or court appearances with Beelzebub, and the few he dragged me to usually turned into brawls or sieges or full-blown assaults meant to catapult our Hell into a war with another.

"She's always hungry for new devil progeny," Corson continued.

"What?" I cocked my head.

"Yep." He ran his hand over his sculpted torso, tracing his fingers over the fine muscles of his body. "That's why I'm one of Mommy's favorites."

I waited for him to finish fawning over himself and explain his answer as the pieces of this madness slowly clicked together.

"I'm not purely spun from her essence." The sapphire of Corson's eyes glowed. "I got a bit of Lucifer inside me, too. The big, famous daddy devil. Well, before his demons conspired and gutted him, ripped him to shreds, and divvied up his essence."

"You're born of two devils," I said.

It wasn't impossible, simply uncommon. Merging essence meant offering vulnerability, even if only during the ritual itself. And devils didn't do vulnerability. But who dared to deny the devil Lilith?

Wally would have no choice but to obey Lillith's whim. And with that realization, my world fell in on itself. What would this do to him? When I ripped the devil essence from my being, it nearly killed me, but somehow, it was enough to resurrect Wally, to heal him, to keep him alive and healthy and always improving. What would happen if he broke off a piece of himself and offered it to Lilith?

What would it mean to me? Every part of me wanted to lay waste to this temple, storm the chambers of whatever room Lilith had taken Wally, prevent any union that meant Wally shared a piece of his soul with another. But I didn't even know where Lilith had gone. And I certainly couldn't fight off a devil.

15

Wally

"Wait…you wanna make a baby with me?" I asked with what must've been the most dumbfounded expression in the history of expressions.

My jaw had fallen slack with shock. My eyes were wide yet locked in on Lilith. Literally zoomed in on her with the power of my essence in the same way I'd done when observing the distant details of Hell. She sprawled across the edge of her bed, posing a proposition to merge our essence while also…well, posing seductively.

"This isn't real."

"It's quite real, Walter," Lilith cooed. "Naturally, I'd want your offspring. It's a fascination of mine to see the wonderful Diabolic diversity different devils bring when our essence collides."

"Could you clarify what you mean by mating?" I asked as my throat tightened. "Like actually pushing our bodies together in a… Well, you know how people push their bodies together. Or actually, maybe you don't. Do Diabolics do sex? Bez does. He's really good at it. But he might've learned that from mortals. See, we've got some cool stuff. And Mora does it, too. A lot, based on the way Kell discusses it. But again, she might've picked that up from people. Hmmm." I swallowed the lump building in my throat from the million other random words about sex threatening to spill out into this very awkward conversation.

"Devils do, in fact, have sex when merging essence." Lilith shifted her position, letting her legs dangle on the edge of the bed. "I adapted it for mergers—a bit of pleasure for the process, an intriguing absurdity that lesser things require. The requirements for procreation are such a foreign concept."

"Oh?"

"When I wish for life, I simply will it." Lilith waved a hand. Essence pooled at her fingertips, curdling inward and transforming into a tiny glowing yellow light that exploded with black tar. Energy coiled around the light, adding a golden hue beneath the sheen blackness of the blob.

Black flames hissed; black lightning sparked; the two elements raged around Lilith's wrist, sizzling when they popped against the atmosphere. The blob itself bellowed and cried and released echoing wails.

"Is that a baby…" I stared at the instantaneous life Lilith brought into this world with a single motion. "The essence has changed."

"Of course." Lilith blew on the blob of energy, soothing the screech and carrying it upward to the ceiling, which opened like an automatic door.

"How?"

"I took a single drop of my being and birthed awareness out of the nothingness still lingering in Hell."

"Whoa." I watched the blob fade into the distance as it floated toward the night sky of twinkling stars. Stars Bez had said embodied all the baby demons of Hell. "You just made a child in an instant."

"I made a demon, yes." Lilith chuckled. "Easy enough after a few trillion."

"I guess that would make Diabolics parthenogenesis—which is asexual reproduction." I nodded. "We have lots of species who reproduce this way. Lower beings and all."

Lilith squinted, then smiled, then let her face fall flat in a way that left me flustered and frightened and fumbling to think of what to say and what not to say.

"Devils would use this parthenogenesis," Lilith added. "Demons don't have the ability to multiply their essence into a new sentient form of consciousness."

"Oh." I grimaced. I suppose I had said Diabolics, which was an umbrella term for devils and demons and all things essence-related. "But intercourse isn't actually a requirement for you? Devils don't need the act—well, I suppose no one needs the act now thanks to the advancements of science—but with the way your essence and magics work, the physical isn't required."

"It most certainly is. There is a primal push and pull mixed with passion as our essence collides. The merger requires we be fully synchronized, enthralled, bonded on the deepest of levels." Lilith leapt forward in a blur, standing behind me instantly. "This should be a benefit, as your species is quite conditioned to coupling in such forms."

"Um…well, I don't know if I'm ready for a child." I stepped back from Lilith, not that any distance would offer me space. Her energy radiated throughout the room, adding a perfume of her presence. "I should probably wait until I have a better understanding of my essence, my devil-hood-ness-ity stuff."

"No, that will not do." Lilith strutted toward me. "I've allowed devils time to contemplate arrangements only for them to perish into the pits of Oblivion before sharing their seed."

"Oh. Um, well, I've escaped Oblivion before, so that's good news." I gave a strained smile. Not that I had any interest in returning.

"Once. I haven't lived this long by gambling. No, we'll do this now," Lilith insisted sharply as if her words had ended the conversation. "Beelzebub's essence is one I craved to cultivate for far too long. Seeing the wonders it's done when mixed with your mortal flesh, I can only imagine the glory our union will bring."

"I see." So this wasn't even about me. She wanted to recapture some claim she sought to have over Beelzebub, the most dangerous devil of them all.

I took a deep breath and tried to remember I was a devil here, too. Lilith wasn't threatening me, and she wasn't looking for missteps; she was making a proposition. A flattering one that I needed to delicately yet assertively pass on. Why did the mere idea of rejecting a devil make my stomach twist into a million knots? That and the horror of having a child.

"It's a big commitment," I muttered. Fuck. Of course I muttered. Guess I needed to just dive right into this polite rejection. "Eighteen years. For mortals. Our standard child-rearing commitment stuff. Well, longer, really. If you're a good parent. Not that I'm planning on being bad. But inexperience is the worst when aiming for success. Probably. In my case. In most of my cases. Gah, Diabolic lifespans are basically forever, so that's an even bigger commitment. Yeah. Lots to learn as a devil myself. I'd probably want a few hundred centuries under my belt before committing to taking care of a child. Or a few hundred years. No, actually, a few hundred centuries sounds right for me. Maybe then kids would be cool. Like one or two. Not a trillion or so like you. But you make it work. Very well."

"I'll tend to the child. Within a few centuries, it'll blossom quite well." Lilith telekinetically drew me closer. "Let us commence."

"This isn't gonna work for me." I flailed momentarily, feeling my essence pluck at the air like the strings of a harp, and as such, I broke Lilith's grip over me. "You're very beautiful, but there are so many reasons I can't do this. For one, performance. As much as I can admire your attributes, it's not something that works for me intimately."

Lilith cocked her head.

"It's nothing about you." I gave her a tight smile. "I just can't, um…you know. Or not. Bez and Mora seem very fluid in all things gender and attraction, but that's only a pool of two Diabolics, which isn't much to go on. But Corson also seems like he would be open to just about…but then there's Orias. Also, several demons I met in this villa. They seemed open but mostly with eating people. Diabolics really are hungry."

Lilith lowered her head and raised her black eyes to meet mine, a wicked gleam in her smile. "We're insatiable."

I gulped.

"But I understand you're explaining your attraction is solely toward the male form."

"Yes," I said with a heavy sigh of relief. Maybe I wouldn't need to drop the other reasons this coupling wouldn't work.

"I can see the appeal. Their bodies are fun in all their limited ways." Lilith extended her arms, flaunting herself as her image changed. Not in the way a glamour shifted the air ever so slightly to cast an illusion. No. Her body mass changed, swelled, grew, and expanded as her feminine shape crumpled away, now replaced by a masculine body equal in stature and shape to Bez's.

In fact, upon closer inspection, her facial features shifted ever so to look less like a male version of the face she'd shown me and more like Bez's with the sharper jawline and the high cheekbones. Her complexion remained a deep purple, but the scales smoothed out. Her shoulder and biceps flexed in the same flirty, flaunty way Bez would.

"Wow. You just shape-shifted, like, everything." I eyed her muscular frame, tearing at the seams of her fitted dress.

A dress she burned away with a flick of her hand, changing the ashes into a new outfit that barely covered her. Bez's outfit. From the warrior's skirt to the identical set of gauntlets he'd picked as accessories. Everything about this body was meant to emulate Bez, down to the definition of her abs. Her. Hers.

"Question." I grimaced. "You've taken on a more masculine form, but are you still—"

"I'm still the God Queen Emperess of Hell, this and any other I lay siege upon," she spoke with a deep, surly voice but held a light lilt underneath. There was command and certainty entwined in the echo of her words.

"Glad we cleared that up." I meekly went to step around her, inch my way closer to the door, which I was beginning to realize didn't exist in this design.

Of course not. She'd magically transported us here.

"As intriguing as I find this—and flattered by the whole altering your form for aesthetic reasons—the intercourse part isn't gonna work for me," I flatly said, biting back a dozen tangents on the lack of preparation I had for parenthood or the fact I didn't see parenthood in my future. "Plus, while the childbirth factor seems quite quick, there's an eternal commitment."

"Quick?" Lilith cocked her head; her curled ram horns framed her face in the same way they did Bez's. "The intercourse alone could last months."

"Months?" My jaw dropped. "But wait. You just…" I pointed to the sealed ceiling, gesturing to the demon she created in literal seconds.

"I have eons of experience," she explained. "Since you don't know anything about untangling your essence from your being, colliding it with the empty around yourself, shaping consciousness from the ether, or merging your entity with another's."

"I know plenty about merging my entity with someone else's," I muttered.

"Do not worry, though. I will fuck my seed into you, and you will spill your essence into me. A drop. A pure, undiluted piece of power meant to merge with my entity."

"No," I said. No edge or concern in my tone. As a devil, I had to hold myself on equal footing with Lilith. She brought me here as an equal. Even if the idea sent trembles through my entire body.

"No?" Lilith's face crinkled with disgust like the word had clung to her tongue with a bad taste. "Fine. If you wish to carry the demon to term, I can renovate this portion of my domain during your stay. A devil-merged Diabolic is usually at least a century. The essence is quite fickle about merging, so you'll need to stay close."

"I can't get pregnant."

"You are a devil. You can do whatever you will. If your feeble mortal body says otherwise, then change it." Lilith flexed her muscles, displaying her broad, firm chest. "Bodies are such limiting things. Do not allow one so simple in its construction to control you, my dear."

"Okay, let me clarify. I'm not getting pregnant. I'm not having a baby. Not your baby. Not anyone's baby." My essence swelled in my chest, making my words breathy and fuming with fury. "And I'm not sleeping with you. I'm with Bez."

"You would reject me for a demon pet?" Lilith hissed like the mere idea itself carried poison.

The air around us turned hot and dry, scorching my skin like I'd fallen into a desert.

"You would reject my proposition, my offering, my essence, after all I have done?" Lilith's voice shifted, and the masculine form withered away as a more feminine serpentine form wriggled side to side. "I have granted you an audience with all my glory. I have given you a Devil's Banquet in your honor. You, Walter Alden, a no-name devil, an abomination birthed not of the nothingness in the universe but of some second-rate pathetic realm barely functioning on the one planet in your vast dimension of unexplored territory."

Lilith's body blurred, rattling so quickly in place her image was difficult to take in. This wasn't her true form, but it was the closest I'd seen by far. Similar to a gorgon with a humanoid upper half and a tail body. But her arms split apart and spread into thin-fleshed wings that spanned the length of the room. Her jaw cracked, and out spilled a hundred tendrils, each whipping around with gnarled teeth and hungry mouths.

"I have been nothing but accommodating." Lilith raged, each mouth speaking the words in an echoed, repetitive loop. Or I assumed they spoke the same words as her many-mouthed tendrils spoke a different language from my world.

Had she taken the time to learn every single language, both mortal and Mythic, before inviting me here?

"I should kill you where you stand."

"But you won't." I clenched my fists, channeling essence and puffing my chest with so much bravado I might actually get myself killed for arrogance. "You speak as if I'm weak, but we both know you're hesitant. Much like myself. My limits, my potential, are unknown factors."

"That so?" she hissed a hundred thousand times over that every dialect of my world reverberated throughout this shrinking room.

Literally shrinking. Lilith drew it in and forced us closer and closer without even moving.

My essence sprang from my pores defensively, coating my hands and feet in claws.

"Please." Lilith's voices knocked me back, the sheer force of the sound. "I could end you with a thought."

She slithered across the room, turning away from me, revealing the long, jagged spikes lining from her neck to the tip of her tail.

"Killing you offers me nothing, though." With a flap of her winged arms, Lilith tore open the wall. "However, taking the filth of your muck and offering it to your better… That will provide me what I've always craved."

The tendrils shrieked with such a fury the entire world trembled. And I did mean the entirety of her dimension. I felt it in the quake of nearby demons, in the essence of those who were broken to pieces and transformed into scenery, in the quake of the stars above, and from the burning of the key Lilith had gifted me. A key which would open her door to Hell and send me home. But I felt her door fling wide open the moment she screeched.

"What've you done?"

"I've invited a new devil to attend," she hissed. "Beelzebub has spent enough time locked away from the universe. I wonder how grateful he'll feel when I restore him with his missing essence."

She unleashed Beelzebub? The devil who'd tormented Bez for as long as he'd lived. The devil who'd waged wars against every other devil for the sport. The devil who currently sought the return of his long-missing piece of essence.

Essence which currently coursed through my being.

16

Everything rumbled. The sky split and shattered into a billion shards, which fell like meteorites. Rage seeped through the air, so haunting and familiar, I almost fell to my knees on instinct. Demons shrieked and fought and clawed and cast against the palpable fury which lashed out erratically. One by one or a hundred at a time, demons erupted into nothingness as their essence was spent and their lives were forfeited.

I stared out at the harrowing sight of an empty, broken sky where the stars cried and war rained down everywhere. A shadowed silhouette of a form I'd never forget filled the darkness, standing taller than any mountain, a sight that'd make titans terrible if any still lived in the deep depths of the earth of the mortal realm. Somehow, someway, Beelzebub had stepped through the threshold and into this world. How?

"How is he here?" I conjured black ice to shield the shards of fiery sky crashing down onto the temple, onto every part of Lilith's dominion, slaughtering tens of thousands immediately.

Beelzebub simply setting foot into this world had sparked destruction. He wasn't even fighting yet. This destruction was merely a greeting. A reminder that everything about my devil roared with war.

"Look out!" Corson tackled me, knocking me out of the way of several purple-scaled spikes that shot out of the floor and ran the length of the corridor before sinking into the ground, much like a shark's fin.

Ominous and alluring and completely out of my purview, with all my attention fixated on Beelzebub's arrival. How'd he get here? How'd he get out of his Hell where I'd locked him in? How long before he realized I was here in Lilith's domain?

I trembled. If he didn't already know.

"You feel so good quivering beneath me, wrapped in my grip." Corson lay on top of me with a fiendish smile of wicked delight.

The spikes sprang up so quickly they nearly impaled me, while Corson of all beings saved me. Not that him shoving me to the ground and landing on top of me was much of a save.

"What're you doing?" I snarled as his hand reached around to comfort me in a hug.

"Can't have my mommy go and kill you before I have a chance to bend you over and bed ya." Corson grinned. "Though, if you prefer missionary, I'll gladly gaze into your eyes as I impale you in such a more satisfying way than my mommy ever could."

"One, get off."

"What do you think I'm trying to do?" Corson winked.

"Two, your mother issues aside, thanks, I suppose." I shoved him off. "Three, how the fuck did Beelzebub end up here?"

"My guess is Lilith, in her feisty omnipotence, determined his visit during your banquet would make for quite the entertainment."

"It's not my banquet."

"It is now. You think your devilish human boy is gonna last long now that the devil he robbed is here?"

"Wally didn't steal…" I growled, furious and frightened and fucking confused. Beelzebub would kill Wally. He'd break my love apart into a billion molecules and devour every ounce of his being to restore his full strength.

"Look, the way I see it is this Hell is going to fall apart. In a day or decade, but with Beelzebub here, let's just say Mommy doesn't remember the wars she sent us into, and he came here himself instead of the buffer of his armies. No, thanks." Corson pursed his lips, then twisted them into a minxy grin. "So why don't we enjoy our time together before we all fall into Oblivion again?"

My insides stirred, anxious at the idea of returning to such a devoid realm. A place of sleepless slumber. A world of silent wails. An eternity of internalized war with my mind while granted peace from the horrors of Hell. Such a tragic afterlife that Beelzebub had dropped me into more times than I cared to remember, only to drag me out gasping and flailing and missing the misery of nothingness because my devil had grown bored and sought torment for his prized possessions.

Corson's smug expression, coupled with the way he slid his leg between mine at the idea slipping more between me.

"Uukk, you realize that's never going to happen?"

"Never say never. Relationships blossom."

I scowled. "If and when Wally and I arrive to a state where we explore an open relationship—"

"I meant ours, not your soon-to-be-dead devil, but it's cute you're considering him and his nonexistent future."

"Point is, I won't be exploring any of it with you."

"Why not? I'll be gentle." Corson leaned in close, his tongue a breath away from my lips. Thank the gods neither of us breathed. "Or rough. Or whatever you want when bent over, darling."

"I don't bend for anyone, and I typically find fellow Diabolics boring in bed." I slapped a hand over Corson's face and squeezed tightly. "Personally, I'd rather fight you than fuck you."

"Why not both?" Corson's teeth chattered, and his body shivered with excitement.

I shoved him away. "Get off."

"I keep trying." Corson stood to his feet and offered me a hand up, which I didn't accept. "Seems mommy dearest has gone and decided she's fully unhinged, letting the most notorious devil into her home while attempting to slaughter the right hand of the devil currently invited here as a guest of honor." He shook his head, tsking. "Madness."

"Madness indeed." I scoured the skies for Beelzebub.

Despite his grand entrance of tearing the sky asunder, he'd vanished just as quickly. If Lilith brought him here and opened the doors to her Hell, then it seemed she never intended on mating with Wally, merging their essence into some Diabolic demon offspring of their devilish union. No, she planned for something far more nefarious. She planned on handing him over to Beelzebub, allowing him to reclaim his glory. Had that been her intention this whole time? Why the grandstanding? Was she actually evaluating Wally's capabilities, or was this merely the whim of a devil?

Corson grumbled. "Oh, fuck me—"

"How many times do I have to say no," I interjected, but it wasn't my quick attitude that silenced him. No, it was the purple smoke coiled around us from head to toe. "Ah, fuck."

In a blink, we vanished and then reappeared at the far end of a tiny bedroom. So quaint and small, it held none of the majesty I expected of a devil.

Yet, seeing how there was barely any room for distance between Wally and Lilith, it dawned on me Lilith warped this place. My essence surged at the sight of Wally pressed to a bed that was being absorbed into a wall. Despite this hovel of space, Lilith had stretched a corridor like putty between me and Wally, where his distance slowly increased, and the flooring slopped in stringy noodled angles.

"Bez." Wally's eyes were black, his hands covered in claws, and his teeth fanged.

I lunged forward at blurring speed, closing the distance of the few yards that separated us, only for Lilith to warp the spatial slack further and further, sending this corridor in twists and loops that only further divided me from Wally. When I paused my chase, the distance closed, but the instant I took a step, the walls and floor rumbled, ready to keep me at arm's length.

Lilith had only brought me here as a spectator. Someone to witness the horrors she intended to inflict.

"You spurn my offer of courtship, so be it." Lilith's teeth turned jagged and layered in her mouth as her head shifted and her mouth transformed into a snout. Or beak. Or something beyond the confines of her mortal guise and into her true reflection.

Wait. Wally had rejected her? The weight of relief, coupled with the heavy anchor of dread that yanked at my insides, was nauseating. I was proud and flattered and honored he stood up to a devil, clearly enough to provoke her. But that was the problem. He pissed her off, and now she'd done the unspeakable.

"Killing you, killing that pet of yours, would offer little recompense for what I am owed." Lilith waved a hand at me, pulling the corridor distancing me closer. "But handing you both over to Beelzebub will finally make him kneel with gratitude."

"Two things Beelzebub doesn't do." I scoffed. "You're either completely delusional or more arrogant than Beelzebub if you think handing over Walter will earn you anything other than a quicker death."

"I don't know." Lilith smiled. "Beelzebub merely needs to be whole again in order to be of use for my needs, so the additional essence bubbling inside The Great Lord Devil Walter Alden"—she gestured a spinning motion at the monotony of Wally's title, one she'd conceived nonetheless—"of the Misfit Mortal Mage Hybridization is really an unnecessary surplus."

She made it sound as if the essence I'd given to Wally had gained more power. Something which wasn't possible. I'd taken that essence from Beelzebub and held a fraction of his being inside me for centuries. It remained exactly as it was the day I'd devoured it on the battlefield of rebellion. The essence hadn't grown or depleted. Yet somehow, when interacting with Wally, the purity of devil essence magnified the possibilities. How?

His aura did feel more Diabolic, but I assumed it had to do with how he channeled his power while defending against another devil.

"I considered handing over the treacherous coward who'd fled with Beelzebub's essence centuries back, but as you said"—Lilith's venomous gaze locked onto me—"Beelzebub doesn't kneel or show gratitude. So what good would returning you, killing you, or keeping you as my pet have ever offered me?"

Lilith had known about me from the very start. Her and likely every other devil out there, and just as the gods they were with entire worlds of their own, they expressed no interest in the meddling or actions of insignificant beings such as me.

"To make use of Beelzebub, I merely need him at full strength, a true devil reborn," Lilith explained. "The extra boost to his power is unnecessary. As I recall, he was unfortunately quite capable already."

"Again," I said through gritted teeth. "Beelzebub will not show you gratitude. He won't thank you. All he'll do is use his power to obliterate your Hell in its entirety, something he's already aiming toward."

The layers of Lilith's filtered dimension had begun to crack, and somewhere out there, Beelzebub ripped apart other regions of this world.

"Yes, his tantrums are troublesome, but nothing I can't weather." Lilith shrugged. "After all, despite everything, Beelzebub is still bound by the same laws as all Diabolics."

I furrowed my brow. What was she plotting?

"I'd always planned on mating with Walter, securing a piece of his essence through sheer bliss. Mortals enjoy their carnal pleasures. But pain is a swifter method to achieving my goals."

I snarled.

"Walter, you will hand over your essence. Just a piece. A piece Beelzebub won't require to be whole again. A piece that will link him to be forever in what your mortal things call a Diabolic bond."

"What?" The question spilled from my mouth along with exasperated shock.

Lilith intended to bind Beelzebub to her will, forcing him to serve her. And she intended on using the very ritual that'd first brought Wally and I together. A ritual we could no longer use, but I still clung to the sensations that synced between us. The accident that originally connected us, offered us a future, would now be used to divide and destroy us.

"Walter Alden, False Devil with Mortal Stain, you will carve out a piece of your ill-gotten essence and offer it to me." Lilith moved the floor, pulling me closer to her grasp. "In doing so, I will offer your pet a quick death. With Beelzebub under my thrall, you will have no fears of the devil plucking your demon's strings and dragging him out of Oblivion."

I growled, teeth barred, claws drawn, tails switching, and wings raised high as if anything I could do would pale in comparison to a single strike a devil unleashed. All the same, I'd go down swinging before I allowed her to threaten Wally. If I only landed one blow before she killed me, hopefully it'd offer Wally a few seconds to flee.

"Don't listen to her," I said, ready to pounce on the devil who'd slaughter me in an instant. "I need you to—"

Purple spikes sprang forward, aimed at my head. Fuck.

Metal clashed, and the spikes shattered.

"Stop it," Wally spoke with ground teeth, his horns sprouting out and growing atop his head like a gnarled tree.

Thin black wires circled me. Not wires. Essence. His single tail split into a million threads, which stretched long and shielded him from Lilith's attack.

"You dare." The devil chuckled. "Oh, simple little thing you are."

"Awkward times." Corson stretched his arms wide like some attempt to bid an offish farewell at a party he'd overstayed. "I'll just see myself out."

"Oh no," Lilith said. "You'll stay."

"It's not like you need my help."

"Help? No, no, no. I plan on slaughtering you alongside this false devil and his phony Beelzebub pet."

"Why?" Corson's brows knitted into a scowl. "I've done everything you've demanded since—"

"You interfered," Lilith interjected. "You think I didn't note your essence strike mine when I went to break this little demon trash."

"Oh, mother, you misunderstand. Deepest sincerities for the confusion." Corson didn't even do a remotely decent job faking his apology. "I merely meant to detain him on your behalf while brutishly ravishing him in the process. You see, I can be a team player."

Lilith's essence moved in a blur, wiping away Corson's smirk by breaking his jaw in one swift motion. "So pretty to look at, so vexing to listen to."

Corson gurgled as his tongue spilled out, and his essence healed the shattered lower half of his face.

"Corson's first words were a lie, and his last have been vulgar and vindictive every time I've sent him to Oblivion to learn a bit of respect." Lilith circled the demon prince. "Perhaps this is the time I leave you there. Focus on future progeny like the splendid spawn Beelzebub will grant me once I make him my true champion. Yes, a being worthy of serving me, unlike the billions of wasted efforts spent on children such as Corson and all the other forgettable demons."

Corson redirected his essence, transforming his hands into blades while locking eyes with me. It wouldn't last long, but perhaps our combined efforts would offer Wally an extra step or two while he fled.

"You two wish to attack?" Lilith held her winged arms out invitingly as flames formed around her. "Do your worst."

"I said stop." Wally's threaded tail looped around Corson too, offering us protection from Lilith while his cherub wings sprang out.

They created a gust of black wind, blowing the fire away. A few of Wally's feathers fell loose, captured in the blaze of wind.

Feathers fluttered, slashing at Lilith and the essence she redirected, nearly striking her as she shuffled away in a blur, dodging the attacks. Of course she would. Wally was a fellow devil, and even if his damage was insignificant, merely a scratch or two, the weakness it'd reveal in her glory would be offense enough.

A feather collided with the threads of Wally's tail that shielded me from the collision. I understood. He'd guarded us not from Lilith's attacks but from his own devil essence.

"You think you can fight me?" Lilith waved away the feathers, the fires, the furious wind. "The gall."

Wally pivoted his feet in a way I'd seen a thousand times over in our trainings. It meant he intended to fall back and flee, which would be wise. But he hunched forward, funneling essence through his tiny wings in a way that suggested he meant to rage in combat. The shadows of his horns twisted in ominous horrors, painting portraits of the anguish he sought to unleash, the torture he plotted, the darkness of his essence.

"You truly think you can fight me alone?"

"Nope," Wally muttered, then clamped his jaw tight.

I wanted to help him, to prove he wasn't alone, yet the threads of his splintered tail acted as barbed wire that held Corson and me in place—protected and immobilized. Not certain Wally fully thought out his shield technique.

"You don't have to face her alone. Wally, let me—"

"Wasn't planning on it," he said, containing the wrath of his horns. "Also, wasn't planning on risking you."

"You wish to do this the hard way, fine by me." Lilith lunged forward, her body crumpling apart as she slithered faster, wings expanding, teeth glistening, and spikes swelling.

She hissed, ready to pounce and strike Wally, when the walls of the room burst wide open, and a giant hand snatched Lilith up like a worm instead of a serpent.

"You were so fixated on me, you didn't even feel Beelzebub thrashing at the barrier you'd placed around the temple." Wally leapt away from the next hand that swept into the room. "Then again, I suppose essence is a tricky thing to sense, and the chaos cast across the entire dimension probably made it impossible for you to pinpoint his next target."

But it wasn't difficult for Wally to track, not with a piece of Beelzebub inside him. Perhaps we could win this thing.

Lilith shrieked, furious and frightened. Her body transformed more and more the longer she remained in Beelzebub's grasp. Soon, it took all four of his arms to contain her as she coiled around his limbs and fought back.

The temple trembled as both devils took full form. Beelzebub towered over the lands as a behemoth of a being who snatched up demons in waves to crush between his fingers before hurling their shattered essence at Lilith. She shrugged off the remnants of her children used as fodder against her and coiled around Beelzebub.

Her wings stretched far, carrying freezing flames and crackling earth in each gust.

Beelzebub snatched Lilith by the razor-taloned blades of her wing tips and snapped off one of the seven to use as a weapon. Her mouths of a thousand tendrils squeezed his arm tight until he released her broken form and then proceeded to redirect her strike to choke him.

Unveiling their purest form shredded the very fabric of Hell's walls, twisting and tearing pieces of reality as their very perfection reflected against the sky.

Wally grabbed my hand. "We need to get the hell outta Hell."

17

Wally

The devils waged a fierce battle. A flick of Beelzebub's wrist set the land as far as the eye could see on fire. And my eyes saw tens of thousands of demons caught in the raging inferno from every direction. I analyzed their agony, shivering at the piercing pain.

Lilith didn't ignore their deaths; each of her tendrilled mouths wailed a symphony at the faltering essence. An absence that washed away the delicate layers Lilith and her team had designed for my banquet. The starry sky faded into abstract shapes of cosmic radiance. Tendrilled mouths snatched up those starlit geometric shapes and devoured the literal atmosphere of the dimension.

Suddenly, Lilith spat fiery comets from her mouths, each gullet burning bright as the tendrils released a steam that cloaked Lilith and Beelzebub. A mist meant to join in Lilith's stranglehold over Beelzebub, but he gripped the steam, literally tearing the gas into shredded physical form. Chunks of steam crashed onto land and exploded, unleashing tidal waves of boiling water that sizzled with everything it collided with, scorching the earth as it washed away Beelzebub's flames.

Was this what devils were truly capable of? What kind of magic could even come close to the onslaught they cast?

I knew devils were powerful. I'd listened to definitions of their strength. I understood the accuracy of the statement that Lilith would destroy my dimension if I didn't attend the banquet. Well, the potential for it. But to actually see the carnage unfold, though…

Bez squeezed my bicep, pulling my attention away from the catastrophic battle, the duel between gods, the death of a world.

"We need to leave this area before the warding falls." Bez eyed the sigils hidden beneath the rubble of the temple.

No wonder this place hadn't been swept away by the destruction. It remained a tiny haven, an island surrounded by a sea of death and destruction.

"Where would we even go?" My eyes darted around, scanning further than any human could, probably further than most demons, as my essence helped study the land for miles in every direction.

Scalding water.

Flames reborn.

Crackling earth.

Essence trapped beneath devastation. Essence shattered beyond repair. Essence purged from existence.

"Wally." Bez jerked my arm, forcing me to look at him, to lock eyes with his steady gaze, his calm crimson irises, his stoic, concerned expression. "We need to leave this world."

"How?" I asked, struggling not to tremble in Bez's grasp.

"I suggest leaving with those nifty keys Mother bestowed." Corson smirked, reminding me of his presence and seemingly unphased by the obliteration of his dimension.

"Keys?" The word spilled from my lips with a fog of confusion almost as dense as the mist that hid Lilith during her next barrage of strikes.

Corson nodded in my direction; his sapphire eyes analyzed me the same way I'd studied the dying land. His stare pierced through the deepest construct of my cells where the tiny embers of Lilith's magic burned. That was right. The flaming key that brought us to Hell still burned deep within our cores, nearly extinguished but enough to see us home for certain.

"Even without the keys," he said with a playful pause. "It seems we're all in luck."

"Luck?" I spat the word. "Bad luck."

"No." Bez looked up at the fractured sky, seeing something beyond the literal broken world. "Seems the door's still ajar."

"Yes, yes. Mommy went and overestimated herself," Corson said, glee in his growing smirk. "Or she underestimated Beelzebub."

"Both," Bez said.

"I recommend you leave now before she revokes your pass."

"If she gets the chance." Bez scoffed. "Chances are the doors will simply seal entirely once Beelzebub slaughters Lilith."

"Shouldn't you leave too, then?" I asked Corson, to which Bez scoffed again. "What? He did save you."

I'd sensed it when Lilith lashed out, casting her essence like a line meant to hook Bez, to hurt Bez. As fast as my essence was, it couldn't reach him from such a distance in time, but Corson shoved him out of the line of fire. Well, the line of protruding spikes.

"He helped me avoid a minor fatality." Bez folded his arms and looked away. "I'd hardly call that a rescue."

Corson turned away from us, looking up to the sky where devils clashed. "I'm just gonna watch this unfold. I've always wanted to see Mother meet her end."

"What if she wins?" I asked.

"She won't," Bez firmly said. Corson snorted in response.

"Mommy's arrogance has granted her eons of success. It's nice to know that bravado will finally be her undoing."

The bitterness in his lighthearted words hit hard. I couldn't say I didn't understand the sour feelings toward his mother, Lilith was much worse, much more controlling and overbearing than mine, but I couldn't understand the willingness to accept dying alongside her just to watch her fall.

"If you stay, you'll be swept into this destruction." I pointed to the rattling sigils ready to give way any moment.

"No worries." Corson knelt, patting one nearby. "I'm only keeping them active until you lot leave. I've never been afraid of a bit of violence."

"You'll die," Bez said. "When Lilith falls, her world will be sealed until the end of time, and Beelzebub will slaughter all on principal."

Corson shrugged. "Fun times."

"Are you sure he'll kill her?" I asked, nervous about what two devils could do to our world.

"Yes," Bez said.

"Wouldn't it be wiser to keep her alive and use her to keep his own Hell portal open?"

"That would require Beelzebub to show humility and a long-standing collaborative partner," Bez explained. "Things he'd never do. The moment Lilith offered him assistance, she signed her own death. Beelzebub would spend eternity rotting in his Hell before accepting assistance from a fellow devil. That'd make him weak. Beelzebub is a god-king to all things. He is anything but weak."

The awe-struck terror mixed with the calm collectiveness that spilled from Bez made my heart lurch. I wanted to hug him, hold him, offer some type of comfort to a wound that'd never heal. But I couldn't do any of that here. We had to escape first.

"Part of why I'm sticking around." Corson turned back with a smirk. "I might not be able to strike down a devil, but I can most certainly enjoy the show. Then I'll go off and be a thorn in their sides."

"Meaning?" I asked.

"Just do your part and make sure you two toss those keys back into Hell once you're home sweet home and all that jizz."

"Jazz," I corrected.

"Whatever." Corson shrugged. "Liked my saying better."

"Wait. Why do we have to toss the Hell key?"

"Hell key." Corson snickered. "Silly name, but it's for a silly tool, so suppose it evens out." He rocked his head side to side, hair swaying as he contemplated. "Lilith is a fool but always one with a plan to outwit any man. Those keys are a piece of her without expressly being a piece of her. Meaning, when fished out across the universe, it forces the door slightly ajar to her Hell."

Bez huffed. "Meaning, even if Beelzebub shredded the bulk of her essence, the door wouldn't close."

"Precisely. Mommy is a paranoid type, so while you two head off, I'm gonna enjoy the show, then go pillage and plunder those keys across the various dimensions she's tucked them away." Corson waggled his eyebrows. "This'll ensure she doesn't get a backup place."

"I'd ask how, but I truly don't care." Bez pulled in the opposite direction. "May your devil's death provide entertainment and yours be swift."

"Oblivion hoping." Corson cackled; lightning above crackled; stars wailed; essence exploded; the world crumbled.

Bez and I stepped forward, falling through the billion layers of dimensional webbing that were met with an agonizing second that lasted ten lifetimes. Then it all fell away, and Hell vanished as the city of home returned.

A night sky hidden by the bright lights of the city.

The reality of the world began to set in. The actual world, not some fabricated setting of a muted dimension or a war-torn realm where two beings collided with such ferocity even armies of millions couldn't create such a degree of devastation.

Once I'd gained my bearings, Bez snatched the energy pulsating within me and gathered it to the core of my chest before ripping out the blaze meant to carry us between worlds. He smothered the flames Lilith offered between his hands and then tossed them into the abyss.

"Where'd you send them?"

"The cracks between worlds." He brushed the soot off his palms. "Eventually, they'll find their way back to Lilith's realm per their default purpose."

"So, it's really done then?"

"Not quite." Bez glared.

With two devils clashing a world away, it was imperative we made every second count. Otherwise, that war might spill over into our dimension.

We flew across the city to Mora and Kell's place. Bez flew. Despite my wings and other Diabolic features being actively present since returning from Hell, without the presence of a threat, it seemed my extensions didn't cooperate. My cherub wings were about as useful as a novelty set. And while I could've used an incantation to create a quick broom to fly on, I wouldn't move half as fast as Bez on my best day.

Bez didn't even contend with the formality of security protocols, zipping over the front gates while I weaved together a quick incantation to counter any of the wards attuned to Diabolic threats. Though despite the obvious increase in defensive measures lining Mora's estate, none of it seemed geared toward Diabolics. Odd. Usually, she kept her protective spells crafted by Kell more discreetly placed. Also, while Mora set precautions for anyone, mortal, Mythic, or Diabolic, I expected Corson's recent infiltration to lead to more demon-resistant traps.

"I dare you." Bez barred his teeth to the guards who circled us once he landed at the front door.

The door swung open, and Mora greeted us dressed in some tiny, bubbly blonde with a face covered in chocolate sauce and fingers coated in Cheeto dust. I gagged at the junk food wafting from her pores like she'd literally swam through a pool of greasy, fried snacks.

I made a face Mora clearly noticed.

"It's a cheat day." She sucked on her orange fingers one by one, slowly pulling them out of her mouth with a loud pop in this bizarre food porn kind of way that I imagined must've had a huge audience among Diabolics and their obsession with eating.

"Your devil takeover kicking in again?" Bez asked, caressing my face with his gray hand and brushing his thumb near my eyes.

The touch made me more aware of the veins around my face, the ones that must've bulged at my enhanced senses. Senses that allowed me to smell every meal Mora had binged recently. But this wasn't a takeover. Or so I thought until my eyes fluttered ever so in an annoying, quick way that almost made my lashes visible before another room came into view.

I'd never adjust to seeing two things at the same time, layered over each other. Faded images of books, not quite silhouettes but lacking full depth, lined my sight as I stared inside Mora's home.

Tony skittered across the collection of tomes, analyzing various spells. He had stacks already annotated more meticulously than mine and piles of discarded texts that didn't serve a purpose to his goal.

What is his goal?

I tilted my head almost like if I lined my neck up just right, I'd see the answer, the thought dancing along Tony's mind. It was there in the corner of my vision. Our familiar bond fully restored since my return and somehow slightly stronger.

Tony clacked his claws. He felt my presence, the return of our connection in full effect. The blossoming improvements that seemed seamless when I made no efforts yet staggered for years when I applied myself. Tony scurried out of the library he'd holed up inside to greet us.

"Devil's takeover." Mora hmphed. "That's a classic."

"Maybe you can share your wealth of knowledge with the class," Bez said.

"Study guides and slumber parties another time," Mora said with an obvious note of sarcasm, but truthfully, that sounded absolutely delightful.

I never got invited to many slumber parties—the few I had were pity invites because of my popular brother or my bully of a mother. And a whole party dedicated to studying? My head swam in the daydream, almost escaping the impending dangers we'd come here to warn about.

"You know, that was a quick trip." Mora gestured, then turned her motion into a movement to telekinetically wave over a cocktail glass. "I expected something closer to six years, not six months."

"Six months?" My jaw dropped. "Seriously? It was like a day there."

Bez tsked. "It was much longer; you just have a very linear perspective on time."

I frowned.

"As an immortal, you should get used to losing track of time. What's in a century, really?"

"So, I take it Lilith didn't scrutinize your every action," Mora said, eyes trained on me as she sipped her drink. "Or in action."

"About that." I bit my lip. "Where's Kell?"

"Must be urgent if you two rushed over to my lil ole home in the middle of the night." Mora waved us inside.

"Dimensional jetlag." Bez shrugged as we followed Mora upstairs and deeper into the manor.

Tony finally crossed paths with us. He scrambled toward me, climbed my leg, and nestled in the curls of my blond hair. His claws clinked against something, and when I looked, really examined myself for the first time in a while, I saw the full extent of my Diabolic features. Well, as best I could in the semi-reflective surface of a glass picture frame hanging a piece of artwork in Mora's hallway.

Tony's claws had hit one of my horns. A tiny set compared to Bez's four curled ram horns. Mine were about two inches, maybe three—not that size really mattered—and pointed upward with a slight curve. They popped with a sheen black, standing out in my blond hair nearly as much as Tony himself. Veins were stretched around my solid black eyes. My wings were small but pulled taught, the feathers appearing thicker and sharper than they had in the past.

In Hell, I'd weaponized them, using each feather as an extension of my being. But now I couldn't even feel them. Not really. Not the way I felt my arms or legs. Not the way I bent my fingers or wiggled my toes. The instinct wasn't there. Or it was when I didn't overthink it. A rarity, truly.

When we finally reached Kell's study, the entire space was covered in half-abandoned projects of things she'd tinkered with and stacks of books. Books that looked similar to the annotated ones Tony had been putting together elsewhere. What had they been doing in the six months since we left?

"Hey, Scorpio," Kell said. "You're supposed to be working, not slacking off."

Tony hissed and nestled deeper into my hair.

"Here, I would've figured you'd be the one slacking off in my absence."

"Wish I had the time." Kell sighed.

"Do you even have time to say hello?" I asked, lowering my head like it'd somehow catch Kell's eyes, which had fallen back to a book. So, I imitated her to show a proper greeting. "Oh, hey, Wally! Nice to see you're back from literal Hell. How was the trip? Did the devil treat you well? Did you bring me a souvenir?"

"Well?" She raised a brow. "Did you bring me a souvenir?"

"Oh, you wanted to know how my meeting with another devil went?" I bulldozed right past her question. "Glad you asked. Lilith was friendly. Really cool theme."

"Tacky, if you ask me." Mora side-eyed my tunic and Bez's warrior skirt.

I sidestepped right around that comment. "She was also super fascinated by lesser worlds and mortal merged devils, so much so that she wanted to mate."

"That's right, Bael used to hold the occasional banquet himself when Lilith would let their child visit his Hell." Mora shrugged. "Forgot what an avid collector she was."

"I bet." Bez scoffed.

"Any who," I continued. "Turns out I was really more of a consolation prize, one she never planned on having to begin with. Her real motive was offering my head to Beelzebub."

"Who she released from Hell," Bez added. "His Hell. Currently, they're both in Lilith's domain."

That immediately caught Mora and Kell's attention. Both women stared wide-eyed with straightened postures and slack jaws as we explained everything about our trip, our escape, and how Corson warned those flaming keys were extensions of Lilith's power so she'd never find herself trapped inside her own dimension like Beelzebub had. It was a preventive measure in case she was ever overpowered by her demons, by another devil, and afforded her an opportunity to regroup and regather her essence.

"So, if she feels Beelzebub will best her in combat—"

"Which he will," Bez interjected.

"Then she's going to flee her Hell—"

"Probably dragging Beelzebub with her," Bez added. "Since he doesn't suffer cowardly foes."

"And since Corson is currently eradicating all of Lilith's other keys scattered across the universe—"

"Which he never elaborated on," Bez said, barring the fact he'd told the prince he didn't care how he did such things.

"Now, we're here hoping to remove any keys that'd bring Lilith—and possibly Beelzebub—into our world."

"Smart idea," Mora said.

"Kell, can you please return the copy of the key you made?" I asked. "I'd like to destroy it just in case."

"Key?" Kell raised her eyebrows.

"You know the one you and Bez insisted would be a great way to seal a devil away and might actually now be the very thing that unleashes one…or two."

Bez rolled his crimson eyes. "When you say it like that, you can make *anything* sound bad in retrospect."

"I'd love to throw it away along with all my hard work put into creating the damned thing, but unfortunately, I don't have it anymore."

What. The. Fuck?

18

Bez

Of fucking course Kell and Mora had dropped the ball in our absence. I practically ran this city in my spare time. Not that the desire met my fancy, but obviously, those kept in line by my presence decided to pounce on the vulnerability of this tragic oasis.

"You can reel back the arrogant bravado." Mora folded her arms.

"Pardon?"

"I can always tell when your thoughts get smug," she said. "Suppose you think you could've done better."

"I'm just saying, the witches didn't strike under my watch." I smirked. "And if you'd let me handle them before my departure, then we wouldn't be in this situation."

A situation that consisted of Kell and Tony working laborious hours to pinpoint the witch coven through scrying spells while creating a thousand different counter-incantations to the slew of traps conjured by a group who'd declared themselves a movement.

A group of witches bent on ruling the Diabolic Oasis, which they'd probably remain something witchy.

I had no idea what they'd stolen from the shop, but based on Wally's increasingly furrowed brow as he ran through the listed missing inventory, it was a lot.

"You're sure about these?" he asked Antoninus, and the scorpion clacked one claw for yes.

Tony had compiled a list of everything stolen—because of course the bug knew more than Kell, who only paid attention to her projects—which allowed them some idea of what the witches were plotting, but apparently, they'd become quite adept at hiding their presence in the city.

"With these items, it's no wonder you can't track them," Wally said, listing off several dozen things while naming various spells or concoctions one could make.

Damn. I hadn't realized we were sitting with such an artillery at our fingertips. To think, I could've been throwing Molotov cocktails from petrified goblin eggs and the shavings of dragon scales this entire time during my training sessions with Wally. Then again, the wrestling really was the best part of the day.

"Why are you smirking?" he asked, growing flustered from his long list of spells he needlessly prattled on about. "I can't believe we were robbed. These witches are the worst."

"We don't have time for witch drama," I snarled. "We've got devils to contend with."

"Devils whom you lot made a problem," Mora noted, pursed lips in a judgy little face no matter whose body she wore.

"People with witchy wives who lose important things shouldn't throw fireballs," Wally added, continuing his evaluation of the inventory list.

"Hey, I'm not responsible for any of this," Kell protested. "I think fireballs should always be thrown. In fact, I wanted to light up all the thieving witches the first time they attempted to steal from me. It was Mora who wanted to play peacekeeper."

"We're running a kingdom here, not a free-for-all."

"You won't be running anything if Lilith flees to this world and slaughters us all as a practice run to regaining her strength," I said.

"No one's getting slaughtered," Wally said. "I just need the scrying board and a few ingredients, and I should be able to locate the coven. Or, at the very least, one of their caches, which might lead to the coven. Or another cache. Or a person they sold part of their cache to. Or—"

"Wally," I snapped. "You're doing the overthinking worry thing again."

"Oops." He grimaced. "Yeah, I can find them."

"If you think you can find them after the countless hours I spent searching for a workaround on their cloaking spells, be my guest." Kell scoffed. "FYI—half of those stolen goods from our store are making it impossible to track them. Well, pinpoint them. The last spell very notably informed me that the witch coven was, in fact, still on earth."

"Geez, you don't even know if they're still in the Diabolic Oasis or not?" I sighed.

"They're in the Oasis," Wally said with the cutest cockiest little grin. "No one steals a basilisk egg and then abandons it. They're the size of a person and weigh about two solid tons. And anyone who would steal it knows it can't undergo dimensional travel without proper preparation, which, if any of you remember, took a long time for me to situate when we bought it for the shop."

None of us remembered because none of us really paid much attention to the rules of magics that Wally loved rambling about.

"You still can't track them," Kell said with a frustrated edge. It was rare to find someone with a spell that could outwit her. The fact this coven had stolen from her and likely used Kell's own preventative measures wasn't lost on me. Oh, how it must've infuriated her.

"I'm not going to track them," Wally said, holding up the list of lost inventory. "There are simple spells to find rarities that no protection wards can deceive. It's just a matter of doing the research."

"You son of a bitch," Kell muttered.

"I won't argue with you there." I pointed at her, smiling until Wally frowned. "What? You are. Your mother's the worst."

The horrors of this situation, the dire existence-ending possibility, fizzled away for a few brief minutes as Wally muttered with aggravation over our aloofness while fighting a smile that came every time he sank into the joy of research. He couldn't help but smile. After all, his nerdy, little obsessive need to study had truly paid off. I settled into this moment, savoring the calm between storms.

I allowed Wally's joy to keep me calm while he prepared his little locator spell, ignoring the fact that if Mora hadn't insisted I not involve myself, then I could've killed these annoying witches before we even went to Hell.

Why does no one simply accept my ruling as truly superior?

Thankfully, it didn't take my budding genius long to pinpoint the enemy. We arrived at a collection of warehouses where Wally led the way, me at his side and Mora and Kell close behind. He breezed through the maze of buildings, muttering probabilities like he was the smartest rat about to snag the cheese until we reached a collection of trees leading to the nearby forest.

"I got this." Kell sidestepped past Wally, confidently taking the lead since he'd solved a riddle in days that she hadn't in the last several months.

Using Nature's Blessing, Kell uncloaked the hidden glamours put in place by the plant life.

"Interesting sorcery," Wally said, examining the plants that shriveled. "What spell is that?"

"It's like the familiar bond," Kell said. "Flowers seeped in magic by witches here and serving as familiars.

"Plants can be familiars?" Wally's puzzled expression quickly tucked that piece away for a later observation. "Fascinating how the pollen carries the Mythic residue of magic in the air."

"Yes, yes, yes, the coolest of the cool," I said. "Can we kill now and study later?"

"Do we really need to kill them?" Wally asked. "If they understood the situation—"

"Fuck that," Mora said. "I tried diplomacy. They can all rot in whatever witchy afterlife awaits them."

"Returned to the goddess," Kell answered. "May they choke on her roots until the end of time."

And with that, she led the way into this warehouse despite the fact Wally's spell directed our path deeper inside and eventually down a set of stairs that took us into a cellar filled with artifacts galore and a group of witches who dropped everything under the direction of one who shouted at them to find their formation.

"Reminds me of the toxic cheer squad I was in."

"Oh. My. Fucking. Goddess." Kell smacked her cheeks with shock. "How am I just now learning you were a cheerleader?"

"I was really just there to be a thrower," Wally clarified. "But weak arms—they expected me to be like Alistair."

"He does have such strong arms," Kell said.

"Anyway." Wally made a pouty face. "Apparently, I didn't have enough pep for the team, so I got cut."

I smirked. "Please tell me you kept the uniform."

"From when I was fourteen?" Wally raised a brow. "No. It wouldn't even fit."

I tilted my head, leaning closer to him. "The number of times you've said that, and yet, we always manage."

"You dare step into our base of operations and make idol conversation," a witch said, still directing the others, so based on his confidence and bluster, I figured him for the leader. "The gall of coming here, behaving in such a way."

"I'll cum where I want, thank you very much!" I winked at Wally, who rolled his eyes.

"Seriously? Not the time. But also, told you I'd find them." Wally nodded toward the coven leader, cocky smile that his research had paved the way, so much so even his tail pointed. A good sign indicating that his essence was syncing up to his desires, even if for basic motor functions.

"You mean fell into our trap," the coven leader said.

"I'd rather not kill your entire coven, Desmond." Mora sauntered in front of Wally and Kell while I remained in the back, seeing as the witches circled us from every angle as if they could flank our position.

"You won't have the option," Desmond said.

"Wow. Didn't realize you were so eager to die." Mora snickered. "But if I don't have an option—"

"No," Desmond snapped. "You won't have an option, as in you won't be given the option to kill us. You'll be dealt with."

I joined in Mora's laughter. The audacity of these simple witches. I understood their bravado in challenging Kell, assuming they could fair against one of their own, but surely, they understood a single coven couldn't defeat one demon, let alone two and a devil hybrid.

"I get the bravado in stealing from me," Kell said, holding back her own chuckle. "Assuming, foolishly, you could challenge one witch and win as a self-proclaimed powerhouse coven, but surely you're not so arrogant to believe yourselves capable of defeating two demons and a devil hybrid."

"This lot wouldn't even fair against one demon," I growled, relishing in the shutter it sent through the coven witches surrounding us. Already, they hesitated, they questioned their predicament, and in a few moments, they'd beg for a mercy I was in no mood to grant. "And they think they can kill three?"

"Why kill you when we can snare you in our trap?" the witch leader asked.

"Please, these sigils won't even stop me." Kell shook her head, a grin on her face and pity in her eyes.

"They're not meant to contain you, wicked witch," Desmond said. "Merely meant to keep your focus split as the real trap unfolds."

"Excuse me, but um, not to be that person." Wally raised a hand because of course he had to be polite even as we infiltrated their pathetic attempt at a coup. "Aren't traps better if they're not announced?"

Mora strutted forward with her hands on her hips. "Hun, never underestimate the hubris of a man who feels slighted because he's not in charge."

"Hubris?" Desmond scoffed. "You are the one with hubris, demon bitch! We finally have a city, a place to gather without Collective oversight. A place with real power. Potential. Possibility."

"You're just saying synonyms now." Mora gestured with aloof dismissal of Desmond's comments. "You're mad because you wish to wage a war against an army of mages. You're delusional because you think one hidden city can offer the Mythics refuge to conspire their assault. You're arrogant because you think you can run this city better. A city that wouldn't exist without me. A city cultivated and culminated by the network of Mythics, mages, mortals, and everyone under the fucking sun that I organized, gathered, saw a glimmer of potential in."

"You're short-sighted, Mora."

"Says the witch who's only considering his vision for the now." Mora shook her head and tsked. "I always think centuries ahead. Eradicating your coven wasn't on the agenda, but alas…it looks like the witches are going to dwindle just a sliver more."

"Sounds like my cue." Kell swirled her arms at her sides, summoning a lavender mist that began to eat away at the sigils warding the room.

"Pretty sure it's mine, too." Desmond snapped his fingers and muttered some spell of sorcery, which conjured a bright light between his hands.

Every witch in the room held their hands around a white light that formed into a ball and took on a glass shape.

My body tensed.

My eyes widened.

Every fiber of my essence recoiled at the sight of each witch in this coven holding a Diabolic orb.

"How?" The word escaped my chattering teeth.

"Like I said, you've walked right into my trap." Desmond extended his arms, holding the orb in one hand.

An orb that was nearly three times the size of the others displayed by the coven. Their orbs were closer in size to the one that had held me for nearly fifty years. Fifty years. Years I lost in isolation. Torment. Horror I would've faced until the end of time had happenstance and timely accidents not interfered.

"These will contain any Diabolic," Desmond said. "Demons, devils, even defective misfit mages merged with essence."

"Bez." Wally's tail reached out, gently coiling around my wrist as if to pull me from my thoughts and back to the situation at hand. A situation which would be our end.

"We have enough of these orbs to contain an army of demons," Desmond said.

"How did you acquire these?" Mora asked, no fear in her voice, but she'd never spent time inside a Diabolic orb.

"I created them after years of study," Desmond explained as a ward fizzled out and the glamour that cloaked the wall behind him faded away, revealing a trove of orbs in all sizes. "Did you really think Magus Remington was the only person Baron Novus shared his contraptions with?"

That annoying Fae noble and his damned demon knight were still proving to be thorns in my side even after dying. They created these horrible tools. And it turned out they handed them over to more than just Abe. Abraham. Magus Remington. The bastard who tricked me into fighting his battles, then locked me away inside an orb and used that betrayal to rise to infamy among The Collective forces.

"But what would an army of demons get me? A bloody war against The Collective? No, thank you." Desmond summoned a fire into his free hand. "I want an insurmountable victory. One that'll have every mage on their knees where they belong."

"You can't control demons with the orbs," Wally clarified. "Only trap them."

The way he said the words, there was no fear in his voice, no realization that trapping us was enough. I wouldn't suffer it. I wouldn't allow myself to be contained by these orbs or any other. Never again.

"Unlike Remington, I was aware of the Fae's manipulation, so I studied the orb given and created modifications. Ones which will allow me to release just a fraction of essence to perform a binding ritual. And that will put you demons under my thrall. Our thrall."

Every witch in the coven raised their orbs, each preparing to attempt trapping Wally, Mora, and myself.

"And just so you know, I won't settle for some trivial demon dressed as a devil." There was an arrogance in the way Desmond presented the orb, the flame, the way he held them in either hand. "No, no, no. Once you're bound, I'll summon Lilith herself and shackle a true devil."

"Kell," Mora called out.

"Busy." Kell's lavender mist had nearly melted away all the sigils when a deep blue smoke slithered into the room like a serpent and wrapped around Kell's sorcery.

"You should be honored, Morax," Desmond said, a bitterness as he said Mora's demon name. "You get to help me carve out a new world order, one where the witches take our rightful place at the top."

"What's everyone's obsession with topping? It's so basic." Mora huffed. "And world domination? So pedestrian, Desmond."

"Enough," he yelled.

"I always knew you were adventitious, but I didn't realize your goals were so lofty." Mora sent a trickle of black lightning to her feet and through the floor, which she'd use to diffuse the threat.

But I couldn't chance it. These witches might've had more wards in place. More defenses at the ready to deflect such a simple strike. Mora's need to minimize the bloodshed would be our ends.

"No," I roared.

I zipped across the room, shattering the wall of orbs behind the coven leader, then turned my attention onto the witches themselves. They moved so slowly, each one lost in Desmond's smokey serpent that battled Kell's lavender mist. The sizzle of black lightning crackled against the concrete flooring. When glass burst in swift succession, the startle lowered their guards, and these feeble witches attempted to flee.

The instinct painted their faces, fear dripped from their pores, and confusion reverberated in their shaky bodies. Gods, I savored their dread, their anxiety, their immobility. It fueled me and pushed down the terror of someone daring to contain me in another orb.

"Never again," I growled.

And with that, I leapt so fast I barely found the time to take joy in the carnage. One by one, I tore apart the coven witches, bashing in skulls, ripping out hearts, slicing off arms to beat others with.

Crunch. Snap. Splosh. Splatter. Clink.

Bones breaking. Blood gushing. Glass crashing. A symphony of death.

The brutality was soothing. The agony as they shrieked brought comfort, even if their deaths were swift. A quick death was boring, certainly, but that boredom ate away at the anxiety in my chest. As the witches fell, they dropped their orbs, breaking the fragile items. Soon, I found myself cackling in unison with the wailing cries of anguish.

"Slaughter. Mayhem. Horror." I grabbed a young witch by the face and squeezed until her head popped with a beautiful crackle and bloody eruption. "Oh my!"

Wally shouted my name. Mora pestered about something. Kell won her battle with the smoke. But I blissfully ignored them, zipping from one location to another.

This coven actually believed they could contain a devil, that they could control an army of Diabolics, but they couldn't even keep up with the movements of one demon. I mean, a demon as grand and skilled as myself certainly made for a real challenge, but they had no spells at the ready. No wards to hinder my assault. No incantations to mend their injuries. No chance of survival. Kell's sorcery had unraveled the simple set of traps they'd lined and really left them completely vulnerable.

"Fools!" I shouted with gusto as I slapped a witch so hard his head spun around, and he toppled over onto one of his frightened friends who crawled away on the ground. Or tried until the dead weight pinned them and my foot crushed their lungs.

"You won't stop me from—"

I darted behind Desmond and jammed my clawed hand into his back, gripping his spine tight until his arrogant shouting twisted into a whimpering, begging screech.

"You talk too much, prick." I laughed as I ripped out his spine.

Wally and Mora screamed "no" at my actions. Not at the anguish on Desmond's face. Not at his bloody bone mixed with meaty bits of muscle that clung to the spine. Not at the blissful delight that came from the Diabolic orb he held shattering when it crashed onto the ground. No, they hollered for another loss.

The flame key copy Kell had created slipped between the fingers of the dying Desmond.

I went to snatch it up, but it fell away into the ether and vanished entirely. "Fuck."

19

Wally

When Bez killed the witches, I tried not to overreact. When Bez destroyed the Diabolic orbs—which could've proved pivotal in researching for counter plans to imminent threats—I tried not to overreact. When Bez literally let the one thing standing between Lilith and our dimension slip between his fingers, I didn't overreact.

I had a history of overreacting, overanalyzing, overthinking, and just over-fucking-whelmingly freaking out about things that didn't go accordingly!

But this last month, I told myself to take deep breaths every time I wanted to scream. Considering I no longer required breathing and finally stopped following the routines of built-in motor functions, I took a lot of breaths this month.

I rolled over, eyeing Bez as he slept comfortably in our bed, in our home, and in our little oasis because nothing bad had come…yet. I took a breath to exhale the million words of anxiety I wanted to spew.

Chances were Lilith died in her battle with Beelzebub. Or she would die. Or the flame key copy fizzled out to nothingness. Or the copy never would've worked because Kell didn't make it properly. Or a million other factors. None of the possibilities assuaged the morning dread of waking up to a new day. Every time my eyes opened, the clarity of reality sank back in, and anxiety clawed at my thoughts.

How could Bez snooze without a care in the world? He slept there with Weather on top of him, two heads nuzzling close for affection while Stormy secured Bez's arm as a pillow. Since returning to our world, he'd remained in his own skin, though moments like this, he'd keep his wings tucked inside his body, retracting the essence like a malleable putty to reshape when he awoke and stretched to shake away the night's sleep.

"You realize that's the only reason he's letting you sleep on the bed," I said to Weather. Sunny cocked his head, inquisitive and cheerful first thing in the morning. "He can't feel your two-hundred-pound butt and all the clingy head nuzzles."

It was weird. A positive sign, I guess, for Bez finally feeling comfortable in his own skin, but the disconnect from sensations sort of made everything he said and did this last month hollow. A hollow laughter. Hollow snark. Hollow passion. Just hollow.

"Or maybe I'm being dramatic."

Sunny yipped in agreement.

"You don't even know what I'm talking about."

Stormy growled as if to say I was always dramatic.

"Which I'm not." I pet Cloudy, the only pup in the house not to betray me for Bez's favor or consider me dramatic.

I needed to stop worrying about everything. Bez. Our world. My devil essence. Lilith.

I mean, she was just a devil. A world-shattering being. One devil who had contingencies for every possibility, including creating escape routes to worlds she deemed beneath her. Plus, one more devil who couldn't technically pass through Hell dimensions since I held a piece of his essence. A piece of Beelzebub, which he definitely wanted back. Returned. Refunded. Recounted in his audit of essence. He probably didn't do audits. I would. If I were a devil. Account for my being. But then again, I wouldn't feel like I needed to focus on bureaucracy if I were all-powerful. Maybe. Not that I'd know since I wasn't all-fucking-powerful, and there were currently two omnipotent beings circling our dimension like sharks.

Wrong. Sharks were sweet. Sweeter than folks realized, at least. Most people didn't understand their habits, their purpose, their—

Dammit.

This was my problem. I got so lost in the details that I often forgot about the… Well, the details.

I couldn't even look at Bez while he slept. Ignoring the problem. Pretending everything was fine. Perfectly content despite the looming destruction at our doorstep any day.

"Bez, you awake?" I asked, turning away from him, yet finding my tail had nudged him.

I might struggle to look at him when overthinking everything, but I still wanted to see him, talk to him, talk until the stress of the entire world faded away.

"I'm gonna head to work."

Work didn't alleviate my stress. It distracted me for pockets of time, a few seconds here when I found myself buried in an intricate artifact, a few minutes there when I got lost in the details of a relic, and then just a return to the gnawing fear of what might maybe possibly happen one day, someday.

It was awful. I didn't understand how people ignored looming threats and pretended they didn't exist. Not me. Not possible.

"I'm going to attempt another locator spell," I said to Tony as I brought out the list of items I'd re-cataloged—which had taken a lot longer than expected given my distractions plus the disorganized mess those witches had left everything in.

"Waste of time," Kell shouted from her back room, one where she'd kept the door open. A possible side effect of her own anxiety for thieves. However, she didn't vocalize it while acting as aloof as she normally did. So it was really just an inference on my part.

"I don't know." I grabbed a stack of books off the counter. "Tony's found some pretty useful texts."

Quite possibly the only person who supported my paranoia. Only Tony wasn't a person.

He clacked his claws. The familiar bond gave just a fraction of his thoughts, his wavelength of emotion, his empathy, his love.

I shrugged. "Close enough. Besides, being a person is overrated."

"The flame is made from essence; Diabolics can't be tracked," Kell continued. "You're wasting your time."

"Maybe." I carried the stack of books down the hallway. "Maybe not."

Usually, tracking demons, sensing their powers, was impossible. It proved beneficial when staying off The Collective's radar. It proved exhausting to locate demon threats on Baron Novus' villa. It turned out not to matter much here in the Diabolic Oasis where most everyone—conspiring witches aside—focused on a 'live and let live' philosophy.

But in Hell, essence worked differently. At least for me. Bez, too, it seemed. There were layers and sensations and a level of intricacy that functioned so much differently than anything I'd experienced. And that was through a filtered lens.

I'd felt and identified essence clearly while in Hell, understanding it in ways I never had before. Maybe if I found a way to tap into my abilities like I had before, then I could track down the flamed key copy, properly dispose of it, and finally put to rest all this fucking stress.

After lots of failed attempts to locate the flame key copy and research that led to more and more dead ends, I decided to take a break. While working out wasn't my go-to way to alleviate stress, I did find myself constantly wound up.

I made my way to the back of the store where Bez trained in the sparring room. He'd come in today. Not that he told me. Not that he planned on working. Not that we really did much of any work around the shop these days. We all sort of just existed on autopilot, doing stuff and doing nothing simultaneously.

It wasn't that I missed the constant training, but I missed Bez. I missed us being on the same page about things. His impulsive move had left a vacuum that turned into a huge, unsolvable obstacle. But right now, the biggest obstacle seemed to be conversation.

"Training?"

"I suppose." Bez used his tails to set up some fitness equipment.

He'd gone back to fully dressed suits even if he hadn't gone back to a human host. A lumbering demon body that always looked about one good stretch away from tearing apart his entire outfit. But the glimmer of his cufflinks told me the suit would be fine. I'd made those with an incantation meant to stitch his clothing when his wings or tails or even his claws shredded his wardrobe.

"Getting comfortable in your own skin?" I asked, playful and light and a little concerned about the distance between us. It was invisible and silent but looming all the same. "Would've expected you to possess someone new when we got back home. Maybe not right away. I know you're picky. And there was so much happening. But now there's this lull…"

"No lull," Bez whispered. "I feel the same dread and concern that's eating away at you."

I widened my eyes, really looking at him but not seeing the weight of stress and panic.

"When we returned, I worried there'd be a devil on our heels before we removed that damned flame key copy," Bez explained. "Then we lost it. I lost it. I foolishly—"

"Bez, it's not your fault."

"It is." He sighed. "And I keep waiting for a devil to swoop into this world and slaughter us all. Lilith on the run, somehow escaping. Beelzebub somehow exploiting the ajar door to Lilith's Hell. Sure, he's missing part of his essence. But an open door to Hell is much different than a sealed dimension."

My heart surged, almost instinctively searching for the rhythmic pace of Bez's. A fast beat he lacked in his demon body, but his voice registered elevated tension, fear.

"I figured Beelzebub would be especially motivated to finish his battle with Lilith and come track me down for daring to escape. For fleeing a battlefield like a coward. For stealing essence from my betters."

"Bez…" I stepped closer, hating the distance between us— literal and otherwise, but cautious because he looked a moment away from collapsing into the fear he kept hidden behind layers of snarky jokes and one-liner innuendos and ever-brave bravado.

He hated appearing weak, hated being vulnerable, hated being anything other than a protector.

"Is that why you're in your demon form? Does it make you stronger?" I asked, letting a small smile creep out. "I know sometimes you complain about the limitations of the mortal coil."

"I just don't wanna feel," he breathed the words like they were suffocating him, choking him on emotions he didn't very much care for acknowledging. "I don't deserve to feel the pleasures of the world. I don't wanna feel the pleasures when I'm in this much pain."

"Oh, Bez."

"I know you're worried they could arrive at any point," he continued. "Tomorrow, a year from now, a century away. It could be a thousand-year battle between Lilith and Beelzebub. It could take a million trips around the sun for the Earth. It could never happen at all. Perhaps they both killed each other. Maybe a scheming devil with wicked machinations sprang on the duel between former supreme rulers, pounced upon them, and brought an end to their reigns."

"You think that's possible?"

"That's the problem." He sighed. "Anything's possible. For all we know, the doors to Hell have been closed off. We could look. I could send my essence out, skulk between the layers of different dimensions, and check."

"Why don't you?"

"I'm afraid to see the answer," he said with a slight tremble in his voice. "It's my fault. My impulsivity."

"It's not your fault."

"It is, Walter." Bez turned away. "I was afraid of being trapped again inside an orb. Forgotten. Forever."

"You will never be forgotten." I kissed the space between his shoulders, soft and gentle. Bez didn't move, didn't react. He just stood there, his wings hanging low and somber. I spun him to face me. "Please don't dwell on what happened. Let's just focus on the now."

"There's no fixing the now."

"I've got ideas. Percolating."

"Such as?" He cocked his head.

"Not saying because you never listen to my rambles anyway." I teased.

He kissed me, sloppy and wet and with teeth, obnoxious and playful and somehow so fucking hot. Then he nibbled on my lower lip, the one I wanted to bite now just so I wouldn't talk, wouldn't ramble, but he already knew how to shut me up.

"I listen to every annoying word that you utter, you beautifully insufferably addictive man."

Bez kissed me again. In seconds, we'd gone from playful to frisky to engulfed in a passionate make-out session.

He grinded against me, the heat of his body burning hotter with each kiss. I found myself lost in his touch, the way he ran his clawed hands down my sides, the smack of his lips against mine as he squeezed my ass, the thrust of his hips as he pushed me back.

I expected him to shove me several feet across the room, stopped only by the wall where he'd pin me in place, but my wings stretched, flapped once, and braced our position. A gale of black wind circled us, adding to the chaotic passion of each kiss.

"Pity I have to pause." Bez pressed his forehead against mine, bracing a bit of distance between our mouths.

"What?" I reached out with my lips, trying to meet his. "It was just getting good."

"Yes, but…"

"But what?" I ran my hands between the fabric of his pants. He'd gone to wearing loose-fitting stretch slacks since his waist had doubled in circumference now that he stayed in his demon form.

"I know, but I wanna feel you."

"Oh, duh." I turned so suddenly, my horn hit his with a loud clink. "Sorry about that. The not realizing you can't feel in this form—not the hitting your horn thing. But sorry about that too. It was an accident."

"No worries." He gently kissed me again.

"Mmm. Tease."

"Plus, I don't wanna break you."

"Break me?" I quirked a brow.

"It's a lot more to handle." Bez ran his fanged teeth against my neck, making me quiver with anticipation for more. He could break me again and again if he wanted. I'd gladly give myself to him in this form. "So, I need to go find a body. Slip into a mortal condom, so to speak."

"Ewwww." I cringed, shaking my head like it'd somehow erase the comment from my brain. "Don't say it like that."

"I know, I know." Bez bucked his hips against mine. "You're a bareback boy through and through but for the sake of your butt— lemme go slip into someone more comfortable."

"You really think I can't handle you?"

"Cocky." Bez smirked. "And as tempting as it'd be to break you, make you eat those words along with my cock, I wish to feel you whimper beneath as I rail you, so alas, I need to dress up."

"Shame." I squeezed his clawed hand, desiring more than anything to feel him inside me and wishing he could feel me this instant. Feel my passion. My lust. My love. My everything. He elicited it all, leaving me hungry and craving him more and more each day.

"Wally." Bez tilted his head, staring at my tail, which traced an incantation.

What?

My body tensed, anticipating a threat. My essence always reacted when danger arrived. But there was usually a sinking pit in my stomach, a sensation of my Diabolic power heating up and spreading across my entire body with a wave.

That didn't hit. The only sensation I got was a slight static shock in my hand and a jolt at the sudden explosion of the incantation.

"Fuck." Bez jerked his hand away from mine. "That stung."

"It what?"

"Wally, what'd you do?"

"I don't know." I shrugged. "I wanted you to feel this. Really feel this. And then…"

And then my essence made it happen. I filled in the gaps without sharing my thousand-fold theories because, somehow, my desire to help Bez feel in his demon form worked. My magic and essence combined to conjure some spell, some unknown layer of reality, some wonderful experience for Bez.

Bez grabbed my face, cupping my jaw between his hands, and pulled me into a kiss. A kiss where he tasted me, felt the push and pull of my lips and tongue and body. We'd gone from testing the motions to savoring every sensation in seconds.

"I'm gonna ravish you." Bez wrapped his wings and tails around me, dragging me to the floormat with a heavy thud.

He kissed me every moment, rolling around together and somehow undressing us just as quickly. He wasn't kidding about ravishing me. His lips tasted every inch of my skin, peeling off my clothes until I somehow lay face down in tattered threads with Bez's tongue sliding down my crack and teasing my hole.

I moaned, quivering at how he played and lapped and breathed, each eliciting a deeper arch in my lower back.

"I forgot how good you taste." He slapped my cheeks and spread them far apart, but when I expected him to trace his tongue on my hole, he grazed his teeth against my ass and bit down.

I whimpered, and he relented, kissing and licking and slapping the cheek again for good measure.

"Fuck." I trembled.

He went back to burying his tongue in my hole, caressing my skin, shoving my face further into the floor with his tails. And then Bez had gone and flipped me over onto my back again.

I groaned, muttering profanities as the ecstasy of his touch simmered. "Why'd you stop?"

"Because the perfect meals should be evenly cooked."

I snorted at the absurdity of the comment. "Was that supposed to be sexy? Bez, I mean, funny, sure, but sexy is—"

He swallowed the entirety of my cock, leaving me a flabbergasted, moaning mess.

I lay there, fully enveloped by the warmth of his mouth and the practiced touch of his fingers, which found their way inside me. I moved my arms, not to control Bez's head—why control the perfect motion? No. I wanted to prop myself up. Sit and bask in the pleasure of Bez sucking me off. But he wrapped a tail around each of my biceps and throat, pulling me down and pinning me in place. When my tail switched defensively, he teased it, taunted, distracted, and left me a blurred mess.

Bez gurgled, his throat making this noise that added to the blowjob, made every nerve on my cock swell.

I tried to bite my knuckle, to hold back my panting moan, but Bez didn't relent. His tails kept me in place as he played with my cock and brought me closer and closer and closer until I couldn't help but shout.

"Wait!" My hips thrust instinctively, seeking satisfaction, seeking completion.

I came down Bez's throat, hips twitching. He didn't relent, sucking and holding the entirety of my throbbing cock in his mouth.

"Bez," I whined.

Finally, he released me, letting me pant uncontrollably beneath him as he stood to his feet.

"Oh, Wally, save your breath." Bez unfastened his slacks. "You'll be screaming my name soon enough."

20

Wally stared in awe as I slid my pants down. I used the tail around his throat, the only one I kept around him, to pull him forward. He crawled toward me, obedient when leashed and completely subservient to my needs because even before I told him what to do, he went to work on my dick.

It would take him a moment to adjust; he knew this much based on how quickly he started playing with the head of my cock, so I savored the moment. He licked and teased and stretched his jaw wider every time he shoved the head in his mouth. Little by little, he gauged how much he could fit in his mouth. All the while, he stroked my long, thick shaft with both his hands.

"You want it all, don't you, you greedy boy?"

He moaned in response, taking in another inch before pulling back as his face blushed.

I undid my tie and stripped off my shirt, standing fully nude while Wally bobbed his head back and forth on the tip of my dick.

"You're gonna have to work harder, Wally." I grabbed a handful of his curls and shoved his head down.

He gagged, his throat bulging at the suddenness of my cock pushed deeper than he expected. His body jerked away, held in place by the fact I had his head.

"Come on now." I lightly smacked his face, pumping my hips at the same time. "You talked such a big game, Wally."

He grabbed my hips and braced himself. I went to relent, recognizing this as a sign he'd use when he couldn't ask or speak or tell me to ease. But Wally didn't back away. In fact, he leaned forward when I backstepped, keeping my cock deep in his throat as he choked, spit drooling down his face the entire time.

"Fuck, you're such a hungry boy, aren't you?" I pulled his head back, forcing him to breathe free without my cock. "Tastes so good, doesn't it?"

He panted, then wiped tears from his eyes, and prepared to say yes, to concur, to beg for my dick back, so I generously obliged.

I rammed my cock all the way back into his throat and savored the sweet satisfaction of his gurgles as he swallowed it all the way to the base. Once his jaw stretched to his limits, I bucked and moved at a steady pace.

Wally looked up at me as I fucked his mouth. Gods, the way tears welled up, the way he gagged and his back curled up with a need to stop, but he pressed on, craving my pleasure and taking my dick so damn well.

"When I'm done with this hole, I gonna revisit your ass."

He gulped and slobbered on my dick in response.

I shoved his head back and forth, making him bob from tip to base until the throbbing that came from enveloping his tight throat nearly made me explode.

It was a new level of pleasure feeling Wally, truly feeling Wally. Our entire relationship, there'd been this layer of film between us, so thin that I didn't notice it. Didn't realize how much distance had truly existed between what I perceived Wally felt like versus what he actually felt like. I wanted to explore it all. I wanted to feel him. I wanted to taste every inch of his body. The sweet and salty of his skin. I wanted to kiss his lips again and again. I wanted to shove my cock, my tongue, my fingers in all of his holes and watch him whimper.

"Off." I pulled his head back and pushed him to the floor.

When he went to sit up, I used a tail to knock him back down, then flipped him onto his stomach.

"Arch."

He obeyed, spreading his legs into position and arching his back with his head and chest on the floor and his ass raised at my preferred height.

I knelt and smacked his ass, the same cheek I'd been playfully abusing since I first started working him over. The light bite mark of my fangs had left lovely red indents, and the cheek itself was bright and oh-so-shocked in comparison to his pasty right cheek.

"I'll have to even this out as I rail you, Wally." I squeezed his butt as I repositioned him.

While he learned how to position himself to my liking, he knew that based on my mortal form. I stood taller now, even on my knees. I needed to line him up differently to truly enjoy the feel of his ass.

Once I had him how I wanted, I lubed his hole and shoved my cock right inside.

"Ah." He gasped.

Before instinct pulled him away, I laid the full weight of my body on top of him, brushing his hair as he whined. Slowly, I let gravity assist, and my entirety filled him. Wally continued to whimper as he adjusted to my girth inside him, every added inch pushed further than he'd grown accustomed to.

"Bez." He moaned.

"That's not the scream I was planning on." I continued remaining motionless, allowing him another minute with just my cock inside him. "Do you wish for me to stop?"

He shook his head.

"Do you wish for me to begin?"

He nodded.

"Are you ready?"

He nodded.

I began slowly pumping my hips while we lay there on the floor. Each time I moved just a bit faster, studying the rhythmic whines I elicited each time. There was a beautiful pattern to Wally's noises of pain and pleasure and panting.

Soon, I found myself arching upward, hands pressed on his back between the joints of his shoulders where his adorable little wings shivered. My tails kept his pinned and writhing as I fucked Wally faster and harder.

He screamed, and I rammed my fingers into his mouth, hooking him like a fish as I pounded away.

"You feel so good." I couldn't stop myself, relishing the way he sent waves of pleasure through my entire body. "Fucking take it. Take it all."

He whimpered as he sucked on my fingers, then I pulled my hand away and jerked his head back, turning him to kiss me.

I wrapped my arms around his chest and stomach and thrust faster, harder, and when he yelled, I swallowed every sound with tender kisses.

Every time I pumped into him, I found myself needing more. Our skin was slick with sweat, sticking together. I never wanted it to end. I wanted more.

"I can't help myself," I growled between kisses.

I pinned my arms over Wally, biting his nape and ramming deeper inside him. Wally gasped, buckling beneath me. He lay there taking my cock. More. More. More.

“I want more.”

Continuing, I lifted off him some, pulling him into a further arch by squeezing his flexed biceps and pulling them back. With his tail more obedient, perhaps under Wally's control, I released one of mine and used it to tie Wally's arms behind his back as I pounded away.

Eventually, I pulled out and flipped him onto his back, his arms uncomfortably pinned behind him as I spread his legs and slipped between them. I enjoyed the shift in Wally's expression. The tension when I pushed the head of my cock back into him. The contorted pain of each inch he took. The way it crumbled away and his face melted into something of pleasure once he finally readjusted to my dick again.

I watched every inch pull out to the tip before I shoved it back to the base. Such a satisfying sight to fill his hole again and again while he whimpered and writhed, taking it.

“Look how hard you are.” I ran my hand over his twitching cock; each thrust brought him closer and closer. I wouldn't even need to touch him, but I wanted to stroke him to completion. I wanted to feel his cock explode. And I did. Three quick tugs, and he came, hips spasming a moment as he shot long pearl strands along his chest and torso.

I played with his flaccid cock, loving the feel of it shrinking in my hand as some of the remaining cum slicked my fingers and made milking him a bit further all the easier.

Part of me wanted to stroke him hard again, make him beg all over, dragging out this pleasure over and over until he couldn't move. But already, I could see his eyes glazed in satisfaction, content, and seeking me to finish.

I hugged him tight, kissing him, licking his neck, nibbling on his skin, and all the while ramming him again and again, harder each time. Every stroke brought me closer and closer until, finally,

I buried myself all the way in and burst. I bit down on his shoulder, tasting him as I filled his hole with my seed.

"Fuck." I growled, laying on top of him and breathing in unison with his panting for the sheer satisfaction of sharing this synchronized moment. "Gimme ten, and let's go for round two. Got to make up for the last month."

"I'm gonna need more than ten." He quivered beneath me, gathering himself.

"Guess I can give you fifteen."

"Bez." He huffed.

"Fine."

I didn't resist Wally's push when he repositioned us into a spooning cuddle. Normally, I'd allow him to be the big spoon. There was something satisfying in being held, being embraced and given that affectionate comfort. But he was clearly worn out and craved his own comfort, so I held him gingerly, scooting in tight and nuzzling my face into the crook of his neck.

We rested here for hours together, and I loved every second of it. I wanted more seconds. Always more when it came to Wally. I wanted all the time. Forever and then a little bit longer because I was greedy for him.

"I love you, Wally." I kissed his neck.

"I love you, too, Bez." He squeezed my hand and pulled it close to his lips for a gentle peck.

How I wanted to ensure we'd have more time. More of this. More sweet cuddles. More fucking until he collapsed. More love. More forevers.

If I wanted those mores, then I needed to fix what I ruined. I needed to ensure Lilith and Beelzebub were truly gone and lost to the universe. I needed to make sure her Hell was locked and every secretive escape route was snuffed out of existence.

21

Wally

We lay together on the floor. Bez teased me with his tails, fingertips tickling my skin, and his mouth kissing and licking and tasting. There was nothing more satisfying than getting fucked by a big bad demon who loved you. But damn, I was tired. I had no energy for his attempt at coaxing me into another round. My throat was sore, too sore to talk to Bez or make snippy comments. My ass was tired, too tired to buck against his hardening dick that he already positioned like a fucking torpedo—quite literally, it seemed. My every muscle was spent to its limit, my essence circulating to compensate for the exhaustion.

So, I ignored Bez's intentionally provocative gestures, forcing him to cuddle.

"How's the search for the flame key copy coming along?" he asked.

"Eh." I shrugged, scooching closer against him in the process.

Bez tiptoed his claws against my tender flesh, then traced his fingertips along the sculpted parts of my muscles. "I can help if you like."

"Feels like a pointless endeavor."

"Oh." His hand stopped, and he retreated a bit, so I turned over and scooted in close again, wrapping my leg over his and coiling my tail from his ankles to thighs, which pretty much kept him snuggly stuck beside me.

I went to kiss him, to tease him, to cuddle him into submission or surrender, but Bez's crimson eyes had turned glossy.

It hurt him. Not the stranglehold on his legs, but my comment, my casual disregard for his help, help he wanted to offer for a problem he blamed himself for. He held onto this like it was his fault.

He didn't make Lilith an enemy. He didn't provoke the witches. He didn't develop the idea of copying the key to begin with. All he did was panic when an enemy unveiled a weapon that could trap him like it had once before. A modified weapon, in fact, one which would extract essence. One which claimed to be powerful enough to contain an actual devil. One that…

"Wait a damned second!"

"I wasn't doing anything." Bez adjusted his dick, which was hard again, and slapped against mine, using the greased lube to begin rubbing them together. "That's just physics, Walter."

"What? No. Not you." I side-eyed him. "Although, you're not fucking me right now. You're not fucking me for a good minute or seven hundred minutes, in fact."

He crinkled his forehead, mouthing the math as he counted on his fingers.

"It's like half a day," I answered. "A full day being 1440 minutes, just a fun fact. But also, a full day in the Diabolic Oasis is actually only 1402 minutes, so that's an interesting extrapolation to account for when traveling between worlds."

Bez blinked several times slowly, utterly confused.

"I had an epiphany. Such an overused phrase, but also, I did reach actual clarity when it comes to our problem."

"Yes?"

"We're focused on the key, the idea that it might be a way for Lilith to escape into our world."

Bez cast his gaze downward like a sad puppy.

"We're under the assumption that the key copy works," I continued. "And under the assumption that Corson found and removed the other copies."

"Unlikely, he's a damn moron," Bez said with an arrogant attitude true to form and giving me the gift of my charmingly hostile boyfriend back.

"Exactly," I said. "We should focus less on ensuring Lilith can't find a way into our world and more on how to deal with her *if* she finds her way into our world."

"Dying seems the most obvious thing to plan for."

"Okay, that's an outcome, not a plan. You don't plan for death." I grimaced. "Well, I suppose you do if you're given a head's up. Which we've technically been given, but not really because we know it'll happen. Just not when it'll happen. Which sort of ties into what everyone knows about death. Everyone's aware it'll happen one day, someday, yet everyone's baffled when it strikes. That opens a whole can of existential proverbial worms, which isn't really what I was talking about, but it's also an important—"

"Walter." Bez snapped his fingers close to my face like pulling me from a daze. "You're rambling. You had an epiphany. Now, deep breath, and exhale all the tangents before sharing your idea."

"Right." I followed his advice and let all the tiny thoughts brewing in my brain fizzle away so I could focus. "We've been focusing on trying to stop Lilith from entering our world. I mean, we've been hoping she's dead but also paranoid she's got some escape plan at the ready. We can't prevent what we're unaware of. However, we can plan for her arrival."

"And how exactly do we do that?"

"We just need the Diabolic orb that can contain a devil."

"First of all, I destroyed those orbs."

"You broke it." I shoulder-bumped him. "Broken things can be restored."

"You are an expert at fixing broken things."

"I can't tell if that's a jab and me or you."

"Six of one, half a dozen of the other."

"Anyway—"

"Second of all"—Bez dramatically cleared his throat—"we have no idea if such a device exists."

"Yes, we do. The witches told us."

"Just because some witch told us doesn't make it true."

"Why would he lie?" I asked. "He planned on using the flame key right then and there to bring in Lilith."

"A fallacy and a lie are not one and the same, Walter."

I huffed. Damn, that was somewhat valid.

"There are people who profess the devil is an angel who reigns over Hell—one singular location, such nonsense—and this devil man assigns demons to torment mortals for all eternity, poking them with pitchforks for being naughty on earth." Bez twisted his face into a sour, judgy expression where he pouted his lips and scrunched his forehead. "People say lots of absurd things they believe to be truth."

"Maybe we just need a little faith."

"Did you hit your head?" Bez asked. "Are you practicing life as a jester?"

"I just don't want to be idle, not when I could do something."

"Okay. What's your plan then?"

"I think we should start by asking the expert in question."

"Expert?"

I grinned, a little giddy at the idea. "The coven leader who made these modified Diabolic orbs in the first place."

"The one I murdered?" Bez nodded affirmingly. "That may pose to be a problem."

"Not with a little dark magic and a doggo pup specifically bred to contain the souls of the dead and damned."

I expected to be more hands-on during this part. Especially since the whole plan hinged on my idea. Mora brought Weather, who spent the whole time seeking approval from Bez, so when I instructed his placement, the pup ignored me until Bez snapped his fingers, prompting Weather's obedience. All the while, Kell turned me into an errand boy, sending me from the stockroom to the front displays to the boxed-up goods we hadn't even accounted for yet. Always sending me to grab just one more thing while she set up a ritualized summoning circle meant to bring forth the souls of the dead.

"You know, I've actually done a lot of research on necromancy," I said. "I'm pretty sure you shouldn't be inverting those symbols."

"They do a lot of soul raising in the Collective?"

"No, but I'm telling you based on—"

"Since only one of us has actually raised the dead, maybe you follow my directive."

"Okay. I see you're skipping around the steps," I said, not-so-quietly judging the messy spell work.

Casting a quality spell was like baking. It needed to be properly measured and accounted for. She hadn't even gotten to Weather's role yet.

I had actually dug up my old essays on forbidden magics when we got Weather. It turned out I had a lot of solid notes on the Mythic species, which I'd hoped would help in properly raising him. But that was useless since he only ever listened to Bez, anyway.

Tony skittered through my hair, nestling again. A gentle reminder that I didn't need Weather, the beast my familiar merely tolerated. Tony was my companion while Weather was Bez's pet.

"Bet you haven't done this with the assistance of a Cerberus." I folded my arms, ready and waiting for her to ask about Weather's role.

"Oh, sweet Wally. I don't need a Cerberus. Just an ingredient or two." Kell raised a hand toward Weather. "Come."

"You want my dog to cum?" Bez cocked his head. "Pervert."

"Shut up." She scoffed, then snapped her fingers until Sunny led the way forward, sniffing her hand.

Kell pet each of Weather's heads, giving Sunny lots of pats, giving Cloudy head scrunchies, and delicately avoiding heavy affection when stroking Stormy's chin. In the process, Kell pulled off a thread of fire from each of their manes. Magically, she weaved the red, blue, and purple flames together and placed them in a jar.

"It's not my first dance with the dead." Kell smiled, smug and so annoyingly versed in all the spells I'd only ever considered hypothetical.

"Are you sure about this, sweetie?" Mora asked, eyes fixated on the flicker of the flame jar in front of Kell. "Didn't Maurice's ex nearly set you on fire the last time you did this?"

"Why are you always getting set on fire?" I snorted. "Maybe I really should be the one casting this spell."

"She said *almost*." Kell rolled her eyes. "Thank you very much."

"Just making an observation since you're quite combustible," I teased.

"He makes a valid point, hun." Mora nodded toward me.

"It's irrelevant." Kell waved a dismissive hand. "I've got an actual Cerberus, so if the flames act up, this good boy right here will keep me safe."

Sunny barked in agreement, tail wagging faster.

"That's right," Kell said with a baby voice. "Who's a good boy? Yes, you're a good boy. Such a good boy. The best boy, huh?"

"Don't deceive him," Bez said, adjusting the sleeve of his dress shirt. "He's an adequate boy most days."

Sunny grumbled and lowered his head with disappointment.

"Wait, which ex?" Bez asked, a hand pressed under his chin to appear musing while he used his tails to pet and soothe Weather. "Not the one I gutted, right? That guy was a bag of dicks."

"Who really knows." Mora shrugged. "That boy's got a higher body count in the bedroom than victims he drained dry."

Maurice was one of Mora's many host bodies that she'd alternate between possessing. An old vampire, in fact. One who Bez apparently had a colorful history with.

Kell finished lining up the last of magical gems and bones necessary around the summoning circle she put together and began her ritual, speaking a mix of ancient languages, both mortal and Mythic, as she evoked the spirits of the other side. It cast shadows across the store, curious lost souls eager to lunge on this summoning, intercept it, and interfere for their own possible gains. But the candles placed around burned brighter until all the wax disappeared, replaced by an aura of vibrant colors dancing around the room. This kept the unwanted away while casting a guiding beacon to the one Kell summoned.

Every word Kell uttered carried a drumbeat that sounded all around us. Weather's ears perked up, heads turning in every direction as he sniffed the magic in the shop.

The inverted symbols Kell traced on the floor lifted up, forming something tangible. They fluttered around us like fall leaves.

She grabbed the jar, pouring the flames out. Red, blue, and purple fire spilled onto the floor. They splashed embers in every direction. One by one, those sparks clung to the floating symbols, lighting them up and adding a fiery spiral of colors to the vibrant aura already in effect.

Bones rattled, adding to the magical drumbeat. A few exploded to dust, merging with the fiery ashes of the symbols.

Sunny tried to grab a floating femur bone but was halted by Bez, who used his tail as a leash to pull Weather back.

Fire whirled in an inferno, sweltering but contained, shrinking as quickly as it erupted. It formed into a human silhouette, fire swelling in and out like lungs breathing heavily until they poofed into smoke, and the ashes fell around the room like snowfall.

"Welp." Kell brushed her hands, knocking away soot. "Hope you had a plan B because we won't be summoning Desmond from the dead."

"Lemme try," I insisted.

"Wally, there is no trying. It's not a competition on which of us is better at casting." Kell flipped her hair and shot me a cocky smirk. "But to be clear, it's obvious that I'm the better spellcaster."

"So you say, I'm telling you if you just follow the directions appropriately then—"

"Nature has claimed him and his coven," Kell clarified. "She's got them bound in the deepest trenches of the earth. And if I know anything about the goddess—which I know everything about her— she won't be sharing the souls of that coven until she feels they've learned whatever lessons she deems appropriate."

"Which would be?"

"Who really knows with her." Kell tsked. "Fickle bitch."

"Dammit." I sighed. "Guess that's that, then."

I really thought this might've worked, might've helped, might've taken the weight of the unknown off my shoulders, off Bez's.

"Maybe we can put the orbs back together ourselves."

"I do love projects," Kell said. "Might take a century or two of tinkering, but we're bound to figure out all that Fae and Diabolic balance and the medley of whatevers Baron Novus used."

Baron Novus would be the real expert opinion here. But like all things involving the Fae, even their spirits remained elusive and impossible for anyone to track.

"There might be another expert you can summon."

I quirked a brow. "Who?"

"Asshat Remington," Bez breathed the name with contempt. "Not sure he'd know how to fix an orb, but he didn't just keep me on the mantle as a trophy. On occasion, when alone, he'd tinker with the device. I assumed he was ensuring I couldn't escape the artifact, but knowing Abe, he was probably trying to figure out the Fae magics involved."

I didn't know what to say, how to express my apologies for his experience, my thanks for sharing this for the sake of my outlandish idea. Magus Remington trapped Bez and held him locked away inside a Diabolic orb for nearly fifty years. He was responsible for so much pain and isolation in Bez's life; he fueled Bez's mistrust of mortals and the mortal world.

But as much as I despised Remington's betrayal, his actions, that damned orb that held Bez for so long, I couldn't help but be grateful for it all. That horror put our paths together. The coup that nearly led to my death several times over properly introduced me to Bez.

22

Bez

I seethed as the smoke and fire breathed in and out, taking the form of Abraham Remington. Flames trickled away from his body, delicately flickering around the summoning circle. He wasn't the decrepit mage who'd withered toward the end of his mortal coil before being struck down during the coup meant to overthrow the Collective regime in Seattle. No, this Abe took on the form of his youth. The sweet smile he shot me with his boyish face was as wicked and deceitful as it was the first day I'd met him.

"Beelzebub, aren't you quite the sight." He ran a hand through his wavy blond hair. "You always did wear a suit well."

My demon body didn't even faze him.

"Well, well, well, Walter, too?" Abe eyed Wally up and down, studying his muscular body, the one he'd grown into since leaving his station in the archives. "Something's different. Did you get contacts?"

"Diabolic essence." Wally shrugged.

"Easier than Lasik, I suppose." Abe nodded approvingly. Sickening. "You look better than the last time I saw you."

"You too. Younger and less impaled," Wally retorted, not missing a beat. Good for him.

"Yes, well, the afterlife is far more relaxing than all the decades I served at the helm as Magus." Abe smirked, arrogant in a way I rarely saw except when alone with him in the archives, when not pretending civility in front of his mage rabble, when not feigning empathy for Mythic plights, when not tricking me into feeling for him.

I turned away, wishing to slaughter Abe's spirit here and now by any method possible. But my impulsivity had already cost us once. I needed to swallow my rage, my regrets, my hatred and allow Wally a chance to discover answers.

"I do hope your mother is fairing well with the position," Abe said nonchalantly, which only made Wally's shocked inhale sharper and louder.

"You knew she was behind the coup?"

"Of course. Keep your enemies close and all that nonsense." Remington chuckled. "Who do you think tipped her off about Ian? If she were ever going to make a move, she needed the right piece on the board."

"You're a fool, Abe." I spun around and spat my words. "You overplayed your hand and died!"

He locked his gaze with me, unblinking, expression stone, then he smiled and released a carefree shrug. "You win some, you lose some."

He had never looked so calm, so at ease, so free. That fucking piece of garbage! He tricked me into waging a war, he professed feelings for me, he manipulated my every thought, and then locked me away inside an orb so he could show me off like some damned trophy. And now—now he gets to find peace in death! It wasn't fair!

"Oh, Beelzebub, you look flustered," Abe said, turning his attention to Wally. "Does he still crinkle his forehead when he finds himself incapable of a proper retort? It was truly the cutest little expr—"

"Silence." Wally held up a small gem that he had removed from the assortment Kell had placed around her summoning circle.

The flames raged high, tightening around the small space provided to Abe.

"Do you know what happens to a soul that burns up to ashes?"

Abe shook his head but remained silent as the fire licked at his translucent skin.

"No?" Wally asked. "That's because no one knows. So, I suggest you don't fuck around unless you wanna find out."

My entire body warmed, and it wasn't the inferno Wally waved around, threatening Abe with. No, it was the steady command in Wally's voice, the cold threat without an ounce of hesitation, the remorselessness in his eyes. Whenever he got like this, murderous and vengeful, I found myself lost in the pure bliss it brought.

It would take everything I had not to mount him here and now.

"And don't think the fire is a one-and-done kind of thing; please understand how the spiritus stones work." Wally held up the ruby. "These are fueled by ancient magics and currently fueled by a witch's spell to enact the summoning." He nodded toward Kell, who remained in a trance-like state during the necromancy ritual. "However, when I add my mana to it or alter the frequency of the casting in even the slightest way, it risks spirit damage. Irreversible damage. Agonizing pain you'll carry in your soul until the end of time.

"Fine, fine, no need for the theatrics." Abe gestured his surrender.

"Now that we have your attention, I have a few questions."

"Honestly, if you wanted to torture me for information, you should've just started up with lectures first." Abe huffed. "Nothing more grating than listening to you drone on about bullshit no one cares about."

That hurt Wally. Visibly stung him because, in all his time working in the archives, he'd only found two people willing to listen to him discuss his findings: an unwilling demon trapped in an orb and the magus who always conversed so delightfully when presented with Wally's research. To learn it was all an act, a lie, a façade meant merely to elicit what Abe sought... I understood Wally's pain in a way much, much worse.

"I've never experienced Hell, but I imagine it's a lot like Walter's lectures." Abe laughed. "Must be why Beelzebub enjoys your company so."

I growled.

"Oh, relax. It's merely a joke."

"You studied the Diabolic orbs, correct?"

"I might've had a book or two noting my research."

"Really?" Wally asked wide-eyed. "Did you ever learn of their origins?"

"You're asking if I know about the Fae manipulation?" Abe scoffed. "The audacity they thought they could turn Abraham Remington into a meager case study."

Wally and I simply stared. He didn't know about the specifics. About Baron Novus.

"The Fae were discreetly revealing these contraptions to mages, witches, other skillfully magical beings. Nothing based in intellect." He eyed Weather.

Sunny yapped. Cloudy huffed. Stormy growled. I petted his heads with my tails to calm the little beast. He wasn't base in intellect; he was the smartest Cerberus out there.

"You didn't even learn of Baron Novus' involvement?" Wally asked. "This is useless. He knows even less about the Diabolic orbs than we do."

"Send him back." I shooed Abe's spirit. "We'll fix the orbs another way."

"Baron Novus? Is that the Fae behind the orbs? Never learned a name or a motive. But I did find several of the Diabolic orbs scattered across our world." Abe raised his eyes. "Learned quite a few things. Even how to restore them. Might've jotted that down in a book or two."

"Liar." I barred my teeth.

"Not a lie. Needed to prepare for any possibility of your escape. Also, my hope was to eventually find a way to harness your essence while keeping you bound to the orb itself. Pity."

The same thing those damned witches wanted. Power hunger mortals and Mythics always searching for a way to exploit Diabolics.

"Despite everything you learned, you never knew that fairy whispered commands in your head, urged you onto this mission," I snapped. "You were just a puppet, Abe. A useless puppet who played his part."

"Aah, so you're wondering if my actions were a result of the Fae's suggestive whispers? Everyone in authority knows the Fae manipulate from the shadows. Only weak-willed fools fall prey to their intrusive thoughts." Abe rocked his head disapprovingly. "I'd been researching ways to contain, control, or kill a devil the day you stepped into Seattle. This Fae noble you speak of merely provided a tool to trap an even easier tool."

I snarled.

"Back to your books," Wally said, an edge in his voice. "What'd they say about repairs?"

"How am I supposed to know?" Abe scoffed. "Unlike some people, I don't sit around memorizing every word I've read so that I can parade trivial facts about as if it'll make for an interesting conversation starter." Abe smirked at Wally. "I actually know how to make small talk."

"Knew," Wally corrected. "Past tense. Because you're dead."

"Still the life of every party I attend." He pointed around the store. "Case and point."

"Where is the book? The one with your notes?"

"Went missing some time ago." Abe's eyes shifted around the room, landing on Mora, who'd propped herself on a stool with her legs kicked up on the front counter. "Mora Mayfaire, always so lovely no matter who you're wearing."

"Remington." She smacked her lips together, applying a fresh coat of gloss as she prioritized redoing her makeup during the ritual.

"If the rumors are true, you found your way into my private studies on more than one occasion."

"Idle gossip." Mora ignored us all, staring at her reflection.

"Much like the rumors you were, in fact, a demon."

Mora popped her lips a few times. "I swear, the things people will lie about. It's criminal."

"Mora, did you steal Abe's research?" I asked.

"What part of idle gossip did you not understand? I can't be responsible for every rumor."

I sighed. "Those books might have the intel we need to repair the Diabolic orbs."

"Oh. Why didn't you say that?" Mora kicked her legs off the counter and strutted around to the back. "Pretty sure they're in Kell's Spring Fling hat."

Mora rifled through the box of witches' hats and grabbed one covered bright pastels.

"Why exactly were you stealing Abe's research to begin with?" I asked.

"I told you, Bezzy," Mora said, rummaging through the hat and throwing Kell's trinkets onto the floor. "I always keep tabs on those studying Diabolics."

"Yes, those wild rumors claimed she even tried to break into my archives once or twice."

"Might've been curious to see behind the curtain."

"Certainly. It was first how Morax…sorry, Mora landed on my radar. Learning the witch Mayfaire fancied a certain Diabolic artifact in my possession," Abe said, so smug and arrogant. "Not that she ever came close to it."

Mora's eyes flitted emerald green momentarily, proving Abe had even weaseled his way under her skin, so much so her demon essence glowed beneath her flesh. Once the aggravation passed and the green of her veins disappeared, she resumed her search for the stolen books.

I simply smiled. Mora cared. Even if she pretended otherwise. At this point, it didn't matter what Abe said or did. He was dead and gone and would be forgotten as quickly as he'd arrived.

"Have fun dealing with Abraham." I used my tails to lead Weather out. "Gonna take the dog for a run. He's been stuck pint-sized for far too long and needs to properly stretch his muscles."

"Something you can't do because you're dead," Mora quickly spat at Abe as if she needed recompense for his cutting comments.

"Oh, Beelzebub. I didn't hurt your feelings, did I?"

"Have a fun rest of your afterlife, Abe. May your spirit shuffle off quickly so I can enjoy my eternity." I waved goodbye to Wally and headed out the door.

"I'll come find you when we have answers." Wally squeezed the gem. "If we get answers."

"The confidence. It looks good on you, Wally. Shame you never found it when it mattered, when you had career prospects," Abe taunted—taunted because he was dead, and all he could do now was gloat.

I could strike his spirit, send him off to nothingness, return his soul to whatever peaceful slumber he received despite being an utter cunt, but impulsivity would only harm Wally, myself, and the rest of the mortal world.

I flew alongside Weather for the evening, hurling fireballs for him to catch until the giant slobbering beast panted with each step. We managed a few laps from one end of the Diabolic Oasis to the other before I wore the hound out, so we casually strolled back to the Well of Wonders. Not that I had any intention of returning until they were done with Abe's intel. But if I didn't get Weather somewhere to rest soon, I'd be stuck carrying him over my shoulder all the way home. Not a hiking trip I intended on repeating for myself.

Cloudy lowered his huge head, whimpering and attempting to rub his head against mine.

"Don't even think about it." I pointed. "Size."

Weather bapped his collar, enacting the sigils that Wally had placed. It shrank the Cerberus to his pup size, making it easier to give Cloudy the pets he wanted. Wally had created incantations to augment Weather's size for any and all occasions. And honestly, as fun as it was having a big train of a beast to terrorize locals, I did not approve of his kisses. The big slobbery beast always demanded kisses. Well, two of his three heads. Stormy was the only semi-decent one among them.

"Good boy." I summoned a fireball, which Sunny immediately went to snatch up. "You're not getting anything yet."

Weather bounced on each of his feet, moving in place with excitement as all six of his fiery eyes locked onto the fireball between my palms.

I twisted the black flames with a mix of rocks I grabbed. "Heel."

He sat down, all three heads smacking their jowls as the Cerberus' mouth watered.

"No treats yet." I nudged a persistent Sunny away. "Rollover."

Weather obeyed.

"Play dead."

Sunny dramatically let his tongue roll out; Cloudy closed his eyes and slept; Stormy glared, growled, and then let his head rest with his eyes wide and lifeless. He was such a drama queen. A real acting flair held back by subpar co-stars.

"Okay, almost there. Now, play killer."

Weather leapt to his feet and snarled, biting at the air and pretending to tear apart a corpse. Brilliant. Lethal. Such a collaborative strike from each head.

"Now, do it properly." I dragged a tail across my throat, gesturing death. "No witnesses!"

Fire swelled between each of Weather's jaws, and he breathed red, blue, and purple flames. Fire, which I snatched up and crushed into my black flames, creating the perfect crispy, crunchy cindered rock embers for the Cerberus to snack on. He loved this almost as much as the molten pup cups I'd prepare for him. Much better than the coffee shop Wally would take him to. Still couldn't believe how many corporations Mora invited into her private city.

By the time Weather finished his snacks, Wally sent a text letter indicating they'd finished retrieving intel from Remington. I should've left the second I proposed the idea of summoning that foul fool, yet I deluded myself into believing it'd offer some type of closure. Him in shambles and rotten, a specter suffering an afterlife of anguish; me, a distinguished, successful, happy, and sexy demon living his true self. Fantasies were better left as possible daydreams. Reality sucked. And not half as good as Wally's sucking.

"Come along, hound." I slapped my thigh and beckoned Weather to trot close by as we went back to the store.

When we arrived at the Well of Wonders, everyone had left except for Wally.

"Mora took Kell home," Wally said, cleaning up the summoning circle. "The necromancy spell really took it outta her, which wouldn't have happened if she performed it accordingly. I have a ton of research explaining…"

I played with Weather while Wally had his tangent, poking the hound with my tails and provoking him into a little chase.

"You'll be happy to know we found some useful information."

"Ecstatic." I sighed.

"To think Kell had all that intel this whole time." Wally shook his head. "Just know, once we don't have devils breathing down our necks, I'll be making Kell clean out all of her hats so I can do a proper inventory of everything she's *collected* over the centuries."

"Good luck with that," I muttered, attention fixed on Weather, who snapped his teeth and nearly grazed my tail.

"Honestly, it'd probably be easier facing off against devils. Multiple."

"Uh-huh."

"Are you even listening to me?" Wally asked as a fireball whirled between my tails and captured all of Weather's attention.

Wally tossed a second fireball down the hall and sent his familiar fluttering on a small gust to join the Cerberus in the back of the store.

"I know that was difficult for you, seeing Magus Remington."

"Annoying is all." I shrugged. "Dead prick really got off easy."

"You did good, rising above."

"I rise above all the time, Walter." I glared. "I'm on the top, always rising above. Very top like."

"I didn't realize you were so glorious. I'm oh so humbled." Wally's sass wasn't lost on me, and the dramatic sway of his hands called into question my glory. "I assumed you'd be a little down."

"You know what they say about assuming things. It makes you an ass for me."

"That's not the expression."

"It should be." I winked.

"It doesn't make any sense."

"It does to tops."

"Fine, I'm an ass." Wally dramatically gestured to himself. "One who was clearly wrong about you feeling down."

"Precisely." I folded my arms, turning my nose up at him.

"So this present I got you was just a big ole waste."

"Exactly." I paused, blinking. "Wait, what?"

"I should just toss it and be done with it."

"No. A gift? For me? Gimme!"

I loved presents. Everything about them was fun. Picking them out. Finding them wrapped. The anticipation. Tearing them open. The surprise when what you demanded was actually gifted. The side-eyed contempt when unworthy offerings were presented instead. Diabolics didn't celebrate birthdays. In fact, we didn't have any holidays in Hell. And granted, mortals had this absurd need to celebrate everything from the momentous to the mundane. Did sporks need a national day of remembrance? No. Did they have one? Possibly. Because mortals obsessed over chronicling everything, which was ridiculous since they all lived such short lives. But alas, they got birthdays right.

"I'm definitely counting this toward your birthday present."

"You are not!" I flexed my fingers with the look of grabby hands.

"Fine," Wally dragged out the word with an expression torn between a smile and a pouty little face. "Can't blame a guy for trying."

Birthdays were my favorite, which was why I gave myself three of them. Based on the zodiacs Wally had introduced me to, I figured I was a Gemini sometimes, a Scorpio most of the time, and on rare occasions, I was such a sassy Virgo.

Wally held up one of the gems. "For you."

"It's not even wrapped."

"Well, I didn't exactly have time." He plopped it into my open palm.

It was the ruby Wally had threatened Abe with. Only instead of a bright red, it had a dark scarlet gloss to it. Pretty enough. But a useless trinket. "Thank you."

"It's a spiritus stone. Made from golems, crafted by goblins, enchanted by specters."

"Super fun." My attention waned because while I knew he wanted to be generous, this seemed more like a gift for Wally. Something to allow him to share random facts, which was fine. Normally. But I got hyped for a present, and now I had this junk.

"Not only do they control the dead, keep them in check, but they can hold souls virtually forever," Wally explained. "Well, not *forever* forever. So long as the stone remains intact."

I raised an eyebrow.

"I figured with everything that Magus Remington did to you, then he should rot in there for at least as long as you did."

"Oh, he'll stay in there so much longer."

All those years left trapped inside that Diabolic orb, placed on a mantle as a trophy, forced to listen to Abe's jabs whenever he deigned to acknowledge my pitiful existence. I contemplated every way I would eviscerate him if I ever escaped. And then I did find freedom. I reached him, I planned to end him, but he'd already been slain. A brutal death but far too quickly. It was nice knowing I had a second chance at vengeance.

"Thank you so much! This is the perfect present." I pulled him close with my tail and kissed him. "You're absolutely devilish, Wally."

23

Wally

"Revenge is not a gift," Kell said as we worked on sorting the various shattered Diabolic orbs.

It was a difficult enough task to put one back together, but in order to do so properly, we had to align the right pieces. It also involved cleaning off a lot of blood that'd stained the glass.

"Well, it's not a gift you just hand out all willy-nilly," Kell continued. "If I offer vengeance as a present, I save it for big anniversary gifts. Mora loves a cold dish of revenge served with a side of captive enemies."

"Bez mostly likes video games, inappropriate toys, and food," I said, already having a list of forty-eight potential gift ideas for his next upcoming birthday. Ugh, knowing Bez, he'd probably want gifts for the birthdays he missed out on during our visit to Hell for six months. "Really, the only thing Bez likes about birthdays and anniversaries is he gets to force me to eat his cooking without protesting…much."

"Did he at least show you how grateful he was?" Kell shoulder-bumped me.

"Oh, yeah. There was some seriously serious gratitude happening."

"Did you leave him sore?"

"Huh?"

"You know, on your journey to topdom," Kell said with a flair. "It's like stardom but for your dick."

My face burned, and I couldn't find the right words. "Oh, um, well, no, not exactly."

"After a gift like that?" Kell shook her head. "You should've had that demon horns down, tails up, legs spread, and put away red. His ass, from the ball slapping pounding."

"Uh…"

"Instead, it's just your face that's red." She pinched my cheek. "Which is also adorable."

I swatted her hand away. "I'm not sure that's gonna happen. I might've overhyped the idea in my head."

Kell had her head tilted, actively listening as she continued sorting glass shards.

"It's just we didn't exactly talk about it. I mean, we did in the heat of the moment, but then—"

"He railed you."

"Exactly," I breathed. "And then we got dragged to Hell, which led to a whole bunch of other stuff, oh damn so much happened in Hell, but there was another semi-hot sexy messing around stuff going on. Although, it was just oral."

"Give or receive?"

"Receive."

"Look at you, working your way to the top."

"I don't know. Not sure if it was ever really a thing or I just made it a thing in my head." I sorted shards, finding it easier to identify the slightest distinctions between broken orbs than figure out what the hell I was trying to say. "I think I'm just gonna keep things the way they are."

It wasn't like I was a vers guy. I'd never been a vers guy. Never been interested in it before. But I'd also never been in love before. Never been in a relationship. Not a real relationship anyway. Since settling down with Bez, I found myself wanting to explore new things. All the things. Everything. And we had the time. Eternity. Presumably. Right now, that depended entirely on whether or not we survived the looming threat of devils.

"Do not give up on bending that boy over," Kell said as she thrust against the table for an added effect. "That ass is too good to quit."

"Yeah, yeah."

"Seriously. Mora spent centuries trying to clap those cheeks before conceding her efforts; you can give it at least a few more months before you give up."

"How is Mora?" I asked, not so subtly shifting the conversation away from Bez and me in the bedroom.

"Smooth." Kell rolled her eyes. "She's fine. She found and dealt with all the loose threads involving the coven. Guess there were a few stragglers elsewhere and some other Mythics who foolishly pledged fealty."

"So, not the only one plotting revenge lately."

"The things I would've done to those witches." Kell crackled lightning around a balled fist.

"Wait, you didn't deal with them?"

"Mora handled it." Kell made a face. "Amicably."

"That's surprising."

"Not really. She acts ruthless—and if it comes down to it, she'll end a life or a hundred—but she's a big ole softy. Don't let her fool you." Kell gestured. "Me, on the other hand? I'll gut a bitch for looking at me sideways. I've got no time for bullshit. Life's too short."

"Aren't you immortal?"

Between the essence Mora shared with her and all the dark magics she cast, Kell had lived hundreds of years and probably intended on living hundreds or thousands more.

"Well, other people's lives are short. Shorter if they piss me off."

"You sound like Bez."

"Thank you." Kell giggled.

We returned to sorting through the glass chunks, setting them apart on trays that Tony whisked into the back for a special rinse that'd delicately remove the blood and dirt and anything else obscurely the etchings without ruining the integrity of symbols.

We studied the glass, coming to the conclusions in our notes as Remington had in his, as I was certain the witch who'd created these orbs must've noted. The materials were unfamiliar, unlike any Fae glass I'd encountered. Granted, there weren't exactly tests to identify the depth of Fae artifacts and relics due to their secrecy, but there were usually hidden signs of their culture, of their power, that seeped into everything they made. Oddly enough, the Fae magic used in the creation of the orbs felt foreign, wedged inside the symbols like a garnish as opposed to an entrée.

It was quiet work for the most part. Sometimes, Kell and I babbled for hours; other times, like now, we silently tinkered, lost in the artistry of salvaging artifacts and decoding ancient magics. Once we'd sorted them all, Kell began putting together the list of ingredients Remington claimed would restore a broken Diabolic orb to its full integrity. Well, he didn't so much say it as his overly simplified coded notes explained it.

I mean, I was working with an added edge since I'd had to decipher his scribbles for years on behalf of my bosses, who didn't have the time for paperwork, so I made a lot of ciphers for the coded writing.

And if it turned out the information provided was less than truthful, the added benefit of giving Bez a one-of-a-kind gift in the form of retribution was it also ensured I could follow up with Remington if he attempted to get one over on us. Though I very much hoped to never see the fallen Magus ever again. I'd allow Bez to throw the spiritus stone in a safe and allow it to rot, forgotten like so many of those trinkets.

"You know, at this rate," Kell said, stacking ingredients into neat piles. "I can probably have a few of these recreated and devil-proofed in a few weeks."

"Let's focus on ready in a few days."

"Darling, I can have one ready by tomorrow." Kell side-eyed me. "Not all of us have a compulsive need to reread the directions three times over at each step."

"It's an invaluable skill that undercuts errors by 72%."

"Did you read that in some silly step-by-step pamphlet on directions somewhere?"

"As a matter of fact—"

Lightning crackled so loudly it rang in my ears afterward. I froze, frightened I'd unleashed my essence in a fit, but there was no sign of my powers lashing out at Kell or the store itself. Lightning popped again and again so many times the black flashes of light outside flickered in here.

The silent sizzle between a thousand furious flurries of lightning strikes ended with an explosive eruption that shook the entire building. We weren't on a fault line. Nothing about our private pocket portal city experienced the harsh extremes of nature; everything down to the temperature was cultivated by spells of the day.

We raced to the front, peering through the windows to find the sky slashed open. Seven long rips that'd literally carved open the dimensional walls. Not to the mortal world but to the ether between worlds, to funnel in a force of sweltering heat that poured into the city like a sludge.

I stopped breathing and commanded my body to cease the familiar routine because fucking hell, every inhale was a battle with humidity.

"I think you're gonna need to get that Diabolic orb ready a lot sooner than tomorrow."

Every secret part of me that yearned for this not to happen burst. The parts that prayed and hoped and wished and craved and wanted my worries to be delusional, typical overthinking, and filled with unnecessary preparation.

"Fuck me." Kell swallowed hard. "Which devil do you think it is?"

24

Black lightning crackled, each strike rippling through the fabric of the world and spilling essence into the city. It fell like a waterfall and splashed in waves larger than most of the buildings. It raged like a tsunami come to eviscerate everyone and everything.

I watched as that swarming essence devoured everything in its wake, miles away from my home, but it wouldn't take long for it to consume everything here. It wouldn't take long for Lilith to consume this tiny pocket world and spill out onto the mortal realm, feasting upon everything there, too.

This was Lilith. This devastation was her way of recovering, restoring what she'd lost in battle with Beelzebub. Her form was nothing more than broken essence, desperate and clawing at life and rubble alike.

A sizzle popped beside me and darted past the balcony where I stood. I spun around to find Mora leaping out of the Diabolic threads she'd laced across the city.

"Hurry, Bez." She extended a hand. "We need to move—now!"

Right. Undoubtedly, Lilith's destruction would soon consume all the threads Mora had placed for fast travel. I'd almost forgotten about them since she refused to allow other Diabolics to spread their essence throughout her territory but freely offered her webbed dimension for anyone who desired it. Personally, I figured Mora was just looking for an excuse to have more people in her at once. Even adjacently like venturing through her threaded essence.

"Hold on." I darted away from her and grabbed Weather, tossing the dog over my shoulder where he secured his front paws on my wings and wriggled in my grip. "Stay still."

"Seriously? Gonna bring the dog?"

"Yeah, he's not like your trinkets; he can't be replaced."

"Whatever, let's go." Mora snatched my hand, and we lunged into her Diabolic threads.

She raced ahead, weaving around others who screamed furiously as they whipped round and round in aimless directions. They looked like Wally whenever he tried to hop into the webbed world. Wait. What were so many people doing in Mora's threaded essence?

"Are you evacuating the city?"

"Best as I can." Mora shoved a confused gorgon out of her path and sent the serpent plummeting between the cracks of the threads, where they splashed through a golden glittery portal.

"What the fuck?"

"I might've mixed a bit of Fae magic with my Diabolic threads," Mora explained. "Contingency plan in case the Oasis was ever infiltrated. Though, I expected Collective forces or pissy Fae, not a fucking dying devil using my city as an appetizer."

There was no way Mora could rescue all the citizens. Despite the amount of energy she expelled, reeling everyone in here for safety, I'd wager it was barely half of the people she'd invited to live in her private city.

Every person floating through Mora's threads ate away at her power, depleting all her essence. Her steps slowed, already pushing past her limits. I wasn't sure she'd make the trip across the city. Already, we'd spent nearly ten seconds in her webbed world for a trip that should've taken no more than three seconds.

When we finally reached the Well of Wonders, Mora ripped through her own Diabolic webs and evaded the waves of devil essence. The huge currents of tar below us weren't the only threats. Tendrils sprang out with gnarled teeth and snapping jaws, eating away the threads of essence Mora had laced everywhere.

"Dammit." She used her telekinesis to steady herself, unable to fly like me, and she did her best to send off as many still caught inside her Diabolic webs to a safe destination. Whoever remained inside was devoured by Lilith.

We pushed past a wall of barriers created by Wally and Kell, who warded the raging tar from consuming the store. Each time droplets of black tar struck the conjured barriers, they ate through the magic with the same force as acid. Wally and Kell spent more time reinforcing the defenses they'd just created than summoning new ones to expand their dwindling territory.

"Take him." I shoved Weather into Mora's grasp and pivoted in the opposite direction.

I soared overhead, whirling round and round above the chaotic essence. The devil essence latched onto the black wind I summoned; it feasted upon the flames I added; it chased the lightning I hurled in the opposite direction. There was no stopping this. None that I could find, but at the very least, I could stall for time.

"Bez!" Wally shouted, running toward the edge of the barrier line.

Dammit. The last thing I needed was for him to throw himself into even more danger because of me. Since I'd done all I could for the moment, I flew toward the Well of Wonders and snatched Wally around the waist for safe measure.

I moved so quickly, I beat Mora and Weather to the front door. As they joined us, Kell poured powders in every color of the rainbow, chanting something under her breath.

"Whatever witchy woo you're saying, it won't be enough to stop a devil's rampage."

Kell ignored me, continuing her spell until roots sprang from the ground. The colorful dust carried in the wind and took the form of spirits. Not fully composed like Abe's summoned soul, but silhouettes of red, orange, yellow, green, blue, pink, purple, and a plethora of shades in between.

"It's an evocation, baby Bez." Kell winked. "Mixed with a bit of wicked magic."

The dust. That was those gems crushed into nothing. I checked my pocket for the ruby Wally gave me. Abe remained tucked away and forgotten.

"Like I said, it's not the first time I've done a bit of necromancy."

"So, you're controlling these souls?" Wally asked.

"Yes and no. I made a deal." She gestured to the spirits collapsing onto the roots, which swelled and torpedoed beneath the ground. "Work with Nature herself and join her ranks. Which I think is a much better fate than collecting dust in one of my hats."

"Nature's Blessing mixed with evocation." Wally stared wide-eyed as the roots burst out of the tar, sprouting into trees with branches made of blades, flowers with fanged teeth, vines in the shape of women, and so much more. Every spirit added to the weaponry a hundred-fold, turning Nature into a front-line defense.

"How'd you convince your ex to help?"

"She's got as much to lose with a rampaging devil as anyone else," Kell said, leading us inside and away from the raging duel between the earth herself. Away from Lilith, a living entity of a dimension of her very own.

"Wait, you dated Nature?" Wally asked, attention fixed on Kell and unwilling to gloss over the fact the witch dated a deity. "Like *thee* Nature. Like she's actually sentient and capable of candlelit dinners?"

"We didn't really do dinners, but her vine work is divine." Kell winked. "Speaking of divine, every witch is currently channeling Nature, offering their magics, their spells, their everything."

"Why?" Mora asked.

"It's happening everywhere," Kell said, a tremble in her voice I'd never heard before. "Essence ripping through reality and consuming anything in its path."

"A matter of hours before she destroys this world," I said. "We need to flee this realm."

"We can't abandon the world," Wally declared. It was met with silence, which made him swallow his anxiety and his chivalry. "Can we?"

"Fuck 'em." Mora retrieved a nail file from her pocket purse. Correction, a dagger that grew to full size once removed from the tiny tote. "I can start fresh anywhere and everywhere. Bez, Walter, I'm more than willing to drop you lot off in any world of your liking, but this is where we part."

"Not a fan of the heat?" I asked.

"Lilith is gonna chase you two to the end of the universe and back around again." Mora stabbed the air, tearing the dimensional lining apart with her blade. "Stay and die nobly with the world if you wish, or leave with me to breathe another day."

"Figuratively," I said.

"Precisely." Mora carved open a doorway. "I love you, Bezzy. And your boyfriend's okay, but I won't be greeting Oblivion for anyone except Kell."

"I can't leave," Kell said. "I can't abandon my world."

"Watching your first world die out and meet its end is sad," Mora explained. "After a while, it's like any other death. Numb. Routine. Inconvenient. Circle of life and all that."

"I'm connected to the pool of witches," Kell said. "I bound my soul and magic to this battle."

"Dammit, Kell." Mora lowered her dagger. "To be clear, I'm pissed by your unilateral decision for self-sacrificing moves of heroism."

"I know, hun." Kell pursed her lips. "Total turn-off, right?"

"The biggest."

"Look out." Wally lunged ahead and tackled Mora as black tar seeped through the tear Mora carved.

The pair rolled onto the floor as Kell and I went to work sealing the dimension and revoking access to this room.

My role mostly entailed slashing at Lilith's essence until it retreated back into the portal while Kell cast sorcery to seal it.

"Oh, fuck me!" Mora shoved Wally off her and brushed her dress smooth as she stood up. "That bitch surrounded the dimension. I thought she was fleeing. Who takes the time to create a barricade around the world that they fled to?"

Mora stomped off, cursing in every language known to mortal, Mythic, Diabolic, and probably a few dozen unknown profanities.

"We need to finish repairing the Diabolic orbs," Wally said. "One at the very least."

"I can focus on that," Kell said. "I'm basically spent anyway since I relinquished all my magic to Nature. And I do mean all of it. Like max out your credit cards and apply for a loan with terrible interest rates kind of spent."

"You okay?" Wally asked.

"Not feeling it now." Kell shrugged. "But if the world doesn't die, best believe I'm gonna be hassling you for spells the next decade."

"Not to be rude," Wally said before barreling into blunt data—I knew he planned on slapping Kell with facts based on how he politely picked up a book to reference. "Piecing together the orbs requires magic. It's in the instructions."

"I'm still fucking up my credit score before anyone revokes my spending habits." Kell waved a hand, conjuring a slew of supplies onto the front counter. "Basic spell work is fine for me. Life or death combat…" Kell snapped her fingers four times before a flame sparked between her fingertips. "Not so much."

"How long will it take you to put together a Diabolic orb?" I asked.

"A few days." Kell shrugged. "If I was bragging."

"How long for the both of you?"

"A few weeks," Wally said. "We have different methods."

"Nonsense." Kell smiled. "You're brilliant."

"I know that. My intellect was never in question." Wally squinted at Kell before turning his attention to me. "We just have different approaches. It collides in the wrong way. But she's got a better grasp on the research than I do."

"So Kell will work on the orbs while you focus on defensive measures." I flexed my muscles, channeling my essence in preparation for combat. For war. For a one-sided battle against a thrashing devil. "I'm gonna stall for time. Get you at least one day."

"I can help distract Lilith," Wally insisted.

"You are helping by securing this place," I said. "Kell needs peace and quiet to work."

"I really don't," she said, tinkering with tools. "I thrive in chaos."

"Well, Weather and Antoninus need somewhere safe to rest their heads." I pointed to the Cerberus and Wally's familiar.

"They'll be in the safest place," Wally said. "Tony, I need you and Weather to go to the well."

The familiar protested with a clack of his claws, but when the essence inside Wally blossomed, the scorpion settled. Claws coated Wally's hands, horns grew three times the size they'd ever been, his tail flicked and snapped against the floor, and his cherub wings swelled and transformed the tips of each feather with sharp blades.

I nodded approvingly. "Someone's finally slipping in and out of his essence with ease."

"The less I think about it, the more naturally it syncs with my desires." He stared at his claws, watching the ombre effect reach his forearms.

"Hey, bug." I stopped the familiar. "Take this with you."

I tossed him the ruby holding Remington's soul.

"On the off chance I don't survive this, I want to ensure he remains in that damn stone." I smirked. "I'm petty like that."

Tony carried the gem on his back and shuffled to the back of the store, toward the well, which served as the safest place in the entire Diabolic Oasis. It had more magics protecting it than the rest of the city combined ten-fold. But since the well held Agatha's Heart, the still beating tool that fueled the dimensional cloak of the city, Mora made it such a priority that no one except for Kell and Wally had access.

"Dog, wait." I patted my thigh, calling Weather over. I gave each head a few pets and then a kiss on their furry foreheads. Cloudy yipped with excitement. Sunny licked my face in return. Stormy growled and pulled away.

"Shut up." I held his head, staring into his fiery blue eyes. "You're gonna accept my kissies, and you're gonna like the kissies."

Stormy huffed and conceded. I gave him the biggest smooch before giving Sunny and Cloudy one more little forehead kiss because, obviously, they'd only whine if I played favorites.

After I sent him off to the well for safety, I found Wally filling a bag with artifacts.

"And what are you doing?"

"Putting together a lethal combination of diversionary magics."

Once he'd filled the bag to the brim, I snatched it from his grasp. "Hey!"

"Is for unicorns, and unless you've got one on hand, you won't be joining me."

"I can help," Wally snapped. "I can actually hold my own against Lilith."

I glared. Quite the personal jab he threw out, but all the same, his luck against Lilith the last time they clashed didn't mean he could hold his own.

Facing a devil on my own would be the end of me. There was no way around it. The only chance I had of surviving, of besting a devil, came down to the fact her focus was divided into so many tasks. Her essence split across the entire world, fighting Mythics, mortals, the Collective, and any Fae who deigned to assist. Probably several thousand, at the very least, who found themselves trapped on this dying rock with Lilith barricading the dimensional walls. Plus, while she escaped Beelzebub, her essence was in a state of decay, barely holding on.

Whether this would kill me or not, I didn't care. Whether the world fell away to dust in the wake of Lilith's rage, I didn't care. What I did worry about was Wally. Even with the strength of a devil, his skills were untested and not nearly trained enough. I couldn't do this, couldn't focus unless I knew Wally remained safe.

"You are helping," I said with a surly edge in my tone, swallowing all the kind nothings I wished to whisper. "Reinforce the barriers. Leave the rest to those of us accustomed to battle."

"I can do more than reinforce barriers."

"I'm not even sure you can manage that much, lil misfit devil boy." Corson barged through the front door, a smile on his face.

His sapphire blue eyes shimmered as two others stormed in

beside him. Mortal in appearance, unlike Corson, who remained in his demon form, but these two were absolutely Diabolic. The glow of crimson eyes from one and emerald from the other indicated that much.

"Ah, Hells."

The last thing we needed was demons invading the realm at the behest of their devil.

25

Wally

Corson stood at the door in tattered armor, not like the Roman gear he sported the last time they crossed paths. He looked more like a knight errant, except his chest plate had several holes, the right arm piece had broken off entirely, and his clawed feet clicked against the floor free of any armor. Though, that might've been an aesthetic choice given his long claws and the hooked arch of his feet, similar to a werewolf. The men on either side of him didn't dress nearly as distinguished or ready for war.

"Those pitiful magics you call a barrier didn't even register our essence," Corson said. "We just waltzed right inside."

"Biggest mistake of your soon-to-end lives." Bez's stance shifted as he prepared to lunge forward.

"We're not here as enemies." Corson raised his hands in surrender. "Just here to help. Starting with the shitty barriers."

"It's devil-proofed," I explained.

"You sure about that?" asked a man with crimson red eyes, indicating a similar aura to Bez's Diabolic essence.

Although, that was where the similarities came to an end. He possessed a slim athletic guy with a deep amber complexion wearing a white crop top and glittery skinny jeans with more rips than fabric to cover his legs and nearly exposed ass. His top revealed his stomach, but his arms were covered in hot pink-mesh sleeved stockings that went all the way to his wrist, where he wore bubblegum pink fingerless gloves that matched his combat boots.

Did he possess the guy in this outfit or modify the wardrobe to his liking upon taking over? His fashion sense seemed as eclectic as Bez's tastebuds.

"We are sure," Kell chimed in, answering the guy's question, even though her focus needed to be locked on the task. "I know my way around essence, and those barriers are absolutely devil-proofed."

"I'm a devil." The guy in the crop top boasted, flexing his washboard abs.

My eyes widened. Lilith. Fuck. She'd possessed this body and slipped right inside with two demons at her side. So much for Corson wishing for her downfall. He'd likely turned on us the second we fled.

"The name's Satan." He grinned.

"Oh." My face dropped, along with my heart rate. I couldn't believe I was meeting Satan. The actual Satan. Again! Properly. Sort of. Considering the whole end-of-the-world thing. "You look different than the last time I saw you."

"We've met?"

"I saw your performance."

"Aww. My dance. Perhaps the only thing I'll miss about Lilith's Hell." He twirled around, performing what looked like a pirouette, followed by a high kick and a flawless bow. "She spared no expense on choreography."

"Your body has some nice moves to it," Corson said.

"Thank you. It's called a twunk, and it specializes in dancing of the grinding variety. Also, gym life, parties, sex, and something called ecstasy." He spun around one more time. "And I found it the cutest little outfit."

"To be clear, you're not a devil," Kell said. "The barriers aren't designed to shield against knockoff devils."

"Yeah, or else Wally would get stuck too." Bez pointed his tails at me.

"Hey!"

"Lilith would never be bested by such a barrier," said the third man, an older, lanky guy with thick salt and pepper hair. "Nothing can fend against her glory."

He clutched his vest, prideful in the way he raised his head high and straightened his posture. There was something incredibly familiar about his emerald green eyes and the lime shade of his whites.

"You're Orias, right?" I asked.

"That I am," he said with the most dignified demeanor.

He was the octopus-like demon who hosted my Devil's Banquet.

"Why are you here?" I asked.

"We're here to help," Orias said. "Obviously."

"You sound quite loyal to the devil currently set on destroying our world," Bez said.

Ours.

For as much as he professed not to care about this dimension or anyone in it, his true feelings occasionally surfaced.

"My loyalty only extends so far," Orias explained. "Beelzebub destroyed half the dimension in their battle, and Lilith devoured the other half to fend him off. Between the two of them, there's nothing left of our Hell. No place to pledge my eternal allegiance."

"So you're all here to help?" Bez asked, suspiciously squinting at Corson.

"Well, currently"—Corson playfully knocked on the door—"I'm here to huff and puff and blow you down."

"Blow your house down," I said with a deep frown. "The expression that you butchered. It's about a house."

"And here I thought it was about squealing lil piggies and big bad wolves."

"I believe he was performing a flirtation ritual of innuendos," Orias clarified as if I needed it.

"I caught that." I glowered. "Just giving him the benefit."

Not that I was opposed to folks hitting on Bez—he's a catch, after all—but the world was literally facing Armageddon.

"I don't have time for Corson's particular brand of come-ons."

"Are you jealous?" Bez asked with a little cocky glimmer in his eyes. Oh, I'd never hear the end of this.

"Of me cumming?" Corson added. "Who wouldn't be? I can cum on just about anyone. No need to fret, misfit devil. I have plenty of cum to go around."

My entire face burned hot, and suddenly, the idea of the world ending didn't seem so awful if it brought an end to this mortifying conversation.

"Wait." I shook away the embarrassment. "Lilith destroyed her own world? The whole dimension? Everything?"

"She attempted to salvage the world in the first century," Orias said.

Corson and Satan tsked.

"But as the battle dragged on for nearly a millennium, Lilith resorted to any measures to distance herself from Beelzebub."

"Which meant hurling her army of children," Satan said.

"Or devouring us," Corson added. "Anything to keep Mommy at peak performance."

My jaw had fallen slack, not from Satan or Corson's commentary or the fact I was actually having a conversation with *the* Satan—who dressed like a slutty circuit boy. No, what left me completely befuddled was how casually they discussed a battle that raged on for centuries.

"That doesn't make any sense," I muttered. "We just left Hell not all that long ago."

"Time works differently in different planes of existence," Bez said in the most patronizing tone.

"I know that." I furrowed my brows. "But when we were in Hell for the better part of one day, more than six months had passed in our world."

I mumbled to myself, trying to account for the reversal of time and extrapolate how it moved in such a fluid way. My thoughts swam in theories and formulas, and eventually, I just surrendered before I ended up drowning in the math.

"It's absurd and makes zero sense."

"Look at my adorable mage trying to find the logic in Hell." Bez playfully patted my head with a tail while holding the other two at my side like I was a little adorable display for him to show off.

"Stop it."

"The only thing that confuses me is why the Great Mother fled to this world of all worlds," Orias said.

My stomach twisted in on itself.

"Revenge, of course." Satan popped his hip and fished a lollipop out of his pocket. "I could hear her shrieking all the way from my cage."

"Shrieking? About what?" Orias asked.

"About the rejection the Devil Mage Walter Human Guy Insert Remaining Accolades Here blah, blah, blah"—Satan gave me a dramatic curtsy then sucked on his lollipop—"gave her."

"You rejected Lilith?" Orias gasped. "The gall."

"She said pretty much the same thing."

"It was the highlight of my existence." Satan smacked his lips around the lollipop, then shoved it back in his mouth.

"I'm less confused about her motive and more so about her methods," Orias said. "How'd she manage to get here? Nearly half her essence has been shredded and obliterated. Her gates have all closed, yet she still ended up here, dragging what remained of her army to this realm."

Wow. Lilith had pulled her forces through.

"It's because—"

"I screwed up," Corson interrupted, sapphire eyes locked onto me. "Lilith has keys placed throughout the universe for safekeeping. A way for her to pass between worlds even while her gates are closed. She had thousands of keys scattered across hundreds of dimensions. I thought I got all the ones here, but she must've had another I didn't document."

"Wait. What?" I shook my head. "No, what happened was—"

"Walter, please," Bez interjected. "Don't be rude. Let the man finish."

"I truly believed I could remove all of them, preventing Lilith's escape routes." Corson sighed.

"How did you intend on destroying them?" I asked.

"She has a map—had, whatever—in her palace that displayed and connected to the various keys she'd scattered across the universe."

"Lilith had a map of the universe?" My eyes widened, wishing she'd shown me that instead of a dinner party with a dance number from a knockoff devil, who currently stood a few feet away, sucking the life out of a piece of candy.

"Yes," Corson said. "It displayed most of her keys, and I thought I knew how to reveal the hidden ones so I could disrupt her connection from her core base of operations, but I obviously deluded myself into such things. Because I clearly missed some here in this mortal realm."

"It's quite shameful," Bez said with a click of his tongue to add to the disgrace. "But at least you're owning up to your failures."

"Bez," I whined because he knew damn well this was most likely our fault. That copy of the flame key Kell made, the one I encouraged, the one Bez allowed, the one we assumed would help prevent a situation such as this.

"So, that's why you dragged me along on this foolish plan?" Satan bit down on his lollipop with a heavy crunch. "A guilty conscience, Corson?"

"No," Corson protested. "We're stuck in this world anyway. We might as well team up with the only living souls to buck Lilith's authority and survive to tell the tale."

"Plus, she is vulnerable with so much of her essence depleted," Orias added. "But we won't win. At least I can have a glorious death to entertain those in Oblivion with."

"This is not the morale boost I was hoping for." I sighed. "Let's come up with a plan and figure out who's best at what."

Much to my protest, Bez convinced me to stay behind at the shop with Orias so we could reinforce barriers. Being the most humble servant of Lilith for longer than I cared to ask, the octopus demon had a lot of insight for tweaking spells so that they'd remain resistant to Lilith's thrashing essence, which lapped at our barrier walls.

Her essence didn't move with a purpose, mainly on instinct. I wondered how much of her was still in there as she fought to regain herself, reshuffle her mind, restore her lost thoughts. This wasn't like the tiny piece of devil essence I had, a piece so small it lacked sentience. But after nearly a thousand years of clashing in a battle against Beelzebub, it seemed to have left Lilith riddled with injuries beyond repair.

Mora strutted outside to join Orias and me as we secured the very shallow perimeter not consumed by chaotic essence.

"How's Kell coming along?" I asked.

Mora shrugged, not exactly informed on the process of restoring a Diabolic orb. I didn't want to distract Kell, and I knew for a fact if I stayed inside, I'd hover and question and point out everything she did or didn't do. Plus, I wanted to be out here, at least able to watch Bez from a distance.

"She would've healed faster in Hell." Mora folded her arms, glaring at her destroyed city. "Any Hell, in fact. Instead, she foolishly dived into a world not suited for essence."

"She didn't exactly have much of a choice with her limitations on the keys." I shrugged.

"She only needed the key to escape her sealed Hell," Mora said. "Once she was in between realms, she could've strolled anywhere. Knocked on Hell doors to one of her allied devils. For fuck's sake, she's got enough."

"No way would Her Royal Supreme dare risk exposing herself to an ally in such a state of vulnerability," Orias said. "She's rightfully fearful one of her so-called comrades would pounce upon her current state, slaying her in an act of grabbing power and securing their station among the hierarchy of devils."

"You know, you're looking as lovely as ever, Orias."

"You two know each other?"

"Long ago, back when I reigned in Bael's Hell," Mora said. "Orias was a young diplomat. He would visit, and I'd entertain him. Though, he did most of the entertaining."

Orias nodded. "I do miss your Court."

"This body suits you. The suit, not so much." Mora grabbed Orias' vest, tugging at the buttons. "I usually prefer a sturdy mortal body in the bedroom, but admittedly, you look so much better with all your limbs."

"Seriously?" I blinked at them both.

"What?" Mora smiled. "You wouldn't believe the things Orias can do."

"Now might not be the time for tentacle porn," I suggested, an edge in my voice.

"Shame. Life or death situations are the best aphrodisiacs."

"If you like, I can accommodate your fancies." Orias dug a clawed hand into his chest, wedging his fingers between his ribcage like he planned on actually ripping open his body.

"Stop, stop, stop!" I demanded. "I am not watching you rip apart your body so you can bang Mora."

"What? These are as strong as they'll ever be." Orias gestured to the barriers. "If Lilith wants in here, she'll break through no matter the stop gaps in place."

"Wally has a point." Mora gently plucked Orias' bloody hand from his chest cavity. "It's important to treat hosts with proper care. I was actually planning on adding this gentleman to my collection. Assuming we all survive this hellish situation."

"Oh. You have a collection?"

"Yes, quite a versatile selection, in fact."

"You must show me sometime."

"Certainly. And you must take care of this body because I hate a torn outfit." Mora adjusted Orias' tie. "I'll have to teach you all the etiquette of building a fine wardrobe if you intend on remaining in the mortal plane."

I ignored them, focusing on Bez, who flew above the thrashing ocean of essence. Corson used telekinesis to stay afloat, albeit without the grace of Bez. Satan, on the other hand, sat with both his legs hanging over a broomstick while he rode side-saddled and playfully stroked the tip of his broom. He breezed through the air quickly and seamlessly. It turned out he'd possessed a misfit mage of his own and utilized the Pentacles of Power to access our traditional flight styles.

Each demon battled against Lilith's essence, helping Nature, who rampaged with the strength of every witch, living and dead.

I growled, biting back my own essence. It surged in my core, ready and eager to lash out and strike down Lilith, to help turn the tide of battle, to clash against another devil. The way I'd instinctively defended against her in Hell, in her Hell, I couldn't help but believe my abilities were being utterly wasted. Sidelined because what?

Bez turned his gaze toward me, and a calm washed over his face despite being entrenched in battle, slashing at essence, summoning elements in flurries, utilizing dark artifacts to lay curses and commands that might've at least stunned their devil target momentarily.

I took a deep breath and exhaled my frustration. As much as I could, at the very least.

Bez needed me here so he wouldn't fret. Our entire relationship, he always worried about me, about how breakable I was compared to Diabolics. But I was a Diabolic now. Adjacently, at least.

He could have his combat with me safely out of the battle if it made him happy. But he best believe we were going to have a discussion about this. I'd saved him on more than one occasion, so I was no damsel who'd die in a fight.

It's not like it's a pattern or something.

My heart pounded in my chest, erratic and pumping blood so fast it boiled. Essence bubbled inside me, defensively swelling, ready to burst through my pores any moment.

"What's happening?" I squeezed my head, trying to calm my thoughts, sway my essence, soothe the power circulating at hyper speed.

The broken sky tore asunder again, the tear splitting wider as four beastly arms barreled their way inside the dimensional walls.

The worst possible thing happened.

"Beelzebub is here."

26

Bez

Beelzebub descended in his full glory, his skin as black as the tar of Lilith's essence but lacking the shimmer against the sunlight. Natural sunlight that pierced through the dimensional walls that Lilith and now Beelzebub had cracked apart upon their invasion.

This made no sense. I turned to an awestruck Corson and Satan, who quaked at the impending clash. To think they could reveal such horror on their faces after already witnessing him duel against Lilith for centuries was a true sign of Beelzebub's tyranny.

"I thought you said Lilith fled, left him locked behind her sealed gates!"

"She did." Corson trembled. "I barely made it through, swept in her wake."

"Perhaps it comes from the essence he stole," Satan said. "He did take a lot of Lilith's essence."

"Impossible." I ground my teeth, fighting off my own fear of Beelzebub's return. "Slipping through a sealed doorway to Hell requires a fully intact devil. Taking her essence wouldn't restore what he's lost."

It was equivalent to grabbing a second sword for battle instead of a shield. Yes, it would help Beelzebub in combat, but it didn't simply substitute for the missing item. Or, in this case, his missing essence. It gave him access to different techniques, nothing more.

"Lilith does it." Satan gestured to her ocean of tar.

"Lilith only circumvented it by her hidden keys across the universe," Corson added.

"Fuck me." The realization struck. That was how Beelzebub got here. "He's stolen some of Lilith's essence, subsequently giving himself access to her power, her private secret portals, the hidden cracks between sealed doors to Hell."

He used her trick to claw his way into our world, where he'd now slaughter us all and restore his lost essence by ripping Wally apart.

Beelzebub's veins glowed a multitude of colors, almost like an enchanting rainbow that coursed over his skin, except each bright array represented an aura from the demons he devoured in Lilith's Hell. Their essence still pumped through his body, fueling him beyond reproach.

"You thought you could run!" he roared in echoing Diabolic tones, voice literally cracking the air around us. His snout scrunched as he snarled and let out more foul growls.

I covered my ears, wincing from the sharp slice of sound tunneling through me.

"You believed fleeing here would distract me, appease me?" Beelzebub bellowed, a horrible mocking laughter of ear-piercing brutality. "Foolish creature. Your vanity beckons completion as a sign of perfection. I require only drops of my essence to be deemed perfect. Worthy. Unstoppable."

Each of his eight wings flapped, sending tornados, fires, ice storms, and waves of elemental destruction in every direction. Not only attacking Lilith but shattering Nature's forces upon contact.

"Bringing me to the mortal world where my lost essence dwells will not deter me from slaughtering you, lowly devil."

Beelzebub began clashing with Lilith. Conjuring flames that burned away the army of plant life. They raged in an inferno that burrowed through the earth, tearing its way across the land. Soon, the fire took shape in the form of giant talons and snapping teeth and hooked whips and a thousand other weapons meant to strike and tear and pull Lilith's essence into one singular location.

"Let us finish this, tragic creature that you are." Beelzebub tilted his head. The sun shimmered against his golden horns that twisted atop his head like a crown.

They were a sign of station, a crown given to him upon his creation, the instant he crawled into existence and declared the universe belonged to him. All would kneel or die. Some would kneel and die. It mattered not to Beelzebub. All he craved was conquest and carnage and claiming everything as his.

In the moments since Beelzebub had arrived, he'd reached out to pluck Lilith's essence from across the world so he could finish this battle. His fiery weapons merged with molten rock and dragged Lilith closer.

Soon, the city she'd laid waste to revealed itself again. In the wake of destruction, her essence retreated. How much of the world looked as disastrous as our city? How much had Lilith destroyed since she fled to our world?

"We need to fall back," Wally shouted.

Wally? I spun in the air, finding him flying beside me while Corson and Satan retreated back to the Well of Wonders.

"Walter, I told you—"

"Yes, stay behind for safety," he interrupted. "Now, take your own advice!"

He extended a hand, and I grasped it gently, intertwining our fingers. It was a momentary relief, allowing the war upon this world to wash away.

I smiled at him, soft and small. Then I yanked his arm and pulled him into a sudden embrace. With our chests pressed together, I wrapped an arm at the small of his back and held onto the hook of his wing where the joint met with his shoulder blades.

With him safely secured, I soared through the sky faster than I'd ever flown before and barreled through the barrier, which would only hold a fraction of a second if and when Beelzebub deigned to acknowledge our presence.

Over the course of the next few days, we sat in the shop watching Beelzebub shred waves of essence at a time, listening to the agonizing shrieks of Lilith as the god-king devil continuously and brutally eviscerated the other devil.

It didn't matter how much Lilith fought back, how much she countered his strikes, how valiant her efforts to regroup and lash out. None of it made a difference against an indomitable opponent. Beelzebub existed only for war, pain, suffering. If something thrived in his presence, it was only because they endured his horrors. And even that was an offense, further encouraging him to find new ways to demean and torment those beneath him.

"How we coming on the orbs?"

"My orbs are always coming." Corson bit the air by my ear.

Using my tail in an uppercut motion, I stabbed him through the chin.

He gurgled, body shuddering as essence poured from his split throat, staining his dreadfully dull sweater.

"You're in my space." I withdrew my tail.

Corson wiggled his lower jaw back and forth until he healed. "Apologies."

"Closer to finishing—not that flirty demons seem to give a fuck when all they want is to fuck," Kell said from her workstation, where she'd remained day and night, using caffeine and magics to delay her need for sleep. That and bitchy comments. By day three, she let out rude little jabs with every breath.

Corson leaned in close again until I thwacked my tail against the hardwood floors, encouraging him to keep his distance. We'd been stuck in this store the entire time, careful to avoid stepping outside where the devils warred.

Despite Beelzebub ripping apart Lilith's essence and dragging her to one central location, it hadn't detracted from the essence blockading the dimensional walls. We used Mora's fancy Fae blade to pierce the veil between dimensions only to find Beelzebub's essence had rampaged, stomping out Lilith's essence and securing the realm in her stead.

So now we all stayed in this tiny store. It'd never felt so small until recently. But with a whiny Cerberus, a hissing scorpion, a chatty witch, an anxious mage, and five demons all wedged together, I almost relished the idea of certain death in battle.

Wally walked back into the room with an air of authority about him. I hated how the world would throw him into these dangerous situations, threatening him with death at every turn, but he truly held such a captivating calm when thrust into combat. His collective cool oozed off him, making even his scent permeate power.

"Kell's almost finished with the Diabolic orb, and it'll cut things close, but I think we need to take advantage of their battle," Wally said. No. Declared. Commanded. Announced like a devil himself in charge of everyone in this room, including me. "If we're gonna have any chance of winning this, then we need to strike while Beelzebub is distracted by Lilith."

"Distracted?" Corson scoffed. "She's been writhing on the ground as he wails on her this entire time."

"Exactly," Wally said. "Despite how exhausted she is, how broken her essence is, he hasn't paid attention to anything else in days. He hasn't acknowledged us. He didn't even react when Nature withdrew her forces to mend the holes left in the earth. The only thing Beelzebub is fixated on is his duel with Lilith."

It was a fair point. He might have an overwhelming advantage against Lilith, but Beelzebub didn't make sloppy moves. While he declared her a weak devil, she was still a devil who was, therefore, worthy of some priority.

"So, what's your plan?" I asked.

"I think we need to exploit their battle," he said. "If we strike Beelzebub while he's distracted by Lilith, we should be able to seal them both in an orb."

"If that thing can actually hold a devil." Corson gestured. "Just because it's big doesn't mean it's powerful."

"I don't know." Satan licked a lollipop. "Size might not be everything, but I'd rather drop a hammer on your head than a thimble."

"Is it just a hammer you wanna slap my face with?" Corson winked.

"I can think of a few things."

The power radiating off the nearly restored orb had a palpable weight. I nearly trembled at the force, the instinctive pull the tool had for drawing in Diabolics. It was unlike any other orb I'd encountered, from the one that held me for what felt like a lifetime to the thousands stored on that magical villa.

"It'll hold," I whispered, locking eyes with Corson. "Surely, you can tell the difference."

His sapphire blue irises widened as he quieted his prattle and allowed himself to feel the gravity of the Diabolic orb. As the only other demon here who spent time bound inside these devices, he must've registered the same sensation.

"Okay." Corson nodded in agreement. "Even if it is strong enough to contain a devil, could it handle two? Could any orb?"

"I believe it's the added advantage to containing a devil," Wally explained. "If they're locked up separately, even incomplete devils, they might have the force to shatter these orbs over the course of time and persistence, and then we're in the same situation. Instead of delaying this slaughter for a hundred years, a thousand, ten thousand, my hope is to keep them busy clashing as they fight for control inside their prison."

It made some sense. Beelzebub would never submit to ally himself with Lilith, even if they were trapped together. And Lilith, being a fellow devil, would never submit to death. To Oblivion. The pair could quite literally fight each other until the end of time itself.

Corson smacked his hands together in a loud clap, a sudden and obnoxious noise. "Sounds like a plan. We finish this orb, then lock those two pricks up forever. Not quite satisfying as sending mommy to Oblivion, but I do relish the karmic justice of imprisoning her in a Diabolic orb."

I, too, enjoyed the idea of trapping Beelzebub in such a way. The way I was trapped, having my essence shredded and fractured and depleted for years on end.

"There's one problem." Wally's eyes turned pitch black, and his gaze drifted beyond us to the battle outside. "Kell is close to completing the orb, but Lilith won't last that long. She'll be depleted soon. Her essence is waning, and the fragmented bits are moving more sluggish each time Beelzebub rips them from her body."

Wally's devil essence pierced a different layer of sensory comprehension, allowing him to glimpse aspects of Diabolic power I never knew existed, something I didn't believe any demon could access.

"If we wait any longer, we risk facing Beelzebub alone," Wally said. "I don't think that's a fight we could endure for very long."

"Minutes at best," Corson said.

"Seconds for you lot," I replied.

"Arrogant of you." Satan snickered. "Hawt!"

"Not boasting," I said. "I'd only live longer as a way to draw out my death. Consider your few agonizing seconds a blessing that Beelzebub wouldn't deem you worthy of suffering."

Satan pouted. "My inner masochist is aroused and offended."

"So, it's decided." Wally swallowed hard, steadying his shaky voice. "We do this now. If a collective unity of demons hit Beelzebub with a barrage of attacks, it should distract him long enough for Kell to finish the final touches on the Diabolic orb. Then we seal up Lilith and Beelzebub and put their prison behind a billion walls of warding magic."

I wanted to protest, to tell Wally not to join us, to demand it. Instead, I nodded in agreement with the other demons because as much as I didn't want him to come to harm, I couldn't protect him from the wrath of devils.

I had to believe in him during any situation. I had to encourage him in all things. Wally was the world to me, the universe itself. Nothing in existence mattered except for him. That also meant the things he cared for mattered. They had to matter to a degree. That was what love meant, what I'd learned in the brief time we'd been together. If I loved Wally, loved him as much as I professed, then I had to be willing to fight for the things he cherished.

27

Wally

What had I done? What the hell had I done? What the ever-living Hell—quite literally—had I done? Somehow, I'd come up with the bright idea we needed to charge into battle and fight Beelzebub so he wouldn't kill Lilith until we had the time to trap both of them inside the Diabolic orb.

I excused myself from the storefront and headed back toward my study, where I could sort through artifacts and determine what would help with…challenging a devil. My breathing hitched when I stepped by Kell and her workstation.

As uncertain as I was about everything, Bez's wellbeing, the state of the world, my own abilities, there was one thing I knew for certain. The orb would work. There was this tension beneath my skin, essence circulating on high alert, ready to fight the threat of the broken artifact. The more Kell restored it, the more aware of its presence, its power, I became.

During the raid on the witch coven, this same sensation had hit. Struck. Sparked a fuse inside me to defend against a looming threat.

But I didn't make sense of it in the seconds that passed when confronted with those Diabolic orbs. Bez shattered them and the witches before I could react, before my essence could attack.

Attack.

I was really going to attack Beelzebub. With Bez. With other demons. Why hadn't Bez said anything about me going on this mission? I shouldn't be going on this mission. I wasn't ready. I'd never be ready. Not with my essence. I wasn't a Diabolic, not really.

I continued rifling through items until I found the case containing the demon-killing blade. Supposedly. Not that I ever personally killed a demon with it. But it hurt Diabolics a lot. Messed with their essence, their healing. It'd help for certain.

"If I could open the damn thing." I pried the latches, somehow struggling to unfasten them.

How could I delude myself into thinking I could help in this battle when I couldn't even open a case?

"I can't even help Kell," I muttered. Not without butting heads. I knew that much; I knew to step aside, to put my ego aside. Why'd my ego convince me to see this plan through? To convince others it was the plan? "I'm a moron."

"Furthest thing from it," Bez said, sculking from the doorframe. He tilted his head just enough to slip his horns under the doorway without hitting his head again. Since staying in his demon form, he stood taller, and the store seemed smaller. "You okay?"

I sighed in response, holding back every agonizing question leaping through my thoughts.

"Look at you, lost in that little hive of a mind." Bez kissed my forehead, calming the wave of anxiety beneath the surface of my thoughts.

But even his touch couldn't soothe my paranoia.

"Why didn't you tell me to stay back?" I asked less a question and more an accusation. "I have zero experience in fighting. I mean,

I have some. But not against Diabolics. Okay, there's a few instances where I fought Diabolics, but never alone. Then again, I wouldn't be alone in this battle either. But this isn't demons. This is a devil. Two devils. More like one-and-a-half devils. Well, probably more of a quarter based on how scattered Lilith's essence is."

I stared through the nearby wall. Literally saw past the brick and stone, glimpsing the writhing clumps of essence dragged back to the city from across the globe, but too bloody and broken to rejoin with Lilith's core.

"And yeah, I'm strong. Definitely strong. But should I really be fighting a devil? Should any of us?" I continued because I had a million things to express, to pour out, to… "I don't even know. My thoughts are swimming with so much confusion and fear and stupidity. I'm not smart enough to be making a plan that challenges the scariest, most hateful devil in existence."

"Are you done?" Bez blinked. "I can let you ramble on until you tucker yourself out if you prefer."

"Aren't you worried?"

"Terrified beyond belief," he said. "Or I would be if I didn't have someone to believe in."

"I am not the person who you put your faith in."

"No, you're the person who I put my dick in."

My face fell flat. "Seriously, Bez? Can you take nothing seriously?"

"I take dick pretty seriously." He smirked. "Gladly take yours if you'll sling it this way."

And just like that, my entire face burned, quite possibly literally on fire. Was I on fire? Had Bez really just said that?

"Now that I got your attention, I want you to know I do fear what comes next. I fear falling short. I fear failing. I fear losing you. But most of all, I fear not honoring you."

My eyes watered.

"You're the smartest, strongest, bravest, brightest, cutest, dorkiest, most-annoyingly ridiculous-est person I've ever met in my long eternity." Bez grabbed both my hands, wrapping his over and under them. "You make me better. You make me happy. You make me believe. I stand by your decisions because if you believe something will work, then I know with absolute certainty we can't fail."

"What if I'm wrong?"

"We could sit here while you do the math on it."

I contemplated what kind of formulas I'd even need to run to evaluate those figures. It'd likely take me weeks to properly discern a proper method that'd yield the best results.

Bez grinned, studying my mouth. I was clearly muttering. Dammit.

I bit my lower lip and squinted. "You're screwing with me."

"If I were screwing with you, you'd know it, love." He smacked my butt with his tail. "I am, however, teasing you."

"It's distracting."

"Good. If that hive of a mind is kept busy, you can't buzz with self-doubt."

I leaned in and hugged him. "Thank you."

He squeezed me back so tight and comforting, it removed all the doubt. All the stress. All the confusion. There was only me and Bez.

I didn't use this time to train, to study, to prepare. Everything about to unfold was unlike anything I'd experienced. We were about to clash with a devil, a being with the power to sway dimensions, consume entire realities, command armies of billions.

There was no preparation that'd ready me for that. So I used this time to hug Bez, to hold him as he held me, to hope and pray and wish and believe our plan worked.

We'd attack Beelzebub. We'd stall him. Keep Lilith alive a little longer. Kell would complete the orb. She'd seal away Lilith. She'd seal away Beelzebub. The end. The easiest of easy plans.

I chuckled anxiously. "We're so fucked."

"You, always." Bez squeezed my ass cheeks. "Me? Only if you're incredibly lucky."

My laughter turned into this bizarre cackle from Bez's utter absurdity.

"And how does one get so lucky?" I slapped his butt and grabbed his firm cheeks just as tight as he'd squeezed mine.

"For starters, that whole confidence thing is really doing it for me." Bez kissed me.

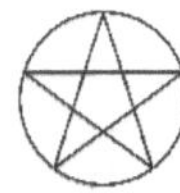

I gathered everyone as the tide of the battle neared its end. Using my senses, I peered through the distance, zooming in at the sight of two devils. Lilith had shrunk, barely larger than an anaconda, wings flapping as she slithered around the confined space where her opponent kept her trapped. Beelzebub had shrunk too, barely a few feet taller than Bez. Quite the stark difference from when he entered the dimension towering over most of the buildings. It was difficult to know if the size morphic change had to do with his depleted essence dueling with Lilith's across the planet or if he wanted to toy with his prey.

"If we're gonna do this," I said with a gulp, one that didn't remove the trepidation stuck in my throat, making every word shaky. "We have to move now."

Each step Beelzebub took had this taunting effect, as if he wanted Lilith to suffer and beg and break before he ended it all. An end that he'd worked toward for nearly a thousand years. The surreal impossibility of it all. The distortion of reality.

I found myself questioning my world's timeline, the biblical truths so many humans believed, and how much of that truth, to a degree, might've overlapped with the history of Diabolics. How much of their accords trickled down to lowly worlds such as ours through the mouths of demons who'd just witnessed a hundred-year battle or a dimension concurred and shared that truth, that history with mortals? With Mythics? With a world so much younger yet the same age as their dimension?

There was so much I wanted to study, to research, to share with the world. No way was I going to die here and now. No way was I going to let the world die.

"How close are you, Kell?" Mora asked.

"Minutes away if y'all just hold on for a bit."

Lilith wailed in the distance.

"We can't." I stared at the handful of glass shards Kell needed to assemble, the remaining steps to invoking the Diabolic orbs' power. "We can hold out for a few minutes."

"We're all going to die." Mora folded her arms. "And just know that I'm going to make all of your lives as miserable as demonically possible when we're in Oblivion."

"Aw, you're making me feel all warm and squishy." Corson puckered his lips.

Mora ran a finger along Corson's sharp jawline, smiling up at him. "Remember that time I murdered you?"

"Didn't take."

"If at first, you don't succeed." Mora winked.

"Enough," I said. "No joking around. I get you're all used to being the strongest person in the room 99.9% of the time. I get that you've all faced death and wars before, but this is Beelzebub. This devil will obliterate the entire dimension, every dimension, if we fail."

"Let's fuck 'em up." Bez flexed his claws and spread his wings wide.

I led everyone outside, and we formed a line as we walked into battle. Part of me wanted to surge ahead, fly quickly, but with each step, I noted the strategy.

Bez stood beside me, unleashing waves of black lightning that crackled against Beelzebub's elements circulating across the city. Jolt after jolt reshaped into electrical silhouettes of Mythic beasts, primal lightning lunging furiously ahead.

Mora stood on my opposite side, strutting in her heels while weaving her hands to trace incantations of the highest caliber. Her technique was flawless, her spells on par with the strongest of mages, which meant her host body must've belonged to someone highly skilled in Collective education. Magic erupted in every direction, countering or redirecting the chaos of Beelzebub's strikes.

Corson walked next to Bez, breathing in so deep that his chest swelled like the throat of a frog. Just when I thought he'd pop, he exhaled black fire. The flames cascaded ahead in a wild stampede, eating away the elements already stunned by Bez's lightning.

Orias strutted in a similar fashion to Mora, eyes trained on her hips as he mimicked the walk. All the while, his tentacles sprang out of the torso of his host body, delicate of the flesh, and he waved his limbs to telekinetically hurl Lilith's broken essence from the grasp of Beelzebub's barrage of attacks.

Satan stayed the furthest out in this lined formation and turned to me.

"We devils gotta make the grand entrances, right?" He swallowed his lollipop—stick and all—then wooed loudly before raising a single arm and shooting a tight black beam from his palm. "In the fine words of a prima donna princess, get fucked posers!"

The energy struck Beelzebub and exploded with a cacophony. Not a single one of the demons I walked beside slowed down. They didn't even appear fazed by the wave of explosive destruction. Admittedly, it was pretty badass walking alongside them through the empty streets of the Diabolic Oasis.

Tar and acid and ice and fire and wind and molten earth sprang forth in every direction, yet not a single demon flinched. None of them bothered to even react once Bez pulled his wings in tight over his chest.

The seconds ticked by, and the bombardment of elements swept in close until Bez unleashed a powerful black gale that sliced and diced the entire attack.

"He's not even treating us like a threat." Bez cocked his head, glaring. "Let's make him regret that arrogance."

"Gladly." Corson grabbed Bez's arm, and the two instinctively spun round and round, no communication required but so synced in their strategy.

Bez released his grip, and Corson flew ahead like a flaming comet.

In an instant, everyone took that as their cue and barreled ahead. Orias moved the slowest, easiest for my eyes to track. His tentacles burrowed deep into the street, pulling out chunks of concrete, which he set aflame and threw.

Mora appeared beside Beelzebub in a flash, evading the swing of his fist and darting back to the safety of darkness conjured by a spell just as Bez used the opening as an opportunity.

Bez stabbed Beelzebub in the chest with the demon-killing blade. The devil roared; he roared so loudly, the earth around the two cracked and crumbled, collapsing to pieces.

Before Beelzebub could attack Bez in retaliation, Corson slammed into him all fire and shock and cackling manically until Beelzebub threw him back with telekinesis.

Not that it did much good. Corson spit fire as he flew back. Satan swept in quickly, using the fire as a cloak. Each swing of his fist and kick of his legs held this majestic acrobatic movement. It was as if he danced circles around the devil, pummeling him in the process.

I watched this all unfold from a safe distance. As safe as ground zero of a world-ending battle could be. I couldn't move. My knees quaked, an instant from buckling. But I didn't need to fight. The five demons moved succinctly, striking Beelzebub at every turn.

Satan remained the heaviest hitter—logical since he possessed a piece of the devil Lucifer inside him. That made him the most vital fighter in their group. Seconded only by Bez, the only demon here actually trained by Beelzebub and used to waging battle with such ferocity.

No. I should've been the second heavy hitter. I had devil essence, too. I had Beelzebub's essence. Not that he'd even deigned to acknowledge me or the loss in power he suffered from that missing fragment.

"*Because you are nothing,*" Beelzebub's voice echoed in my thoughts, a roar of echoes surrounding his words, the Diabolic tongue.

What was this? My heart surged, my eyes fluttered, and everything around me twisted into gnarled, warped images of decayed plants, putrid air, and rotten corpses. The world spun in every direction, showing me the entire planet in destructive glimpses.

How? No. This wasn't real.

I grabbed my head, squeezing away the Diabolic nightmare he'd cast. When? It didn't matter. I needed to break free of this. I screamed, lashing out with essence and magic and spells to wash away the nightmares. Nothing worked. They continued spinning faster. I fell to my knees, hyperventilating.

"Relax." Bez held a steady hand on my chest.

In the seconds since I'd fallen, he was covered in injuries; one of his wings had been sliced off.

"Bez."

He wasn't the only one in pain. Satan thrashed about, covered in flames. Orias had lost three tentacles. Mora stood riddled with open wounds, blood and essence spilling out faster than she could heal. Corson dragged himself forward on the ground, barely able to move. Had it been seconds? Had more time passed? This was the power of a devil at work. We weren't even able to buy time.

"You all really believed you could challenge me? Five pathetic demons." Beelzebub roared. "I have faced armies of millions. Slaughtered worlds of billions. Devoured dimensions of trillions. You are nothing."

He withdrew the demon-killing blade, the one that'd remained embedded in his chest the entire time he fought off Bez and the others. It didn't even faze him. With telekinesis, he crushed the blade, snapping the metal into a thousand tiny pieces that were forced into a small ball of trash for discarding.

"I'm more than a demon," Satan hissed, finally free of the fire.

"Yes, a paltry fool with a few drops of Lucifer's essence." Beelzebub snarled, his snout revealing his fangs. "Lucifer was as inferior as Lilith, vain devils content with the gift the universe granted them and only interested in trivial foolery meant to make them memorable."

"One demon with a piece of the devil might not frighten you, but how about two?" Corson propped himself up with his arms, sapphire eyes glimmering.

I needed to help. Needed to move.

Corson held up a piece of Lilith's splintered essence, letting the tar drip down his forearm.

"How long I've craved this moment." Corson scoffed, cutting a piercing glare at Lilith, who merely lay on the ground unconscious. "Mother isn't even aware of such a momentous victory."

He stuck out his tongue, stretching it nearly a foot in length, and wrapped it around his arm, lapping at the piece of essence he'd taken. A fraction, a tiny molecule of power ingested, but once he gulped that fragmented power, his body surged. Injuries that'd left his body mangled a moment before vanished almost as quickly as he had.

In an instant, Corson sprang out of shadows weaved by Diabolic webs and punched Beelzebub across the jaw, cracking one of the exposed fangs at the end of his snout. It didn't end there. He swooped back into the shadows and darted out from a different direction, rampaging against Beelzebub.

Satan raced ahead, joining Corson's futile attacks. They moved in a flurry, swiftly striking Beelzebub. The devil moved his four arms quicker than the demons, blocking their hits, countering their blows, knocking each of them back, and pummeling them until they collapsed.

It didn't matter what we did.

"Fall back," Bez said. "Reinforce the barrier."

"What, no." I hadn't even fought yet. Hadn't moved yet. Hadn't found the courage to face a devil.

Lilith lunged from her spot, recovered enough from the time we stalled, and furiously bit Beelzebub's throat. With her fangs set in deep, anchored into his flesh, she wrapped her serpent body tight, coiling around his arms, torso, and right leg.

"I need to help." I traced incantations in the air, flipping the sigils and inverting signs to make this healing spell adaptable for Diabolics. I couldn't offer much, but I could mend Bez's injuries, speed up the recovery of his essence, support those fighting.

Lilith wailed, and the air itself shattered like glass, crumbling away chunks of the dimensional walls. An icy wind blew. I shivered. Such a stark contrast to the scalding heat that radiated off the devils to collide with the frigid chill of the world outside this hidden city. A broken city now. A dying city in a dying world in a dying dimension.

I ground my teeth, grinding out the self-doubt. I needed to focus, to fight, to buy time for Kell.

"Look out." Bez shoved me, not fast enough.

The shriek a moment before. Beelzebub had broken Lilith into pieces, dropping her to the ground in seconds. Now, he barreled forward, a moment from hitting Bez, who braced in front of me.

"No!" I screamed with as much fear and malice and hatred as Lilith had unleashed a second before.

Unlike her, my energy didn't wane. The broken walls of the dimension fell like glass shards, yet when the decibels of my Diabolic voice reached them and everything else, time slowed. Froze. Even Beelzebub. An awareness met with a furrowing brow and snarled snout.

Run. I needed to run.

With Bez in my grasp, I dodged Beelzebub. Again. Again. Again. Each time, shouting with my essence to stall the devil's pursuit until he vanished from my sights altogether.

"Good job, Wally." Bez shrugged off the stillness, the scream that continued to delay time around us. Living, dead, non-organic, magical or not. All of it seemed affected.

I spun around, searching for Beelzebub.

"Look out." Bez shoved me away from the approaching darkness.

Beelzebub knocked Bez away, reopening every injury I'd just mended with magic.

"Manipulating the flow of time." Beelzebub looked down on me. "You've learned how to wield my essence well."

I went to run, but the ground itself encased my hands and feet beneath gravel. Beelzebub leaned close, a clawed hand gripped my face, and his snout pressed against my cheek.

"This is more essence than what was taken." He sniffed, deep and confirming Lilith's suspicions about my essence evolving.

His essence.

No. Mine.

Using my tail, I cracked apart the rocky shackles which bound me. Then I balled a fist and decked Beelzebub across the jaw with spiked knuckles.

"It's my essence now." It had evolved with me, for me, grown and changed in ways devils never had before. He couldn't have it back. He couldn't win this battle. He couldn't destroy everything simply because he lusted for destruction.

Without hesitation, without pause, I swept ahead and found myself clashing with the devil.

I hit him with every spell I'd learned. Incantations one after another. Saturation of the atmosphere itself, turning the air and earth and molecules in between into my territory of combat. The familiar bond to Tony offered a pantheon of knowledge and insight into things about nature only witches accessed. I harnessed every element in my repertoire, and those I didn't have access to, Tony assisted with. I glamoured myself approaching Beelzebub from a thousand directions, each illusion obvious. I wouldn't win with stealth, but if I spammed his senses, then it might offer an edge for a second.

All I needed was another second. Another landed punch. Another critical spell. Another fatal injury. Another—

With a sudden and single snap of Beelzebub's jaws, he shattered every incantation I'd cast. The swing of his lower arms sent the elements burrowing into the pits of the earth. His menacing exhale broke my control on the area. And he ignored my illusions, unfazed by pain, real or imagined.

In an instant, he towered above me, pummeling me from every direction. Hit after hit. It was brutal and blurring and bloody, and I couldn't think anymore.

…

…

…

He kept hitting…

…

…

…

It hadn't stopped…

…

…

…

I didn't know what to do…

…

…

…

I gasped, awaiting the next onslaught. The next brutal assault. The next bone-breaking strike.

But relief struck when Beelzebub tired of me and knocked away the demons who bombarded him in a frenzy. I needed more time. Everything faded in and out with each blink of my swollen eyes. Orias tracing sigils of wicked spells. Mora using one-of-a-kind artifacts that could slaughter a nation. Satan sent waves of darkness. Corson cackled chaotically, still high off the taste of a devil embedded with his essence; it pulsed and thrummed with every attack he attempted.

I lay there, defeated and incapable of continuing.

The ground crunched beneath Beelzebub's footsteps, and I wheezed. I needed to move. Fight. Harness my power. If he took another step, I'd be dead. We'd all be dead. Everything would end. The world. The dimension. The neighboring realms. The universe. Beelzebub would strike it all down.

Lilith shrieked.

I flinched. Beelzebub paused. We both turned to see Lilith's crumbling body.

Her scream didn't hold the fervor of resistance it had every time it had before. No. Her voice echoed with fear and defeat and an inability to stop the inevitable.

Kell approached, chanting with the Diabolic orb in hand. She'd made it here. She'd finished the orb. I panted, relieved and exhausted and struggling to mend all the damage dealt.

Kell stood silent with the orb raised high, unrelenting as broken bits of Lilith's essence funneled from all across the city. Each writhing piece slashed at Kell, sliced deep, tore chunks of flesh, and did everything in the devil's power to resist the eternal prison awaiting her.

In one blink of an eye, Lilith raged against the orb. In the next, she'd fallen prey to the indomitable artifact.

It worked. It held. It still had power, power Kell directed toward Beelzebub. She chanted the song meant to contain him, enacting the symbols on the Diabolic orb and giving her all to end this battle.

"The absurdity of twisting an angel's tears into a prison," Beelzebub growled. "To think such a thing exists."

Angels? What?

Beelzebub lifted off the ground, not resisting the pull of the Diabolic orb but instead using the momentum to lunge at Kell.

NO!

Mora leapt at Kell, knocking their footing out of Beelzebub's path but also breaking the gravitational pull of the Diabolic orb.

"Angels?" Kell asked, as perplexed as me.

"The Angelics are long since lost to the universe," Mora explained, her eyes glowing emerald green. "Very few still breathed when I was born."

"They were admirable in combat but soft." Beelzebub stood tall again. "They challenged the glory of the devils, and as such, I removed them from existence."

"Lucifer loved his angels." Satan punched Beelzebub, knocking his balance off, but not enough. "One of his few admirable qualities. You haven't tasted love until you've tasted an angel."

Beelzebub went to strike Satan, only to miss when Orias wrapped a tentacle around Satan's waist and pulled him out of range.

"Lilith never stopped talking about how much they glittered." Corson struck Beelzebub from behind. "It seems you owe me a few centuries of whiny lectures endured about the times before."

When Beelzebub turned in rage, another tentacle snatched up Corson from the devil's grasp.

Soon, Mora and Bez joined the fray, each demon antagonizing and retreating again and again with Orias' aid.

I gathered my bearings, doing my best to heal the injuries endured. Between my essence and magic, it didn't seem to make much of a difference.

Each demon fought with a fury, using the catalyst of the Diabolic orb to push them past their limits. Slowly, it dragged Beelzebub inward. His essence could only fight so much. Every time a demon landed a lucky strike, a piece of Beelzebub was sealed away. But he warred and raged and refused to go quietly.

Surrender from the incarnation of violence seemed impossible, but I wanted to do my part. Moving was too much work, so I shared my power, weaving sigils with my tail—the only part of me not entirely numb—and created every top-tier incantation I knew, which made for a lot of spell weaving.

The demons moved faster, harder, ruthless and unyielding. I threw more spell work at them. More. More. More. Anything to bring this devil to his end.

The devil's lower arms transformed into blades, and he lunged directly for me.

Bez intercepted him, stopping him from impaling me. Two blades thrust through his chest, another breaking his remaining wing.

"Takes more than that, bastard!" Bez spit at Beelzebub, dragging himself off the sword arms.

Without hesitation, Bez resumed his attacks, the same each of the demons before had attempted. Bit by bit, he ripped apart Beelzebub's essence. Small fragments, but enough to lure them into the orb. If he could keep this up, if the others could, if I could, then it'd bring a final end to Beelzebub.

"Whenever you fail me like this, I just send you back to

Oblivion so you can contemplate your disgrace." Beelzebub unleashed such tremendous fire it incinerated Bez to nothingness.

Instantaneous. Even the ashes were mere wisps. Impossible. Bez couldn't... Bez wouldn't... Bez... Not Bez!

I screamed so loudly I shattered the broken shards of the dimensional wall Lilith had cracked apart. They sprinkled like snowfall, glittering around the ashes of Bez. Those flakes were fueled with magic both new and ancient. I took a deep breath, drawing in all that stray mana. More than any misfit mage or not could contain. My essence clawed at my insides as furious as me. It needled throughout, repurposing the magic we'd taken.

My shadow swelled before Beelzebub, horns growing into gnarled twists much like a demonic stag.

"I'll end you." In a flash, part incantation and part essence, I appeared behind Beelzebub.

Without a word, I hacked and slashed and ripped into every weak point Bez had exposed. I tore chunks of Beelzebub out, releasing them back into the pull of the orb. I dug my claws into Beelzebub, burrowing into the spots Bez had already chiseled away at.

Bez had pushed his former devil to the precipice of defeat, and I gave the final shove. I wanted to drag out this agony. I wanted to make the devil suffer a fraction of what I felt. But more than anything, I didn't wish to give him the glory of a final battle.

"May history forget you, you worthless fuck!" I kicked him in the chest.

Beelzebub roared, thunderous and godly, as the Diabolic orb contained his essence, shredding it into microscopic pieces, pieces which swam alongside Lilith's essence. The two collided, their beings warring even in this prison.

I tumbled forward and nearly collapsed on the ground. I took deep, exhausted breaths, each exhale returning and restoring pieces of the city. It'd need a complete overhaul, maybe just a wrecking ball to finish the job, but I didn't want to see this place die. I didn't want to see anyone die. No death. Not B… I bit my lip. I couldn't say it. Couldn't think it. Couldn't feel it. Not now, not ever.

Mora and Kell walked over, each using the other as a prop to stand as their legs trembled with exhaustion.

"There isn't a hole deep enough to drop these two." Mora stared at the orb, studying it cautiously while wrapping her arm around Kell's waist.

"There's one place we can send them," I said, fighting back every sob ready to burst out.

I couldn't process Bez's death. I wouldn't. I wouldn't have to.

"We can send them to Oblivion." I stood to my feet. "Drop them into the nothingness where they won't be a threat to anyone."

"I can see those gears turning, Walter. It doesn't take much to know what you're thinking." Mora studied me, careful and cautious in the way she sidestepped. "I'm sorry about Bez, but we can't open Oblivion."

"Yes, we can. Bez pulled me out of that place with devil essence, I can do the same."

"He pulled out your consciousness," Mora explained. "He waved a little flag of devil essence which retrieved your mind."

"And I'll do the same," I snapped.

"Bez is gone on a cellular level, mind, body, and soul cast into the nothingness of Oblivion," Mora declared it so nonchalantly, so callous, so flippant about the situation. "It takes a devil, a true and complete devil, to open the doorway to Oblivion and pluck out a deceased demon."

"I'm unique, a hybrid devil unlike any other." I barred my teeth. "I'll open Oblivion and pull out every fucking demon if that's what it takes."

"You're powerful, Walter. More powerful than I think any of us realize quite yet, but you can't open Oblivion. You wouldn't even know where to look for the door to Oblivion."

"Where is it?"

"I don't know," Mora hissed. "It's nothingness—not sure it has a fixed location. I wouldn't even know where to begin."

"They would, though." I stared at the orb. "I can leash Lilith or Beelzebub, form a Diabolic bond with one, force them to do my bidding, and open Oblivion."

"They're both broken, incomplete devils, incapable of opening the doorway on their own."

"Then I'll form a bond with both of them," I shouted. "I'll make them obey, make them work together. Two partial devils could surely be strong enough to open one damn doorway. Stop coming up with reasons this won't work and help find a fucking solution!"

"I might have a better idea than taming the shrew and her eternal cuckold." Corson propped a foot on the orb, a cocky grin on his smug face. "Why make deals with devils when you can dance with demons?"

"I don't have time for riddles or annoying come-ons."

"I want to be rid of Lilith permanently, and I very much enjoy your idea of dropping her into Oblivion, where she's left me to rot many times before," Corson said. "The beautiful thing about falling into Oblivion over and over and over again? You start to memorize the trail leading to nowhere."

Was this real? Was this really going to happen? Were we going to rescue Bez from death?

My heart surged. "Let's do this."

28

Bez

Damn. Dead. Again. It'd been so long since Beelzebub had struck me down, shattered my being to nothingness, that I'd forgotten the sensation. The agony of burning. So much fire. Blistering heat that seared every cell of my being.

Merely a handful of seconds, yet this excruciating phantom burn clung to me as I drifted in darkness. Everything was nothing, dull, but Beelzebub made sure I'd hold onto this radiating icy cold grip of death.

My only hope was that his vindictive spite was a sign of his faltering success against the orb. Gods, I hoped it held. I hoped Wally and the others managed to defeat him without more loss.

"Dwelling on the world—any world—of the living will only make your time spent here painful," a feminine silhouette of lavender light stepped from the shadows. "Seek solace from Oblivion's embrace, and this world can offer you clarity, peace, and even happiness."

Great. Was this demon about to give me a tour? I'd protest, but I couldn't recall the fundamentals of stitching together my being to speak through the shadows.

I floated silently, studying every curve of lavender light, the sculpted face created, the talons, tails, and soon the details formed a memory.

I recognized this demon. Agares.

"That's what they used to call me, yes," they replied to my thoughts because the filter between thinking and speaking didn't exist here in Oblivion. Even without a mouth or a voice, I still expressed myself.

"You're an ancient demon." Eligos had told me harrowing legends of Agares and the way they bucked Beelzebub's authority, escaped his world, carved out a name for themself a thousand dimensions away.

Perhaps it was what motivated the fallen knight in his venture for glory, his dream to give voice to the demons. Perhaps it also encouraged me in some small way to run and hide and build a new name for myself.

But seeing the truth of things, seeing how this ancient demon of legend hadn't lived so happily, hadn't escaped Beelzebub and exchanged his Hell for freedom. No. They ended up bested by Eligos, locked in an orb by that Fae Novus, and now they lay dead and forgotten in Oblivion like me and trillions of others.

"To hear my eons of life surmised in such a swift and sullen manner frames quite the picture," Agares said, shifting around the darkness, offering the gentlest of lavender light.

"Apologies."

"No need. You know of me, in part," they said. "And I know you, favorite child of Beelzebub."

I tsked. "Favorite to slaughter, to cast down here again and again and again. To drag through dimensions, paraded for my shame."

"A project he never gave up on," Agares said. "Unlike so many of us."

Shadows slithered all around me, and whispers echoed everywhere.

"When Beelzebub found himself bound to his singular Hell, bested in a coup against a weaker foe, he slaughtered every demon in his dimension." Agares extended their arms, casting lavender light on the moving darkness.

"And they're here for their revenge." I sank into the darkness. "I abandoned them, fled, left every demon locked behind a doorway."

"There is no resentment," Agares said. "Winning a war against Beelzebub was never in their future. Many see that now. Understand they were always meant for Oblivion. We are here to embrace you."

What?

"We're honored to meet you…" Agares paused at my name, a name I felt on the tip of every tongue. A thousand souls. A billion. More. Each calling out a name that didn't belong to me anymore. Each biting back a name that shouldn't have been given to me. A name that wasn't me. A name I'd heard in a thousand lives, lives I didn't recognize. Not anymore.

"I expected my next trip to Oblivion to be met with malice."

"This is not Hell," Agares said.

"There could be worse ways to spend my eternity."

"And there could be better ways still." Agares lifted their head, face locked on a moving glimmer in the distance. "Something tells me it'll be a much longer wait before we're reunited—"

"Bez!" Wally's voice sliced through the shadows, a beacon calling to me and silencing the millions of nearby souls.

"Not you, too." I sank into myself, watching Wally descend into the dark nothingness with me.

Beelzebub had taken everything from me, even Wally's life, his future, his happiness. I could only hope to hold onto myself long enough here to shield him from the somber existence of no longer existing.

"I'm so glad I found you," Wally said, his bright smile lighting up the darkness.

In fact, everything about him illuminated this place. Wally's entire form held tangibility, physical shape, a breath of life. His devilish features shimmered, providing power and precision as he navigated this nothingness.

Wally hadn't died. Wally had leapt in here the same way a devil would.

"How? How did you get here?" I swam around Wally, incorporeal and fragmented energy with no body to speak of, to speak with, but I had the sheer will to ask.

"You'd be amazed what three partial devils can do." He grinned, no hidden anxiety in his expression, just a face brimming with confidence.

Satan and Corson. They weren't partial devils, merely demons trotting about with stolen essence.

"It doesn't matter what they are," Wally said, making me swallow my own thoughts because, in this void of a world, nothing was hidden. "It was enough to carve a path here, enough to retrieve you, to save you."

"You tore into Oblivion to save me?" My eyes watered.

I hated how Walter made me feel…feel seen. Feel at all. I loved hating it. Loathed that I couldn't accept it at value. Hated how much I enjoyed resisting his genuine spirit. His kindness. His loyalty. His love. But more than anything, I appreciated it, wanted to explore it forever and ever and more than time itself could offer.

"There you are." He reached out, hands cupping around my face, running them down my shoulders, caressing my silhouette, and giving me a shape outside the shadows. "We need to go."

"You in a rush?"

"Maybe. Only a fully intact devil is supposed to be able to open Oblivion, so I'd rather not test the timer." Wally held my hand, pulling me ahead. "Plus, we dropped Lilith and Beelzebub down here. Up here? Between? The location is very unspecific. Point is, while I don't imagine them working together to break loose from the orb any time soon, I don't want to be here if or when they do."

"Do not worry about that, Wally." Agares fluttered between the shadows, taking deliberate steps. "We demons reign in Oblivion, enjoying the slumber it offers. No devil dwelling here has a voice. They will sleep. We will make them."

"Thank you, Agares." Wally nodded, careful about his horns, which had grown and swirled in odd directions, symbolizing what I imagined as the maze of his thoughts. "It's nice to see you again."

That was right. They briefly encountered each other when Wally died. Dead. Fallen into Oblivion.

"May our paths never cross again," Agares said. "But if they do, know you are always welcome in Oblivion, Walter Alden."

With that farewell from an ancient demon, Wally flew through the shadows, holding me in his grasp and moving faster and faster until light split the darkness away.

"Wait." I pushed away. "I have to say goodbye."

"What?"

I sank back into the darkness, whispering every thought I'd ever had as loud as fucking possible until a glimmering orb appeared in the shadows before me.

"Everything you did to me." I floated toward the orb, watching broken essence swirl round and round. "Everything you did to control me. To make me yours. To own me. To kill me. To break me."

Essence ripped at itself. It was Beelzebub shredding Lilith, knocking her presence away as he moved closer to the edge of his glass prison.

"It failed," I said with tears welling in my eyes. I needed him to know that after everything, he meant nothing. I needed him to know because I needed to leave this hatred, this regret, this poison, this passion, this rage in the depths of Oblivion. "I will forget you. Whether it takes a century or a thousand, you don't own me. You don't control my happiness. You don't haunt my dreams. You don't stir in my memories anymore."

Wally descended, hovering close behind me but allowing this moment between me and the devil who'd haunted my eternity.

"Last time I ran away from you, locking you up in your Hell. This time, I am running toward something, toward someone." I backed away, letting Wally hold me, carry me away. "Someone who knows me in ways you never understood. Someone who loves me more than the world itself. Enjoy Oblivion. May you be forgotten until the end of time."

The broken essence sank into its orb, not fighting, not furious, but finally accepting failure.

I smiled, free from Beelzebub's grasp, and ascended through the depths of nothingness until the world took hold of me.

Everything burned. I gasped. I roared. I thrashed and raged and collapsed into muck.

"His essence is still too broken," Mora shouted. "He needs a body, something to stabilize his recovery."

Wally shouted something. I turned to see but found only light in his face. Light everywhere.

Then darkness again.

"Wakey, wakey, sleepy head." The voice was faint, gentle.

Wally.

His hand caressed my cheek, then traced along my jawline, and finally worked its way down to my pecs, getting a good solid grip on my chest.

"While I very much prefer you in your own flesh, this suit is awfully cute, too," he said with a light cackle.

"Motherfucker." I shot up in the bed where I lay, tails out and piercing Corson's wrist, his throat, and his heart. I should've aimed for his crotch. "You handsy prick!"

"I was a total gentleman." He puckered his lips. "I just needed you to wake up before I headed out."

I retracted my tails, coiling them back inside this mortal body where my essence continued recovering. Getting dragged out of Oblivion often left demons drained; I recalled several occasions where Beelzebub had pulled me out and thrown me back onto the battlefield of some war. And while exhausted for certain, I usually wasn't this busted up.

"Guessing three makeshift devils don't know how to bring back a demon the right way."

"Is there a wrong way?" Corson cocked his head. "You're alive again. Yippee. A little worn down but nothing some R&R inside a tight little body won't fix up in no time."

He wasn't wrong. This actually felt a lot like when I broke free from the Diabolic orb. That required a few weeks of restoration inside the mage body I possessed. Who did I currently possess? I stared at the pale hands, focusing on the energy of this host. There was mana for certain. Some unfortunate mage, it seemed.

My heart raced. A mage? I was inside a mage's body.

"Where's Wally?"

"He's nearby." Corson tiptoed his fingers along my thigh. "Closer than you think."

No. This wasn't the case. Wally wouldn't. He was never a fan of me possessing folks, but he didn't protest it either.

"Wally." I shoved Corson off and crawled out of the bed, searching for a mirror, something to prove the worst hadn't happened. "Fuck."

I sighed, instinctively exhaling frightened breaths. This host body belonged to someone I didn't recognize. Though, part of that could've been the composite already taking effect, manipulating the features to slip into my aesthetic.

"What's your deal?"

"I thought…" I laughed a little to myself. "I thought something very silly happened."

"I'm gonna miss you, pretty boy."

I scowled, letting my horns stab through the head of this host and ruffle the brown hair I'd need to darken with a glamour soon enough. Chestnut brown wasn't for me. Black and orange all day, please.

"You're leaving?" I asked, making my way back to bed because exhaustion had settled back in.

I wasn't sure how long I'd lay here recovering, but I wanted to sleep for another few days, a few weeks, maybe a solid year.

"Yes. I find this dead town boring," Corson said. "Satan and Orias are dragging their feet about it, claiming this place merits some interest, but I've assured them the rest of the dimension has much more to offer."

"So, you're staying here?" I asked, referencing the world, not the Diabolic Oasis, which I gathered from context meant the city had survived—even if left as nothing more than rubble.

"We weren't the only demons Lilith dragged through the doors of Hell in her wake as she fled from Beelzebub." Corson shrugged. "Maybe I'll find some of them. Play a game. Kiss, kill, or recruit. See where that takes me."

The rest of the world must be somewhat intact, too. Not that three demons would complain about exploring a dying hellscape.

Who knew what Lilith and Beelzebub had done to this world before they were dropped into Oblivion? Gods, Beelzebub was locked inside a Diabolic orb and dropped into Oblivion.

Oblivion.

Beelzebub was truly gone. He was a defeated devil, bound in the void of nothing until the end of time itself. He was gone forever.

I smiled. Genuine and relieved. There was this hidden weight on my shoulders that eased. This tension I carried at all times, so constant and aching I'd grown accustomed to it. Numb to the pain. And yet, with Beelzebub forever out of my life, truly gone and no longer a looming threat in the shadows, I found relief.

"Did you even hear what I said?"

"I wasn't listening." I chuckled, still musing over Beelzebub's absence. His torment. The horrors he must be experiencing. Not at the hands of the many enemies he'd dropped in that void over the eons. None of them could hurt him as much as he hurt himself.

It must be awful for him, locked in that orb with his shame of failure, failure for all to see, failure he'll never escape.

My chuckle transformed into a vindictive cackle of delight. I only wished I could mock the bastard. But I'd have to settle for living my best fucking life forever and ever with my mage.

"Where is Wally?"

"Here," Wally answered, rushing into the room.

"Yes, I'll miss you too, asshole," Corson grumbled, still rambling on about his demon road trip as if I were listening intently to what he had planned.

"Thanks for getting me when he woke up." Wally glowered.

"I wanted to, but Bez looked worn for wear, and I feared your ceaseless prattle would send him back to Oblivion." Corson smirked. "Then I'd have to rescue him all over again."

"That's not the expression," Wally said. "And—"

"And enjoy your trip, Corson," I interrupted. "Goodbye. Now."

"Thank you," he replied with a flourished bow. "Maybe in another century or two, your little misfit devil will be willing to share the cutest demon in all the Hells that ever Helled."

I rolled my eyes.

"First, you ripped out my heart; now, you own it." Corson winked and then turned his attention back to Wally. "See you around, Walter Devil Boy of Great Mortal Human Things, First of His Hybridization or whatever and all that jizz."

"Goodbye," Wally said with pure malice in his heart. It was intoxicating. "Try not to maim and murder."

"Toodaloo." Corson waved as he left. "If I do, I'll think of you."

With that, Wally telekinetically slammed the door shut.

"He's frustrating."

"Pretty sure you said that about me…a lot."

"Yeah, but…" Wally paused, taking a deep, calming breath. "He's worse. Much. The last three months were excruciating. I kept waiting for him to leave. Satan and Orias were ready the second the dust settled, but Corson… So obnoxious."

"Three months, huh?"

"Give or take." Wally shrugged nonchalantly like he wasn't mouthing the time I slept down to the very second.

"And you decided to put me in a host?" I stared at my hands, extending my claws momentarily to test their limits. "Guessing from Mora's collection since the selection is probably limited here in the city."

"Yeah. She's already called in her favor for that one, too."

"At least you got me a cute body." I gave Wally my best smoldering expression, something to draw him closer, calm his nerves, elicit the right tension. "I'm just surprised you lot put me in a body to begin with."

"You were in really rough shape, Bez." Wally got quiet for a moment, biting his lower lip. "We're not exactly experts on reviving demons. I swear, Corson intentionally led me in circles when searching for Oblivion."

"Well, it all worked out," I said, dragging Wally away from whatever somber feelings he almost stirred up. "I'm just surprised you were cool kicking some poor fool out of his own skin for my sake. After all that work you did so I could feel sensations in my own body. But seeing as I didn't have much of one left, thank you for your valiant efforts."

"To be clear, I only helped you feel in your own demon skin so you could feel in your own demon skin, you know?" Wally's expression quirked into this confused, frowny smile. "I just want you to be comfortable with who you are. If you're comfortable as a sexy brute of a demon with killer abs, flawless gray skin, and a thick build in all the right places. Then that's great."

He winked, then giggled, because it was Walter, and despite all he did to be charming and sexy and suave, he was still a little geeky nerd who blushed when sex came up in idol conversation amongst others. Funny, considering how demanding he was behind closed doors and the number of frisky ventures he jumped at exploring.

"But also, if you prefer rocking out in mortal flesh while flaunting your tails, your wings, your horns, and your claws, and the crimson eyes, and wow, you really do show off a lot of your Diabolic features now that I think about it. Hmm…uh, the point is, I want you to be happy, Bez."

"Well, I'll be happy once I break this body in." I lifted the blanket a bit, eyeing myself beneath the covers to draw Wally's interest. "The composite is slipping in nicely, so we'll have to test my stamina soon."

"Oh?" Wally's eyes widened. "What'd you have in mind?"

A scratch at the door caught his attention before I could answer. The whiny sniffles that followed made it clear the hound had realized I'd awakened and come to pester me for fiery treats. I bet that was the only reason Weather bothered to come begging. Wally didn't make fireball snacks nearly as well, always worried he'd burn the Cerberus' tongues. Like a beast born of fire and meant to serve over the gates of the underworld needed to worry about too much heat.

"Don't," I protested as Wally went to open the door. "He can wait five minutes."

"How much stamina were you planning on testing?" Wally shot me a judgy smirk.

"I literally just came back into existence a few moments ago." I folded my arms. "You'd think I could enjoy a quick blowjob in peace."

"He's missed you, though." Wally opened the door, allowing the three-headed mongrel to barge inside, sniffing everything inside the room, tail wagging and paws ambling about aimlessly in the room. "But I will say in your absence, I finally won Weather back to my side."

"Is that so?" I squinted.

"Oh, yeah." He nodded. "You wanna see? Sunny and I have six tricks mastered."

"Psst." I gestured a wave of demonstration. "Proceed."

Sunny was easy to train and win over. He was an attention whore, doing anything for pets, smiles, affection, acknowledgment, a snack, a treat, an extra serving in his bowl, and really anything that said he was the center of the universe.

"Let's show Bez the new trick I taught you," Wally said with a side-eye of cockiness. "One that doesn't involve pretending to murder folks."

"Who's pretending?" I grinned.

"Weather—"

"Sit," I interrupted.

Sunny's ears perked up, but he kept his eyes trained on Wally. All the same, the Cerberus sat down. When Sunny whimpered apologetically for Wally's plight, Cloudy nudged the center head, and Stormy growled. It took a few seconds longer than usual, but the beast remained obedient.

"Yeah, you definitely won him over."

"One out of three." Wally huffed.

I whistled enough to command Weather up onto the bed. "You better get over here, Walter, unless you want the hound to take the best cuddling spots."

Wally slipped beside me, wrapping his leg over mine before Weather plopped down. The Cerberus lay with Stormy on my hip, Sunny on my stomach, and Cloudy resting on Wally's side.

"So, what's next?" I asked, clearing the hoarseness from my voice, which Weather mimicked like it were some type of game. Either that or the hound was mocking me for being unwell.

"Literally whatever you wanna do," Wally answered. "We can chill at home or get back into the shop routine. Oh, we could explore the city—restoration has been going well. Mora's completely obsessed with getting the Diabolic Oasis back to 100%. We could travel, too. The rest of the world seems fine. I mean, from what I've heard. Kell's explored some. Seems Nature kept most of the destruction at bay, and the Collective is doing its part to glamour away a near apocalypse from the minds of the masses. Honestly, not sure people really noticed how close to the end of the world they really were."

I scoffed. "Are they ever?"

Wally didn't respond. He just had this pensive little expression mixed with an inquisitive gaze. All the insight he shared was secondhand knowledge. The state of the world. The repairs on the city. Everything. Because it seemed this entire time I'd been gone, all of Wally's efforts were focused on opening Oblivion to pull me free.

"Do you want to venture out there?" I asked. "Check on your family, friends?"

"No. Like I said, Kell kept me updated," he said with a hug. "Now, things can go back to normal. Or whatever we had before Hell. Before devils."

We lay together in this cozy half-sleep, and I found myself truly at peace in Wally's embrace.

29

Wally

Bez had taken less time to recover than I preferred, accompanying Mora on her ventures to secure the city now that the threat of devils had passed. I was pretty disappointed in the Collective using the gaps in the dimensional walls of the Diabolic Oasis to attempt slipping infiltration units inside, and while I didn't approve of Mora's kill first, show leniency second philosophy, I understood the sentiment. We'd endured a lot. This city had wounds of its own to heal. We didn't have time for mage drama.

Tony hissed. Not aloud, but through sheer thought rattling through the familiar link we shared. It rang through from the other side of the city, proving our bond continued blossoming and would hopefully grow over the centuries.

I unveiled my wings and soared through the skies, calmly searching for Tony's location.

While my essence prevented me from forming a new bond with any other animals, it helped sync my scorpion and me on a different level altogether. So long as I lived, fueled by Diabolic powers and magical forces, so would Tony. He'd thrive and grow and evolve. I couldn't wait to study all the amazing things he'd accomplish with magic, with essence, with me.

I glamoured myself once I reached the pinged location.

Tony skittered up the wall to join me on the rooftop, where we watched a group of mages slip between the cracks of the city's protective barriers, magics we hadn't restored. Once inside, they glamoured themselves poorly. Even without my essence to sniff out their magics, I could've seen through these poor tricks before mastering the Pentacles of Power.

My guess was that the most elite forces had been wiped out during Lilith's attack on the world, or they were still recovering from the ordeal. Not sure why I hoped for the latter. I wasn't part of the Collective anymore. I didn't like the way mages sought to control every aspect of magic in our world and sometimes the areas outside it. Still, I couldn't slaughter these fools. Despite Tony's insistent thoughts and subtle clacks of his claws.

I leapt off the roof and landed amidst the center of their apprentice-level formation.

"Seriously, how long have you lot even been out of the academy?"

None of them answered. Their faces were frantic and frazzled as they honed their mana, reinforcing their glamours like I hadn't seen through this travesty.

"Guys, gals, and mage pals. I can see you." I waved my hands in front of their faces. "Can you see me? My Diabolic features? You might not have heard of me. I'm Walter Alden. Legendary misfit. Bound to a devil. Only he's not a devil. So much better. But I'm a devil. Sort of. It's actually a really long story."

With a thwack of my tail, I shattered the incantations one of the mages behind me traced. With a stomp of my foot, I overwhelmed their attempt to saturate the ground and lay claim to this terrain.

With Tony in the wings, their familiars had already fled back through the cracks of this pocket dimension.

"Okay, enough of this." I took a deep breath and exhaled fire. Partially for a new trick, I planned on winning Weather's love, even if bribery seemed like the wrong way to win a pet over—I wasn't above it. The other part of me liked showing off my advanced control over the elements.

In all my years as a mage, a legacy, a student, an apprentice, and an aspiring practitioner, I'd never shown mastery in a single skill from the Pentacles of Power. Now, I wielded each with ease alongside my Diabolic abilities. My devil powers.

The flames didn't burn the mages, merely licked at their mana and burned away their glamours.

"I'm going to ask you to leave now." I raised my clawed hands. "Collective forces are not welcome here. If they continue their attempts to infiltrate, they'll incur the wrath of a Diabolic army. The same army which halted two devils."

An exaggeration for sure, but no one knew how many Diabolics were involved in the battle against Lilith and Beelzebub. Honestly, fewer would believe five demons, a misfit hybrid, and one wicked witch managed to avert the end of the world anyway. Plus, with Corson, Satan, and Orias out and about, likely making names for themselves in all the wrong ways, it'd give the Collective reason to pause. If those were merely three members of our Diabolic army, they'd surely hesitate. Not that we needed an army at this point.

"He's just one—"

I smacked their leader across the face with my tail, tracing an incantation with my tail tip in the process and conjuring a metallic seal that welded his mouth shut. He hit the ground face first with the heavy clink of the steel screwed over his lips.

"It'll fade," I said with a sly smile. "Sort of like dissolving stitches. Which, fun fact, that metal plate I spelled over your mouth was originally a medicinal spell created to help injured golems."

Another mage lifted an enchanted sword, hacking at my back. With a simple flutter of my wings, I shook loose three feathers. One to slice through the sigils lining the sword, another to break the blade itself, and a third to hold to the mage's throat.

"I'm trying to be nice. Show restraint." I glared at their fallen leader, who struggled to counter the spell that welded his mouth shut. "If I ask again, I'll simply send your corpses back with a finely written note explaining my demands."

My shadow swelled over him, horns growing into gnarled horrors I intended to unveil if they didn't accept my offer.

Their group leader froze. Each of them stilled. Their mana. Their breathing. Every muscle of their body stiffened, too frightened to even tremble.

"Leave or die." I tilted my head, letting the light hit my horns; the shade cast darkness over my eyes and gave them what Tony considered to be the most menacing expression of all time.

It helped to have his thoughts synced to mine, feeling his words as a vibrant emotion in the back of my head. It also helped me register the attitude I gave those mages worked when their frantic faces fell into horrified expressions, and they fled without taking all their supplies.

"Oooo." I retrieved one of the bags. "I wonder if the Collective sent them with anything rare. I feel like a mission of this caliber qualifies for unique artifacts."

"Why is it you keep sparing Collective mages?" Mora asked, slipping through the hidden thread of her Diabolic webs she'd recemented throughout the city.

"Killing them only results in more mages sent in their stead," I said, keeping my voice steady despite the fact Mora had a super startling presence and always managed to catch me off guard with her arrivals. "Sending them with a message—a warning—that's what's gonna stop Collective forces in the long run."

"You say that, yet this is the fourth, no fifth, time you've intercepted my investigations on infiltrations." Mora sauntered toward me. "It's funny because you didn't have a problem with me handling matters in my own fashionable choice the last month or so."

"The last month or so, it seemed like a brutish but effective method." I shrugged. "Now, it seems futile. The Collective would likely respond better to amicable treaties. We'll begin with threats, sparing the forces sent to infiltrate and open for discussion. By the time we have negotiations on the table, our walls will be restored, and this topic will be moot."

"Really?" Mora placed a hand beneath her chin, feigning deep contemplation and giving off actual irritation. "Right as Bezzy began joining my scouting missions, that's when it became a futile effort? Hmm. Suspicious."

"I'm sorry…was that a question?"

"The question is, are you really interfering because you think your plan will work, or are you simply shielding Bez from combat?" Mora asked, hands on her hips and attitude wafting in the air. "Are you worried he can't handle himself?"

I wasn't worried about Bez. I mean, obviously, I worried about Bez. But I wasn't worried about how he'd fair against Collective mages. Well, maybe a bit. Not in such a patronizing way that Mora insinuated with her tone. I just didn't want Bez rushing into combat to prove himself. He'd fought two devils. He'd survived Oblivion without the aid of a devil. Not a fully intact devil's restoration. He didn't have anything to prove.

"Well, Walter.?" Bez slipped out of Mora's demonic threads woven across the city. "Which is it?"

"Huh?" I bit my lip, stalling for a few seconds to think and keep from blurting the wrong thing.

"Walter?" Bez seethed; crimson eyes locked onto me with a hateful glare meant to wash away what he perceived as pity.

"Um, well, you see…"

Bez huffed louder than the ruffle of his feathers and flew away before I could scramble to put together one concrete sentence.

"Oops." Mora placed her hand below her mouth, face wide with fake surprise. "Did I go and cause strife with the lovebirds?"

I furrowed my brow and growled, the essence stirring in my chest and ready to roar.

"Oh, you look so furious with your forehead all scrunched up with angry eyebrows." Mora playfully plucked one of the hairs from my brow. "I miss you with glasses. You used to look so cute and confused. Now, you just look menacing and mean."

"We're not done," I said through barred teeth.

"I'm sure we're not, Wally." Mora wiggled her fingers in a farewell wave. "Go find your boyfriend. I'll deal with Collective drama. Amicably, of course."

I flew off, chasing Bez.

It didn't take long to find Bez. I followed his trail, flying past our home, around the city, skipping over most of his haunts since they were still under construction, and finally arriving at our store. The Well of Wonders also remained closed during this restoration period, even though it was one of the few places not entirely decimated by the devil attacks.

Bez trained in the back of the store, making use of his mostly untouched training room. A place where we used to spar regularly. A place that was meant to help me unlock and control my Diabolic abilities. A place I ignored now that I'd found my footing and gained an understanding of myself and this new path my powers had carved out on their own.

"I'm sorry."

"For what?" Bez had the sleeves of his dress shirt rolled up as he struck a heavy training bag with his fist, rhythmic punches meant to hone his skills.

It wasn't exactly a standard training bag, given we'd supplemented it with materials that'd withstand daily strikes from Diabolics. Even so, I routinely had to reorder the supplies and make new ones for the room. Guess after today's training, I'd need to contact our old vendors, see if they were back in business after the near apocalypse.

"I wasn't trying to protect you or anything," I said. "If that's what you're thinking. I know you're capable of—"

"I'm not worried about you shielding my feelings or my life." Bez continued his punches, using his tails on several nearby speed bags. "I'm worried that I can't keep up with you."

"What?"

"You've always been so strong, Wally. You just couldn't see it. Now you can. You are one-of-a-kind powerful. Beyond measure."

"No, I'm not." I folded my arms over my chest, trying to think of how to downplay Bez's comments. "I've gained some understanding of skills, but I'm not one-of-a-kind. I mean, my essence is. But even so, it's not that special."

"It's not the essence." Bez stopped his training. "Yes, that adds to who you are, to what you can do, but you've always been one-of-a-kind special. I've known it since I first laid eyes on you. You weren't like other mages. You weren't like other Aldens. You weren't like other misfits. You were Wally. My Wally."

I almost collapsed into a puddle of mush. Bez always knew the right thing to say.

"You know, these punching bags can't offer the real training I need." Bez loosened his tie. "And honestly, you've been getting a little lazy lately. Might need to smack you around until you remember your training."

My face fell flat. Bez also knew how to say the absolutely wrong thing, too.

"Alrighty, demon." I stretched my legs, flexing my foot in my hand as I limbered up. "You wanna change first?"

"I do my best work in a suit." Bez leapt ahead in a blur, not even stating we were going, and attempted to strike me with his claws the instant we began.

I pivoted out of the way, dodging his movements as I slowed the perception of my senses. It allowed me to focus, to take a figurative breather as Bez struck furiously fast, even with time seemingly stalled.

His tails looped ahead of him, slithering at my feet in an attempt to trip me.

If I kept backing up, I'd end up crashing into the wall, but I could already see the fire building in Bez's palms, ready to scorch me from whichever side I darted. With no other options, I jumped forward, and we tumbled to the floor together.

We ended up knocking into each other, rolling on the ground until I found myself on top of him. Bez dug his claws into the mat, using them to secure his position, and bucked his hips in an attempt to throw me off him.

Swept in the heat of the fight, I slashed his chest.

Bez winced, stifling a shout but visibly frustrated.

"Sorry." I retracted my claws from his bloody chest, staring down at him below me.

"Don't be." Bez whirled his legs so he could wrap them around my neck and lock me in place. "We're training. I'm fine."

We flipped around, him on top of me, and my eyes fixed on the blood dripping down his slow-healing wound.

I couldn't allow this. It consumed me. His injury. His pain. His neglect for his own well-being just to prove he could keep up.

"You're right here, right beside me." I forced myself up, pushing between his legs until I squeezed my shoulders through his clenched thighs that held a rock-hard grip on my chest and back. He kept one arm locked, too, but I brought my free hand to his injury.

I bent my thumb as far as it'd go, then let the claw grow and curl inward until I reached my palm.

"What are you doing?"

"Trying something." I sliced through the skin, letting blood spill into Bez's injury, but it wasn't the blood I wanted to share. "A long time ago, I sliced my palm, and your essence spilled into my open cut. Now, I'm trying to reverse that."

"What?"

There it was. A sliver of essence come to restore the injury on my hand. I sliced it from the whole of my being, letting a single drop fall into Bez's nearly healed cut.

"What have you done?"

"Given you a piece of the devil essence inside me."

That single drop multiplied and swelled into several, mixing and merging with Bez's demon essence. It called to me, roaring within Bez's body, breaking down and rebuilding all at once. It was unlike any sensation I'd ever felt.

Bez loosened his grip, letting his legs slide down to my waist with his butt resting on my thighs. I moved my hands to his waist, pulling him closer to me, sitting upright.

"I need you to understand I'm not one-of-a-kind." I bit my lower lip, breaking the skin in my search for the right words.

There were no words to truly convey how complete my life was with Bez in it. He was unlike anyone I'd ever met, challenging me in the best ways possible, keeping me excited and eager to explore new experiences, all the while helping me stay grounded so I didn't float away on a tornado of overthinking anxiety or a whirlwind of self-doubt or a gust of too many metaphors meant to express what I'd already said.

"Wally, I'm not worried about being left behind. Not truly. Just a little frustrated with myself is all. I don't need you to share your power, your success, your—"

I kissed him, letting my blood swirl between our lips, carrying over a few droplets of essence. "I'm merely half a person, completed by your presence, your belief, your love, your loyalty, your existence. Without you, Bez, I'm nothing."

Bez's eyes welled up, and he kissed me again, fiery and aggressive and with a bite. One I reciprocated.

We rolled around on the mat, kissing and thrusting and pinning each other in place. I couldn't tell if we were making out or wrestling or both, but I couldn't stop. Couldn't submit. I needed to shower Bez with love.

He groaned as I twisted my body over his, holding him beneath me. His tails went to snatch me up, break my grip, but my single tail split into a thousand thin threads and pinned his tails with ease. I smiled, having finally found a way to counter that move he used any time I came close to besting him. His tails, his techniques, his tenacity always outsmarted me when we practiced. Not now.

"How's it feel?" I asked, teasing him as I nibbled his ear. "Having me inside you for a change?"

"Oh, Wally thinks he's grown up?" Bez rolled me over, pinning me beneath him as he straddled my hips. "Finally *come* to take charge?"

I ran my hands up his thick thighs, the firm muscles making me throb. In an instant, I spun in the air with Bez in my grasp.

He growled when I slammed his back against the wall. I ignored it. Ignored him. All I focused on was his lips. His taste. His perfect fucking body covered in clothes. I stripped them away piece by piece. I ripped open his shirt. I tore off his slacks. I slid off his dress shoes in a combination of using my tail and lifting him off the ground by gripping his ass and the back of his thighs while holding him against the wall.

Every kiss. Every step. Every time I locked eyes with Bez during this flurry of passion, it only drove me further. Passion consumed me. Lust fueled me.

Soon, we'd flown from one wall into another. This time, I took the brute force, letting my wings buffer the collision as Bez straddled my waist, kissing me the entire time. I didn't want to break apart our lips, but I needed to see.

"Dammit." I turned momentarily, using my tail to rifle through a drawer while still holding Bez with my hands. "Got it."

I fished out the lube Bez kept stocked and zipped to the center of the room. I threw Bez down, stripping off my own clothes as quickly as I could.

By the time I'd removed my shirt, Bez had sat up on his knees, hands pulling down my pants and mouth playing with the head of my cock.

I stood there, harder by the second, as Bez swallowed every inch. Wrapping a hand through his hair, I grunted in unison with his gurgle as I choked him, and then I pulled him off and pushed him onto his back.

"Not the hole I plan on using." I dropped to my knees.

"Well then, little mage. Show me what you have in mind." Bez spread his legs on either side of me, ready to slide in close, but I gripped his ankles and flipped him onto his stomach.

I readied him, using the lube quite generously both for his comfort and my ease since this was new.

"Have you ever?" I asked, not wishing to pause or ruin the moment, but I was worried I'd bust two strokes in.

"This is as new for me as it is for you." Bez positioned himself on his knees, doing his best to properly angle himself, and far too high.

I smiled a bit, adjusting him, pushing his back down so it didn't arch like a mountaintop. Once everything seemed just right, I slowly made my first attempt at topping someone.

"Whoa." My mouth fell wide at the sensation of pushing inside Bez.

He cleared his throat loudly, groaning.

I moved slowly, afraid if I went too quickly, it'd be over, and also allowing Bez a chance to ease into every new feeling of pleasure and pain and submission. Gods, he felt fantastic.

Each time my hips bounced against his ass, I found myself moving a bit faster, a bit harder, and soon the slap of skin had this enticing rhythm that further fueled me.

I thrust deeper inside Bez, relishing the sound of his moans and this bizarre connection as my essence coursed through him. It snapped and broke away from me, coursing through Bez's veins and becoming his.

Here we were, linked and bound by devil essence, which had evolved and changed beyond measure. How I looked forward to exploring the unique properties of our being, how it'd function in a year, how it'd flourish in a century, how it'd keep us together forever.

But for now, I wanted to enjoy the feel of being inside Bez.

"Arch." I pressed my knuckles to the small of Bez's back.

He obeyed instinctively, obediently, and I thrust harder in him, placing a hand over his mouth to stifle a shout he let out from the sharp pain of my pounding.

"Sorry." I kissed his nape. "You just feel too damn good."

I continued kissing him as I pounded him, getting in a rhythmic and intoxicating pace.

"Let yourself enjoy it."

Bez groaned into my mouth, and I swallowed every sound, eliciting a thousand more as I fucked him. Gods, he felt amazing. I wrapped my arm around his neck, holding him close. Our skin was slick and sticky with sweat. I slid my other hand down and squeezed his ass.

Using this position, I pushed him forward all the way, pinned beneath me, and thrust deeper into Bez.

Every time he moaned, I nearly burst, so I finally pulled my cock out and let him rest. I teased his hole, slapping my dick against his ass as I took deep breaths. Calming breaths. I was about to climax. I needed to wait. Savor this. Enjoy Bez's perfect bubble butt.

"You feel it, right?"

"You?" He panted. "Yes."

"No, I mean, yes—obviously, I'm amazing."

"And cocky."

"You love it." I pressed the head of my dick against his hole. "But what I meant was the essence. You can feel it merging with you, right?"

This wasn't like when Bez had shared his essence, where it linked us together, where it required regular rituals to keep the bond strong.

"How've you done this?"

"I don't know." I used my hands to spread Bez's cheeks, slowly sliding back inside him, moaning from the euphoric pleasure. "When it became mine. It changed, evolved into something unlike any devil before. Now, a piece belongs to you, untethered from the rules set by all the devils before, and turning you into something completely unique."

"Something like you." Bez released a beleaguered groan once I slipped all the way inside him, letting my dick rest and offering him a breath to adjust.

"I look forward to what we are becoming, growing together, and changing." I wrapped my arms under his, digging my claws into his shoulders as I looped around and secured Bez in my grasp, then I rammed him harder and faster until he grunted and buckled beneath me. "I'm different than any devil, you're different from any devil, and there's no one I'd rather share this experience with than you."

I pounded Bez until he whimpered, body convulsing underneath me, held in place by me.

Bez lay there, taking every swift thrust. Freeing one of my hands, I slipped it between Bez's hip and the mat, finding his throbbing cock and stroking it in unison with my thrusts. Eventually, I held my hand still, letting his dick slide back and forth with the motion of mine that controlled the sway of our bodies.

"Wally," Bez whined, unable to bite back his pleasure, and he came onto my hand.

That excited me beyond measure. I tried to stop myself, to slow myself, but my entire body washed over with this blissful warmth. I pressed my forehead between Bez's shoulder blades and groaned as I came inside him.

"Fuck me," Bez said as I rolled off him and rested on my back.

"Pretty sure I just did."

"Is that what I've been doing to you all these years?"

"You're not as gentle." I chuckled.

"Well, fuck." Bez rolled into me, wrapping his arm over my shoulder. "I'm definitely gonna make you earn the top in the future. Not handing this ass over lightly anymore."

"Sparring for top?" I smiled. "You sure you wanna go straight to being the full-time bottom in this relationship?"

"Arrogant." Bez squeezed me into a tighter embrace. "I think I need to show you now how often I go easy on you."

"I'm just saying, we both know I've got better control over devil essence than you."

"Walter, I had devil essence for centuries before I graced you with such gifts."

"But we know I sort of flipped over the board and made my own rules." I used my tail to tickle him until his sour frown turned into an annoyed smile. "Sort of like how I flipped you over."

Bez got quiet for a moment.

"Sorry. I'm just teasing."

Bez didn't respond.

"I'm not even that into topping. Like strict roles for us. I like that for us." Which was true. But I'd found myself curious for more with Bez. He always brought out my curiosity for more. More of everything. More of him.

Bez smiled. "I can't think of anything better than spending an eternity at your side, watching the misfit mage and his devilish desires unfold over the course of forever."

Bez kissed me, soft and sweet.

"You're a dashing devil again." I kissed him back. "You realize that, my darling demon."

We lay naked in a sweaty embrace with our whole lives ahead of us. I couldn't imagine anyone better to spend forever with.

30

I helped around the shop over the next few weeks, finding myself drawn toward Wally more than usual. Since spilling his essence inside me, filling me with his power, sharing a piece of his very being, things had changed. Positive changes, but still too early to fully wrap my head around.

When close to him, like now, I found this humanity crawling beneath my skin. Not the same as the way I'd always felt when stuffed inside a mortal body. That sensation came with a gloved touch.

I went to the sparring room in the back of the store and trained these new feelings.

Now, everything carried this extra layer of vibrance. A breath inhaled. A stretch of my back. A flex of my muscles. Everything hit deeper, grounding me here and now. When I sniffed and the metallic odor of my fitness equipment made my nostrils flare. When I wiped the sweat pooling on my brow. When I swallowed the piece of caramel-coated panko popcorn that'd finally wiggled loose from my teeth. The human form was no longer a mere guise to gleam the mortal realm but a true extension of my being through and through.

That came from Wally.

This essence came from Wally, it linked me to Wally, but it was mine entirely. I couldn't explain it. All the same, I understood it. At least I understood something about this essence.

Part of me contemplated calling Wally out of his study and shaking his stiff bones loose to spar with me. But since our last training match ended with Wally besting me in more than one way, I didn't need him exploiting his advantage and understanding of the essence we shared. I decided to hold off on calling him in lest I end up pinned and pounded out again by a wicked, devilish mortal with an insatiable appetite.

I needed to work through the learning curve of this essence. It didn't work the same way as Beelzebub's had when connected to me. It altered how I used my own essence. It'd take time to adjust, but I looked forward to the journey.

Having eased into a nice warm-up with the basics, I decided to move into something more advanced. Summoning primal elements in an enclosed space wasn't Wally's favorite thing. He worried too much about dusty old trinkets people had long forgotten about, but since he'd already warded the room with countless incantations just in case my training ever got a bit too destructive, I took full advantage and let loose a cascade of primal passion.

Once I'd unleashed a frenzy of elements, I let loose with my speed and zipped around, evading my own casual destruction as sigils popped with defenses meant to absorb or eradicate my attacks. It added an extra layer of training, endurance, education. I had to outsmart Wally's wards and best my own chaotic casting while not actually ruining the sparring room or my host body.

After a few rounds, I worked on summoning my Diabolic features and maintaining them during my training. My tails flicked without snapping apart. My wings flapped furiously without losing feathers to the gale force I summoned. My claws slashed through every obstacle I encountered without retreating back into the cuticles of my mortal nails.

It seemed the devil essence had fully restored my own, rejuvenating me beyond measure, and every bit of training helped me cultivate a small understanding of what life had in store.

The day escaped me, training nonstop with no breaks and no need to stop, but when the setting sun hit the gem I kept on display, it created an irritating glare during my last round of cardio.

"How'd I do, old friend?" I panted, allowing the endorphins post-workout to course through this body. My body.

Remington's ruby didn't respond, though the shadows of deep crimson adjusted ever so, altering the lighting. I'd kept him close, placed upon a mantle for no one to view except me.

"I'd love to stick around, testing my limitations, but I've got a dinner to make." I winked at Abe.

There was a satisfaction like none other, knowing his spirit found no peace as he dwelled there in the same way he'd imprisoned me. Forgotten.

"Hope you enjoyed this show as much as the one I put on for you last time." I slapped my ass cheek. "I'll be sure to give you all the deets on this evening. I'm enjoying dabbling in versatility, but I plan on railing the ever-living Hell out of Walter tonight."

And step one came with the perfect dinner.

I excused myself from the store, which neither Wally nor Kell objected to, each lost in their own projects and incapable of tearing their eyes away to even acknowledge my comment.

After a casual flight home, I began to prep dinner. I'd done my best to pick something incredibly flavorful and very mortal-y, which seemed like such a waste of good ingredients. Still, this was a dish Wally rambled about regularly, and as far as mortal dishes went, I supposed it had some nice textures and tastes.

I kept the dish simmering a little longer than anticipated. I'd assumed I left room for Wally's "just one more minute and then I'll leave" antics, but he must've found himself entranced in a particularly exciting artifact this evening.

Finally, the loud clanks of the front gate unlocking indicated Wally's arrival. I zipped around the table, setting everything up and casually taking a seat when he came inside holding a half dozen bags of trinkets to work on if he found the time.

He wouldn't be finding the time tonight.

Antoninus hopped out of Wally's hair and scuttled away to join Weather away from the dining room as agreed upon. He was even polite enough to whisk away Wally's bags.

The aromas of tonight's meal made Wally's face light up with excitement.

"You got takeout." He nodded approvingly. "And you made it fancy."

"I didn't get takeout. There isn't a place outside of Seattle that makes these fritter thingys." I pointed to a crispy fried squid Wally loved—bizarre since they tasted much better raw and covered in chocolate as opposed to grease, but to each their own.

My recipe came from some of Wally's favorite takeout dinners he had longed for since leaving his home to be with me.

"You made Pad Thai and red curry from scratch?"

"And so much more."

Wally stared at the assortment, eyes fixed on the crunchy spring rolls. "How'd you make all this?"

"I cooked it, obviously."

"Since when do you cook?"

"I cook all the time."

"Yes, but this looks…normal." He sniffed, nostrils flaring as he searched the lingering aromas for every ingredient. "You didn't add anything…well, Bez-like."

"Ugh, the restraint that took." I groaned.

"Are you not eating?"

"I'm eating."

"Yeah, but you never cook normal stuff." Wally squinted with suspicion. "What's the special occasion?"

I had no intention of telling him, so I smirked, silently staring back as he chuckled. That laughter began lightheartedly but quickly evolved into something with an edge of anxiety.

"Wait. What is the special occasion?" he asked, frantically mumbling to himself. "What is today's date? What have I forgotten?"

"You haven't forgotten anything, Wally," I replied.

"No, there's something. You're not telling me something. What's going on? Is the essence reacting poorly?" Wally tugged his curls. "This is my fault. You're eating human food because I broke your terrible tastebuds. I'm so sorry."

"First off, I eat human food all the time. You make me sound like Weather with his puppy chow and fire rocks."

Walter grimaced. "I mean…"

"Secondly, I'm not broken. I'm happy."

"Because there's something special about today?" he asked with his brows raised, searching my expression for the slightest reaction.

"You're impossible." I sighed. "There's nothing special about today's date. Nothing yet, anyway."

With that, I slid out of my seat and dropped to one knee.

"I was hoping we could change that."

I'd hoped to share this news with him after dinner like I'd rehearsed, but Wally's beautiful hazel eyes widened and washed away my desires. All I wanted was to see him happy in this moment.

"We talk about eternity all the time, and I want to make that commitment official. I want to scream my love for you in front of everyone."

"Yes!"

"You didn't even let me finish."

"That's what she…never mind." Wally giggled.

"I had a whole big speech. There were drafts and papers, and the bug helped me practice."

"And I wanna hear it all. I wanna listen again and again and again." Wally fell to his knees in front of me and pulled me into a kiss.

"You know I cooked and everything?" I panted between kisses.

"And it looks delicious." Wally ran his tongue along my neck and nibbled. "But I'm only hungry for one thing tonight."

He squeezed my ass, not so subtly indicating where he planned to redirect this evening. I'd had the same plans but after food. After my full speech. After making Wally gush like a weepy little bitch overjoyed by the proposal.

Instead, I found myself entangled in his embrace, locked in fiery kisses and grinding against his body. Not that I was complaining.

Fuck this felt great. The whole thing. The kissing. The shared essence. The synced sensations. The devilish nature unlike any other before. The eternal commitment to Wally. Wally. Everything with Wally. I wanted this feeling forever and ever and ever.

His lips were soft yet rough, consumed by the passion of this moment yet already adrift. I pressed my body against his, allowing the friction of our firm muscles to steer him back to the task of carnal pleasures. And he reciprocated, but the taste of his lips came with the bitter note of distraction.

As much as I loved the highs, there were other pieces to our relationship I'd grown to love, even if they weren't my favorite parts.

I paused, taking a breath so I could breathe him in. His scent. His happiness. His quirky little obsessive brain.

"Your little hive of a mind is already planning things, aren't you?"

"What? No. Okay. Maybe. Just venues." He smacked his lips against mine, rough and wordy. "Those book years in advance; I wanna decide on the best location."

I could spend a million years listening to him talk about anything and everything in existence. Excessive details. Meticulous notes. Fascinating anecdotes. I wanted all of it. But right now, I wanted Wally's lips. His mouth. His body. His touch. His satisfaction.

I grabbed him by the waist and rolled on the floor, sweeping him into a heavy make-out session, running my fingers against his skin, sending a slight jolt of electricity to elicit arousal.

"Where were you thinking of having this?" Wally asked. "Here? Or were you thinking a destination wedding? I guess anywhere would be a destination wedding, depending on who we invited. I should probably invite my family. Do you think my family would attend? I wonder if the Collective would allow them to attend a devil wedding. Obviously, not my mother. Not that she'd be on the invitation list. Oh, I need to craft some invitations. There's some amazing incantations to create biodegradable confetti. Delightful and environmentally friendly. It can also be turned into a mulch, which is good for woodland Mythics in nearly any ecosystem."

I lay back, surrendering to Wally's unstoppable chatter. He didn't even notice, prattling on and making a mental checklist of things he wanted to look into. I unzipped my slacks and fished out my cock, playing with it. Still nothing, which made my erection wane.

"You're oblivious."

"Huh?" He turned and stared at my dick. "Dammit. I didn't mean to get distracted."

I played with the head of my cock, rubbing the precum on my thumb.

"It's that mouth of yours, always running wild." I teased him, pressing my sticky fingers on his lips. "I think we need to occupy it, fill it with something far more satisfying than words.”

He leaned forward, licking my shaft. A slow, seductive move while he kept his eyes locked on mine. “To be clear, though, words are quite satisfying. I mean—”

I rammed his head down onto my cock and savored the gasp as he choked all the way to the base.

“That’s better.” I grabbed a fistful of curly blond locks and forced his head up and down.

He planted his hands on my thighs, squeezing them to steady the bob of his head. His eyes watered the deeper I pushed my dick. I pounded faster into his throat, making him gurgle and gag and groan, which only made me wanna ram my dick in again and again.

“You fucking love it.” I used both hands to control his head as I thrust upward, face fucking him. “Once I wear out that throat, I’m gonna fuck that adorable little ass of yours until the only words you speak are my name.”

Wally took that as a challenge, attempting to move his head at the same swift pace of my control, an entertaining sight. I moaned as I continued bucking forward, smacking his face with my lower abdomen each time I shoved my cock into his tight throat.

“I can do this forever,” I growled. “And I plan on just that.”

My cock throbbed, closer and closer with each stroke. Wally grabbed my ass cheeks and squeezed them while holding the entirety of my cock in his mouth.

He twisted his neck just enough to tease me, continuing to bring me closer and closer until I came.

“Fuck.” I slapped the back of his neck, holding him in place as I filled his mouth with my cum. “Swallow.”

He obeyed, his Adam’s apple bulging as he gulped.

“Good boy.” I released him, and he crawled forward, kissing me. I tasted what remained of my cum in his mouth.

“Quick question.” Wally grinned, boyish and inquisitive and

obnoxious. "Will we be Mr. and Mr. Alden? Will you be Bez Alden?"

I raised a questioning brow and scrunched my face. "Yuck. I don't do last names."

"Oh, going for the whole mononymous vibes." He nodded, practically ready to give me a lecture on the qualifications for only being known by one name. "I dig it."

"You're still far too chatty."

"I believe there was a promise of screaming."

"More of a threat."

"Yes, please."

I tore at his clothes, watching him giggle and roll on the floor as I stripped him. Once I had him on his stomach with his ass exposed, I slapped it.

"Behave, misfit."

"And what happens if I don't?"

"Then I'm gonna have to teach you some respect."

"You know I love a good lesson."

I smiled down at him, playing with his cheeks and spreading them.

"I love you, Wally."

"I love you too, Bez."

THE END

ACKNOWLEDGEMENTS

I want to thank everyone who followed Wally and Bez on their journey! It was such a thrill writing this series and sharing these two with readers. This is the final installment in the Diabolic Romance series for now. I may revisit the boys in smaller projects in the future or release a new trilogy with some fan favorite characters (allowing Wally and Bez to cameo while they enjoy their HEA). For the time being, there are some other projects I've got in the works that I'm really excited to dive into, and I hope that you'll enjoy those stories too.

If you enjoyed this book (or even if you didn't), I'd love if you left an honest rating and/or review. They really help with exposure and as a queer indie author, every shout out makes a huge difference in more readers finding our stories. Thank you for taking a chance on my words! I can't express how much that means to me.

AUTHOR'S BIO

MN Bennet is a high school teacher, writer, and reader. He lives in the Midwest, still adjusting to the cold after being born and raised in the South.

He enjoys writing paranormal and fantasy stories with huge worlds (sometimes too big), loveable romances (with so much angst and banter), and Happily Ever Afters (once he's dragged his characters through some emotional turmoil).

When he's not balancing classes, writing, or reading, he can be found binge watching anime or replaying Baldur's Gate 3 for the millionth time.

Author website:

https://www.mnbennet.com

Amazon page:

https://www.amazon.com/stores/MN-Bennet/author/B0BLJJK5NF

Goodreads page:

https://www.goodreads.com/author/show/23017668.M_N_Bennet

Patreon:
patreon.com/MNBennet

Newsletter:
https://mailchi.mp/e2ee2caea89a/newsletter-sign-up

Find All My Stuff:
https://linktr.ee/mnbennet